Gorilla Beach

Nicole **Snooki** Polizzi

Gorilla Beach

A Novel

GALLERY BOOKS

New York   London   Toronto   Sydney   New Delhi

G

Gallery Books
A Division of Simon & Schuster, Inc.
1230 Avenue of the Americas
New York, NY 10020

First Gallery Books hardcover edition May 2012

GALLERY BOOKS and colophon are registered trademarks of Simon & Schuster, Inc.

For information about special discounts for bulk purchases, please contact Simon & Schuster Special Sales at 1-866-506-1949 or business@ simonandschuster.com.

The Simon & Schuster Speakers Bureau can bring authors to your live event. For more information or to book an event contact the Simon & Schuster Speakers Bureau at 1-866-248-3049 or visit our website at www .simonspeakers.com.

Designed by Joy O'Meara

Manufactured in the United States of America

10 9 8 7 6 5 4 3 2 1

Library of Congress Cataloging-in-Publication Data

Polizzi, Nicole
    Gorilla beach / by Nicole "Snooki" Polizzi. — 1st Gallery Books hardcover ed.
        p. cm.
    1. Seaside resorts—Fiction. 2. Seaside Heights (N.J.)—Fiction. I. Title.
    PS3616.O56775G67 2012
    813›.6—dc232011052765

ISBN 978-1-4516-5708-1
ISBN 978-1-4516-5710-4 (ebook)

Dedicated to Jionni

There are a lot of gorillas down the Shore,
but you're my Number One Gorillah.
You're my husband and I love you, Pewp!

Acknowledgments

Thanks as always to my parents. Mom and Dad, I love you! You've always supported me and I'm so grateful. Book number THREE! Woo hoo!

My pets are my inspiration. Special shout-out to Rocky the cat who lost a leg this year, and can still jump on the bed. Go hard, Rocky!

A million thanks to Team Snooki: Scott Talarico, Danny Mackay, Aaron, Joey, Brad, Stacey Wechsler, and Scott Miller. You guys make it all happened and I'm so lucky to have you in my corner.

Everyone at Gallery has been incredible. Lauren McKenna, you're the best editor evah. Lisa Litwack, Erica Feldon, Jen Robinson, we're killing it!

My best friends, Steph, Ryder, and Jenni are always there for me. I love you!

I ♥ my fans and tweedos. Keep being yourself and you'll rule the world, just like me.

Huge thanks again to Valerie Frankel, my hawt Jerzey girl contributor, for helping me turn my ideas into a funny, sexy, rockin' story.

Lastly, to everyone who loves going down the shore and having a blast as much as I do. This one is for us.

Chapter One

Like a Slutty Virgin

Giovanna "Gia" Spumanti stepped out of the dressing room in a white Bangin' Bride costume. It consisted of a lace-up corset, a tulle micro-miniskirt, thigh-high stockings with a garter belt, and a veil that Gia flung back over her pouf. "I know brides are supposed to wear white," she said. "But it'd be so much hotter in leopard."

Gia and her cousin/best friend Isabella "Bella" Rizzoli had just arrived in Seaside Heights, New Jersey, from their off-season home in Carroll Gardens, Brooklyn. Their first stop down the Shore? The Pleasure Chest, a sexcessories boutique.

Holding a bouquet of white plastic roses, Gia strutted the length of the store aisle between racks of bondagewear and a wall of stripper wigs. She did a dramatic pose, arching her back. Her barely holstered boobs popped out of the corset.

"Nip slip!" said Bella, laughing. "You look like a slutty virgin."

"Ooops." Tucking herself back in, Gia said, "I'm wearing this to my own wedding. Just to make sure all eyes are glued on me."

"They would be if you wore a burlap sack," said Bella. "We don't have a lot of time. Maria's bachelorette party is in an hour."

As the official Bitches of Honor at Mary "Maria" Agatha Pugliani Stanzo Manzitta Crumbi's upcoming nuptials (she was calling the event 4x4, her July 4 fourth wedding) to Stanley Crumbi, Gia and Bella should have hosted the bachelorette party themselves. But Maria thought it'd be a hassle to have the cousins organize the event from Brooklyn. Maria's new bestie, Donna Lupo, the wife of one of the groom's business associates, insisted on planning the party anyway. Knowing Maria, who gargled with tequila and had been known to grind a lamppost when drunk, the bachelorette party would rock no matter who hosted it.

The betrothed couple had a special place in Gia's heart. She considered Maria and Stanley her "down the Shore" parents. Maria had been her boss at Tantastic, the hottest tanning salon in Seaside Heights. Stanley was the cousins' Seaside landlord. The couple had already been married and divorced before. Thanks to Gia's matchmaking and guido makeover skills, she'd helped them get back together last summer.

Big Italian weddings were a blast and a half. Gia's excitement about the event was slightly tainted. She was in the middle of a sexual dry spell, and not happy about it. Her relationship with Frank Rossi, a Seaside Heights fireman, aka the Hose, iced over during the winter. The two broke up on New Year's Day, but the end had been coming for a while. The long-distance relationship was tough. With his schedule, it was hard for them to get together. She really disappointed him when she canceled on coming to Seaside for Christmas and went to stay with her estranged father, Joe, his wife, and their new baby in Philly instead. Georgina "Gina" Spumanti was a few months old. Gia wanted to make an impression on her half sister, as well as repair the splintered relationship with her dad. Frankie grumbled, but he said he understood. She should have stuck with her original plan. All week, Joe lavished attention on his new daughter, but ignored Gia. Before the divorce with Gia's mom five years ago, Gia and Joe were as tight as sausage casing. After the split, Gia moved to Brooklyn with her mom. Joe met and married Rhonda and moved to Philly. Gia hoped her visit would revive their former closeness, but it was useless. Joe seemed unreachable. Frankie of-

fered to come to Brooklyn for New Year's. They went to Times
Square to see the ball drop and kissed at midnight. Their last kiss.
No spark. No feeling. It was like kissing a store mannequin. Gia
feared her emotions had gone numb after Philly. Frankie had had
enough of being kept on a string. They ended it officially the next
day. She hadn't seen, texted, or spoken to the kid since.

"Attention Pleasure Chest shoppers!" said Bella to get Gia's attention. "I lost you for a second there. Where were you?"

"Gorilla Island," said Gia. "I was surrounded by a pack of
juiceheads, and they were fighting over who got to bring me Jell-O
shots and fried pickles."

"If only such a place really existed."

"We can dream."

A shopgirl came over. "Need any help?"

"Does the Bangin' Bride costume come in leopard?" asked Gia.

The woman's mouth twitched. "It's white. As in *bride*?" She
gave Gia the "one meatball short of a hoagie" look. Gia got that a
lot.

After she walked away, Bella said, "She's a snob about selling
stripper clothes in a sex store?"

"Forget her," Gia muttered. She knew what was what, that she
wasn't winning any prizes for her brains. Not everyone was born
to put on a rubber apron and split atoms in a kitchen with a meat
cleaver. Some people contributed to the world in a different—no
less important—way. To bring fun and energy and . . . oh, screw it.
Gia's mood was wrecked, flattened like a beach ball under a dump
truck.

Two years of college had been enough. She wasn't a great student and didn't see the point of prolonging the struggle. Since
she'd dropped out (due to a lack of funds and interest), Gia had
bounced from job to job. The only one she'd been good at was
working for Maria at Tantastic last July. When Gia returned to
Brooklyn in August, she was full of confidence and pumped to

reboot her life. At night she lay awake, dreaming of managing her own salon, of being the bosslady.

Reality squashed the fantasy. Forget a manager position, Gia couldn't get any job, anywhere. "No openings," they said at the salons she applied to. She'd spent the year ripping tickets and selling candy at the local movie theater. Her mom's boyfriend ran the place. Nice boss, good wage, the job still sapped her spirit. She hated spending so much time holed up in dark rooms that stank of fake butter. She craved the spotlight.

Never thought she'd ever hate the smell of popcorn.

"What's wrong now?" asked Bella.

"Nothing." Gia's mood was like an old man's balls—swinging out of control. She didn't want to complain on their first day of summer vakay. She'd been looking forward to their trip to Seaside Heights—her "true" home—all year. Now that they were finally here, she needed an attitude adjustment. Drawing herself to her full height of five feet tall (plus four inches of platform espadrille and four inches of pouf), she said, "Brilliant idea. Let's go to the bachelorette party as Bangin' Brides!"

"Really?" asked Bella. "Do you think Maria would like it?"

"She'd freakin' love it!" said Gia, her enthusiasm growing. "Come on, Bells! Just picture it! We'll stomp into the party like slutty virgin-bride bookends. It'll be hilarious! Maria will piss herself laughing."

"She won't be embarrassed?"

"Have you *met* Maria?" The bride never saw a plunging V-front, skintight, Lycra, camo-print jumpsuit she didn't crush on hard. Her acrylic nails were longer that her fingers. Her pouf defied the laws of gravity. "She doesn't know the meaning of the word *embarrass,*" said Gia. "Neither do I."

"Sold," said Bella, smiling, warming to the idea. She called to the snooty shopgirl, "Hello? Yeah, we need another Bangin' Bride costume."

"What size?" asked the woman, smiling.

"A medium." All shopgirls loved Bella. She was tall and athletic, with perky silicone half-melon boobies.

Gia was a small. Shapely, soft, and perfectly proportioned with a generous rack, she measured sixty inches of sexy. But, by any conventional standard, Gia didn't compare to Bella's sinewy, streamlined body that looked awesome in *anything*. Suddenly, Gia had second thoughts about the two cousins wearing the same costume.

Do not go there, she thought. Whenever Gia had one of those shaky body-image flashes—the kind that went, "I wish I was taller . . . skinnier . . . had a tiny waist . . . longer legs . . ."—she immediately squashed it and replaced it with something positive, such as, "My tan is mad hawt . . . I heart my juicy badonk . . . My boobs are total boybait . . . ," etc. Having had some eating issues in high school, Gia was careful to keep her thoughts positive. Turning the negativity around was her secret trick, and it worked.

The shopgirl brought Bella the costume on a hanger. "Should I put it in a bag?"

"I'll wear it out," said Bella, and took it into the dressing room to change.

"We need a dozen penis pops, too. And a leather whip, and these pink, fur-lined handcuffs," said Gia. "Do you gift wrap?"

Chapter Two

That Sicko Freak Happens to Be My Son

"This is it," said Bella, pulling up to the curb at Boulevard and Sumner, only a block away from their favorite Seaside clubs, Karma and Bamboo. The sign out front read THE COWBOY CLUB, with a corny neon silhouette of a man in a ten-gallon hat, boots, and spurs. Bella cringed at the sight. "You sure about the address?"

"Yes," said Gia defensively.

"Just checking." Bella had a right to ask. For one thing, this club looked as if it'd beamed down from Oklahoma. For another, Gia wasn't exactly reliable about addresses, start times, or phone numbers. Granted, she didn't screw up every time, only 70 percent.

They got out of Bella's 1996 Honda. Bella closed the door carefully, afraid it might fall off if she slammed it. The Cowboy Club looked dead. Unlike every other place in Seaside, it had no line or bouncer checking IDs outside.

Gia noticed, too. "Nine on a Friday, and there's no one here?"

Bella shrugged. It was weird. She pushed the padded doors to get inside. They entered a cavernous main room. It was dark, except for spotlights aimed at giant posters of western scenes on the walls. Dry prairies, buffalo herds, and the Dallas football-team cheerleaders. Country music blared, loud. The girls cupped their hands over their ears to block the sound.

"Arrrgh!" screamed Gia. "My ears are bleeding!"

The tune was awful. Some mopey hayseed whining about his truck or his dog or how his wife left him for a horse. Each twang struck Bella like a steel guitar to the skull.

For Maria's sake, they pushed onward. The interior didn't improve as they crept into the belly of the club. The bar was big, but understocked. At a glance, Bella counted only a few bottles of booze. What kind of club had only a few vodka options? And where was the bartender? Ceiling lights flickered across the dance floor in tune with the "music." No dancers, though. The banquettes against one wall were empty, too. Bella felt self-conscious about her Bangin' Bride costume now that not a soul was around to appreciate it. She pulled down her miniskirt, tugged the corset up, and followed Gia, who could move surprisingly fast in four-inch heels.

"It's like a ghost club," said Gia.

"This can't be the right place."

Toward the back, they noticed movement. A peal of laughter rang over the music. They noticed a small gathering of . . . bears? No, women in fur coats. A tight circle of them. Bella could make out their dark silhouettes.

"Is that the bachelorette party?" asked Gia.

They moved closer. The women in fur were howling and screaming at the top of their lungs. Some seemed to be kicking at something in the center of the circle. A big pouf of blond hair rose up over the top of the women's heads for a second, then disappeared again. It rose and fell. Each time it became visible, the woman screamed and kicked.

To Bella, it looked as if this posse of women were kicking the crap out of someone. Her karate training kicked in, and she felt her muscles tense under the Bangin' Bride costume. Bella could not stand to see an unfair fight.

She strode toward the circle and pushed a few of the women—

middle-aged femooks in designer clothes, furs, plastic faces, and killer heels—to get to the center of the circle.

Bella had to blink. What in the name of cowboy Christ was she seeing?

"What the fuck?" asked Gia behind her.

At the center of the circle, a blonde was riding a bucking mechanical . . . what *was* that thing? Bigger than a sheep, smaller than a cow. A mechanical juicehead dwarf pony? The woman in the saddle was writhing on top of it as it jerked back and forth. She held on to the horn of the saddle with both hands, screaming with orgasmic joy. The women hadn't been gang-stomping her. They were kicking at the foam padding around the pony ride that came loose with every swivel.

"Kinky," said Gia, nodding at the blonde. "Doesn't that hurt your vagine?"

"Who the hell are you?" asked one of the spectators. She took a pull on the bottle of Cristal in her hand as she narrowed icy blue eyes and arched her thin black brows at the cousins. Her hair was black, stick straight, with cropped bangs. It looked like a Chinese wig. Bella didn't know designers, but her dress looked expensive. The fur jacket looked real. Around her neck, she wore a six-inch, diamond-studded gold cross.

"Gia!" shouted the blonde on the bucking machine. Her words came out herky from the jerky ride. "It's. Me! I'm. Ride. Ing. A. Frig. Ing. *Bull!*"

"More like a goat," said Gia.

"That's what I thought!" Bella said, laughing. Wait, the blonde on the . . . thing . . . was Maria? Bella wouldn't have recognized her if she'd punched her.

"You. Guys. Have. To. Try. This!"

No. Thank. You, thought Bella. Not unless there was an on-site gynecologist.

The machine slowed and then stopped. Maria kicked one bare

leg over the side of the pony, then fell over the other side onto the foam padding.

Cupping her crotch, she said, "There goes the wedding night. I feel like I just had sex with a tuba."

"Me next!" shouted Gia, jumping up and down, clapping.

The femooks helped Maria to her feet. She was shaky, but able to gather Gia and Bella into a three-way hug.

"Princesses," Maria squealed. "You made it! Dressed to impress, too. What took you so long? You're an hour late. You didn't recognize me at first, right? I made a few changes."

Some changes? She'd bleached her raven hair with a skunk stripe into a Hollywood yellow. Formerly soft and curvy, Maria had dieted herself to bony, which wasn't a good look on anyone. Bella guessed she'd had a nose job and a face-lift. And her dress! It was black, classy, and draped. The Maria of last summer preferred clothes that were loud, shiny, and supertight. Glancing at her feet, Bella spotted another major change. No wonder she seemed shorter. The former devotee of six-inch stilettos and patent-leather, high-heeled booties, Maria now wore kitten-heeled strappy sandals.

The most shocking change of all? Maria was . . . pale. Maybe the blood had drained from her face after the bottom-pounding she'd just taken. Even still, it appeared Maria hadn't been on a tanning bed in months.

This woman wasn't the chronically tipsy, leathery, bronzed mystic tanning queen they knew and loved. The new Maria looked like Victoria Gotti after crawling a hundred miles on a bad road to a sketchy plastic surgeon's office.

Another woman had crawled onto the horny-pony ride, and the creature was bucking away again, the women howling and screaming. Each woman, Bella saw, was holding her own bottle of champagne.

Gia was still blinking in shock at Maria's shocking transformation. Maria frowned at her and said, "You look like you've got gas, honey."

"I'm fine," said Gia, giving her old boss another hug. "It's aweome to see you! Congrats on your wedding!" She reached into the Pleasure Chest shopping bag, grabbed a handful of condoms and foil packs of lube, and threw them in the air like confetti. A few of them bounced off the writhing mechanical pony and flew across the room. A couple hit femooks in the face.

Maria said, "Come sit down, girls. I love the outfits."

The bride brought them to a booth in back. As they squeezed in, Bella whispered to Gia, "An hour late? You couldn't make it two hours?"

A few of the other ladies joined them, including the hard-ass with the Chinese-wig hair. She stared at the girls and weaved a little. *Drunk and pissed off,* thought Bella. Not a good combo.

"We have bachelorette-party gifts," said Gia, breaking the tension. She gave Maria the Pleasure Chest shopping bag.

Maria reached in and withdrew a cellophane-wrapped goody.

Gia said helpfully, "It's a penis pop."

"I can see that," said Maria.

"Cherry. Your favorite."

The other women were silent. They seemed to be waiting for the China-wig brunette to react. She squinted at the pop for a few beats, then she barked. From the relieved smiles of the other women, Bella guessed she was laughing. The tension deflated, and the other women started laughing, too.

"You girls are too funny," slurred the brunette. "You're the cousins from Brooklyn. Gia and Bella, right? Maria told me all about you. You're so young! How old are you?"

"We're both twenty-two," said Gia.

"I like your style. You need champagne. Everyone needs champagne!" Banging on the table, the brunette bellowed, *"We need more bottles out here!"*

Bella cringed at the volume. Gia cupped her ears again.

"I'm Donna Lupo," said the brunette, holding out her hand with the perma French manicure and a couple of doorknob diamond rings. "I'm married to Luigi Lupo, who is Stanley's best friend from the neighborhood, like a brother. This is Antonia Diana Ravioli, Luigi's cousin Bobby's wife. Here's Carmela Incantanta Fortunata, who's married to Alonzo, Stanley's second cousin. Over there on the bull is Adriana Tagliobulo, wife of Carmine, an associate of Luigi's and Stanley's . . ."

While Donna introduced the group as if she were reading the Italian phone book, Bella took in their outfits. It was as if the spring collections from Neiman Marcus had fallen off the back of a truck and landed on these ladies' backs. All wore fur jackets or vests. All had stick-straight hair in various shades of Paul Mitchell, with cropped bangs and subtle highlights. No skunk stripes or poufs for this crew. They each wore clanging gold crosses that nestled snugly into their cleavage. Their makeup consisted of mascara, gloss, and five spackled layers of nude foundation.

Gia asked suddenly, "Isn't it too hot to wear fur?"

Donna wore a lynx jacket, the white fur tickling her jaw. "It's *never* too hot to wear fur," she said. "A toast! To air-conditioning!"

The ladies lifted their bottles and guzzled until they'd drained the champagne inside. Then they threw the bottles and belched thunderously in unison. Then they started laughing like jackals. Such behavior wouldn't shock Bella among her own friends. But to see middle-aged women like this? Yeah, it was like an episode of *Mob Wives*. They'd probably start tearing each other's hair out next.

Donna pounded on the table and screamed, "More champagne!" like the Italian-American princess version of Henry VIII. Bella glanced around, looking for a cocktail waitress or a bartender. None in sight.

Donna's attention swiveled to Maria. "So tell us about the wedding. Did you arrange the tables like I told you to? I hope you didn't seat me with Annette Camponati, because I freakin' hate that backstabbing bitch."

Maria said, "You and Annette are on opposite sides of the room. I did everything like you said."

Bella and Gia made eye contact. Maria seemed afraid of this Donna person. Bella felt intimidated by her, too, and she was no quivering violet. Bella could make brown-belted juiceheads quake at her karate-sparring gym. But Donna had a fearsome presence. Bella shuddered, imaging what it'd be like to get on her bad side.

Had Donna pressured Maria to make the physical changes to fit into their crew? Bella would never change herself for anyone. Sure, she'd had her boobies done, but she did that for herself. The Girls had been her twenty-first-birthday present to herself. If anyone had told her to do it, she'd've been dead set against it.

Gia, apparently, didn't feel intimidated by Donna. "Where're the male strippers? This is a bachelorette party. Don't tell me the closest thing we have to a hot gorilla is that tin-plated kiddie ride over there."

"Are you saying I don't know how to make a party for my friend?" Donna's blue eyes flared.

"No offense to you. But this club sucks. You can't dance to this country crap. The bottles are kicked. No hot boys. Let's go to Karma to dance. We'll torpedo the place."

"We can dance to this!" Donna said. "Come on. I'll show you." She gestured for all the women to follow her to the dance floor. "Get in lines," she demanded.

"Stand in a line—on purpose? Is this the DMV?" asked Gia.

"*Do it!*"

The cousins got on line with the others. Donna stood in front and tried to teach the ladies some country shitkicker moves.

Gia and Bella could not follow. Bella's body simply would not do-si-do. The entire experiment was a do-see-don't. Bella zoned out, barely paying attention, while the other women mimicked

Donna's steps. Bella's mind drifted back home, to her mom's face when she practically pushed Bella out the door. She hadn't wanted to leave her mom. There was too much to do, and Bella had been the coper in the house all year. Along with powering through her classes at NYU, Bella cared for her mom after the uterine-cancer diagnosis. Bella filled out the health insurance forms and made the chemo appointments. She held her mom's hand, cleaned up after her, kept the house in order, cooked their meals. Her dad? Where the hell was he during all this? He bailed. He let them all down. A bitterness rose in Bella's throat at the memory of her father, slumped in the living room armchair at home, refusing to help Mom climb the stairs after a chemo treatment.

No, thought Bella. *Do not go there. You're supposed to be having fun.*

Bella grabbed Gia's wrist and pulled her out of the line, saying, "We have to use the bathroom."

They ran toward the restroom sign, and down a short hallway farther back into the club. Bella said, "Holy shit! Maria drank Donna's Kool-Aid."

"It's like she's a completely different person," agreed Gia.

"We have to do something." Bella punched open the door marked with a cowgirl silhouette.

The room was dark. Bella groped for the light switch, turned it on, and saw a man sitting in one of the stalls, the door wide-open, his eyes wild as if he'd been caught stealing.

Or whatever else he might be doing in the ladies' restroom. By himself. Alone. In the dark. With his pants down.

"Ewww," said Gia.

The cousins clattered back to the main room. Gia shouted, "There's a creepy, sicko freak in the bathroom! Call the cops!"

"Wait!" shouted the male voice behind them. The kid was pulling his jeans up and fixing his belt. He had waxy skin, black eyes, dark hair greased back, and a five o'clock shadow that probably took him five months to grow. Through the armholes of his black skank tank, Bella could see how scrawny he was. Maybe twenty-five, he was tall, with a long pencil neck and bobbing Adam's apple.

"Can't I get a minute's privacy around here!" said the kid.

"It's a public john, not your bathroom at home," said Donna, weaving over, line dancing on hold.

"I went into the cowgirls' room *by mistake*."

"You know this freak?" asked Gia.

Maria was shaking her head frantically. A warning?

Donna said, "Gia, Bella, this is Fredo, my son, and the manager of this club."

Ohhhh, so that's why we're here, thought Bella. They could be at Karma, really celebrating Maria's last night as a single lady. But, no, Donna the alpha lynx had to support her son's crappy club.

Maria, the peacemaker, said, "It's an honest mistake, Donna. Gia didn't know Fredo was your son. She'd never have called him a creepy, sicko freak otherwise."

"Yeah, I would've!" said Gia. "He was in the pitch-black women's bathroom, grunting."

"I thought it was the cowboys' room!" protested Fredo.

Cowboys' room? It was so corny. "Why in the dark?" Bella asked.

He blushed and looked at his Pumas.

Donna said, "My boy has issues. He doesn't like to see his poops. Even when he was a baby, he'd cry hysterically as soon as his diaper was full. . . . What? Don't look at me like that, Fredo. You're anally retentive. It's just who you are, and I love you anyway. Did I embarrass you? I'm sorry, sweetheart. Let me give you a hug."

Donna steamrolled toward her cringing weirdo son and mauled him with kisses. It was sickening to watch. Bella squirmed sympathetically for Fredo. Poor kid, still caught in his mama's French-manicured clutches.

Gia whispered, "Okay, that's disgusting."

Bella's marathoner leg muscles twitched to get away from the uncomfortable relationship on display. But she feared making any sudden movements. Having grown up in a hard-core Italian neighborhood, she knew never to come between a Sicilian mama and her favorite son. It was like poking the bear with a stick. Or a Taser.

Finally, Donna released Fredo, who stumbled backward a few steps and wiped at his skank tank as if he were trying to brush off the hug. Donna gazed at him with pure love and adoration. "My boy. Isn't he handsome?"

Dead silence.

"He's going to the wedding, too," said Donna. "Maria, didn't you seat him at a table with the girls?"

Maria nodded. "I did, Donna. Right between Gia and Bella."

"Good," said Donna. "I heard you girls are both single right now. Fredo can be your date to the wedding. You two should be thrilled."

"Waaaa," Gia said. "I mean, yay!"

Bella glanced at Maria. She looked apologetic and silently pleaded with the cousins to go along. Gia read the message in her eyes clearly. Sighing, Gia said, "Great. We'll rock the wedding. Like we're rocking this club. Whoopee."

Donna beamed. "Wonderful. Fredo, more champagne!"

Chapter Three

Home Sweat Home

"You'd think Stanley would do better by us," said Gia, looking up at the concrete building at the corner of Hancock and West Central Avenue. It looked like a stack of giant gray bricks with black, square windows. Not many windows, at that.

Bella parked and switched off the Honda's ignition. This was to be their new summer digs? Stanley had made the arrangements for them. The bridegroom owned half the broken-down beach rentals in Seaside and arranged for the cousins to spend their July in "a state-of-the-art two-bedroom condo with a Jacuzzi and ocean views," as he described it on the phone last week.

"It might rock on the inside," said Bella.

Gia snorted. "It *is* a rock, inside and out."

The cousins—still in costume—hauled their luggage up three flights of stairs. Bella used the key Stanley had mailed to them, and they went into their top-story condo.

"State-of-the-art? More like state-of-the-fart," Gia whined.

"It's clean," said Bella.

True. But since there were no curtains or carpeting and barely any furniture, what could look messy? There was a Jacuzzi—in the living room—with two legs-up water bugs in it. They must have died from disgust at how scary ugly the place was. Also in the living room: a sticky-hot leather couch patched with gummy duct tape, a cigarette-burn-scarred coffee table, and a TV bolted to the ceiling like in a prison. The "kitchen" in the corner of the living room had a minifridge, toaster oven, and microwave.

Gia cringed at the sight. Not that she cared about cooking. Bella had grown up stationed in her family's Italian deli on Smith Street and equated "home" with "kitchen." Making sauce and shaving garlic was how she relaxed. Without a proper oven, stove, and counter, Bella might freak out. Gia would do anything to prevent that. Her cousin had had a rough year, including her mom's cancer diagnosis and her parents' split. Gia, who lived with Bella's family in Brooklyn, had watched the nightmare un-fold. Gia's number one goal for this summer? See to it that Bella had a good time. Her number two goal? What else? Find a juice-head gorilla and smush like it was the Mayan apocalypse.

"A toaster oven is just as good as a real oven," Gia said.

Bella scoffed, "I guess I can make bruschetta."

"Guys love that! You'll have them eating out of your hand."

"They'll have to," said Bella, opening empty cabinets. "No plates."

They dared to explore the rest of the place.

The bedrooms looked like prison cells with cinder-block walls and concrete floors. One dresser, one small closet, a chair, and a bed covered in plain white sheets and an itchy brown blanket.

"Is it hot in here?" asked Bella.

Even at midnight, with all the windows open, the top floor of the cement building was sweltering. No air-conditioning. Gia's sweat dribbled between her boobs and pooled in her belly button.

It'd been an endless night. They'd hung in there at Maria's party for hours, gamely trying country line dancing and listening to Donna Lupo brag about Fredo, the kid squirming the entire time. The only way Gia got through it was by guzzling champagne and doing shots of amaretto. She even took a turn on the grinding pony. That was the highlight of the party.

The sight of their apartment was sobering. The heat had turned her tongue into sandpaper. Obvy, she needed a margarita ASAP. Gia was just about to suggest going to the boardwalk to a bar when Bella stripped off her stripper gear and flopped down naked on the bed in the small bedroom. "I'm gonna crash."

Gia could take a hint. She gave Bella her privacy, lugged her suitcase into the bigger bedroom, and remade her bed with her own sheets and her leopard-print bedspread that went everywhere she did. She laid her stuffed animal, Crocadilly, on top. Her bed-clothes didn't brighten the depressing space. Gia's heart sank.

"Fuck it." Barging back into Bella's room, she said, "We're not staying here."

Bella sighed. "Should we sleep on the street?"

"We stay here until after the wedding tomorrow. As soon as it's over, I'll get on Stanley to find us a better place."

"Aren't they going on a honeymoon?"

Gia shook her head. "Stanley refused to leave town before Labor Day. Too many summer rentals to deal with. I bet he's just putting it off to avoid paying for a trip." They snickered over their landlord's epic cheapness. "Okay, the condo sucks. But we're in Seaside. It's Friday night. Let's destroy this place!"

"We'd need a wrecking ball to destroy this place," said Bella, rapping on the concrete floor with her knuckles.

Gia was on a mission to wipe the mope off Bella's face. The girl needed to shake off her winter blues *now*. "The place sucks, but the location isn't horrible. We're a few blocks from the boardwalk. I can smell the corn dogs from here."

Bella sat up. "Are you going to annoy me until I say yes?"

Gia nodded and clapped her hands. "One drink, I swear!"

Before Bella could change her mind, Gia hurried her to throw on the first thing they grabbed out of their suitcases. Bella pulled out a purple cotton jersey T-shirt dress with peephole slashes low enough to show a hint of her tramp stamp. Gia yanked free a black tube dress with a wide pink belt. To give their feet a break after the Bangin' Bride stilettos, they wore rhinestone-covered flip-flops. Gia pulled Bella out the door before they lost an hour redoing their hair and makeup. They might look like sloppy wrecks, but so would everyone else out there.

"Inca?" suggested Gia as they hit the boardwalk.

"Really?" asked Bella. "We're going skank?"

"Is tonight different from all other nights?"

The Inca Bar was a dank hole. Rusted water marks on the ceiling. Puke stains on the floor. The walls were crawling with mold and dark specks that Gia didn't want to think about. As gross as the place was, Gia had memories there—some fun, some funky. At this very bar, last summer, Gia nearly lost her shit—literally. Two nasty pieces of work, frenemies from her high school days in Toms River, fed her laxative-spiked Jell-O shots. Gia eventually got her revenge, sweeter than Nutella smeared on a fried Oreo. Just thinking about that victory made her almost unbearably happy.

Tonight at the Inca, the mold smell wasn't so strong. The DJ was spinning house music. A sweaty, packed crowd of dancers jumped up and down in a solid mass of humanity. Gia sneaked a peek at Bella, to see if she was soaking up the energy and good vibes. Sure enough, Bella was swaying, her graceful hands dancing away in front of her. Gia smiled. Yes! Her best bitch was back.

Barreling to the bar like a bowling ball, Gia yelled, "Emergency! Tequila shots! *Stat!*"

The cousins raised their glasses to each other. Gia said, "To summer!" They clinked, shot, and slammed their glasses on the bar.

Chapter Four

Follow the Bouncing Meatball

"You drive," said Bella, too hungover to open her eyes. Their one "Welcome to Seaside" tequila shot at the Inca had turned into two. Three bennies from Staten Island convinced them to try "the Verrazano," equal parts Patrón, Red Bull, and Frangelico. Gia and Bella had one. Then three. They crawled back to the Prison Condo at four in the morning. Bella woke up with red, white, and blue Manic Panic streaks in her hair.

Gia had them, too. "You don't remember? When we got home last night, we decided to do it. For the wedding and July Fourth."

As shocked as Bella was, she liked how her hair looked tie-dyed in "I heart America" colors. It matched their flashy bridesmaid dresses. The top part was covered with silver and red beading. The A-line skirt part was made entirely of red emu feathers. Legs bare, they had matching red patent-leather peeptoe pumps.

So Bella's hair and outfit were bangin'. So was her head, unfortunately. By the time they finished dressing and went down to the Honda, Bella was in serious pain. As a general rule, Bella drove. The Honda was sensitive and Gia drove the way she danced. All over the place.

Grabbing an opportunity to get behind the wheel, Gia took the keys from Bella's shaking hand. "Love to! I know the way. I went to about a dozen sweet-sixteen parties at this place." The wedding would be at Neptune's Hideaway, a catering hall in Toms River, only a ten-minute drive from Seaside Heights.

Bella climbed into the suicide seat (quake) and closed her eyes. Gia had some trouble getting the Honda started. "No worries!" she said, which naturally terrified Bella.

Gia pulled onto Route 37, no problem. Bella dared to peek at the road. Their exit was coming up soon. Gia was in the far left lane, booming down the highway, humming a Rihanna tune.

"Exit on the right," said Bella.

"I'm on the right."

"The other right! Hurry up! We're going to miss it."

Gia switched lanes, looking over her shoulder, pouring on the gas, then stomping on the brake when she nearly hit a passing car. She swerved, righted the car, and managed to get in the right lane. Bella's heart was pounding as hard as her head.

"Ya see? I can do this." Gia put on the blinker to exit, slowed down, and turned to blow Bella a kiss. In that split second, Gia overshot the exit ramp, pulled hard on the wheel, and wound up crashing into the yellow plastic barrels at the corner of the exit ramp. The water inside the barrels exploded out of the tops and drenched the Honda like a dirty ocean wave. When the water sloshed off the windshield, Bella saw smoke rising from the Honda's hood.

Bella turned to Gia, whose hands were gripping the wheel for dear life. "Are you okay?" Thank God they were wearing seat belts.

"I'm fine. I'm like a rubber meatball. I bounce. You don't look too hot."

Bella checked herself for damage. Since they were going slowly when they hit the safety barrels, Bella hadn't felt much of an impact. No air bags in the Honda (yeah, it was that old). If Bella looked bad, it was because she was worried about Gia's being hurt.

Slowly, carefully, Bella opened the passenger-side door. She was shaking when she checked the car. The front bumper had fallen off, and the engine was pouring smoke.

Gia was out of the car, too. At the sight of the mangled bumper, she covered her cheeks with her hands. "Did I do that?" she asked, shocked. "It's not my fault! The exit came up so fast, and then I turned too sharp, and . . . I'm so sorry, Bells!"

"We have to call someone." Bella wasn't going to dissect what happened right now, although it was obviously Gia's friggin' fault. *Stay focused,* she told herself. In a crisis, Bella's mind turned into a practical, logical machine. "Call Stanley," she said, already back in the car, looking in the glove compartment for her insurance info or a roadside-assistance hotline number.

"I kind of lost my phone," said Gia. "Um, can I borrow yours?"

"Fuck!" said Bella, exasperated.

"I'm sorry! I'm a walking disaster area. There should be orange highway cones surrounding me at all times. I wouldn't blame you if you hated me forever."

"I don't hate you."

"Maria will if we don't get to Neptune's Hideaway in the next five minutes. Maybe we should've let Fredo Lupo drive us."

"No service. Friggin' AT and T," said Bella, trying her cell.

"We could walk. It's only a mile away."

"And leave the car?"

Gia said, "See the upside. Maybe it'll get stolen, and you can collect insurance."

"Oh, yeah, that's the upside of crashing my car and stranding us on the highway? Maybe my car will get stolen?" The Honda was a piece of crap. But it was Bella's piece of crap. She bought it (used) when she was seventeen. She and the Honda had been through a lot together. Another loss. She bit her lip. She was not going to let herself cry.

Gia looked concerned. "I'll buy you a new car. I swear."

Right. Like *that* was gonna happen. Bella closed her eyes and counted to ten. Friggin' *one.* Friggin' *two.* Friggin' *three. . . .*

A red pickup truck pulled to a stop on the shoulder in front of the exit ramp. The driver, in a gray suit, climbed out of the front, waited for traffic, then jogged over to them.

"Is anyone hurt?"

"Always coming to the rescue," said Gia to Frank Rossi, her ex, a local firefighter. Last summer, he loved nothing more than throwing Gia over his shoulder in the fireman's carry to take her to the safety of his bed.

And here he was, doing his hero act again. Gia said, "You look good in a suit. Where're you going? Firemen's Ball?"

"What the hell happened?" he asked, assessing the Honda's damage.

"We're fine," said Bella. "But we need a tow."

It was like she hadn't spoken. Frank was on Gia now, checking her for breaks, squeezing and prodding her body. "Watch the dress," squealed Gia. A few of the feathers came off, flew into the highway, and got run over by a beer truck.

Gia seemed more frazzled to see Frankie than by the accident. "You look awesome," she said, hugging him hello. "And you smell good, too." The top of her head came up to his nipples.

Frankie made a quick phone call. After he hung up, he said, "I called the Troublino Body Shop for a tow. Should be here in half an hour."

Tony's grandfather's garage, thought Bella. Great. Now she'd have to deal with *her* ex when she went to get her car from Giuseppe's body shop. "Thanks," she said.

Frank ignored her. His eyes were locked on Gia. "Can I give you a lift?"

"Yes! We're late already," said Gia, hurrying in the truck's direction. When she took a step, she teetered and yelped.

Frankie caught her in his arms before she fell on the grease-smeared highway. He picked her up and held her like a baby. Gia instinctively wrapped her arms around his neck. "Ankle?" he asked, concerned.

"Heel." She extended her foot. One of her patent-leather pumps' four-inch heels had snapped off. "Can you carry me to the truck?"

Bella stifled a laugh. Gia had a sexual quirk about being carried. She got off on it. Whatever. Bella liked it when boys bit her neck like a vampire. To each her own.

Frankie smiled and hoisted Gia up higher. She squealed and giggled. Turning to Bella, he said, "You might want to get anything of value out of the car."

While Bella grabbed their purses and emptied the contents of the glove box into a plastic bag she found in the backseat, Gia said, "This is sick luck that you drove by. We're going to Neptune's Hideaway for Maria's wedding. We're the bridesmaids."

"I figured that from your matching dresses. I'm going to the wedding, too."

"You . . . why didn't you tell me? I didn't know you and Stanley were close."

Frank hesitated. "We're not. I'm going because—"

Suddenly, a bronzed guidette appeared in the truck window. She banged her hand on the side of the door and hollered, "Hey, Frankie! What's the holdup? Let's go!"

"Who's that?" asked Gia about the girl yanking Frankie's leash.

"That's Cara Lupo. She's Mario Lupo's daughter."

"Related to Donna and Fredo Lupo?" asked Bella.

"Cara is Fredo's cousin. Donna and Luigi's niece. Mario and Luigi are brothers."

Of course they were. "What do they do, exactly?" asked Bella.

"Waste management."

"Are you with-with her?" asked Gia.

Frankie frowned. He seemed to be debating which way to go. He went with honesty. "Cara is my girlfriend, yeah."

"Put me down," said Gia, suddenly cold.

Frankie did as he was told. With an anxious glance he said, "I'll wait in the truck," and jogged back to it.

Gia crawled into the backseat of the Honda where Bella was prizing a quarter from under the floor mat. "Did you hear that?"

Bella nodded. "You told me six months ago you were done with Frankie."

"Just because I'm done with him doesn't mean I want him to be done with *me*," whined Gia. "It took him forever to get over his breakup before me. I figured he'd stay single for a while."

"And you'd just start up again, like nothing had happened?" said Bella, shaking her head. "You thought you had a sure thing?"

"You mean, 'a shore thing'? Okay, I was wrong. I'm a friggin' idiot. Do I look like one?"

"No. You look hawt. Frankie is eating his heart out right now."

The cousins walked (Gia limped on her broken shoe) to the pickup truck with their purses and the bag full of salvaged paperwork and junk. It was a tight fit, the four of them in the front cab. Frankie pulled out.

Frank made hasty introductions. Cara, pretty and vapid in a tight blue dress and black pumps, asked, "You're Giovanna Spumanti? Didn't you and Frankie, like, hook up last summer?"

The girl made it sound like a casual fling. Was that how Frankie described their intense six-month relationship? Bella eyed Gia protectively. Instead of setting the kid straight, Gia said, "You could say that. Do you live in Seaside?"

"Toms River. I just graduated."

Bella didn't know any college in Toms River. "What school?"

"Toms River High."

High school? That would make Cara eighteen. Frankie was twenty-eight.

"She's ten years younger than you. Is that even legal?" asked Gia.

"I'm young, but experienced," said Cara. "I've seen a lot of crazy shit."

"I'm seeing some crazy shit *right now*," said Gia. "What was your first date? Lunchables and juice boxes at the playground?"

Bella laughed. "They went to the Build-A-Bear Workshop."

"No, Chuck E. Cheese," squealed Gia.

Cara steamed, her slutteen arms crossed over her chest. Frankie's face was fire-engine red. Friggin' should be embarrassed! He took the turn into the Neptune's parking lot on two wheels. "We're here," he said. "Glad to help you girls out. I'll just park and—"

Cara said, "Actually, Frank and I met at a Halloween party last year. I went as Hannah Montana."

Gia would've snorted till she puked, but then it hit her. "Wait, Halloween? In *October*? Two months *before* New Year's? That's pretty frickin' interesting. Did Frankie come to the party dressed as a cheating, lying *asshole*?"

Frankie raced out of the truck as soon as they parked and pulled Cara out after him. Over his shoulder, he yelled, "See you later."

"See you in hell!" called Gia after him.

Bella and Gia climbed down from the truck, Gia teetering on one heel. Bella said, "You okay?"

Gia took a deep breath and smoothed down her ruffled feathers. "Let's get frickin' married."

Chapter Five

Girls Just Wanna Have Rum

"Do you, Stanley Kowalski Crumbi, take this woman as your lawfully wedded wife—again?" asked the priest.

Stanley, in a navy-blue tux, said, "I freakin' do."

"And do you, Mary Agatha Pugliani, take this man as your lawfully wedded husband—again?"

Maria, in a white satin minidress, short in front with a massive bustle and train that went on for miles in the back, said, "I freakin' do, too."

The priest said, "I now pronounce you husband and wife. You may now kiss the groom."

Everyone laughed, and Maria went for it big-time. She planted a slobbering, open-mouth spit-swapper on Stanley. Gia, standing at the altar at Maria's side, hooted and clapped, hopping up and down on the one good heel.

Maria and Stanley came up for air with a loud gasp. The audience applauded as the happy couple walked down the aisle. As they were instructed to do, Bella and Gia followed the newlyweds out of the "chapel" room, then into the bridal chamber, where Maria had had her hair and makeup done before the ceremony.

"You coming?" Maria asked Stanley as she opened the door. The plan was for Maria to put on the second of her three dresses for the event and make a grand entrance into the Trident Lounge for the predinner cocktail hour.

"I gotta check on some things," said Stanley, already punching keys on his phone. "The plumber was supposed to be at the Sheridan Avenue house an hour ago, but he never showed up. I might have to go over there to unclog a toilet."

"Unclog a toilet on your wedding day," said Maria, her voice frosty. "Why don't you and the plumber go on a honeymoon together?"

"Maybe I would if I knew where the fat fuck was," snarled Stanley.

Ah, wedded bliss, thought Gia. "Stanley, we wanna talk to you about our apartment. You know that place sucks. We need a major upgrade."

"I'd take a minor upgrade," said Bella.

He waved them off. "You're giving me shit at my wedding?"

"Uh, yeah," Gia replied.

"How about you stop breaking my balls just for one freakin' day? Respect the tux, girls."

"Come on," said Maria, pushing the bridesmaids into her dressing room. "Stanley, you better not leave the building or I'll kill you."

"Whatever you say, Wife." He wandered off, texting frantically.

Inside the ornate bridal chamber, a bottle of Bacardi 151 sat in an ice bucket on a table. Maria checked the card. "'*Buona fortuna,*'" she read. "'Love, Donna.'"

"She's your new bestie?" asked Gia, a bit jealous.

"Help me get out of this thing," said Maria. They unzipped her gown and tugged it off. The bones in the corset had left indent marks on Maria's back, and the inside of the white dress was streaked orange. Bronzer skid marks.

"You better than anyone should know to let bronzer dry for ten minutes before you get dressed," said Gia.

"I did wait ten minutes! That's what happens when you go to a new place. Friggin' Soleil. I should've sprayed myself at home."

Gia frowned. "Why go to Soleil? You have Mystic booths at Tantastic."

"I didn't tell you? We sold the equipment and gutted the salon. Stanley and I did the math and realized if we renovated the building, we could rent it for four times as much as I brought in at Tantastic."

"But you loved the salon," said Gia, shocked. If Maria had said, "I'm Jewish," Gia wouldn't have been more surprised. "Tanning was your life."

"I got a new life." Maria found her cigarettes and lit one. "I'm married now. I've got new friends. Since Stanley went into business with Luigi Lupo at Fongul Industries, he's making more money than ever. Not that you could tell by the way he dresses. But look at me! I'm part of Seaside society. I went blond."

"We noticed," said Gia.

"And you had work done?" said Bella, touching her nose.

Maria patted her cheeks. "I had my skin tightened. A few turns of the screw. I feel like a new woman. I *am* a new woman."

"Honestly? I kind of miss the old cougar," said Gia, pouting.

"Nah," scoffed Maria. "The old me was needy and desperate. Those days are in the past. I'm taking some long-overdue me time. My last three marriages—including the first time with Stanley—I worked my ass off to take care of my deadbeat husbands. My plan this time around is to be a wifey. Get my nails done, have a mimosa with breakfast every day, and let someone take care of me for a change."

"Great for you, but where am I gonna work this summer?" Gia had been counting on a job at Tantastic, and another summer of stenciling tantoos and spraying tantags on beachgoer backs and bellies. Even with cheap rent, Gia needed an income. Bella hoped to get her old job back, teaching beat up the beat dance classes at the gym in Toms River where her ex Tony Troublino was the manager. Gia had a sneaking doubt that would work out, though. Tony and Bella's breakup last fall hadn't been friendly.

Maria poured shots for each of them. "No offense, Gia, but your employment isn't my problem. Today is *my* day. Let's keep the focus on *me*. And, right now, I wanna have a shot of rum."

Gia took her glass and said, "I take it back. You haven't changed."

"You'll find a job. You can always work the Shoot the Freak booth on the boardwalk or sell fried clams." Maria took a drag from her cigarette, exhaled. "My first cigarette as a re-re-remarried woman. Tastes *great*." She raised her shot glass. "To love. *Per amore*."

The cousins said, *"Per amore."*

They downed their shots.

Bella asked, "Do you find it ironic that you got married on Independence Day?"

"I'm hoping to see some fireworks on my wedding night, if you get my meaning, nudge, wink, squee."

"Ewww," said Gia.

"Maybe one of you will get lucky with Fredo tonight."

The girls cracked up. "You mean the kid who's terrified of his own turds?" asked Bella. "I like a man who's a little tougher than that."

"Be nice to him, for me? He's awkward, but he's a good kid," said Maria. "Just a little overshadowed by his mother."

"More like bulldozed," said Gia.

"How're your moms?" asked Maria, who'd met Alicia Spumanti and Marissa Rizzoli last summer.

Gia glanced at Bella and saw her eyes cloud over. The truth was, Aunt Marissa wasn't doing so well. Better now than she'd been in the fall, winter, and spring, but still recovering. Bella rarely, if ever, discussed her mom's cancer. The very thought of it was emotional kryptonite. Gia changed the subject. "It's *your* day, Maria, remember? We're all about you, you, you, and then more you. Whatever you want. We hear and obey."

"Well, then, I want another drink."

Gia poured the rum. "To good health."

Maria said, *"Alla buona salute."*

They drank again.

Knock. Maria screamed at the door, "I'm naked in here!"

Gia wasn't sure if that was supposed to lure someone in or frighten him away. Maria took dress number two off the hanger and stepped into it. The royal-blue, strapless number was jarringly un-Maria-like. It was a proper lady's dress. Solid color, no shine or animal print. Knee length. Total cleavage coverage. Since Gia had seen enough of Maria's cracked, sun-damaged cleavage to last a lifetime, she wasn't sure why she missed it now.

"I'm decent!" hollered the bride.

Sad, but true.

Donna and her posse burst into the room. Each was draped in fur, and dripping with diamonds on their earlobes and fingers. Gia had to blink from so much bling in such a small space. Maria doled out shots of Bacardi for her friends. "To the beautiful young bride!" said Donna.

Gia nearly choked on her rum. To be honest, she had no idea how old Maria was. Anywhere between forty and dead. The ladies passed the bottle around until it was gone. Gia tried to imagine her mom—same age as the Real Housewives of Seaside—sucking down rum the night after a champagne binge. Ugh. The ladies fawned over Maria, going a million miles a minute about how fantastic she looked. She gobbled up the attention. Antonia and Carmela got in a baby slap fight over who got the honor of escorting Maria to the Trident Lounge. They each took one arm and pulled on Maria like a wishbone.

"Are you two excited about your date with Fredo?" asked Donna while they watched the Battle of the Bride.

Bella said, "*Excited* isn't the word."

"So what is?" asked Donna, her blue eyes challenging and crackling.

"*Disgusted?*" Gia said.

"*Repulsed?*" said Bella.

Donna's face froze, then she burst out laughing. "You girls are *adorable*! So freakin' cute."

"Okay, I'm ready to make my entrance," announced Maria.

Antonia on one arm, Carmela on the other, the bride left her chamber to greet her guests. The rest of the furry ladies followed. Gia and Bella were left behind. So that was how it was gonna be.

Bella asked, "Cocktail?"

Gia nodded. "Double."

Chapter Six

May I Cut the Cheese for You?

Fredo Lupo walked through the ballroom at Neptune's, head swiveling on his pencil neck, searching the crowd for his dates. He'd circled the cocktail lounge three times before heading into the main banquet room. Gia and Bella were the bridesmaids, for Christ's sake. They had to be here somewhere.

Were they avoiding him, even hiding from him? He swallowed a lump of anxiety that made his Adam's apple bob. He'd do one more lap, then he'd find his mother. She'd smoke out the girls.

Then he saw them. The DJ had only just started spinning, and the dance floor was empty except for Gia and Bella. They were holding drinks and dancing around a pile of their shoes and purses. The tall one—Bella—had magnificent knockers. The little one—Gia—had the cutest face he'd ever seen. The face of a dirty angel. A wider circle of goombahs watched them, saliva practically foaming around their lips.

Gia swayed to the music, arms pumping, hips shaking. The red feathers on her dress floated up and down. If she kept flapping like that, she might fly away. On the edge of the dance floor, his cousin Cara stood next to some juiced-up meathead, pointing and laughing at Gia, who either didn't notice or didn't care—totally oblivious. Fredo flushed with embarrassment, remembering Gia's round, dark eyes when she saw him on the crapper at the club last night. Anxiety spiking, Fredo reached into his pocket for his pill vial. One Ativan, down the hatch. He dry-swallowed it and willed himself to relax.

Girls made Fredo nervous. He had femalephobia. Not that he didn't love women. He worshipped them. But whenever they came too close, he nearly jumped out of his skin. Gia seemed like a harmless nutcase. But Bella with the boobs that just. Didn't. Quit? Terrifying. Hardbodies sent him into a panic attack. Models made him faint.

He needed to sit. Checking his place card, Fredo found his table. He sat. Eventually, the girls would get thirsty or hungry and join him. He didn't dance. It was just too physical for him. While he waited, he looked around Neptune's. He'd been to a hundred christenings, confirmations, weddings, and other family func-tions here. His father, Luigi, had a piece of the place. Other rooms in the huge catering hall looked as if you'd stepped into the Ital-ian Renaissance. Gold leaf everything, marble columns, ornate paintings of cherubs and vineyards, overstuffed velour couches, and gold-painted chairs. This particular banquet room took the Neptune's Hideaway theme to extremes. The theme was Under the Sea, with swimmy, coral-hued tablecloths and silver metallic paint. LED lights under the dance floor changed from blue to green every few seconds, which gave the impression of moving water. A light was under each individual table, too, making the coral tablecloths glow. A dozen mirror balls hung from plaster medallions on the ceiling, each with a blue beam shining on it. He focused on the blue light. It was soothing.

His cousin Cara walked by his table. He smiled at her. Uphold-ing a lifelong tradition, she said, "Eat me, dork."

Simply cutting. Elegantly humiliating. Cara was the biggest bitch he knew or ever would know. Although he should be used to her teasing by now, her mean remark made his pulse race. Self-conscious, he felt other people's eyes on him, the lonely dork sitting alone. He prayed his mom wouldn't try to dance with him, hug him like a baby, as she did at every family event.

Calm down, he told himself. Tonight, he would not be undermined by anyone. He had two sexy girls as his dates. He'd get them drinks or cut their meat—if they let him. He just wanted a chance, the opportunity, to serve. It'd be his honor.

"There he is," said Gia, her brow beading. She plopped down in the seat to his right. "You look good, Fredo. Better than last night."

Bella pulled up the chair on the other side of him. "Did the waiters come by yet? Maria said choice of prime rib, chicken, or salmon. I'm going for prime rib."

Gia said, "Me, too."

Fredo watched in amazement as these lovely creatures gnawed through dinner rolls and picked their teeth with their nails. He might've been staring.

"Say something, Fredo," Gia demanded. "You're freaking me out."

He opened his mouth, but nothing came out.

Bella said, "You're freaking *him* out, Gia."

"I have to ask you, Fredo," said Gia. "What's so scary about the sight of your own crap? I love looking at mine. I can't wait to see how big it is. Honestly? I'm proud of them! I'm poop positive. You should be, too."

"Stop! We're eating," said Bella, laughing. "I totally agree with you. But, damn, not during dinner."

Fredo stammered, "I . . . I . . . I think you both look smokin' tonight." One of his prepared lines.

"You look fresh, too," said Gia, licking butter off her knuckle and burping.

Were they making fun of him? They didn't seem to be. Fredo made the conscious decision to take them at face value. Unlike every other woman here—except his mom—they didn't seem to be creeped out by him.

"Your hair is very patriotic," he said of their red, white, and blue streaks.

"And yours is superslick," said Bella.

"How's the suit?" he asked.

"Too much black," said Gia. "With the skinny tie and white shirt? It's like you escaped from *Reservoir Dogs*."

"He does have a young Steve Buscemi vibe," said Bella. "Do you get that a lot?"

Fredo nodded, even though he'd never heard that before. "I can see it." This was a bona fide conversation! Progress!

The music was interrupted when the DJ announced, "Ladies and gentlemen, your first course is now served." House music was replaced by Sinatra, aka tunes to eat by. Plates of mozzarella, tomato, and basil appeared before them.

"May I cut the cheese for you?" Fredo offered Gia.

The girls burst out laughing. Gia said, "I'm pretty sure I can cut the cheese all by myself."

A small spark of happiness lit in Fredo's chest. He'd made the girls laugh, even if by accident. He decided to laugh along. It wasn't easy, but he was making the right sounds. Bella patted his back. A friendly gesture?

"Are you choking?" she asked, with a sharp whack between the shoulder blades.

"I'm fine, thanks."

Gia said, "If you do choke, Bella knows the Heinielick maneuver."

"The Heinielick?" said Bella, laughing. "It's called *Heimlich*."

Oh, God. The visual—a tongue and a tush—flitted across Fredo's brain. He reached for his water glass and nearly choked for real this time.

"I gotta ask something else," said Gia. "What's with the cowboy stuff, the country music and western decor at your club? Where did you get that pony?"

Fredo nodded. He could talk business. "You mean the mechanical stallion? I hired a guy to modify a kiddie ride, like you see outside of Wal-Mart. It was originally a dinosaur."

"I humped a dinosaur," said Gia. "Kewl."

"It's a very popular attraction at the Cowboy Club. There's no other country-western-themed place in Seaside," Fredo continued. "It's always been my philosophy to find a hole and fill it."

The girls laughed again. "You and every other guy on the planet," said Bella.

"I mean . . ."

"I get it," said Gia. "But did you ever think there was no country-western club in Seaside for a reason? People hate that shit."

Fredo felt stung. He was proud of his club and was desperate for it to succeed. "Country happens to be extremely popular."

"Maybe in Wyoming," said Bella.

"It's not Jersey," said Gia. "How many people do you know personally, your friends, who like it?"

Fredo liked it. Anyone besides him? Well, he didn't have many friends to sort through. Frowning, his mood took a turn for the worse. Gia was daffy, but in this case, she was 100 percent right. He suddenly felt crushed. Had his parents—and investors—known that his choice of theme wouldn't play in Seaside? Dad probably did. Why not tell Fredo his real opinion?

But Fredo knew why. His parents didn't want to hurt his feelings. Given the relentless bullying he'd endured at school, his parents were overly protective. When he was a child, he needed the buffer. But now, he wanted advice, not protection. It occurred to Fredo that he needed more brutal honesty in his life. He was hungry for a triumph, but his instincts were a bit off. He was sure he could be a success if someone told him the unvarnished truth, no matter how harsh, about his ideas. Someone like Gia.

The DJ spoke into the microphone again. "Your attention please! Now, for the first time as husband and wife—"

"The second time!" someone yelled. The room filled with titters.

"The *second* time as husband and wife," corrected the DJ, "Stanley and Maria Crumbi!"

The newlyweds swept onto the dance floor and took their bows. Stanley and Maria waited for the music to start for the traditional first dance. A song came on, and everyone started laughing.

"What?" asked Fredo.

Gia said, "It's 'Bad Romance' by Lady Gaga."

That *was* pretty funny. Gia and Bella liked the song. They grinded in their seats. After a verse and a chorus, the dance floor filled up. Fredo's cousin Cara and her boyfriend crossed right in front of their table. A few times, Cara glanced over at him. Or was she checking out Gia?

"Tell me about that skinny bitch," said Gia.

"My cousin?"

"She a good kid, or a rancid bitch?"

Anyone who knew their history wouldn't fault Fredo for hating Cara. When they were kids, she filled Fredo's soda with liquid soap. Cara once locked him in the basement and didn't tell anyone where he was for a whole day. When Fredo was in junior high, she printed up and distributed FREDO IS GAY T-shirts to his enemies. If anyone deserved to be hated, it was Cara. But telling an outsider such as Gia would violate a family trust.

The expression on his face said it all. Gia frowned. "Let's dance," she said. "Bella, you coming?"

Bella shook her head. "You go. I'll get drinks for us."

Gia grabbed Fredo's wrist, kicked off her shoes, and pulled him onto the dance floor, right next to Cara and her townie. Gia began her kooky moves, shaking her peaches and writhing her hips. Fredo was so stunned to be out there, he could barely sway to the beat.

"You have to move, Fredo," encouraged Gia. "I feel like I'm dancing with a potted plant."

Behind him, someone said, "Dork."

Fredo spun around, but couldn't catch who made the comment.

A new tune came on. Gia really liked it and cheered and bounced up and down on her bare feet. She raised her fist and started punching the air to the beat.

Fredo could do that, if nothing else. He mimicked her odd motion. It felt . . . good. Really good. Energy flowed up from the reverberating floor, charging through the length of his body, up, up, and out of his pounding fist.

"That's it!" yelled Gia. "Pump it hawd!"

Fredo got into it. All the anger, sadness, and self-consciousness that had weighed him down his whole life got lighter with each pump. Before long, his other arm got in on the act, too. He closed his eyes and let the house music pulse through his heart. His legs starting moving, too.

"Ouch!"

Fredo opened his eyes. Cara's furious face was inches from him. She screamed, "You stepped on my foot, dork."

Gia pushed between them and said, "Frankie, your date's having a temper tantrum. Maybe you should give her a time-out."

The beefy dude frowned and said over Cara's head to Gia, "You want to do this now? Fine. Let's get it over with."

"Out of respect for Maria and Stanley," said Gia, "outside."

She cut a swath through the crowd of people and marched in her tiny bare feet out of the banquet hall, through the front doors of Neptune's, and into the damp parking lot. Fredo rushed to keep up. Half the reception guests followed them, including Frank and Cara.

Fredo realized suddenly that Gia hadn't asked him to dance just for fun. She had unfinished personal business with Cara's boyfriend. God, Seaside Heights was a small world. The lines between families in this town were like a sticky spiderweb. Right now, Fredo felt a bit like a fly.

Gia and Frankie squared off. A small crowd formed around them. Fredo stayed close behind Gia. She was radiating waves of scorching-hot anger at this guy. He was amazed such a small person could generate so much heat.

"You're the one who left Seaside, Gia," shouted Frankie. "And you never came back down! You said you'd come, but you were always too tired or busy or just plain lazy. Yeah, I said it. You're lazy and spoiled. I was willing to meet you halfway, but you expected me do *everything*! I treated you like a queen, but you refused to cook for me, even after I drove two hours to Brooklyn for one night when I had to work the next day."

"I get it. You think I'm lazy and spoiled, so that makes it okay to *cheat on me* with a teenager? This is how you treat a woman like a queen? So what if I don't cook? Not every woman is a wifey. And you know exactly why I couldn't leave Brooklyn. My family needed me at home, as I explained to you every time you whined about it. You can't blame me for the *fact* that you're a lying, cheating, child-molesting douche bag."

The crowd reacted to that with taunts and jeers. Frank vs. Gia was like the mountain vs. the mouse. The mouse was winning. Frank stammered, chagrined. After you've been called out for hooking up with a high school girl, where can you go from there?

Cara butted in, "You can't talk to my boyfriend like that."

Frank said, "Stay out of it."

"Can someone please make Frankie's toddler stop crying?" said Gia.

Cara hauled back, her bony fist then launching forward. Gia darted left. Cara's punch sailed through space and landed squarely on Fredo's jaw.

"Fredo!" shouted Gia. "You bitch! No one punches my date."

In a haze, Fredo sank to his knees. He watched a fuzzy movie of a mouse in a red-feathered dress grabbing a handful of his hateful cousin's hair and yanking it hard. Cara screamed in pain, which made him smile. His vision blurred. On his back now, Fredo stared at a thousand shimmering lights from a dozen mirrored balls. But then he realized they were the stars.

Chapter Seven

Guidar on the Fritz

The bar was across the banquet room, next to a giant ice sculpture of Cupid shooting an arrow through a heart. Maria must have pushed for this. Stanley probably looked at it and saw dollar bills melting.

If Bella ever got married, she'd . . . scratch that. Why give yourself to someone who would break your heart at the first sign of trouble? When she let herself think about her father Charlie's actions last winter—refusing to help Marissa when she was sick, then walking out on their family when they were at their worst—Bella's heart felt like that sculpture. A block of ice.

"Drink," she said to herself. Man, did she need (another) one. The shots of Bacardi might as well have been poured down the sink for all the good they did her.

To the bartender, she said, "Tequila."

He set up a glass and poured. She shot it, replaced the glass, and said, "Again."

He refilled her glass.

"Can I join you?" asked a kid standing next to her. In his early twenties, he was dressed in black jeans, motorcycle boots, a gray T-shirt with a white skull on it, and black blazer. His skin was pale. The hair? Jet-black with spikes. He must have emptied a can of Deluxe Aqua Net to keep the clumps sticking straight up. Around his sky-blue eyes, he wore as much black eyeliner as she did. *A punk? In South Jersey?* The kid took a wrong turn somewhere around the Lower East Side of Manhattan. Not her usual type, but cute. Sexy.

"Free country," she said.

"Two hundred and thirty-six years old today." The punk nodded at the bartender and downed his shot. "Happy July Fourth. Happy wedding. Excellent bridesmaiding. You didn't fall down or drop the bouquet. Congratulations."

"Thanks. Standing up for ten minutes straight is a tough job. But some bitch has to do it."

He smiled. His teeth were charmingly crooked.

Bella found herself smiling back at him. She felt an old urge to sketch his face. She used to draw a lot, back in high school. Bella had taken a few art classes and would have liked to do more. But her dad didn't see the point of pursuing art, or college for that matter. His plan was for Bella to marry a kid from the neighborhood and spend the rest of her life shitting out babies and cranking out sausage at the family deli. Bella begged to go to college for three years and was on the verge of giving up when Charlie sold the deli, leaving Bella without a solid plan for the future. Thanks to Mom's subtle manipulation, Dad agreed to pay some of Bella's college tuition. She'd enrolled at New York University in Manhattan's Greenwich Village last fall.

Her freshman year was a struggle. She'd had a vision of walking through Washington Square Park in thigh-high leather boots, her hair extensions blowing in the autumn wind, shopping at the Bebe store on Fifth Avenue with new friends, drinking espressos in Little Italy, reading, studying, having deep conversations about literature and art. Never happened. Bella found it impossible to make friends. She tried. But the kids at NYU wanted nothing to do with her.

The decision was made early on that instead of living in a dorm with the other freshmen, Bella would live at home. She'd take the subway into the city for her classes. Not living on campus hurt her socially. She was also a few years older than the other freshmen, having deferred college for three years. And then some intangible factors set her apart. Her working-class roots. Her boobs. Her Brooklyn accent. Her slutwear and winter tan. Bella fit like Lycra in her own neighborhood. She felt at home in Seaside, too. But at NYU? She was a freak. The snobby girls looked down on her. The boys swarmed like flies on roadkill. But they only wanted one thing—and it wasn't her opinion on the use of imagery in Dante's *Inferno*.

Throw into that stew Mom's shocking cancer diagnosis, Dad's abandonment—and her breakup with Tony.

"Are you okay?" the punk asked gently.

Bella swallowed her anger whole. She had a talent for keeping her feelings locked up. She both feared and admired Gia's ability to express herself. Her emotions spilled out uncontrollably, as if her tiny body couldn't contain them.

"Not okay. Too thirsty."

"We can take care of that."

She watched him flag down the bartender. His eyes were incredible. Not sky blue, actually. Electric blue, like neon. She'd never seen eyes that color before.

"How do you know the newlyweds?" she asked.

"I don't," he said.

"Crashing a wedding?"

"I'm delivering a gift. I was hired to paint a portrait of the bride and groom."

"You're an artist?" she asked, instantly intrigued.

He shook his head. "I hate that word. It makes me feel self-conscious."

Bella nodded. "Do you have a pen?"

Without asking why she wanted one, he reached into his inside jacket pocket and withdrew a black ballpoint. Bella studied his

profile and did a quick line drawing of him on a cocktail napkin.
The pen tore the paper a little, but the sketch wasn't terrible. "For
you."

"This is pretty good. You can draw," he said admiringly. "Let
me do you."

She raised her eyebrows. "You want to do me?"

"Who wouldn't?" Another boy would blush or stammer if
Bella made a sexy comment. But this punk was supercool. Taking pen to cocktail napkin, he quickly drew Bella's face. It took all
of a minute. With just a few lines, he somehow captured her es-
sence. The upward tilt of her eyes, her graceful cheekbones, pretty
pointed chin, and full lips. The long, straight hair, and hoop earrings. But what impressed Bella the most: he'd added a detail, a
flower in her hair.

"A rose?" she asked. "That's my favorite. How did you know?"

"I didn't. I like roses, too. They open slowly. One petal at a
time. I don't trust anything that opens up too quickly."

"You prefer to go slow?" She raised the shot glass to her full
lips, traced the rim with her tongue, then drank, never taking her
eyes off him.

"I'm William Lugano."

"Lugano? You're Italian?" She would never have called that.
Her guidar was on the fritz.

"Half. My dad's family was from northern Italy, which is practically Switzerland."

"Isabella Rizzoli. Do you go by Bill, Will, Liam?"

"Will. And you? Izzy, Lia, Bella?"

"Bella."

They shook hands. She noticed the letters L-O-V-E were tattooed on his knuckles. "Let me guess. On your other hand, you've
got the word *hate*."

"Hate isn't the opposite of love."

"It's not?"

He held out his left hand. Across the knuckles and the space between them were tattooed the letters *R-E-G-R-E-T*.

"That's deep." Bella's tone was sarcastic. But the idea—love and regret as opposites—was definitely provocative. "So where's the wedding portrait? Can I see it?"

"It's wrapped. I'm supposed to present it when the cake is served."

"Give me a sneak peek. I won't tell anyone." He wavered. Bella gave him her pleading eyes, batting her extra set of lashes. "Don't be a twat tease."

He raised his eyebrows. "A *what*?"

"Come on. Lemme see."

"If Donna Lupo finds out, I'm in deep shit."

Christ, not her again. "You're not afraid of Donna Lupo, are you?"

"Yes!"

"Me, too," said Bella, laughing. "Don't worry. I promise to keep my trap shut."

"It's outside."

In his car? Bella listened in her head for the siren of doubt. She'd learned firsthand last summer that you can't be too careful going anywhere with a stranger. She'd fought off a date rapist. Even though she clobbered the little shit, the memory still shook her up. "I'm a brown belt in karate, so if you're luring me out there to rape or abduct me, you're gonna eat pavement."

"Duly warned." Will led Bella into the parking lot. He stopped at a vintage silver Ducati motorcycle, propped up on its kickstand by the side of the building. Strapped with bungee cords to the seat was an eleven-by-fourteen-inch package wrapped in brown paper.

He rode a bike. Bella felt a twinge in a sensitive spot. What was it about motorcycles that was so freakin' sexy? "You brought the painting on your bike? From where?"

"I live in Atlantic City. I've done work for Mrs. Lupo before."

"Are you famous?"

"Ha! I wish. No, she must have googled 'cheapest portrait painting in Atlantic and Ocean Counties.'"

He unpeeled a taped corner of the brown paper, then another. Holding the painting up to the security light swarming with mosquitoes, he showed her his work. The image was of Maria, the new version with blond hair and a vacuum-sealed face, in a red, Valentino-style dress, reclining on a bearskin rug, her legs about twice as long as in real life. Her arm rested in Stanley's lap. He was seated on a black leather couch, in an Armani-style gray suit, a superstudly bulge in his trousers, with his gold-ringed hand on top of Maria's head.

Although it reminded Bella of something out of *Scarface*, the likenesses of Maria and Stanley were amazing. The drapes looked like real damask. She could almost feel the tickle of bear fur. Most of all, the tacky motif cracked her up. But if she laughed, she might hurt his feelings.

"It's okay to laugh. It's supposed to be funny," he said. "Ironic. A reference to Michelle Pfeiffer and Al Pacino in—"

"I was *just* thinking *Scarface*! I swear!"

"So you get it," he said, his blue eyes gleaming. "Whew. That's a relief. No one has seen this but you. And me."

Bella felt another flutter. Not sexual per se, but inspirational. This kid had talent. His downplaying it only impressed her more. After her first boyfriend, Bobby, and then Tony, she'd had all the guido bluster she could stomach. Granted, her year had been too tumultuous to think about romance. But now, standing in the parking lot, dried seagull-shit smears underfoot, the faint smell of Dumpster in the damp July air, Bella felt that part of herself coming back to life.

Will replaced the portrait and retaped it. Unable to resist, Bella put her hand over his. His skin was warm to the touch.

"It really is good," she said, and leaned toward him.

A shout echoed in the night. Then more. A commotion rose in the parking lot. Their heads snapped toward it. Bella thought she saw a flash of Gia's red-feather dress in the fray. The crowd pressed into a circle, blocking Bella's view.

Of course, Gia is at the center of it, thought Bella. Her cousin was a drama magnet. Bella rushed forward and elbowed through the gawkers to see what was going on.

By the time she got through, Fredo was on his back on the ground, eyes open but unfocused. Cara was holding her head, mascara running down her face. On her knees, Gia was bent over Fredo, gently patting his cheek and saying his name. A voice boomed behind her, "My son! Where's my Fredo!? No! What did you do to him?"

Frank's tartlet, Cara, pointed at Gia. "She started it, Aunt Donna."

Gia said, "It wasn't my fault!"

Donna Lupo pushed Gia out of the way and cradled Fredo's head in her cleavage. While rocking, she sobbed, "My boy! My only boy!"

The tableau of a mother holding her immobile son reminded Bella of the Renaissance paintings of the pietà she'd studied in art history class. Mary holding Jesus after he was pulled from the cross.

Someone said, "Luigi Lupo's son, flattened by a girl."

Snickers spread like a virus. Maria and Stanley broke through the circle of spectators and took in the situation.

"A fistfight at an Italian wedding," said Stanley. "This has to be a first."

"*Now* it's a party," said Maria, clearly hammered. She raised her glass and shouted, "Who needs a refill?"

The newlyweds managed to herd their guests back inside. Bella went to Gia and helped her to her feet. Bella had to step over Fredo's outstretched legs on the way. Awkward.

"I didn't start it," said Gia to anyone who'd listen. "Cara threw the first punch."

"Don't speak to me!" barked Donna. "Get away from my son!"

Bella glanced around for Will, but he was gone. He wasn't kidding about being afraid of Donna Lupo. Bella put her arm around Gia. They went back inside. Once safely away from the pietà in the parking lot, Bella said, "I think the polite thing—and the smart thing—would be to grab our purses and shoes and get the hell out of here."

"But they haven't cut the cake yet," said Gia. "Did you see it? It's the shape of New Jersey."

"I love wedding cake," said Bella, reconsidering. "Okay. We stay."

"Yay! But just one piece. My badonk is ridonk."

Chapter Eight

No Badge, No Beach

Gia woke up with a ferocious cake hangover. Bacardi plus choco-late equaled a death-by-sugar headache. Added to the throbbing skull, the shock of waking up within the cinder-block walls of her bedroom gave Gia a flashback to her short but traumatic afternoon in the Seaside Heights jail last summer. She ate three peanut-butter-and-jelly sandwiches while behind bars. God as her witness, Gia would never touch sugar again.

Although, an ice cream sandwich would really hit the spot.

Crawling into the living room, Gia found a note on the kitchen counter: *Went for a run. XXOO.*

How the hell could Bella drink all night, then subject her body to torture? Only way Gia would go running in this heat? If Sasquatches were chasing her. What Gia needed was her instant hangover helper: a vodka-and-cranberry smoothie. She opened the fridge door, hoping the ingredients would magically appear. But the shelves were as bare as her bottom.

The plan: Get dressed. Go to the Starlite Diner for breakfast. Since Tantastic was no longer an option, she'd have to march up and down the boardwalk, looking for a job. She'd take anything. Standards? Low. Having landed and lost two dozen jobs in the last few years, Gia knew it was easier to trade up for a better job if you already had one.

Agenda settled, Gia put on a camo tube skirt, a T-shirt that said DOWN WITH CLIMAX CONTROL, and a pair of pink flip-flops. In the bathroom, she washed her face, brushed, flossed, and twisted her patriotic hair into a model's day-off topknot. Next, Gia's version of a five-minute face: two sets of false lashes on top, one on the bottom, black liquid liner all the way around. Pink frosty lips. Stepping back, she appraised her look in the full-length mirror. Simple yet slammin'.

One problem, though. Gia hadn't gone tanning in a week. Her skin was barely darker than a paper grocery bag. She'd planned on getting a custom full-body myst at Tantastic. Biting back a sob, Gia mourned losing a full summer of free tanning. She'd have to find a new salon. But in the meantime, she'd tide herself over with a bronzer blast.

Closing her eyes and pressing her lips closed, Gia held the tan-in-a-can spray bottle twelve inches from the tip of her nose and pressed the nozzle.

Nothing happened.

Friggin' thing. She pressed harder.

The nozzle broke off under her thumb, and the aerosol erupted, coating the cinder-block ceiling with creamy foam. It looked as if the wall were sweating cappuccino. The brown splatter rained onto the floor. Should she clean up? More to the point, like, *how*? With a wad of toilet paper, she dabbed, but that was like trying to soak up the Atlantic Ocean with a tampon.

Fuck it, she decided. She was too hungover and hungry to deal. She'd clean up later. Or, maybe, if she ignored it hard enough, the mess would disappear. Ten minutes later, she sat down at a table at the diner. She waited for someone to take her order.

And waited.

Finally, a server noticed her. "Breakfast's over. We reopen for lunch in an hour."

Starving and disappointed, Gia walked out, dragging her

Hello Kitty purse on the sidewalk, feeling as if she were cursed. Honestly? From the minute they arrived in Seaside, their luck had been all bad. Was destiny trying to tell her something? Gia refused to believe that.

"I'm a good person," she said to herself. "I deserve to have a good time."

Commitment to fun affirmed, Gia went to a food stand and bought a box of fries and a strawberry daiquiri in a plastic cup. The sun was strong. Gia would go old school—dawn-of-time old—and lie out under the sun for a tan. She headed for the beach entry ramp with her goodies.

A kid in a ramp booth stopped her. "Badge."

"I left it in my room," she said.

"No badge, no beach."

Hating to sound like a name-dropping douche bag, Gia went for it anyway. "Do you know Rick Shapiro? The head lifeguard in the Seaside Heights Beach Patrol? He's a really good friend of mine."

"Then you know he's spending the summer in Alaska."

Shit. "I *did* know that. And he told me to tell anyone to let me on the beach until he got back."

"I'll vouch for her," said a familiar voice.

Gia cringed. Destiny was kicking her ass today. It was almost cruel.

Seaside Heights was pretty freakin' small, even at peak summer season. Spend an hour on the boardwalk or the beach, you'd run into just about everyone in town, including the police. Captain Morgan, officer of the law, looked pretty much the same as last summer. "You grew your mustache back," she said. "Looks Hitler-ish."

"I had a nightmare last night that the entire town burned to the ground. I woke up in a cold sweat, and I thought, 'Pink Slippers must be back in town.'"

He called her Pink Slippers. Long, cute story. "I promise I'm not gonna destroy Seaside this year," she said. "I mean, I'm totally gonna destroy it. But I won't damage private property. I hope." Last summer, she'd burned down a house. By accident!

"Stanley Crumbi told me he parked you and your cousin in a fireproof building on Hancock."

Stanley, that scumbag! "Yeah, he's a real sweetheart."

"I'd tell you to stay out of trouble, but we both know that's the impossible dream. I'll be keeping my eye on you. No alcohol on the beach."

Captain Morgan ambled away. The kid in the booth smirked at her.

Oh, God damn it. Now she had a foul taste in her mouth. She dumped the daiquiri in the trash.

Her cell phone vibrated in her pocket. "Gia!" screamed Bella. "What the fuck? You sprayed bronzer all over the bathroom!"

"The frickin' bottle blew up in my hand. I'm suing the manufacturer! It wasn't my fault!"

"Giuseppe Troublino left a message on my cell phone. I can't face him or Tony. You have to go to the body shop and pick up the Honda."

"But . . . I need a tan."

"Get the car, then get the tan."

Bella hung up. *Jeez, you paint the room bronze and your best friend goes apeshit.* Gia headed for Boulevard, hailed a cab, and sulked in the backseat all the way to Giuseppe's garage.

She walked through the open bay doors. The garage was what she expected. Tools, rags, grime, nudie pinup calendar on the wall. In the back, an office with a window. A car was up on the hydraulic lift. Another parked below had its hood open. No sign of the Honda, or any people. "Hello! I'm here!"

An old man rolled out from underneath a car. He was wearing jeans that were more grease than denim, a T-shirt that might've been white in the seventies, and an American-flag bandanna around his wrinkled neck. He sat upright and wiped off his hands with an oil-saturated rag. Gia noticed that the half-moons of his fingernails were black.

When he saw Gia, though, he grinned brightly. Took a decade off his craggy face. "How can I help you?"

"Are you Tony Troublino's grandfather?"

"I prefer to call myself Anthony's handsome and virile father's father. But, yeah. Who's asking?"

"I'm Gia, Bella's cousin. I'm here about the Honda."

Giuseppe frowned. Uh-oh. "About that, I've got some sad news. The Honda died this morning. I'm sorry. We did everything we could."

Gia was overcome. She'd killed Bella's car! This was unforgivable. How could she ever make it up to her? "Can I see the body?" she asked. Paying her respects was the decent thing to do.

"Are you sure you're up for it?"

She nodded, and braced herself. He brought her behind the garage, to the car morgue. There was the Honda, the bumper off, side door crushed, and the roof dented.

"I told Tony last summer that this car wouldn't make it another thousand miles," Giuseppe said. "I can give you a couple hundred for the scrap and parts."

Jesus. One day you had wheels. The next day, you had lunch money. "Cash would be good," she said, wiping away a single tear.

"You're very brave. If there's anything I can do . . ."

"Yeah."

"My wife Tina should be in the office. She'll give you the money."

Gia found the place all right, but instead of Tina, Tony, Bella's ex, sat at the desk. He wore Air Jordans, gray track pants, and a red tank top ironed to a neat crispness. The hair was trimmed short. His bulging, muscular arms and chest were waxed and oiled to a fine sheen. Tony was an advertisement for the GTL lifestyle. Gia was momentarily blinded by the buff.

"You look good, Gia," he said, smiling, standing to give her a hug. "Sorry about the Honda."

What would she tell Bella? "Still managing the gym?"

"Sure am," he said. "You?"

"Currently between dead-end jobs."

"I hear you." He paused for a beat. "How's Bella? I'd ask her myself, but she refuses to talk to me after she dumped my ass for no friggin' reason."

Whoa! He cut right to the heart of the matter. He must miss her bad. "You don't have a clue what you're talking about."

He held up his hands. "Fill me in."

Gia bit her frosted-pink lip. What to do? Bella had made her swear not to tell Tony about Aunt Marissa's cancer because Bella didn't want his pity. Gia would have told everyone she knew because that's what friends are for, right? To give you sympathy and support. But it was Bella's decision to keep her family's crisis to herself. Out of respect for Bella, Gia had to stay silent.

But the desperation on Tony's face! It'd been nine months since Bella had broken up with him, and he still didn't know why.

Gia took mercy on the poor bastard. "You know that Bella's parents sold their deli and planned to spend the money traveling in Italy, right?" He nodded. "They never left Brooklyn. Aunt Marissa went for a checkup two days before their flight, and the doctor noticed something. They postponed the trip so she could get some tests. It turned out she had cancer. She had surgery, chemo. Bella gave up her dorm room to stay home and take care of Aunt Marissa. We all pitched in, but Bella did the most. She insisted on it. Doing a double shift—school and home—would have been okay. Bella can handle just about anything. But Uncle Charlie completely freaked out. He couldn't handle the stress. When Aunt Marissa had her first surgery, he wasn't even at the hospital. He ran off to the nearest bar and stayed for three days. When she started chemo, Uncle Charlie made excuses not to take her to her appointments. He acted like nothing was wrong, as if she was completely healthy. He yelled at Marissa if the laundry wasn't done or if dinner wasn't on the table. It was psycho."

"Prick," said Tony under his breath.

Gia remembered that Tony had had his share of family hardship. He'd lost his parents when he was five and was raised by Giuseppe and Tina. "That's not the worst of it. In February, Charlie left. Packed his bags and moved out. They're getting a divorce."

Tony sucked in his breath. Fighting in families was to be expected. Treating a spouse horribly? Feeling disappointed and disillusioned? It happened in the best of marriages. But divorce? It was rare in the Italian-American community. Not so rare in the Spumanti/Rizzoli family, though. Gia's parents had divorced, too.

"Help me with the timing," said Tony.

"Remember the day you called Bella and started yelling at her about some bullshit? Aunt Marissa had just come home from the hospital after surgery."

"No wonder she told me to drop dead and never call her again. Why didn't she say what was really going on?"

Good question. "Bella's like her dad in some ways. He refused to acknowledge that anything was wrong. And she refused to talk about it."

"I don't even remember what pissed me off that day, or why I went off on her. She was right to dump me. I should've been in tune with her feelings and sensed something was wrong." Tony covered his face with his hands. "I feel like a piece of shit."

"You have to swear not to say anything to Bella. I only told you because you looked so pathetic."

He thought about it. And thought some more.

"Tony," Gia warned. "You better not screw me over. Bella thinks I've got a big mouth as it is."

"You do have a big mouth. Don't worry. I won't say anything."

"Good. Now. Can I get two hundred dollars for the Honda?"

He mumbled, "Sure."

"And a can of Coke from the machine?"

"Okay."

"And a lift back to the boardwalk?"

Chapter Nine

B-I-M-B-O, and Bimbo Was Her Name-O

Not a nibble after nearly a week of job hunting. Bella must have filled out twenty job applications, from funnel-cake fryer to skee-ball ticket taker. Gia had been searching, too. No luck.

They'd burned through Giuseppe Troublino's $200 on the basics—food, vodka, beach badges, and laundry. Gia was starting to have withdrawal symptoms from tanning deprivation. To save money, Bella was attempting to cook dinners in the toaster oven.

A vacation wasn't fun when you were broke. A week in Seaside, and they'd seen the inside of only one club: the Cowboy Club. As for cocktails, they were stuck mixing their own cheap vodka cranberries in the Prison Condo. If one of them didn't find a job—any job—soon . . . Bella didn't want to think about it.

Bella's cell phone vibrated on the condo's living room table. She grabbed it, doing a silent prayer the call was from her future employer. "Hello?"

"It's Mrs. Stanley Crumbi. The sexually satisfied newlywed."

Cringe. "TMI."

"What're you girls doing tonight?"

"IDK. Making frozen pizza at the Prison Condo, I guess."

"The Prison Condo? Come on. It's not that bad."

"I bought a plant, to add some life to the place."

"Great idea."

"It died."

Maria said, "So come out tonight. I'll take you to a thing."

"A party? With Donna Lupo? No thanks."

"She won't be there. And it's not exactly a party. You'll have fun, though. It's a gathering. Of women. Mature women. In a church basement to play bingo."

"I'd rather eat sand," said Bella. "Actually, considering what we've been eating, sand doesn't sound that bad."

Maria exhaled. "It's not a request. Mama Lupo insists. She's Luigi's mother, the family matriarch. She's going to make a ruling on you and Gia."

"We haven't done anything wrong."

"Doesn't matter. Cara Lupo is telling everyone Gia is responsible for embarrassing Fredo—and, by association, the family—at the wedding."

Bella said, "Gia knows she's innocent. Fredo knows. What difference does it make if his parents don't believe us?"

Maria paused. "How's your job search going?"

"Sucks! I can't find anything. It's like we've been blackballed or . . . wait, are you saying what I think you're saying?"

"No one in this town is going to hire you until you make peace with the Lupos."

"FML."

"Enough with friggin' letters," said Maria. "I hate that shit. I never know what you're talking about. Just come to the game tonight. This is a rite of passage for Seaside Heights society. I came a few times with Donna. You show up, make a donation. Mama will give you her blessing. By this time tomorrow, you'll have jobs. And I'll talk to Stanley about moving you to a new place that doesn't kill plants."

What choice did she have? "Okay," said Bella, and took down the particulars.

The toilet flushed and Gia emerged from the bathroom. "I

could have framed that one. Fredo has no idea what he's missing."

"Get dressed. We're going to church."

"Our Lady of the Perpetual Sorrow?" asked Gia, reading the plaque on the outside of the stone church. "Oh, yeah! This place *rocks*."

Bella was in her "straight but not narrow" outfit of a black Lycra dress, a ponytail, and "flats," or two-inch pumps. She took in her cousin's outfit. Jeans short shorts with a black, studded belt. A black, off-the-shoulder T-shirt that read PASS THE BRACIOLA, a leopard-print jacket, and midcalf, furry, black boots. "The boots might be a bit much."

"They're the only shoes I've got that aren't flip-flops or peeptoe heels," she said. "Toe cleavage isn't Catholic."

"It's twenty bucks per person. Maria's going to cover us."

"You mean Our Lady of the Perpetual Booze Breath?"

Laughing, they went through the arched doors. At seven o'clock, it was still light outside. Entering the church was like walking into a cave, the only light coming from candles and the stained-glass windows. Bella inhaled the scents of wax, wood, and lemon Pledge. A regular churchgoer as a kid, Bella had stopped attending as a teenager. While her mom was in surgery, though, she'd gone to the hospital chapel and prayed like she played.

Her prayers were answered. After months of treatment, Marissa was in remission. For now. Her mom had a fifty-fifty chance of a recurrence, which would be a virtual death sentence. If Marissa stayed healthy for five years, she'd be considered "a survivor."

Gia read Bella's mood. "You're My Lady of the Perpetual Balls. You blew my mind this year. No one's as tough as you."

Bella looked down at Gia's huge, dark eyes and felt the love pouring out of them. That did it. The tears came. She sank into a pew and cried. Until this moment, Bella hadn't let herself sob for her mom. Consciously or not, she thought crying meant Mom was dying. If she held her tears inside, everything would be okay. It was a superstitious bargain she'd made with herself.

Blubbering, Bella said, "Our Lady of the Perpetual Mortification."

"You mean me?" asked Gia.

"No, me! I'm crying in public!"

"It's not public. It's a friggin' church. And you have to let out your feelings, Bells, or you'll get emotionally constipated."

"I have feelings," said Bella. "That doesn't mean I need to broadcast them."

Of course, Bella was upset about her mom! She would love to scream at her dad for being an incredible tool. She'd love to smack down the girls who rejected her at school, the boys who treated her like a stupid slut. But Bella's tendency was to bottle and cork the anger. Gia was Bella's human corkscrew. Everyone agreed Bella was dangerously repressed about her hell year. Marissa pushed Bella to go to Seaside for July. She said, "You need some down-the-Shore-time with Gia. Have fun. Do all the things I was afraid you'd do last summer. Get drunk and hook up with boys. It's unwind or unravel, Bella. You have to unwind."

Weak as she was, Marissa practically shoved Bella out the door. Yet, this was how she honored her mom's wishes? Crying in church?

"I'm okay," said Bella, pulling herself together.

"Ready to destroy this place?" asked Gia.

"Biblically."

"Huh?"

"Forget it."

They followed a trio of blue-hairs to the basement and found the "games" room. The windowless space was devoted to bingo, with five long tables and dozens of chairs facing a small table in the front of the room. On that table was a metal cage contraption with a plastic hand crank and little white balls inside.

The girls scanned the crowd. Had to be forty women here. They seemed to fall into one of three distinct categories. The *Godfather* grannies bore a striking resemblance to Mother Teresa. The Real Housewives of Seaside Heights were Donna Lupo–type femooks dressed modestly for church in slacks and silk tops, but with full hair and makeup. Furs and diamonds were not allowed in the house of the Lord, apparently. A dozen or so women looked homeless, nut-ward escapees dragging plastic garbage bags of empty cans and bottles, wearing oversize, pilly sweaters in July.

"Don't they seem a bit old, snotty, and grubby to be playing a game called Bimbo?" asked Gia.

"Bingo," said Bella.

"I know, right?"

"The game is called bingo, not *bingo* like 'you nailed it.'"

"You mean this game is called bingo? Like the talking lizard in the Johnny Depp movie?"

"I think that was Ringo," said Bella. "Or is that the Beatle?"

"Eww. Lizards *and* bugs?" Gia groaned. "I hate this game already."

Maria was in the back row, waving her arms to get their attention. It was still a shock to see Maria as blond as Donatella Versace.

Gia said, "Hottie!" and clomped in her boots over to Maria for hugs and kisses. The *Godfather* grandmas watched, eyes twitching, clucking their disapproval. Bella followed Gia, smiling and nodding at the ladies of the perpetual stick up their ass. She tried to figure out which of them was Mama Lupo.

The girls sat next to Maria. She said, "Listen, I need to tell you a few important rules of the game."

Bella turned to the homeless woman on her other side. She smelled like a urine-and-saltwater cocktail. "Okay if I sit here?"

"Touch my bingo card, I'll cut you," she said, brandishing a plastic fork with only one prong.

Meanwhile, another church regular was petting Gia's back like a cat. "Nice kitty," said the obviously crazy lady with wild eyes and insane wiry hair. "Where's the nun?! I'm gonna adopt you."

"She's human, Ruby," yelled Maria. "Human. It's just a leopard-print jacket."

"Meow," the woman cooed, right up in Gia's face.

"Ignore her," said Maria. "She's released from the ward only once a week for this game."

"Mooowwll!" said Ruby more emphatically.

"It's kinda hard to ignore her when she's meowing in my face," said Gia.

One of the RHOSHs clapped her hands right in Ruby's ear. "Back to your seat! Back!" Ruby scurried away. The RHOSH smiled with perfect white teeth, flipped her sleek, straight black hair, and said, "Are you Gia Spumanti? I've heard so much about you."

The warning siren went off in Bella's head. The woman looked familiar, although she hadn't met her yet. Maria looked worried, too. But Gia didn't register danger. She said, "Hey. You look just like this bitch I met the other night. A real top-shelf skank whore named Cara. Do you know her?"

The RHOSH's face turned white under her mask of blush and mascara. "That top-shelf skank whore happens to be my daughter."

Making friends wherever she went, thought Bella of her cuz. Maria put her head in her hands. Her plot to get Gia and Bella off the Lupo enemies' list was not going as planned.

A seriously bent old woman in a black veil came over to their table. Cara Lupo's mother nodded at the geezette, then backed away, bowing at the waist as she retreated.

"Good evening, Mrs. Crumbi," the old lady said to Maria.

"It's an honor, Mrs. Lupo," said Maria, jumping to her feet, taking the woman's withered, gnarly hand and kissing her ring.

So this was the big mama. Hardly taller than Gia, she hooked like a human question mark. In ninety degrees with no air-conditioning, Mama Lupo was swaddled in a black shawl, black dress, black tights, and black orthopedic Skechers. Her wrinkles were deep enough to plant corn. Her hair and skin were the same shade of gray. "Are these the girls who humiliated my grandson at your wedding?"

"Mrs. Lupo, this is Giovanna Spumanti and Isabella Rizzoli from Carroll Gardens, Brooklyn. They're dear friends of mine. They feel shame and remorse about any trouble they might've caused. They want to make amends and pay their respects to you tonight."

The lady nodded, her eyes half-closed and suspicious. "I appreciate that. My Luigi would appreciate it, too."

Gia said, "My condolences about your husband."

"My husband, dear?"

"The veil." Gia gestured to the mourning clothes.

Mama seemed confused. "My husband, Sunny, died thirty years ago. He was gunned down at a tollbooth on the Garden State Parkway. I'm in mourning for Alonzo, my Burmese. He died two years ago, bless his little soul."

"Cat," whispered Maria.

"I love cats," said Gia. "I'm part leopard. Just ask Ruby over there."

"Which part?" whispered Bella.

"The part that purrs."

"Have you made a donation?" Mama pointed a crooked finger toward the straw basket next to the metal cage.

Maria said, "We did. All three of us."

"You girls don't seem like the disrespectful sluts my daughter-in-law said you were," said Mama.

"We're not," said Gia. "Disrespectful."

Mama patted Gia's shoulder and returned to her front-row seat. Gia rubbed where the old woman touched her. "Her hand is ice-cold."

"Vampire?" asked Bella, excited.

"Maybe zombie."

"Girls, I gotta tell you the rules quickly before the game starts," said Maria. "First thing, you have to stay completely silent during the game. . . ."

A priest swept into the room. He wore a floppy black hat, a black cape, a purple silk scarf, a black suit with the traditional white collar, and a few thick chains with heavy gold crucifixes. "Good evening, a-ladies," said the priest with meataballa Italian accent. Was it fake? Couldn't be. Dude was a priest! "I see we have-a some new a-people tonight. My name eez Father Guido Sarducci. Ciao."

"Ciao!" chorused the a-ladies.

"His name is Guido?" said Gia, awed.

"Shut *up*," mouthed Maria.

"Is Guido a name?"

"It's Italian for Joe," Bella said.

"Joe? *My own father is a Guido?*" Gia shouted.

Forty women shushed.

"We-a get started? I take one a-hundred dollar for the church off-a da top," said Father Guido, removing five twenties from the collection basket and slipping them into his pants pocket. "Here-a we go. We pass out-a the cards. Take-a the chips. Now-a, my favorite part. The spin! Here-a we-a go."

He turned the plastic crank, and the numbered balls inside the metal cage bobbed and jumped. After a few turns, he stopped the cage, opened the trapdoor, and removed a single ball. "Ze first-a number eez B6."

The women checked the cards placed in front of them. Each

card had a grid of boxes, five rows up and five rows across. Inside each box was a number, 1 to 100. On top of each vertical row were letters (*B, I, N, G,* and *O*). Bella checked all the boxes in the vertical row under the letter B for the number six. She didn't have it, but Gia did.

"Put a chip in the square," whispered Bella.

"Got it," said Gia.

"Touch my card, I'll fork you," reminded the bag lady to Bella's left.

Father Guido spun the cage again. "Ze second number eez N28. N28."

And so the game began. Bella nearly dozed off about three minutes into it. Gia, however, was on the edge of her plastic church chair, rapt with anticipation when Father Guido spun the cage, and bouncing with excitement if she got to put a chip on her card.

Bella was jerked awake when Gia screamed, "Friggin' bimbo! I mean *bingo*! I win!"

A *Godfather* grandma gasped and started fanning herself. Every woman in the room shot daggers at Gia. Maria groaned.

"But you-a can't win," said Father Guido, shaking his head.

"Wrong! Check my card," said Gia, rushing her card covered in chips to the front of the room.

Father Guido confirmed Gia's win, the whole time shaking his head. His skin got even paler. Bella wondered if it was against priestly modesty to tan. Meanwhile, Gia did a backflip (ex-cheerleader) for joy.

Gia reached into the collection basket, counting the twenties into a neat pile, held it over her head, and waved the stack. "Seven hundred bucks, bitches!" she sang.

Bella's jaw dropped. Seven hundred? That was enough to keep their summer vakay rolling. Plus, they'd played the game, which had earned them the seal of approval from Mama Lupo. Cool jobs, like pole dancing at Bamboo, coming right up.

Maria, meanwhile, looked as if she'd just tongued a cactus. You'd think she'd be happy for them. Bella rushed to give Gia a hug. Together, they celebrated the win, dancing to music only they, dolphins, leopards, and the saints could hear.

"I *love* this game!" Gia told Father Guido. "Can we play again? Like every freakin' week?" She kissed him, leaving a pink lipstick mark on his clerical collar. "We've had nothing but bad luck since we got to Seaside. I prayed for our luck to change. God *does* hear my prayers, even if they're slurred from vodka."

Gia released him, and he reeled backward into the table behind him. The metal cage fell on the floor, and balls scurried across the floor like albino cockroaches.

One of the old ladies screamed as if they really were bugs.

"We really should wrap you in yellow plastic police tape," said Bella, shaking her head.

Cara Lupo's mom yelled, "Stupid idiots!"

Ruby said, "That leopard has rabies!"

Mama Lupo was flapping her black shrouds like a zombie bat.

But Bella and Gia barely noticed. They skipped out of there on a green cloud, singing—"and Bimbo was her name-O"—with relief and happiness.

They were saved! It could only happen in church.

Chapter Ten

A Six-Piece Set of Emotional Douche Baggage

"To Hell's Bells Rizzoli," said Gia, raising her cocktail. "The hottest bitch in the whole freakin' world."

Five juicehead gorillas clinked their beer bottles to Gia's glass and chugged. It was a slow night at Inca. But it was early yet, only nine o'clock on a Thursday. The place would fill up soon enough. Meanwhile, she had $700 in her pocket, money she'd *won*. She'd never won anything before. Not even a stuffed Rasta Banana on the boardwalk.

"Next round's on me," said Gia, slapping a few twenties on the bar. "God wants us to party."

"Save some of it," protested Bella. Then she rethought it. "Oh, what the hell. We should celebrate."

The bartender brought Buds for the boys, refreshed Gia's vodka, and poured Bella another shot of tequila.

One of the gorillas put his hand on Gia's exposed thigh (her short shorts could pass for a thong). He squeezed as high as he could get without giving her a free pelvic exam and said, "Let's get out of here."

"What's your name again?" She knew he'd told her already, but she forgot. A few letters splashed across her vodka-flooded brainpan. "Kevin? Keith? Kelvin?"

"Try Gary," he said, smirking.

Was he making fun of her? Another jerkoff who thought she was stupid because she had short-term memory lapses? "Get your hand off me. I'm not interested." The kid took his beer and walked away. Gia called after him, "You can say 'thanks' for the beer, *Gary*." To Bella, Gia said, "Every guy who likes me is a complete scumbag."

Bella did her shot. "They do seem to flock in your direction. I still can't get over Frankie. He really seemed like a decent guy."

"I'm starting to think I can't trust anyone. The douche bags from my past are giving me a complex. It's like I'm carrying around the distrust with me."

"A six-piece set of emotional baggage."

"Emotional *douche* baggage," corrected Gia.

A man's voice from behind them weighed in, "That's a pretty good line."

The girls spun around on their bar stools. "You again?" Gia said to Captain Morgan. "Who do I call to report a stalker? You?"

Captain Morgan nodded at Bella. "Ms. Rizzoli, evening."

"Right back atcha."

"There's an all points bulletin out on you girls."

"For being too pretty?" asked Gia.

"You stole from a church," he said.

"*What?!* No way. I won that money!" said Gia. "There's a roomful of witnesses, including a freakin' priest!"

"The priest corroborated Mrs. Lupo's account," said the cop. "You're from out of town, so let me explain how this particular bingo game works. It's rigged. You're supposed to pretend to play until Mrs. Lupo wins. Then she donates all the cash to the church. That's the way it's been played for twenty years. No one else *ever* wins. The game is a just a pretense for giving money to the church."

"So I was supposed to throw a bingo game?" asked Gia.

"The church depends on that cash. And Mrs. Lupo likes to win, even knowing that it's rigged. Losing on purpose is how the other players pay their respect to her and her family."

"How were we supposed to know that?" asked Gia. "No one told us."

"Maria kept trying to explain the rules, but the game started before she got the chance." Checking her phone, Bella groaned. She held it up so Gia could see the dozen messages from Maria. Bella played the last one on speaker—Maria's panicked voice: "Fuckfuckfuckfuck . . ."

Officer Morgan said, "That about sums it up."

"Are we in deep shit?" asked Bella.

"When *aren't* you?" He sighed. "If you return the cash to Our Lady tonight and apologize to Father Guido, I'm sure he'll drop the charges."

Gia felt like crying. Even when she won, she lost. "What would happen if we kept it? You can't arrest us for being ignorant of some secret Seaside tradition. To hell with them."

"You did not just say 'to hell' with the church," said Captain Morgan.

Bella asked, "Can we keep *any* of it?"

"Where's the money?" he asked. Gia pulled out the stack. "Is that all of it?"

"Minus eighty bucks," said Gia.

He groaned. "You'll have to write a check to make up the difference."

"I don't have a checking account," said Gia.

"Mine's empty," said Bella.

"For Christ's sake! How do you girls *live*?" Captain Morgan tugged on his mustache. "I'll cover the eighty bucks. But you owe me. Big-time."

"Make it a hundred," said Gia. She peeled off a twenty and gave it to the bartender. "I'm a big tipper. I have a reputation to uphold."

"That's my twenty! And I tip for shit!" complained the cop.

"That is true," muttered the bartender.

"Watch it, Harry!" said the cop.

Gia slid off her stool. She pulled her shorts down as far as they'd go (not far). Two guys at the bar spilled their beers. Bella got up, too, and arranged her dress's halter top, having to shake her boobs into the right position. Four guys fell off their stools.

Captain Morgan said, "Did you two dress like . . . like *that* to play bingo in church with Mrs. Lupo?"

"What? Too prissy?" asked Bella.

"I'm surprised they let you in the door," he said. "And now I've gotta take you back there? Lawd have mercy."

Chapter Eleven

The Short Good-Bye

"It's your landlord. Open up!"

"Stanley?" Bella had only just rolled out of bed. The sound of his banging on the door woke her. She let him in. "What're you doing here?"

Stanley Crumbi rushed into the apartment, quickly closed the door behind him, and plastered his body against it as if he were being chased. "Who's here? Just you and Gia?"

"We don't bring guys home *every* night. Just Saturday through Tuesday."

He didn't laugh. He was too busy scanning the living room/kitchen, then darting around to peek into the bathroom, Bella's bedroom, then Gia's. When he was satisfied they were indeed alone, he said, "Here," and thrust an envelope into Bella's hand.

"You got it backwards," said Gia, rubbing her eyes, shuffling out of her bedroom in a leopard-print robe and her trademark pink slippers. "You're the groom. We're supposed to give *you* a gift."

Bella opened the envelope. "It's four hundred dollars."

"Your rent," he said. "I'm giving it back to you. Minus the week you stayed here. And a few expenses, water, heating . . ."

"*Heating?* It's a brick oven in here," complained Gia.

"Also, there are two coupons for a free pizza at Three Brothers and a half-off ticket for the water park."

"You, Stanley Crumbi, are giving money *away*? What's wrong with this picture?" asked Bella.

Stanley ran a hand over his comb-over. He seemed manic, more so than usual. "You know I got a fondness for you girls."

"Oh, crap," said Gia, plopping down on the couch. "This can't be good."

"I really appreciate you getting me and Maria back together, even though you burned my house down. Maria is crazy for you, too. From the bottom of my heart, with all the love and respect in the world, get the hell out of Seaside and don't come back." Gia and Bella laughed. "I'm friggin' serious! You two have to leave town by noon *today*. Start packing."

"This is about that stupid game?" asked Gia. "We gave the money back! I personally handed it to that priest. He blessed me and said he'd pray for my soul."

"Wouldn't take your confession, though," said Bella.

"He didn't have all night," said Gia.

"Don't take it personally," Stanley said. "The Lupos are extremely sensitive people. Look at them funny, it's like you shat on their ancestors' graves. I'd say, 'Screw the Lupos,' but right now, I'm in the middle of some things with Luigi. Things I can't get out of. I stuck my neck out for you about the fight at the wedding. Maria vouched for you with Donna. But Mama Lupo makes the final cut—and I don't want it to be your throats."

Both girls reached for their necks and gulped. "Let me get this straight," said Gia. "You didn't come by to take us out to breakfast?"

"No."

"You're not here to move us into a cozy bungalow on the beach?"

"Hell, no."

"You're delivering the warning to leave town, with no car, and hardly any money," Gia said.

"You can thank me later."

Bella said, "This is bullshit."

"I know Seaside looks like paradise—"

"Meh," said Gia.

"—but there's a greasy underbelly most people don't know about. You girls are rolling around in it. I'm doing you a huge favor." He checked his phone. "I gotta go. Just leave the keys on the counter. I'm sorry. Maria's sorry. But we'll all be a lot sorrier if you stay." On that scary note, he scurried out.

In a way, Bella felt relieved. Her emotions about coming to the Shore were mixed to begin with. Even though her mom practically threw her out of Brooklyn, Bella felt guilty about leaving her.

Gia, however, didn't mix emotions like cocktails. "That's it? I look forward to our trip for months, and it's over before it even got started? I haven't smushed a hot guido yet!"

"I'll call a cab to take us to the bus station," said Bella. "The ride back to Brooklyn is only an hour and change."

"No way. We have some money. Let's go to Point Pleasant or Belmar."

"Can't you read the signs? We've been cursed since we got here. Destiny is screaming at us to pack it in and go home."

"I don't believe that."

"Name one thing that has gone right all week."

"I won at bingo."

"But the other players were throwing the game."

"I still won."

Bella shook her head. "Whatever. We can't stay here."

"I refuse to go home. What's there for me? My job at the movie theater? I love Vin Diesel to death, but *Fast Five* lost its appeal after the hundredth time." Gia folded her arms across her chest and dug herself into the couch. "You'll have to drag me back to the city."

"You're being impossible."

"And?"

They faced off. Neither spoke. Tension grew. A car horn blasted from the street and made them both start. Someone called their names.

Bella ducked behind the "kitchen" "counter." "They've come for us already!"

"I recognize that voice." Gia got up and leaned out the window. Waving, she said, "It's Fredo! Whoa, he's driving a slick white Caddie convertible."

"Are you freakin' crazy? He's one of them."

Gia yelled, "Come on up."

"You're inviting the wolf into the henhouse."

"First of all, we're not hens. We're chicks. And, second, Fredo's totally harmless. He's a wolf puppy."

The puppy was now at their door, probably holding a blunt object. Gia welcomed him inside. Bella had to admit, with the purple bruise on his chin and his skinny neck, the kid didn't give an impression of dangerousness. Bella's arms were bigger than his.

What was she afraid of? She had skills. She'd been tested. If Fredo came at her, she'd swat him down.

"I came by to say how sorry I am," he said. To Bella: "Why are you looking at me like that?"

The kid cowered. She hadn't realized she was in ready position. Relaxing her stance, she said, "Tell your family we're going."

"I swear to God, I told my parents that Cara started the whole thing. But when she's around them, she's totally different. It's not fair that they believe her over me. I'm furious at them."

Gia said, "Don't you get in trouble, too! You're the vic."

"You're the vics. I should have forced my parents to believe me. It's my fault you got the order. I feel horrible about it. You guys have been great to me. Gia, you're the only person who's ever defended me against Cara. You have to let me make it up to you."

Bella and Gia made eye contact. This could be worth listening to. "How?" asked Bella.

"I want to go with you. Before you say no, hear me out. You two are the luckiest girls I've ever met. I have an idea how we can use your luck to our mutual advantage."

"I think you have us mistaken for two other bitches," said Bella.

"You won the bingo game," he said to Gia. "Do you know that, in twenty years, no one has *ever* beaten my grandmother before? Twenty years. You're, like, a miracle."

Gia said, "Well, actually . . ."

But Bella put her finger to her lips, silencing Gia. "So what if she did?"

"We can go places with your kind of luck. I've got a big car, a fat wallet, a full tank of gas, and snacks for the road."

"What places?" asked Bella.

"What snacks?" asked Gia.

"Just pack your bags. We're going to Atlantic City."

Chapter Twelve

Too Pretty for Sin City

Fredo steered the Caddie into the underground parking lot at Atlantic City's premier hotel/casino, Nero's Palace. He'd already reserved a suite. It had two bedrooms, although, if his wildest dreams came true, all three would share one king-size bed, and he wouldn't hyperventilate from nerves.

Uh-oh. Wood. He maneuvered the Caddie into a spot. If he got out of the car now, they'd know in a second. Why did he always get excited at the most awkward moments? He did the one thing he knew would deflate his, er, situation.

He pictured his mother, waving him in for a kiss.

Ecch. Problem solved.

The girls were already pulling their luggage out of the trunk. He'd never seen zebra-print hard-shell suitcases before. Unlike the women in his family, who expected the men to do everything for them, Gia and Bella hauled their own stuff.

Gia said, "Think I'm too pretty for Sin City?"

"Totally," said Bella. She pulled Fredo's duffel out of the car like a sack of feathers. "You need help carrying your bag, Fredo?" asked Bella, holding it for him.

"Of course not." He took the duffel from her and nearly fell over from the weight. She rushed to help him. "I got it," he insisted.

They walked into the Nero's Palace lobby and were instantly awed. Looking up, the ceiling was painted like a blue sky, with clouds. "This place is incredible!" said Gia, shuffling along in furry, black boots.

"I always stay here," Fredo said. "Nero was *paesan*." Gia looked confused. She got that deer-in-disco-lights look a lot. "*Paesan*, meaning 'countryman.' Italian."

"Wrong," she said. "Nero was a *Roman* emperor. Like Caesar. Everyone knows that."

Fredo whispered to Bella, "Nero was Roman, but not Italian?"

"Just let it go," she said.

In Roman-amphitheater style, the lobby was a huge circular room with columns and marble statues around the perimeter. The statues were of Roman gods and goddesses, including an enormous twenty-foot-tall Jupiter, the king of gods, posed heroically on an island surrounded by a moat. Gia wheeled up to the fenced-in statue and said, "Something's moving in the water."

Fredo took a closer look. "Are those alligators?"

Sure enough, a pair of small gators floated to the water's surface, their snouts and eyes visible. Gia pointed at another statute, of Juno, Jupiter's babe. "Check it. The world's first pouf!"

Bella said, "I relate to Minerva, goddess of wisdom."

"I'm Diana," said Gia, pointing at a sculpture of the hunter goddess. "I hunt gorilla."

"You're both Venus, goddess of hotness," said Fredo. "Friggin' obviously."

The girls thought about it. Gia said, "I'm down with Venus."

Bella agreed. "And you, Fredo, are . . ." She searched the statues for his likeness.

"Apollo, the sun god," he suggested.

"Maybe the sun dog," said Gia.

"Bacchus, the party god?" he said. "No! Vulcan. God of the underworld."

"That one," said Bella, pointing at a sculpture.

They read the carving at the base with the god's name. "Uranus! That's you, Fredo," said Gia, laughing.

"Very friggin' funny."

"Just kidding, Fredo," said Gia, taking his arm.

Bella took the other. "You're our Apollo, okay?"

The three of them walked over to check in. A hot girl on each arm, Fredo felt a dizzying spike in blood pressure—only natural, given his anxieties and the situation. In fact, he was surprised he wasn't a lot worse off. With any other girls, he'd have fainted by now. But he could really talk to Gia and Bella. They seemed to like him, too.

The male concierge smiled at him when Fredo handed him his credit card. As well he should! Fredo was checking into the superluxe penthouse suite with two hot girls. He'd never before felt like such a pimp. The suite cost $1,000 a night. That'd be a lot of paper to drop. It was worth it to feel like this, and to get away from home.

He'd replayed in slow motion a hundred times Cara's fist coming at him. Each time, he felt a little more humiliated. If only it'd happened in private! Why did his worst-case scenario have to unfold in front of his entire family? His father was embarrassed by proxy, whether he'd cop to it or not.

Luigi told him he didn't care what anyone thought, and that what mattered was how Fredo felt about himself. But Fredo knew Luigi would prefer a badass for a son. What man wouldn't? The only way Fredo could redeem himself in his own eyes? Leave town mysteriously and return to Seaside Heights with a ton of cash to offer his dad as a tribute. Thus far, Fredo had been a siphon on the Lupo wealth. The Cowboy Club was his most recent failure. In hindsight, he should've known some of his ventures would fail. Like Cup O' Meat, a boardwalk scrapple stand. And Chunk, the plus-size-stripper lounge on the outskirts of town. It had some hard-core regulars, but five chubby chasers weren't enough to support the place. Truth be told, the Cowboy Club was his last shot. His dad couldn't keep shoveling money into the Fredo black hole forever.

This time around, he had to succeed without family support. His plan was to harness the greatest power in the universe and exploit it for his personal gain. What was this cosmic unstoppable force of nature?

Dumb luck. And Gia Spumanti had it up to the eyeballs.

Fredo distributed key cards to the girls. They went up to the suite. The porter brought their luggage on a cart. Fredo, the big spender, tipped him a $50. Bella noticed, approved, and gave him a wink.

Ohhh. Wood again.

"Oh, my freakin' Gawd!" screamed Gia. "Look at this place! I'm in *lurve*!" The main room was pretty sweet, like the Guccione version of a Roman bordello, with columns and pillow-covered lounges for reclining and nibbling on grapes and olives. Gauzy drapes floated in the breeze from the open balcony door.

Gia ran around the suite, pointing at the attractions. "Giant flat-screen TV . . . minifridge, stocked . . . maxifridge, stocked . . . ocean view."

She flung open the balcony's screen door and stepped outside. Fredo followed. They were on the thirtieth floor. The people on the boardwalk scurried like sand crabs. Gia screamed, "Hey, bitches!" A few people looked up and waved back at her. Fredo inhaled the ocean air, deep into his lungs. They expanded, and he relaxed. Gia beamed at him. "This makes up for everything in Seaside, times a hundred." The warmth in her eyes went straight to his chest.

Bella called for them. Gia let go and ran back inside. Fredo followed. Bella handed him a glass of champagne. "The bedrooms are sick," she said. "The closet is bigger than my bedroom at home. The bed is round, covered with white satin. The bathroom has a gold-plated tub, and also one of those fountain toilets that real Italians use to clean their assholes."

"Classy!" said Gia. "From Prison Condo to Imperial Freakin' Palace. I'm never leaving this suite. You can't make me."

Bella held up a hotel brochure. "I found this. Listen. 'Nero's Palace presents the Roman Orgy Salon Package.'"

"Combining sex and manicures?" said Gia. "Gives new meaning to the phrase *hand job*."

Oh, shit, thought Fredo. Wood again. He wouldn't last long with these two if every time they made a dirty joke, he got excited.

Gia lifted her glass of champagne. "The whole first week? That didn't happen. Our summer vakay starts right here, right now."

They clinked and drank. Fredo sipped his. He wasn't much of a partyer, really. He had to go slow, or he'd be facedown on the bed in no time

Bella squinted at him. "Are you sure you can afford this?"

"No worries," he said. If they lost at the tables, then he'd have to pull the plug on the room after a few days. But if they won . . . they'd stay as long as the girls wanted to. Speaking of winning— "Are you guys ready to hit the tables?"

"Already? We just got here. I want to chill and change. There's a sink full of bath products. The shower's got five nozzles, including one that shoots water up from the floor," said Bella.

"More hands-free asshole scrubbing?" asked Gia. "Fredo, this place is right up your alley."

"As it were," said Bella.

Fredo laughed. And then realized with a shock that he was laughing *at himself*. Another breakthrough for him, and it felt even better than being a pimp.

"What now? Fredo, are you *crying*?"

"No," he said, wiping his eyes.

"Aww. I think he likes hanging out with us," said Gia. "We like you, too, Fredo."

Chapter Thirteen

Gorilla Ground Zero

After their showers, Fredo stayed at Nero's to scope out the casino while Bella and Gia hit the boardwalk. They aced AC style in monokinis, short shorts, hoop earrings, floppy hats, and platform wedges. The ocean and beach were to their right, and the boardwalk empire to their left. "Every store is either a fortune-teller, massages, tattoos, or souvenirs," said Bella. "Where's a jumbo hot dog when you need one?"

"Plenty of candy shops," said Gia as they passed Fralinger's, the hundred-year-old taffy puller. "Check out all the strollers for adults."

The scores of wicker rickshaws did resemble strollers. Tourists sat on the roof-covered bench seat, and the operator pushed the contraption on wheels from behind. *They couldn't walk down the boardwalk?* thought Bella. She and Gia were doing it, in heels. God, people were friggin' lazy.

"We can't all be marathoners like you," said Gia, reading Bella's mind. "So they want to take a ride. It's hot out. Don't be so judgey."

"There's a another psychic. Maybe we should ask Madame Olga if I'm too judgey."

"But we already know you are."

Bella felt a tug toward the fortune-teller's storefront. It was absurd to ask a rip-off artist for advice, insight, or information from the great beyond, but she had the urge anyway. "Let's check her out."

"I'd love to. But, you, Bells? Really? Waste money on a *fugazi*?" Meaning, a fake.

Ordinarily, never. But they were standing right in front of the place, it was vakay, they had time to kill and some cash to burn. And Bella was curious. She wanted to be fed bullshit positive answers to her questions. It'd give her a glimmer of optimism to cling to.

"Bust my balls later. Now, we're going in," said Bella. They walked into the airy salon. The purple-painted room was divided by a red curtain into two separate mini "reading rooms." For privacy, each room had strings of beads hanging in front. Behind the bead divider, each space contained a small, round, gold-painted table, two metal folding chairs, also painted gold, and a poster of a palm with captions explaining what each line signified. Under the table, on the floor, was a painting of the round yin-yang symbol. A woman sat at the table in the open booth, reading a novel.

"Madame Olga?" asked Gia.

She looked up from her book. With a Russian accent she said, "I know why you're here."

"She *is* psychic!" said Gia.

"Sit down," said Madame Olga.

Bella had expected a crone, like a craggy Gypsy in werewolf movies. But Madame Olga was attractive and decently dressed. Bella put her around fifty, slender, streaked caramel hair in a tight bun on top of her head. She wore a strapless dress that showed off tan shoulders and gave zero boobie support. Bella predicted something about the psychic's future: if she didn't wear a bra, her breasts would one day swing to her knees.

"I can do tarot, palm, runes, I Ching. I've got a crystal ball around here somewhere," said Olga.

"What about the playing cards?" asked Gia. A deck was on the table.

"That's for solitaire when I'm bored."

"We just want a basic palm reading," said Bella. "How much?"

"Three questions, twenty bucks."

"Me first!" said Gia, sitting in the chair opposite the psychic.

The woman smiled—Gia's enthusiasm brought that out in everyone. "Give me your hand."

Gia put both hands palm up on the table. The woman examined them and said, "What do you want to know?"

"Will I meet the man of my dreams, and does his last name end with a vowel?"

The psychic checked Gia's palms. "Yes, you will meet a man. Very soon. Not someone you know now, but you'll feel like you've known him forever. He treats you like a queen. And, er, his name ends with a vowel. An *i*. Or a *u*. Maybe an *o* or *a*."

"Yay! Okay, next question. Will I have tan babies?"

"Um, yes. You will have tan babies. Four or five of them."

"When I get old, like, thirty, will I be a MILF?" asked Gia, eager, on the edge of her seat.

To her credit, Madame Olga nodded seriously and closed her eyes. "Yes, I see you will be a sexy mama. You will stay attractive until the end of your long, happy life."

Gia beamed. "Great reading!"

Madame Olga accepted her praise. Bella, a cynic, didn't doubt she had a horde of repeat customers who came again and again for a sunny forecast. Gia vacated the hot seat, excited and energized by the news that she'd get everything she wanted, and soon. Reluctantly, Bella sat down and put her hands on the table.

Madame Olga looked at Bella's palms and frowned. "You have a hard life."

Huh? Where was the prefab prediction, like, "I see travel in your future"? Bella shifted nervously. "I didn't ask anything yet."

"You have had much pain. You worry terribly about a loved one's health. Someone you trusted recently betrayed you."

Bella snatched her hand back. Fiercely private, she was rattled. If Madame Olga could see at a glance that Bella's world had been turned upside down, that her most sacred relationships had been shattered, maybe anyone could. Bella felt naked suddenly, and itchy to get away.

"That's enough," she said, plucking two twenties from her wallet and leaving them on the table.

"Are you sure? I have answers for you, if you're ready to listen."

Unlike the doctors, Madame Olga could tell her if her mom was going to live or die? Right. "Another time," said Bella, her voice shaking embarrassingly. Then she walked away, Gia jogging alongside in her wedgies to keep up.

"Don't say it," warned Bella.

"I was going to say that you could probably use a drink." Pointing at the large sign for a place nearby, Gia added, "This place has everything we need. Better not to be false advertising."

The sign read GORILLA BEACH BAR and had an arrow pointing them toward a long ramp from the boardwalk. They trudged along the ramp, through dunes and sand-friendly tall grass, all the way down to, presumably, Gorilla Beach. The closer they got, the louder the music, the thicker the scent of Axe body spray. They passed a particularly tall dune, rounded a corner, and the bar was revealed like something out of a dream.

The place sat on a wood-planked riser and appeared to float a few feet off the beach. It was open air, but protected from the sun by a palm-frond-thatched roof. Tables with and without umbrellas were bustling and busy, full of laughing, tan people with more tattoos than clothes. Waitresses in tiny red bikinis raced around, carrying trays laden with beers and umbrella drinks.

"Is it my imagination, or is every single person here freakin' gorgeous?" asked Bella.

"I've dreamed of this," said Gia, her jaw unhinged. "It's my own personal episode of *Fantasy Island*. Slap me."

"What?"

"This can't be real. Slap me."

Bella shrugged. She didn't see what reality and slapping Gia had to do with each other, but whatevs. She slapped Gia's cheek. Lightly. Just enough to make a nice sound.

Gia shook it off. "Felt it. I'm awake. And there's still a fuckton of gorilla here. Like two thousand freakin' pounds of beef. Okay, I know I said I was never leaving our suite before. Well, I'm never leaving this bar."

"You might want to reconsider," said Bella, pointing toward Gorilla Beach itself. Gia and Bella found seats by a low railing overlooking that section of the Atlantic City beachfront, making puddles of drool watching a stunning parade of hardbodies go by. Bella, in all her days of gym and beachgoing, had never seen such a dense population of smokin'-hot juiceheads with hairless, tan, rippling abs and shoulders.

A guido in a red T-shirt with a GBB logo gave them a bowl of pretzels. He was dark and yummy as rum with soulful, deep-brown eyes that made Bella forget how to talk.

Gia was equally transfixed. "Are you, like, a mirage?"

"I'm your flesh-and-blood bartender/waiter. You guys ready to order?"

Even the waiters were dimes? AC was the greatest place in the entire universe. "Am I dreaming?" asked Bella.

"A wide-awake shot? You need a Dragon Bomb. Vodka, Red Bull, grenadine, and lime juice. And for you," he said, turning to Gia, "a Pink Bikini. Vodka, peach schnapps, cranberry, and Red Bull."

"Perfect," the girls agreed.

"I'm Tanner, by the way."

"Screw you, we just got here!" said Gia.

"My name. It's Tanner." He showed his name tag and left to make their shots.

"Tanner is a frickin' name?" asked Gia. "First *Guido*. Now *Tanner*. What next? A guy named Gym?"

"You called?" asked another waiter. Name tag: JIM.

The breeze, the music, the busy bar scene, and Tanner's tasty beverages quickly dissolved Bella's raw nerves. Gia's nerves, however, were getting rubbed the right way. Only a few feet away, a pack of gorillas were doing push-ups on the beach, their backs bare, bronzed, and glistening with oil. Others were throwing a Frisbee, running and jumping in the sand. Gia watched, mesmerized. "That's it. Run. Run for the Frisbee! Jump! He caught it. Sweet sausage, that's hot." Her eyes big as mussels, Gia said, "We've landed at Gorilla Ground Zero. Look at that monster!"

Bella was already staring. "If we were animal researchers searching for gorillas in the wild, we'd have to alert the media with news of a secret, previously unknown cluster of gargantuan specimens."

"Officially, no regrets about leaving Seaside for AC," said Gia.

If Seaside was a gorilla petting zoo, AC was a friggin' jungle.

Tanner placed a pair of frozen margaritas in fluted, two-foot-long plastic glasses with red straws, and cherries on top. "Care of those guys," he said, gesturing to a table with six shirtless juiceheads.

Meanwhile, a six-foot-five, 250-pound wall of solid muscle with abs that shamed the marble statues in Nero's lobby lumbered by the bar and caught Bella's eyes. He stopped in his tracks and said, "Hey, girl," in a voice as rumbling and deep as thunder.

It was an embarrassment of riches. Outrageous fortune. They honestly did not know where to look.

Gia waved to the juiceheads to thank them for the drink, took a sip. "I'm going over."

Bella said, "And give up our prime seating? Don't you dare move. Wait one second." She uncrossed her legs, got out of her chair, and bent over it as if she were searching for something in her purse on the floor, giving the entire bar a spectacular view of her barely covered, tanned ass.

Fifteen gorillas suddenly swarmed the two girls, baring their teeth (smiling), offering drinks and back rubs, and sending off powerful animal pheromones.

"Calm down, boys, I speak gorilla," said Gia. "Just grunt twice if you like to party."

A dozen started grunting at the girls, scratching their sides and hopping from foot to foot in a primal dance. It was like a scene out of *Rise of the Planet of the Apes*, minus James Franco. Bella and Gia looked at each other and started giggling, hard.

It was Bella's first belly laugh in months. Man, she needed that.

Chapter Fourteen

Always Bet on Tan

Fredo exited his bedroom in the same black suit he wore to the Crumbi wedding, what Gia called his *Reservoir Dogs* look. Granted, it wasn't as slick as that of a lot of the players he saw when he scoped out the casino earlier in the day. But it was a suit, and not a dirty T-shirt and cargo shorts with a fanny pack, which was how most of the tourists dressed.

Gia and Bella were attacking the maxifridge when he came into the living room, plowing through little wheels of cheese, crackers, and sliced salami. They'd spent the whole day at a beach bar and grill, but were acting as if they hadn't eaten in weeks.

"Aren't you getting dressed?" he asked.

Gia glanced up, crumbs around her adorable lips. "You're not wearing that, are you?"

Bella wiped her mouth with the back of her hand. "Oh, Jesus. The undertaker of Atlantic City."

"You said you'd be ready by nine," he whined. Fredo was excited to get to the tables. He couldn't wait to test his Dumb Luck theory, see if Gia had it, in spades.

"Give us twenty minutes," said Gia.

"Make it thirty," said Bella.

They disappeared into their bedroom, giving him brotherly pats on the head as they walked past him. He'd take brotherly.

He'd talk friendly. As long as he got to hang out with them, he was happy. Gia and Bella had "it," a quality that he couldn't define, that made them magnets for attention. The only attention Fredo had drawn thus far had been the wrong kind. He'd reacted by trying to make himself invisible to the people who hurt him. Everything he wore, did, and said was about fading into the background of life. The boring black suit. The shyness. The avoidance of girls and social situations. He had a secret hope that spending time with Gia and Bella would break him out of the shell of his own design. Maybe some of their "it" would rub off on him. Not in a sleazy way (oh, shit, not wood knocking again!). He just hoped they liked him, really. They seemed to.

He'd better not fuck this up, he thought nervously.

Fredo spent the next twenty minutes imagining the many ways he could offend his new friends. Then forty. Finally, an hour after they went into their room, the girls came back out and erased any negative thoughts from his mind.

Bella nearly took his breath away in a black wrap minidress with a deep V-neckline, and a wide leather belt, and four-inch-high, glitter-dusted black pumps. Gia wore a leopard-print dress. Short, tight. Did he mention *short*? When she walked, it rode up, so she had to yank it down. Cute. She'd put on six-inch leopard stilettos to complete the look.

In her hand, a can of hair spray. "Fredo, we're not leaving this room with your hair like that."

"Like what?"

Bella said, "Like an oil slick. Dude, it's gross." From behind her back, she showed him a damp towel. "We're doing this for your own good. Now, just sit back and let us do what we do."

Frightened now, he asked, "Will it hurt?"

"Hurt so good," said Gia.

They pinned him. Bella used a lot of muscle to rub the pomade out of his hair. "My mother said it looked good like this!" he complained.

"His mother," muttered Gia. "She wants you to be a virgin forever."

"I'm not a virgin!"

Crickettes. The towel was over his face so he couldn't see their reaction. If they could see his expression, they'd know for sure he was lying.

Suddenly, the towel was gone, and Gia had a blow-dryer in her hand. "I'm going to blow you now, Fredo. Which is not nearly as sexy as it sounds."

Actually, the feel of her fingers in his hair was plenty sexy, but more soothing. When the whirring and spraying sounds stopped, he reached up and touched the top of his head.

It was stiff, and his hair was sticking up, like a crown. The girls were looking down at him on the couch. "Well?" he asked.

"It's a start," said Gia. "Once I start a makeover, I can't stop until I reach full guido power. Do you submit?"

Ach, why did she have to use words like *submit*? It was like an electric shock to his junk. "I . . . okay. Just don't make me wear too much gold jewelry. I get a rash."

"Are we good to go?" asked Bella, one last spray for herself.

Gia doused her hair, too. "Ready."

They took the elevator ride down from the penthouse to the casino floor. "We start small. Just a hundred bucks," said Fredo as he led the girls through a maze of slot machines toward the table games.

"Look at all these suckers," said Bella. "You might as well set your dollars on fire."

A girl on each arm, Fredo escorted his women to the casino floor proudly. He could feel people staring at the girls. He was like the invisible man between them, but it didn't matter. He had to admit, the crown of his hair made him feel taller, cockier. Like a big shot. "We'll play with my money, and split the profits three ways," he told them. "You don't have to worry. You're not risking anything."

"Shiny! Sparkly!" said Gia, distracted by the flashing lights like a six-year-old with ADD.

Fredo felt an all-too-familiar flash flood of anxiety. Was she up for a night of betting? Would her brain overload from the blinking, buzzing, and blazing of a thousand lights on the casino floor? This was exactly what casino designers had in mind. If gamblers were distracted by the bells and whistles, the free drinks, and skimpily uniformed waitresses, they'd lose their concentration and make mistakes.

He reminded himself that Gia didn't need a brain. She just needed to stand there, look pretty, and let luck flow through her. If she could beat his grandmother at bingo, she could play the simplest casino game.

They stopped in front of a green felt table with a roulette wheel. The guy behind it turned the wheel and spun a small white ball in the opposite direction in the inside edge of the wheel. They watched as it went round and round. Other gamblers frantically placed colored chips on individual numbers inside a rectangular grid or along the outside in spaces marked odd, even, etc., red or black.

The wheel slowed. The ball inside hopped around the numbered slots, finally setting. The operator said, "Thirteen."

A woman whooped. The operator placed a Lucite paperweight on top of a pile of her chips in the square for thirteen. After doing the calculations, the operator pushed a massive pile of chips in her direction. One turn of the wheel, and the winning player just paid for her room and drinks for the night.

Fredo examined Gia. She seemed to be paying attention. He searched her face for a glimmer of idiot savant. *Rain Man* magic.

What he saw, though, was a Kewpie doll with a huge pouf, giant eyes, and a rockin' pair of gazongas. Was this guidette really a conduit for Dumb Luck? They'd find out soon enough.

"Red or black," he asked her, his voice cracking.

"Love 'em both. If I had to choose, I'd wear black."

"Agreed," said Bella.

Fredo took a vial of pills out of his pocket and swallowed one. "I mean the color to bet on. Red or black?"

Gia seemed confused. "Can I bet on tan?"

Chapter Fifteen

The Right Way to Hug a Guido

Gia took pity on Fredo. He looked panicked, as if his life depended on her answer to . . . er, what did he want again? "Can you repeat the question?"

"Should I put the money on red or black?" he said, high-pitched, but really slowly.

"I'm not retarded. You can talk like a normal person." She smiled at the other people around the roulette table. "He's not my boyfriend."

"Or mine," said Bella.

"Gia, please," said Fredo. "Close your beautiful eyes. Take a few deep breaths, and let your mind go blank. Empty it out. It might take a while, but if you—"

"Done."

"Oookay. Now, let a color pop into your head."

"Leopard print." Whenever Gia closed her eyes, she saw spots.

"You're killing me," whined Fredo.

"Bet on black." Weird as it might seem, when Gia closed her eyes and meditated for a split second, a velvety curtain of midnight black appeared in her head.

Scrambling, Fredo dropped two $50 bills on the felt. The roulette operator said, "Changing a hundred." He started to give Fredo ten yellow chips worth $10 each.

"I hate yellow," said Gia. "We want pink."

The dealer said, "Changing a hundred in chips," taking back the yellows and replacing them with pinks.

The pit boss, a freckled redhead—her name tag read ERIN GOBRAUGH—watched the chips swap. She nodded at Gia, as if she approved of her color choice.

Fredo put five chips on the black bar, worth $50.

"Just five?" asked Gia. "Bet 'em all."

Bella said, "What the hell, Fredo? Go big or go home."

Fredo moved his entire pile into the black square.

The ball was in motion. Gia made the sign of the cross and blew a kiss at the wheel. She chanted, "Go, black! Go, black!" To the dark-skinned man standing next to her, she added, "No offense."

The wheel slowed. The ball bounced. Fredo held his palms together as if he were praying to the roulette gods. Gia's pulse raced, too. Bella seemed bemused.

The ball came to rest. The operator said, "Thirty-three, black."

Gia jumped up and down, clapping her hands. "Yay! We won! I saw black in my head, and it came up. I'm psycho!"

"You mean *psychic*," said Bella.

"*Duh,* that's what I meant. I've got the sight! I'm mutherfocking *gifted*, yo!" Gia closed her eyes again, and that same curtain of color shimmered in her mind. Except—superstrange—it was green???

"What's the matter?" asked Fredo, seeing her confusion.

"Okay, not gifted. The signal from the universe is jammed."

"Did you see anything? A number?"

"The color green. Makes no freakin' sense."

Fredo jumped into action. "Two hundred on green!" he said, moving a stack of chips into a bar that had the numbers 0 and 00 in it.

The dude next to Gia said, "I'm in," and put some of his chips on top of Fredo's. An old lady did, too, and a few others.

The operator said, "Run on green."

Erin, the ginger pit boss, came over to watch the spin. Gia said, "Wait! My ritual." She made the sign of the cross, then kissed her fingers, then blew a kiss at the wheel. The operator spun it.

"Double zero," he said when the ball fell into the slot. "Winners!" A cheer went up around the table. Double zero, in this case, was not two times nothing. Fredo's pile of pink chips turned into a magenta mini–Empire State Building.

"How much is that?" asked Gia.

"We started with a hundred," Fredo said. "And now we've got . . . over six thousand."

What?" It'd take Gia months at the movie theater to make that much. She'd won a fortune in five minutes? Not possible. How could casinos stay in business if they gave money away like that?

Gia couldn't help herself. She threw her arms about Fredo and pulled him into a tight hug.

"Ack!" He went rigid in her arms. Froze stiff, then started jerking uncontrollably.

Gia backed off, repelled. To Bella she said, "He's having a seizure."

He whispered, "No, I . . . er . . . I have a phobia about hugging. I do it this way." Fredo stood at Gia's side and put his arm around her shoulder, pressing their sides together, but not touching the fronts at all.

Bella laughed. "Whaddaya call that?"

He blushed. "My mom calls it the Safety Sidehug."

"Safety from *what*?" asked Gia. "From touching icky girls and yucky boobies? With hugging, safety doesn't come first. It doesn't come at all. We do Full-Frontal Guido Hugs."

She grabbed him. Showed him. Bella clamped onto his back, making a Fredo sandwich. "More than two people in a Guido Hug is a Guido Hump," said Gia. "Or you could say Group Hump."

"Don't say *hump*," he whimpered, struggling to escape as if he were afraid something terrible would happen.

And it did. Gia said, "Oh, my, Fredo! You *are* excited about winning."

Then the girls let him go. Fredo popped another pill. He seemed freaked out by the contact. Gia suddenly understood. The kid wasn't just shy. He had a real tit terror. She flashed back to the embarrassing moment when Donna hugged him at the Cowboy Club and he squirmed frantically to get free. Maybe Donna forced him to breast-feed until he was twelve or something.

"You okay?" she asked him, concerned. Had she taken a joke too far?

Frazzled, he said, "Maybe we should call it a night."

"You can't leave now," said one of the other players. "You're on a roll."

"We're taking a short break," said Gia. "Can you guard our chips for ten minutes?"

"Of course," said Erin, the pit boss.

"Bella, we have to give Fredo a crash course. To the nearest bar!" Gia took one of his elbows, Bella took the other, and they dragged him to Circus Max, a horseshoe-shaped bar near the roulette tables.

"I'm fine," he protested.

"Just one practice Guido Hug," said Gia. "You have to do a shot of Patrón first." To the bartender, she held up three fingers.

The shots appeared. "Down the piehole," she said. The girls showed him how.

Fredo drank his, made a face as if his tongue were on fire. Then Gia nodded at Bella, and they grabbed the kid and pressed their boobies against him. "Just let it happen," encouraged Gia. "They're just big mounds of fat and tan."

"And silicone," said Bella.

"Nothing to be afraid of."

He nodded, a bit frantic. "This is good," he croaked. "I'm totally relaxed."

They held for a ten-second count. Took a rest and tried it again. Fredo did seem to take it better the second time. A guy at the bar in a suit asked, "Is it my turn now?"

Fredo exhaled deeply. "Can we play more roulette now? I've had all the hugging I can stand."

The girls said, "Okay." Gia felt as if she'd accomplished something.

They returned to the table. Someone said, "The psycho girl is back." He offered her a chair and pushed it right up to the table so she could see better. She settled into the seat as if it were a throne. This was more like it. She was the center of attention, exactly where she belonged.

Gia closed her eyes and waited for the colored curtain in her mind to appear. When it did and she shared her vision, a dozen gamblers scrambled to place their bets.

Chapter Sixteen

Is That a Sharpie in Your Pocket, or Are You Just Glad to See Me?

Bella ran from Nero's to the north end of the boardwalk, past the Taj Mahal, Resorts, the go-carts pier, and then turned around to run back the other direction. The sun was scorching already, at noon, but she liked to sweat. After last night, she needed to feel the strain of pumping muscle and moving joints. It was predictable and normal. What Gia did at the roulette table? That was out of this world. It was crazy. Totally mind-boggling.

The kid hit nearly every bet! She missed about 25 percent of the time, but Fredo was smart and never put all their money on any one single bet. The stacks of chips kept getting taller and taller. By the time they packed it in, they'd won $18,000. A huge crowd of people were betting with them and doing Gia's signature ritual, the cross and kiss blowing, during each spin.

If Bella were a casual observer, she'd've believed that Gia did have a gift, or some kind of psychic power. But Bella knew that wasn't possible. Or was it? Maybe such abilities did exist. It occurred to Bella, following that line of thought, that perhaps Madame Olga was the real deal. If Gia could accurately predict the spinning of the wheel, maybe Olga knew, for sure, whether Marissa's cancer would come back.

Her mind occupied, she jogged past Nero's. When she realized she'd gone too far, she stopped to look around and noticed she was standing right in front of Madame Olga's storefront. Clearly, her subconscious had brought her back here. If she had any courage, she'd go inside and listen to what the woman had to say. While deciding what next, Bella stretched her legs.

"Hey! Bella!"

She turned to the sound of her name. It seemed to be coming from Madame Olga's. From out on the boardwalk in the glaring sun, she couldn't see into the store unless she went closer. She took a step, and a boy stepped out of the dark and walked toward her.

"Will Lugano?" she said, recognizing the punk artist from the wedding.

"You're in AC," he said, stating the obvious.

"It got a little hot in Seaside."

"Hot out here, too. Come into the shade."

She followed him into Madame Olga's. The psychic wasn't there. As if sensing her confusion, he said, "I share the stall with a psychic. She does readings; I do drawings. And she helps me with my website, too."

"You have a website?"

"Cheapestportraitartistinatlanticandoceancounties.com. I told you. Have a seat."

Bella sat down. "What happened to you at the wedding?"

"When people start throwing punches in parking lots, I'm ready to leave."

"Well, your portrait was a hit. The bride loved it."

"Good."

Bella looked at Will's setup. Stacked up against the walls and on the tables were cartoony portraits on white paper, mounted on cardboard, and wrapped in plastic. Leaning against Will's chair was a heavy sketchpad and a box of black Sharpies.

"That's Kim Kardashian," she said, pointing at one of the

caricatures. "You nailed her ass. And this one is Tom Cruise? On a spaceship?"

"Flying off to meet L. Ron Hubbard on Planet Crazy."

Bella squinted at another cartoon of a girl with big eyes, a huge pouf, caterpillars for eyelashes, a cocktail in one hand, and a can of hair spray in the other. "Who's that?"

"Snooki from *Jersey Shore*?"

"Never heard of her."

"You must recognize this one." Will pointed to another of the portraits for sale.

"It's you." A punk with jagged black hair, black liner around light eyes, in a motorcycle jacket and boots, holding a heart-shaped grenade in one hand, and a guitar in the other.

"I'm flattered, but it's not me. It's Billie Joe Armstrong of Green Day."

Er, who? "You did all these?"

"My other part-time job: I also do three-minute caricatures for tourists. Twenty bucks a pop. Here's my latest." Will turned the sketchpad around. It was Bella in her jogging outfit, stretching. The high, long ponytail, and the angel wings tattoo blazed across her shoulder blades, gave her away. He'd drawn her profile with just a few lines, but somehow captured her.

"How do you do it?" she asked. "I've been to art classes, but all we learned to draw were still lifes and nudes."

"Did you do gesture drawings? Lines that show movement? That's what I did for you with the stretch pose. The caricatures are just glorified cartoons. Big head, small body. I look at the face and find the one feature that stands out. I play it up, throw in some props and details, and I've got twenty dollars in my pocket." He handed her the sketchpad. "If you have any chops, it's easy. Try it."

"I'm not good enough."

"You are. You did a good job with a ballpoint pen and a cock-tail napkin. I'd love to see what you can do with a Sharpie."

"I'll watch you," she said as a family approached. A mother, father, and two kids, a girl and a boy. Judging by the towels and bathing suits, they'd spent the morning at the beach.

The girl said, "Daddy! I want a picture of myself. Please, please, please . . ."

Will whispered, "Gotta love the brats."

The father was hot and sandy and sunburned. He'd have said yes to anything to get the kid to shut up. "Make it quick," he said.

The girl sat on the portable stool in front of Will. She smiled big, showing a couple missing teeth, which was, to Bella's eyes, her most distinctive feature.

The mother said, "She's gorgeous, right? Same face as Angelina Jolie, but softer."

The girl did have big lips and straight dark hair. But the similarities ended there. The girl was average. Not a siren or a mysterious beauty. But mothers loved their daughters. They saw beauty where little could be found.

Will's Sharpie flew all over the page of his sketchpad. The marker had a thick tip on one side, and a fine point on the other. He'd uncapped both ends and wielded the pen like a samurai with a blade. Bella was amazed how quickly the caricature took shape. He threw in tiny details that made it unique, such as a freckle on her nose, and a lock of hair behind her ear. He took another Sharpie out of his pocket, light gray with an extrawide tip. He used it to shade the black lines, instantly adding dimension. Three minutes from starting, he was done.

The facial feature he'd emphasized? Not the missing teeth, as Bella thought. He highlighted her cat eyes, which Bella had barely noticed. But now that he'd called attention to them, she could see that the girl's eyes were special. That was the Angelina Jolie part of her face that the mom adored.

Will signed it and sprayed the paper with smudge-proof sealer. He tore it off the pad, removed the perforated edge, and handed the page to the girl. Her cat eyes glowed when she saw the image of herself. "It's so cool!" she said, absolutely thrilled.

Mom was happy, too. "It looks just like her!"

Dad said, "Great. Can we go in now? The game's about to start." He peeled a damp twenty off his wad and handed it to Will.

Will deadpanned, "Go, Mets."

The father grunted. The mom and daughter thanked Will again, and they left.

Bella said, "That was incredible. You just made two people really happy—in three minutes flat. That girl's going to keep the portrait forever. I can see it framed on her bedroom wall."

Will shrugged. "Or it'll get ripped or stained and she'll throw it out. Daddy will be pissed he wasted twenty bucks. He'll go to the store for cigarettes and never come back. Or head to the bar, drink himself into a coma."

"You've got a real sunny, optimistic outlook on life."

"About as optimistic as yours, I'm guessing."

"Hey, I *am* sunny," she said. "Just look at my tan."

"If you say so."

"You don't know me," said Bella, starting to get annoyed.

Will flinched at her clipped tone. "I'm sorry. You're right. I can be bleak. It's a bad habit, assuming most people are lying, selfish scumbags."

"That's been your experience?"

He fiddled with the lace on his black high-tops and didn't answer. They fell silent. Bella thought, *Someone fucked this kid up but good.* As talented as he was, he had major trust issues. Especially about fathers, she noted. Bella's caregiver impulse kicked in. Instead of probing—didn't seem as if he'd open a vein right here on the boardwalk—she put her hand on his shoulder and squeezed.

"What the . . . do I feel a muscle?" Squeezing his biceps, she added, "Yup. Definitely something going on here."

This brought a splash of pink to his cheeks.

"Why are punks so pale?" she asked.

"I don't have security clearance to speak for all of us, worldwide. But, for me, I've got no choice. I have fair skin. My real hair color is dirty blond. I'm only half-Italian. My mom's side is Dutch and I burn to a crisp in seconds—like a vampire in daylight." Facing her, giving Bella a full blast of his blue eyes, he said, "Now you tell me. Why are guidos always tan?"

"Not cleared by Guidette Authority to speak for all of us . . ."

"Of course."

"I just feel naked without a tan. I've been using bronzer since I was, like, ten, so it's a habit. Even if I didn't use product, I'd lay out. My skin soaks up the sun like focaccia and olive oil. It wants to be dark. I spend a lot of time outside, too. I run and love the beach."

"So you're an outdoors person with a caring heart," he said. "And I'm an indoors-type misanthrope. We're made for each other."

"Really."

"Yin and yang," he said, pointing to the symbol painted on Madame Olga's floor. "Question is, which side are you? The white side, because you're kind? Or the black side, 'cause of your tan?"

"You're the black half. But you've got that white dot in the middle. Part of you, a small part, believes the world is a decent place."

"And part of you," he said, pointing to the black dot in the center of the white paisley, "is a rageaholic."

She nodded. He was right. Bella watched as he drew a few more portraits, pocketing twenties. His customers loved the sketches, and Will seemed to enjoy pleasing them. It was fun to watch. Before long, though, her stomach growled.

"Whoa, that was loud," he said, laughing. "One more drawing to make my daily minimum, and then I'll buy you Atlantic City's famous version of a Philly cheesesteak."

Her stomach rejoiced. "If you hate people so much, why do you spend all your time studying them?"

"I'm searching for potential. Everyone has some."

A couple walked by. The girl said, "Ohh, let's get a picture of us together."

The guy smiled at his girl and kissed her. To Will and Bella he said, "We're on our honeymoon."

"Congratulations," said Will. He pulled out a second collapsible stool and had the couple sit together holding hands. "You're in luck today. As my one-thousandth customers, you get two portraits for the price of one." He found another sketchpad in his pack and gave it to Bella along with a spare Sharpie.

"No, Will, I suck."

"You're good," he said with such conviction, Bella believed him. She studied the subjects and started drawing.

They smiled so big and hard, Bella's lips ached in sympathy. But it wasn't fake. They were genuinely happy to be together, to be alive. Bella drew rays coming out of their heads. Their hands were a tangle of fingers, resting on his thigh. She drew it as a big ball with lines, like a monkey knot. For their bodies, she gave the bride a gown, and the groom a tux.

Glancing to her left, she saw Will was putting on his finishing touches with the gray Sharpie. He sprayed it with the smudge-proof sealer, tore it out, and handed it to them.

The bride gasped. Bella looked at the drawing, afraid he'd made the earnest couple look corny. She stood up to look at it. He hadn't done a cartoon for them, but an impressionist portrait.

"This is . . . holy shit, dude," said the guy. "I can't believe you did this in, like, two minutes. You're amazing."

Will shrugged. "Just trying to impress a girl."

The new bride flashed a smile at Bella and asked, "Is it working?"

Bella hesitated. Could she fall for a punk? In what friggin' uni-

verse would that happen? She glanced again at the gorgeous portrait he'd just created, and at the bashful dip of Will's head. "Yeah,
I'm impressed."

The bride took Bella's cartoon. "Yours is good, too," she said,
and thanked her profusely. Then they walked off, careful not to
bend the souvenirs of their honeymoon. These two would frame
Will's drawing and hang it proudly. When they had kids, they'd
tell the story of meeting a punk and a guidette at the beach on
their honeymoon in AC.

Bella felt a glow inside. Forget what Madame Olga did, or
whatever ability Gia thought she had. Will's talent was a *gift*. The
real thing. And for the last hour, she'd basked in it. Bella felt honored.

"You okay?" he said. "You look misty."

Shaking off her sentimental moment, she said, "More like hungry. You said something about a cheesesteak?"

Chapter Seventeen

Happy Daze

Gia had been chilling at Nero's Palace rooftop pool since noon. Fredo had stayed in to count the cash. Bella went for a run. Gia sought tanning time, but it'd been two hours and she was restless. After the adrenaline rush of last night's triumph at the wheel, she'd thought lying around at the pool by herself was exactly what she needed. To take some time to reflect on how she wound up here, on this orange lounge chair as comfy as her bed. But thinking was way overrated. Her brain didn't want to analyze. It wanted to replay moments from last night. The ball falling into the right slot on the wheel, again and again. The players who bet with Team Gia cheering her on. It was even more exciting to remember what had happened than it'd been last night when she was actually living it. Gia thought there might be a deep and useful insight somewhere in there, about how the past affected the present and the future. She could maybe write a book about it. She'd name it something smart and deep, and a little slutty. *Remembrance of Flings Past*. That had a certain bling to it.

A true highlight of last night was the expression on Fredo's face each time they won a spin. He lit up like a tiki torch. He got flushed and his eyes shone as if they were burning. Gia would bet all her winnings that he'd never had as much fun before in his entire freakin' life. As happy as that made her to give him the gift of fun, via her own gift of psycho-sight, it was kind of pathetic that his existence before he hooked up with the cousins had been so bleak.

WTF, that hugging anxiety? Fear of spiders, Gia got that. She felt dread when she imagined herself alone in vast empty spaces, like on a mountaintop or on a boat in the middle of the ocean—worst frickin' nightmare. But being afraid of human contact? Gia was terrified of not getting enough of it. She knew that everyone had his or her own demons. Fredo's seemed weirder than average, though. Boobies and poopies? This kid seriously needed to get his smush on, and keep it on. But, Gawd, his clothes! Looking like an awkward embalmer, he didn't stand a chance. Gia and Bella would have to give him a guido makeover—hair to nuts—ASAP.

She put her finger to her forehead and used her gift to picture a transformed Fredo. It was harder than choosing a roulette color. Gia wondered how her gift would play in other areas of her life, now that she knew she had it. She could use it to see, ahead of time, before the interview, if she'd get a job. That would save a fuckton of time! She'd just skip 99 percent of them. Or maybe, here was a thought, she could use her gift to make money! Besides gambling! Like, be a relationship consultant. She'd let her gift tell her if a girl's new boy was going be a serious soul mate, or if he'd turn out to be a major loser she'd regret ever laying her eyes on.

"Excuse me, are you the girl who killed at roulette last night?"

Gia glanced over her heart-shaped sunglasses at the man standing over her lounge. She liked what she saw. In his mid to late twenties, he had thick, dark hair, sprayed and blown guido-style, dark, sexy eyes, and cheekbones sharp enough to slice bologna. A big nose, which she was already imagining getting around for a kiss. Big nose meant big in other places, too. His lips: juicy and dusky pink. Shirtless in black swim shorts, he was big, buff, and tan all over.

"You were there?" she asked.

"Me, and about fifty other people." He smiled, showing rows of white teeth. Hollywood flawless. "Sorry, by the way."

"For what?"

"For interrupting you."

She'd already chased away a few lean cuisines who offered drinks and conversation. But this new hottie was worth keeping around. "I'm glad you came over."

"I saw you from the pool bar, recognized you, and had to congratulate you. Can I buy you a drink?"

The yummy bro was hitting her up, big-time. She felt a flutter in her chest that, in a few hours, could lead to throbbing in another body part. Could he be the man of her dreams, the one Madame Olga predicted she'd meet "very soon"?

"What's your name?"

"Arthur Ponzirelli."

"Ponzirelli ends with an *i*, right? Not a *y*?"

"*I* for 'Italian.'"

Just as Madame Olga had said. Gia *knew* that woman was for real. "That's too long. I'll call you Ponzi. I'm Giovanna Spumanti. Gia." She reached to shake his warm, rough, tan man-hand. "You're staying at the hotel?"

"Trying my luck," he said, nodding. "I play in a high-stakes poker game. What can I get you?" He flashed the teeth again. They looked like an ad for a cosmetic dentist. He must have grown up rich. Gia didn't see too many smiles like his in Toms River or Carroll Gardens. Her own teeth, the bottom ones, were slightly crooked. She felt self-conscious all of the sudden.

Nothing a cocktail wouldn't cure. "Vodka seltzer," she requested.

"Be right back."

He walked over to the bar. His backside was as scorching hawt as his front. Ponzi's leg muscles rippled as he leaned against the bar. Gia decided that he was the one. The man of her dreams, or the man of the moment? Either way, she felt the old familiar flicker of anticipation. She was gonna get it in!

If he'd fit.

While his back was turned, Gia sat up and arranged herself on the edge of her lounge, crossed her legs, combed through her hair with her nails, and arranged her black monokini to show more of her cleavage. Not hard to do. Monokinis were made for maximum boobage. She arched her back and held the pose.

Chapter Eighteen

On Your Mark

Ponzi couldn't believe how well that went! He ordered two vodka martinis at the bar and tried to calm down. She had great legs. Dynamite boobs. And those eyes! Like he'd walked into a Fellini movie. The fun-size brunette stole his breath. Which was *not* good. Ponzi needed to stay in complete control.

He'd been trying to figure out how to meet her since witnessing her truly unbelievable run last night. The pit boss changed the roulette operator every fifteen minutes to break her streak, but the girl kept winning. She had two friends with her last night—the gawky kid with the weird hair, and the butch chick with the wings tattoo. Where were they now? He had to make his move before they showed up and took her away.

By his count—a rough estimate, since he was parked at a slot machine twenty feet away—the girl and her friends brought in somewhere in the neighborhood of $20,000 last night. A rich neighborhood. And Ponzi would love to ransack it.

Usually, his particular con was Seduce and Siphon. He'd charm rich divorcées and widows and slowly bleed them of cash in the form of goods and services. And they'd enjoy the goods and services he provided for them. He saw it as an honest exchange, a fair trade. Some might say he had a grift gift, or that he was grifted.

But, however successful he was, his reserves were running low.

Ponzi was under pressure to make a sizable score. He knew he was a wanted man up north and was playing with fire by staying in the country, much less the state of New Jersey. While he watched this girl, Gia, rake it in last night, he decided to change his approach to Seduce and Steal. New suits and gold watches wouldn't get him safely out of the country. He needed cold, green cash. He wouldn't mind seducing Gia for some of hers.

If he weren't planning on robbing her blind, Ponzi would probably have gone after Gia anyway. She was definitely his type. Petite, busty, and dark. He'd put in too many years charming the pants and wallets off middle-aged fatties and slumming dyed-blond sorority girls on spring break. They were the type of women who loved a beefy devil like him. But he wasn't really attracted to them. He deserved to have sex with a girl he actually desired, too. He'd been thinking about how to meet the roulette goddess when he came up to the roof pool for a swim. And there she was, splayed out on the lounge chair, as if she'd been deposited directly onto his lap.

Sometimes, he got the feeling God loved swindlers, too.

Ponzi had spent the afternoon at the pool bar, sipping seltzer, watching as his new mark told a few hopeful horny chodes to get lost. She'd shuffled in her flip-flops to the bar twice already, and Ponzi tried not to stare at her one-piece bikini that stuck to her curves like wet paint. When she flung out her towel on the lounge once, she bent at the waist. Her bathing suit rode up the crack of her ass.

Ponzi's breath caught.

He broke out in a sweat.

Then he recovered his composure. That was bizarre. He'd had a spontaneous involuntary reaction to the sight of a woman's tush? Cruising the casino capitals of the world, Ponzi had seen more ass than a New York City subway seat. Many of the booties he'd beheld (and held) were bolder than this girl's. So why in hell had he reacted so strongly?

She seemed clueless of her wedgie. The black suit, the tanned, sweetly rounded butt, and her adorable artlessness struck him in a tender spot, the place where Ponzi used to have a heart.

Careful to keep her from noticing him (as females tended to do), he watched her out of the corner of his eye. She flipped through magazines and put them down. She played with her flip-flips and floppy hat, wiped a trickle of sweat off her nose and from between her boobs.

He'd been smooth when he finally talked to her. Now he just had to keep it going. The bartender brought their drinks. Ponzi turned back around, flashy smile on his lips.

Then he saw her. While his back was turned, she'd rearranged herself in a sexy pose that, frankly, stunned him. His jaw dropped, and the cocktails slipped out of his hand. The glasses shattered on the pool patio.

Gia laughed at him. He wasn't sure if he should give up now for being so uncool. But, no, he realized. She liked his lapse of composure. She smiled at him, long and slow. Oh, yeah, she was definitely his type.

Chapter Nineteen

WWGD

"I swear, I would've smushed him right there by the pool, but he had a poker game to get to," said Gia that night, on the cushioned chair at the mirror in their luxury-suite bedroom. She was flat-ironing her hair, getting ready to go out for dinner. "His last name ends with an *i*. Madame Olga called it. He wants to meet up later tonight in the casino."

Bella nodded, perfecting her makeup. "I was back there today, and I ran into that kid who painted Maria's portrait. Will Lugano. For a punk, he's not bad. I invited him out with us tonight, too."

Stopping mid-bronzer-spray, Gia turned toward her cousin. In the tan fog of her own new crush, she'd failed to pick up on Bella's smitten vibe. Now that she did, Gia felt both excited and wary. Bella had had a stinker year. As tough as she looked and acted, Bella was an easy mark for guys. They got their hooks in her and didn't let go. Gia opened her frosted-pink-lipsticked mouth to say something, but then decided, for once, to keep her mouth shut. Their luck had obviously taken a turn. They deserved to enjoy it.

Gia would try to get to know Will tonight. If she got a bad feeling about him, she'd say something then.

"Ready for dinner?" asked Fredo, coming out of his bedroom wearing the freakin' black suit, with the same droopy hair.

"Not again," said Gia. "Sit down. First, the hair. Then we're going shopping. After we get you some new clothes, we're going to burn that suit."

The kid was clueless! She had to take control of his look, for his own sake. And, heh, Gia had some personal motive, too. She couldn't resist a guido makeover.

"I like my hair," Fredo protested, but gave in anyway.

"I've got scissors," said Bella. "I used to cut my ex-boyfriend's hair. I can do a five-minute special."

Gia nodded. "Let's do it." She threw a towel over Fredo's shoulders and fastened it with a tramp clamp behind his neck.

"I'm not sure about this," he said. Bella came up behind him, smiling. "Are you positive you know what you're doing?"

"Just hold still," said Bella. "Trust me."

After only five minutes, Fredo looked ten times better. Bella got to the close work, snipped a tuft near his ear, and—

"*Arghhh!*" Fredo screamed as if he'd been stabbed with a hunting knife.

"Sorry!" gasped Bella.

"You cut me!" he ranted, and clutched his ear. "Am I bleeding?"

Checking his ear, Gia didn't see a thing. Maybe a tiny dot. Bella leaned in to look.

Gia patted Fredo on the back. "Don't worry about it. You don't need both ears, right? That's why God gave us two of them."

Fredo went white. Whiter. He swooned. "I'm Vincent van Gogh!"

Bella groaned. "Now that dude was pale. Stop it, Fredo. You barely got nicked. You're not bleeding. Now sit still and let me finish."

Gia kept a hand on his shoulder to calm him, and Bella made a few more snips. After a bit of hair spray, Gia said, "Whaddaya think?"

"It's okay," he said.

"It's fresh to death," said Gia. If Bella ever needed a fallback career, she could always work as a barber. Except for the suit and his pale skin, Fredo looked . . . well, he still looked pretty twisted. But progress had definitely been made.

The trio walked along the boardwalk to the Pavilion Pier Shops, a mall of about a hundred stores. Gia said, "I grabbed two grand out of the safe, and we're spending it right now on you, Fredo. First stop, Lucky."

They went into the jeans mecca. Gia felt as if it were an episode of *What Not to Wear*. She made Fredo try on jeans, then explained to him what was good and bad about each pair. "Those are too tight in the crotch. I can see your braciola!" or "Those sit nice and low on the hips. You have a nice belly, Fredo. You should let the girls know."

They settled on three pairs of inky-blue jeans. Next stop, a shoe store, where Fredo put down a few benjamins for two slammin' pairs of Pumas, black and white. They blew through a few menswear stores and bought T-shirts, button-downs, a black belt, and a new leather jacket. Lacking big muscles, Fredo's body looked rock-and-roll cool in black leather. Although Gia loved big muscles on guys, when a huge juicehead wore leather, it was like he was impersonating a bull.

"Something's missing. Besides a tan and any muscles," announced Gia, sizing up Fredo in his new clothes. "You need bling."

"One signature piece," agreed Bella.

They found a jewelry store on the second level, nestled between a Bebe and a Victoria's Secret. Gia almost lost interest in her makeover project when she walked by the Bebe windows. Ohh, there was a gold-lamé, off-the-shoulder dress with keyhole cutouts all over it. Ponzi's eyes would explode out of his head when he saw her in that.

But first, Fredo. They tried on a bunch of gold chains and gold-filigreed pendants. "They're too heavy and long," he complained.

After some coercion, he agreed to buy a midlength chain with a lightning-bolt pendant. "Like Jupiter," he said.

Gia said, "That's nice. Er, look, Bella and I need to run next door for five minutes, okay?"

"I'm starving!" said Fredo. "Does shopping always make you hungry?"

Bella said, "I'm kind of hungry, too."

"Are you shop-blocking me?" asked Gia in shock.

"You look smokin' hot," said Bella. "You can get that dress to-morrow."

True, Gia thought. She was wearing a black leather corset mini-dress with gold studs around the waist. "But, but . . ."

"I've got a great idea," said Bella. "Let's get gyros to go and eat them on Gorilla Beach."

"You bitch," said Gia. "You know all my weaknesses."

It was still, just barely, light outside. The sun was falling. They had to hurry to get to the beach before the gorillas scattered for the night. Fredo carried their food, and his shopping bags. The girls carried their shoes. Gia's shoes—clear-plastic platforms with rhinestone-encrusted straps that wound halfway up her calves—took some time to remove. Bella slipped off her stiletto sandals in a flash. Her black tube dress, Gia noticed approvingly, was so short, you could see every inch of Bella's long legs. They both wore their hair long and straight, the red, white, and blue streaks add-ing pops of color to their all-black outfits.

"Here?" asked Fredo. They found a spot on Gorilla Beach that was close to the water, right between two different minipacks of guidos. "Sit on my old suit." He spread out the *Reservoir Dogs* jacket and trousers on the sand.

Gia said, "Thanks. Now, Fredo, I want you to look around. Tell me what you see."

"Ocean. Sand. Garbage. Drunk people. Hot girls in bikinis."

"Very good," said Gia. "Now, take a look at the guys."

"Eww. No way."

Bella laughed. "Just do it, Fredo. It doesn't make you gay to look."

"I want you to see how hot guys behave in their natural habitat." Gia glanced around. "Observe." The gorillas in their midst were both easygoing and tense with alertness. They carried their extreme bulk with savage grace and lightness.

Fredo said, "They're tan."

"Oh, yeah," said Gia, spying an especially tan, beefy guido on a nearby blanket. She smiled and waved.

"They're hairless."

Bella made a yummy sound.

"They have really white teeth," said Fredo. "Which I can see because fifteen of them are grinning at you two like they just found diamonds in the sand."

"They did," said Gia.

"More like rhinestones," said Bella.

"I want you to come here every day, Fredo. Observe and learn. Get it in your head to think, 'What would a gorilla do?' We could get you a rubber bracelet with the intials WWGD. By the end of the week, you'll be as crazy cool as any guy out there. You're already fifty times sexier than when we got here. We've got a sweet, uh, *suite*. We've got cash. You've got new clothes."

"And gyros," said Bella. "Speaking of, can you pass one over here, please?"

Fredo passed around their spicy sandwiches. "I want to thank you guys. I know we've only known each other for a few days, but I already feel really . . . you know . . . like we're becoming . . . that's not to presume you feel the same way about . . . oh, shit."

Gia could see how hard it was for the kid to say what he felt. It made her like him even more. "Do you think any of these juicehead gorillas would hesitate to tell the girls in their lives how they really feel?"

"No. But I'm not them!"

"Try it," said Gia, smiling at him, willing him to make that leap, to trust her enough to express himself.

"You can do it," said Bella.

Fredo took a long, deep breath. "I'm just happy that we're all . . . that we've become . . . friends." He got the word out. Poor kid was visibly exhausted from the effort.

Gia said, "We are friends, Fredo. You bet your ass." She held up her gyro. "To new friends!"

Bella and Fredo lifted their sammies. In unison they said, "To new friends!"

Chapter Twenty

Living in the Pits

Erin Gobraugh surveyed her domain. All four of her roulette tables were surrounded with suckers and drunks—happy drunks, the best kind. She made a silent prayer none of them would get weepy or angry as the night wore on. The gamblers could not *wait* to drop chips on the felt. When each round was done, the operators swept a clicking mountain of chips back into the casino coffers. Maybe one gamer would hit a number and win big. Meanwhile, fifteen others would lose, then try again.

Although her standing wasn't connected to how much revenue her particular casino turf generated, Erin was on a mission to double and triple her station's take.

Peeking at the black-glass bubble affixed to the ceiling right over her head—aka the eye in the sky—Erin tried not to look smug. Inside the glass bubble were four cameras, one aimed at a roulette table. They never blinked, never rested. It was almost like being on a reality TV show. Cameras rolling 24–7, someone watched her every move.

It might seem paranoid. But the casino had to be careful. Despite the triple-checking of employees' backgrounds, an honest dealer or operator could succumb to temptation. Seeing all that money move around so quickly, Erin felt a natural impulse to pluck, say, a $100 chip from a pile of them. What stayed her itchy fingers? Stories about pit bosses and dealers who got caught.

The Boom Boom Room in the basement was notorious. Cheaters walked in and crawled out. Or rode out on stretchers. Or in garbage cans. As hard as the casino's thugs were on card counters, dirty employees got off worse. If they lived through the interrogation and beatdown, they never worked in this town—or any other casino in the world—again.

Given the risks, Erin could still see how respectable employees snapped. It was the constant contact with what you couldn't have. Like in that famous poem about the ancient mariner with the albatross around his neck: *Water, water, everywhere, nor any drop to drink.* Desire was desire. Thirst was thirst. Water or money, same thing. No one was above suspicion. She had to keep her eyes peeled for employees and gamblers who might be cheating in ways she already knew about, and ways she couldn't possibly imagine.

Erin had been working at Nero's for five years. She was a blackjack dealer for two, transferred to roulette operator, and was then promoted to pit boss. Her next spot up the ladder was area manager, or overseeing four pit bosses. Which would be a nice salary bump. But it wasn't her dream job. In her fantasies, she was the manager of Midnight, the Nero's Palace nightclub. She dreamed of that job nightly. It would be a joy and a relief to work hard for people's fun, instead of their financial loss. The job was within her reach. Another year or two as pit boss, proving her loyalty. The only thing that could ruin her chances? An unforeseen disaster. A major fuckup. Some crazy downturn of fate.

If she were to spend a hundred years imaging the size and shape of the disaster that would crush her ambition, Erin couldn't have pictured a cute girl with thick lashes, a leopard-print dress, and a pouf. That kid killed Erin's revenue for the night. It was her worst take since she took the pit boss job.

Giovanna Spumanti was officially on Erin's watch list. At the table last night, Erin checked Gia's ID twice and ran her driver's license number through the New York State DMV to confirm her age. The girl was legal. Twenty-two. Never gambled before in her life, she said. This kid did. Not. Miss. It was freaky. If Erin had been on the other side of the table, she'd've backed Gia, too.

This morning, Erin used the casino computers to do a thorough background check. Gia was a law-abiding, tax-paying Brooklyn resident. She didn't own property or a car. No outstanding liens or bench warrants. One arrest last summer in Seaside Heights for creating a public nuisance, charges dropped. Erin sized her up as a party-girl borderline drunk with gobsmacking beginner's luck.

Gia's financial backer, however, wasn't as squeaky-clean (from a criminal perspective). Frederico Lupo, son of Luigi Lupo and nephew of Mario Lupo, the notorious "coin collectors" of Seaside Heights. If the only son of Luigi Lupo was in Atlantic City, the management at Nero's was obliged to show him every respect. But if Fredo (who, frankly, didn't look notorious in the least) was up to something, Erin's boss, Vito Violenti, would have to intervene with the Lupos. The situation could get ugly.

Hopefully, Gia and Fredo had had enough fun and planned to leave Nero's today and never come back.

A pipe dream. After a triumph like last night's, the gambler's mentality would kick in. Believing themselves "lucky" or "talented," they'd return to the table. Maybe they'd win again. But eventually, they would lose. Attempting to replicate the intense emotion of that first victory, they'd bet more, risk more. Unless they mustered the strength to walk away, they'd steam through all their winnings and more. Erin had seen many tragic defeats. For an addictive personality, winning was the first kiss of death.

Greed was a hungry monster. Without it, Atlantic City would be a deserted ghost town. Fredo Lupo had managed his greed carefully last night. He never went "all in" or "let it ride." He had brains in that egghead of his.

Did Gia have brains, too? Well, she had spunk. Hall of Fame

beginner's luck. But smarts? Erin wasn't sure if she should file the girl under "idiot savant" or "idiot."

At ten o'clock on the dot, they returned. Gia, Bella, and Fredo. The girls were in supertight, supersexy dresses and rhinestone-covered six-inch heels. Bella was over six feet tall tonight. Gia's chest arrived at the table five mintues before she did. What a trio! One and a half bombshells, and a geek.

"We're back, bitches!" sang Gia.

"Welcome," said Erin as they took seats around the roulette table. She couldn't help noticing that Fredo looked a lot sharper tonight. New clothes, and his hair wasn't standing straight up. It was brushed back neatly, less of a weird distraction. He looked good. Not such a geek after all.

"Thanks again for the tip last night," said Steve, the roulette operator. Gia gave him $1,000 in chips when she cashed out. She gave Erin the same amount. Most winners threw the dealers a hundred, or a fifty. Or a fiver. Gia tipped well.

Steve asked, "Feeling lucky again tonight?"

"You bet your ass. Ready for your mind to get blown?"

"His mind? What a waste," said Fredo, which was almost funny. He was much more relaxed tonight. Maybe he'd already taken a couple of the pills she saw him swallow last night. "Let's start small," he said. "A thousand in hundred-dollar chips, please."

"Changing one thousand dollars," said Steve.

"Noted," said Erin. "Give them pink."

Steve pushed a stack of pink chips across the felt. Erin smiled and thought, *In ten minutes, that'll all be gone.*

Fredo said, "Okay, Gia. Do your thing."

Like last night, Gia closed her eyes, showing off glitter-dusted, purple false eyelashes. Fredo, Bella, Erin, Steve, and a few of the other players waited for her to speak.

"Black," she said, her eyes opening, frosted-pink lips smiling.

To Erin, she said, "I need vodka, ASAP. It opens the psychic door in my head."

Erin pictured a spidery, dust-covered cellar trapdoor creaking open, and a swarm of mice scurrying out.

She flagged down a passing cocktail waitress. *Getting drunk couldn't possibly improve Gia's luck,* thought Erin.

A handful of players put chips on the black bar along with Fredo. Steve put the ball in the track and turned the wheel. Gia did her ritual, the sign of the cross, kissing her fingertips, then blowing a kiss. The wheel slowed. After a few hard bounces, the ball dropped into a slot.

"Twenty-four," said the spinner. "Black."

Gia screamed and banged her little-starfish, tan hands on the table bumper.

Bella said, "Incredible."

Fredo whooped, "Here we go again."

By the end of her shift at 3:00 a.m., Erin was frazzled and exhausted. She clocked out and plodded to her bedroom on the hotel's staff-accommodations level. The guido crew hit hard. Every spin, every win, pushed Erin's night's numbers further down the toilet. Gia called about 70 percent of their bets. A huge win percentage. Erin had never seen anything like it.

Her cell vibrated. She answered it while standing by the service-only elevator bank. "Erin Gobraugh."

"What the fuck is going on down there?"

Erin's throat tightened. She recognized the voice of Vito Violenti. The *capo di tutti capi.* The boss of bosses. Looking up to speak to the eye-in-the-sky glass bubble on the ceiling, she said, "Just an incredible run of luck. It'll change."

"They're cheating. And you got dirt on the face."

He was watching her, of course, on a monitor somewhere. Rubbing her cheek, she said, "I was eyeing them like a hawk. I can't see how they're doing it."

"On the chin."

She wiped off a crumb of the sandwich she'd scarfed down a short while ago.

He said, "Show me." The guy was OCD about crumbs. Erin pointed her chin at the camera. "Good. I don't want my personnel walking around with shit on their faces."

"I'm sorry, sir."

"Why would a pair of dimes hang out with that ostrich?"

"Fredo's actually pretty funny," said Erin. "He's a smart bettor and he treats the girls with respect, too. He doesn't grab or even touch them."

"He's a loser, you're saying," barked the cell. "As of right now, you're on recon. Figure out how Lupo's doing it. You get answers, and I'll give you the Midnight manager job. Do what you have to do."

What? Had he just offered up her dream on a plate? "Yes, sir. Thank you!"

Then he hung up.

Chapter Twenty-One

Dance, Dance Evolution

Fredo Lupo sat on one side of a banquette at Providence, with a bottle of Dom on ice in front of him. After the night's work at Nero's, the crew piled into his Caddie and drove to the Tropicana to check out the city's premier dance club. Directly across the banquette, Bella sipped champagne and held hands with a punk named Will. Next to them, Gia performed an emergency tonsillectomy using her tongue on some kid she picked up at the pool.

Will said, "They're drooling on my boots."

Bella added, "It's like the first reel of a porn movie."

"You think they can breathe?"

Fredo watched and listened. The house music blasted, making his insides thump. The club's blue and purple neon lights made everyone look sexy—even him. When he caught his reflection in the mirror behind the banquette, he thought he looked border-line not-hideous. He had a pocket full of cash, two hot girls for friends, and a marathon run of luck. For the first time in his life, things were going *right*. Fredo had never been happier than he was at this moment.

It felt bittersweet. Fredo knew—with the certainty of gravity—that such crystalline joy could not last. He didn't know when, or how, his happiness would end. But it would.

At least when the fun came to a screeching halt, he'd have new clothes. He'd done some shopping damage today. More of a do-over than a makeover. Tomorrow, he would get a haircut, a shave, and, if it wasn't too painful, a body wax. Contrary to what Cara, his slutteen cousin, said, Fredo did grow hair on his chest, even if no one saw it. But maybe that would change. Why shouldn't Fredo hook up with someone, too? Gia and Bella found dates after one friggin' afternoon. How hard could it be for him? He had cool clothes, cash, and a posse. If he gave a woman the slightest reason to, she'd touch his penis, for sure. Erin, the cute redhead pit boss with the sprinkle of sexy freckles, didn't rear back in horror at the sight of him. He caught her smiling when he made a joke or placed a smart bet.

"Fredo, I remember you from the Pugliani/Crumbi wedding," said Will.

Fredo squinted. Why was he there? "You from Seaside?"

"I've done some work for your mom," said Will. "The wedding portrait, and a painting of you a few years ago."

Fredo froze. He knew the painting. It was his twenty-first-birthday gift. A replication of a grainy old photo. The painting was currently at the bottom of the Atlantic Ocean. He'd chartered a fishing boat to take him a mile offshore, and he threw it overboard after weighting it down with fifty pounds of sandbags. The painting was of ten-year-old Fredo, running naked down the beach, chased by a massive and enraged rottweiler, the remnants of Fredo's torn-off swim shorts in the dog's teeth. His mom thought one of the most terrifying and humiliating experiences of Fredo's life was "precious."

"Small freakin' world," Fredo coughed out.

"Sorry, man. I just did what I was hired to do." Will understood Fredo's feelings, unlike his own mother.

Fredo waved away the kid's concern. "Objectively, I thought the artwork was very good."

"Your mom has some strange ideas."

"Could be worse."

"You got that right," Will replied. Fredo got the feeling the artist had harsh experience to back up his words.

Suddenly, above the music and banter, Fredo heard a giant sucking, slurping sound. Gia's and her boy's lips had detached.

"I love this song!" said Gia. "Come dance with me!"

Bella agreed, pulling Will along with them. They ran onto the dance floor. Fredo watched the girls shake their peaches like there was no tomorrow, and clumsy Will shuffled back and forth in his motorcycle boots. Which left him alone in the banquette with Gia's date, Ponzi.

"You from Jersey?" asked Fredo.

"No," said the kid bluntly.

"In town for vacation?"

"Work."

"What kind of work?"

Ponzi glanced around. "Poker game."

"High stakes? Like in the movies?"

"Sure."

"What game? Hold 'Em? Five-card stud?"

"It's five-card *draw*, stud."

This kid sneered at him! Fredo's junior-high insecurity kicked in. The cool kid barely tolerating a conversation with the dork. But screw him! The new Fredo didn't take shit from anyone. Even if the kid was paying.

Before Fredo could say something, though, Ponzi quaffed his champagne, then finished the contents of every glass on the table, except Fredo's.

"Should we get another bottle?" asked Fredo.

"You get the next one," grunted Ponzi. "Gia's not a cheap date."

Fredo felt queasy. Gia was many things, but a gold digger? Not even close. If she were a greedy bitch, she wouldn't throw generous tips at every waiter, bartender, and dealer she came into contact with. Fredo felt a wave of protectiveness for his little cash calf. Not only because she had powers, or whatever she called it, "the sight." But, after a few days of hanging out with her, Fredo considered Gia a good friend, and she had a good heart.

"I'm gonna hit the can," said Fredo, slipping out of the banquette. He had to get away from Ponzi. Bad vibes. As he skirted the dance floor, heading to the men's room, he thought he spotted a cloud of red hair behind a column. Erin?

"Where're you going?" asked Gia, shimmying over to him. She'd grabbed his belt loop and yanked him onto the dance floor. "Dance with us, Fredo. I swear, this time, you won't get pounded by a wasted teenager."

She put her wrists on his shoulders and started shaking in front of him. No Full Frontal Guido Hug action. She kept a safety space between them. "Tree branchin', baby!" said Gia.

Next to them, Bella and Will moved to the beat of the music. While Fredo and Gia danced without excessive touching, he saw Will and Bella bend into each other and take their first kiss. It only lasted a few seconds. When Will and Bella pulled apart, they grinned sweetly at each other with heat and warmth.

Gia yelled, "Fredo! Fist pump!"

Responding to the call, he started beating up the beat. His three friends joined him. They danced in a circle, pounding the air in sync, laughing. Fredo realized he'd been wrong before when he thought he'd never been happier.

This was the happiest moment of his life. Right *now*.

Chapter Twenty-Two

Won and Done

Ponzi navigated Gia through the Nero's lobby and up in the elevator while wildly making out. He hadn't appreciated the extra-curricular benefits of being in a perpetual lip-lock with a girl. His face was obscured to witnesses and cameras.

"Where's my friggin' key card?" whined Gia, rummaging in her purse.

It was in the inside pocket of his jacket. While Gia and her crew were dancing at Providence, he'd been left in charge of their purses. It was like throwing meat at a lion. What was he supposed to do? Ignore it?

A housekeeper came by with her cart, and Gia said, "Lucy! Thank Gawd. Can you let me in? I lost my key card."

"Of course, Gia." The housekeeper unlocked the door and held it open.

Ponzi whispered, "You know the maid's name?"

"Duh! She cleans our toilet, for Christ's sake. I know her *kids'* names." To Lucy, Gia said, "Come in for a sec. I have something for you."

She ushered the maid and Ponzi inside. Gia went to the room's closet safe. "We won so much money, I'd feel bad if I didn't spread it around. Won and done," she said while typing in the secret code. The safe door opened. Gia took out a twenty and gave it to the maid.

"No, Gia."

"Yes, Lucy. I'm gonna make you take it." Gia folded the bill and put in inside the maid's uniform top. "Keep it in your bra. Surprise your husband later."

The woman laughed. "Thank you," she said, and left.

Once they were alone in Gia's suite, she threw her arms around Ponzi's neck, jumped up to encircle his waist with her legs, and shouted, "Happy Smush Day!"

Before he could figure out what she was talking about, she started kissing him again. His mind turned to soggy mush. Was that what she meant by *smush*?

She climbed down to kick off her heels. Arms outstretched, she came at him for another kiss. He was happy to supply it. He wrapped his arms around her and lifted her off her feet. "There. I've given you back the four inches you just lost." Then he planted a smooch on her pink-frosted lips.

This had to be the sweetest gig he'd ever played. Gia was definitely the sexiest mark in history—and endearingly clueless. Like swiping candy from a babe. More like the babe was giving her candy to him—and it wasn't even Halloween. He was too, too lucky.

But he had work to do. Stealing her money wouldn't be achieved by smushing alone. He'd have to win her loyalty and trust. That meant buying her clothes and meals, aka the tried-and-true method of "softening the mark." He'd been softening her all day long and had already dropped nearly a grand. He squeezed her ass. Yup, just the right kind of soft.

Which made him rock hard.

Easy tiger, he thought, reining himself in. After he built trust, he had to separate her from her other allegiances, so she thought he was the only person in the world who cared about her. He had to drive a wedge between Gia and her friends, aka the people who'd raise warning flags to her about him.

"Let's sit," he said. Ponzi and Gia sank into the plush sectional couch. Their kiss intensified. In fact, calling it a *kiss* was liked describing a porterhouse as *beef.* This was the Cadillac of kisses. The Marilyn Monroe of makeouts. The heat rocketed from her lips to his hips. He had to touch her nakedness or he might burst into flames.

Gia broke their kiss to gasp for breath. "How old are you?" she asked, and plunged in for another taste.

His mind heard a question. But he was too turned on to think of the truth, let alone a lie. What did she want to know? If it was anything other than "Do you have condoms?" he didn't care. "I'm twenty-seven." Shit! It was his real age.

"You have a North Jersey accent."

"Hoboken." Another fact! Five minutes of groping fully dressed, and he'd told Gia more about himself than he'd shared with another human being since his last arrest. And then, he'd only told the cops the truth because they knew it already. At this rate, she'd have his real name before night's end. That would be bad. Attempting to keep his lips shut, he bit down on them, cutting Gia off.

"What's wrong?"

"Nothing. Just a dry throat."

"Let me get you a drink," she said, standing, ambling cutely in her bare feet to the suite's fridge. "Oh, that feels good," she said, leaning her chest into the fridge for the cold air. "I can't believe I'm saying this, but I think I got too much sun today. My skin's burning." He watched, agog, as she propped her rack on the refrigerator shelf, just like a pair of melons. After grabbing a bottle of beer, she closed the door and walked back toward him. Her slightly chilled nipples popped like turkey thermometers and were pointed right for him.

Her boobs at eye level, she handed him the beer. The view was overwhelming his senses. He couldn't think straight.

"I have something important to say," she announced. "I have STD."

A chink in the armor. "Which one?"

"Huh?"

"Which sexually transmitted disease?"

She looked shocked. "That's not what I meant! I'm totally clean down there. I have EST."

Eastern standard time? "Do you mean ESP, extrasensory perception?"

"Exactly. A song pops into my head, and then I'd hear it playing somewhere. Or I'd think of a scene from a movie, and the next night, I'd be flipping through channels and hit on the same scene on cable. An old friend's face pops into my head, and then she'd give me a shout-out on Twitter. Like that."

"You're special, Gia. It's obvious."

"That's what I think!" she said excitedly. "It's a gift, like, being good at sports. I was born with it. My whole life I've been waiting to find out what made me special. And now I know, thanks to Fredo. The point is, I'm getting a psychic feeling about you."

Uh-oh. Did she know he was a grifter? "What are you picking up?"

"I'm getting a confused feeling from you. Like you want to get it in, but you're not sure you should. If you're worried about my reputation, don't be. Hello? I'm a slut already. I have standards, though. I don't get with just anyone. And I want you."

She peeled off her dress and threw it across the room. Standing naked, but for a matching zebra-print thong and bra set, Gia looked scrumptious. A sugarplum of juicy ripeness. Moving on their own, his hands wrapped around her trim waist. He could almost span it with his fingers. "You're so small here."

Gia smiled. "I killed myself with a trainer this winter. But the pain was worth it for the look on your face right now."

"I'm the first guy to see you in your drawers?"

"First in a while, yeah."

"So nothing going on with Fredo?"

"He's a sweet kid, but nothing romantic," she said.

"So he's just using you for your ability."

Gia frowned. "I wouldn't say *using*. It was his idea."

"And he's pimping out your psychic power for money. And Bella is taking a share of the money for doing nothing? You're a good friend to them, Gia. A lot better friend to them than they are to you."

"You don't know what you're talking about," said Gia coldly. "I've known Bella my whole life. She's not like that. And Fredo has plenty of his own money and doesn't need to use me."

She stiffened under his hands. He might've taken a misstep, trying to rattle her about her friendships too soon. Did he underestimate her loyalty to her friends? "Forget I said anything. I'm sorry, but I see what I see, and I care about you. I don't want anyone to take advantage of you. It helps to have a friend with an outside perspective. You might not be able to see the situation clearly yourself. Money has a way of distorting reality."

"That's true, but not Bella. She doesn't care about that. Fredo is as gentle as a lamb. I get that you're looking out for me. But you've got to be more trusting, Ponzi! I wonder why you're so suspicious. It makes me sad for you, what you must have gone through in your life to think the worst of good people."

She'd hung with him for how long? A day? And she'd hit the nail on the head. He *was* distrustful, and he had good reason. This girl understood him. He felt himself soften—not in the dick, but around his heart. He lifted her by the waist and deposited her on his lap. Between kisses on her bare shoulders, along her slender, bronzed arm, he said, "You're sensational. Let me treat you like a queen, like you deserve to be treated." He lingered on the inside of her elbow and wrist and felt her shiver. When Gia sighed, his heart bounced into his throat. He felt a sudden, bizarre urge to please her. To actually do the things he was promising.

If he didn't slow down, he'd lose control. If he got emotionally involved, could he steal her money? This issue had never come up before. Real emotions? He didn't have any. Or he thought he didn't. Gia triggered something real in him. Ponzi forced himself to squash his emotions and operate on a practical level only. Gia was a mark with a safe full of cash, and he had a mouth to feed—his own.

Inside his head, sirens blazed, lights blared. Or was it sirens *blared* and lights *blazed*? Jesus, he *was* confused! She was right about his feelings. Maybe she was psychic.

"I'm . . . I'm gonna take off now," he said.

"What? You can't! It's Happy Smush Day."

"My . . . my high-stakes poker game starts in a few minutes. I left half a million dollars on the table. If any woman alive could keep me from it, it'd be you, Gia."

"It's four in the morning."

"Really? Then I'm late." He stood up, leaving her in her undies on the couch. Stepping away from her hotness, he gained a measure of self-control. The greater distance from her gravitational pull, the clearer his mind worked.

"Can I see you tomorrow?"

Gia shrugged. "Sure."

She stood in the doorway watching him leave, frowning. He'd made her unhappy—the opposite of how a mark should feel when he left her.

Chapter Twenty-Three

The Brazillionaires

The next day, Gia and Bella sat side by side in throne chairs at Cleopatra's Retreat, the hotel salon. They'd already had their patriotic streaks dyed over. Bella went for her natural shade of chocolate brown. Gia got a new weave, platinum with leopard spots. Took for freakin' ever, but worth it! She'd had a Brazilian wax, a mustache wax, an Egyptian milk bath, and a sea-salt body scrub. A Russian manicurist was, at that moment, gluing acrylic nails to her fingers. Gia picked square-shaped tips with a leopard-face design, green-rhinestone eyes and a red-rhinestone tongue. Each tip was airbrushed by a local miniatures artist and sold exclusively to the salon. Meanwhile, a pedicurist was rubbing chocolate pudding on her feet.

"And then he left," said Gia to Bella. "I don't get it. He was definitely into me. He said he'd find me today."

"I would have told him off," said Bella from the chair next to her. She was getting a honey-and-cornmeal facial.

"I'm letting it slip. Honestly? I think I scared him. I came on too strong."

"You? Impossible."

Gia closed her eyes and fell into a coma of being pampered, jerking awake when the manicurist filed the nail tips. It was loud! Like sandblasting graffiti off blacktop.

"So what next?" asked Bella.

"A *dieci mani* massage. Ten hands on my body at the same time. I might have a flashback to college. Then I'm soaking in that huge hot tub in the Roman Baths spa. Clothing optional."

"I mean, what's next for you and Ponzi?" said Bella from under the amber mask. "The gunk on my face is starting to get hard."

"That's what she said."

The manicurist, facialist, and pedicurist laughed.

"I like Ponzi," said Gia. "He's hot, and except for running out last night, he treats me like a queen. It bothers me that Fredo doesn't like him."

"I'm not sure if I like him, either. I have to say, he's kind of right to say Fredo's using you—in a harmless wolf-cub way. But still."

Gia shrugged. "But Fredo does all the betting. If it weren't for him, we'd be on a bus back to Brooklyn, instead of sitting on a throne with chocolate pudding between my toes. It's a mutual use, and totally on the table. Nothing sneaky going on at all. I don't blame him for seeing talent and using it. If I could use me for my gift, I would, too."

"You'd use yourself?" asked Bella. "Would you regret you in the morning?"

The salon girls laughed again. Gia smiled contentedly, feeling that she was fulfilling her life's purpose of spreading her unique brand of joy to the people of the world.

"What did you think of Will?" asked Bella with stiff lips as her mask hardened.

The manicurist painted on the last coat of clear polish and started blowing on Gia's tips, holding her fingers up close to her lips. "Oh, jeez. I just got excited." The manicurist stopped blowing. "No, I like it." Turning to Bella, Gia said, "Will is a good kid. But he's not exactly your type. He's small, no tattoos, and he's so white! Like a piece of chalk rolled in glue with baking soda sprinkled on top."

"He's definitely different. But I haven't had so much luck with gorillas. Bobby turned into a stalker. Tony turned on me when I was at my lowest point ever. All of my boyfriends were cut from the same cloth, and I'm thinking it might be a good idea to try something new."

Gia rolled her eyes under the brand-new peacock-feather lashes she'd glued on earlier. "I know you, Bella. You're attracted to gorilla juiceheads. The kookah wants what the kookah wants. You can't convince yourself to fall for someone."

"Will has real talent. I can learn from him. I want a man to inspire my soul, not just my kookah."

"Okay, okay. Take it easy, or you'll crack your face. I'm just saying . . . you had a rough year, and you might latch onto the first person that comes along. You might not be seeing things as clearly as you think you are."

"Can I get this off?" Bella rapped on her face mask. The facialist peeled off the honey mask. "You want to be treated like a queen? Well, I want to be treated like an equal. I expect you to back me up, no matter what, even if I made a horrible mistake. That's what best friends do."

Then Bella stormed off. Gia's stomach sank. It was the first bad feeling she'd had since she arrived in AC. Well, second, if she counted being left by Ponzi last night. That really wasn't so terrible. A guy who wanted to take it slow? Obviously, he respected the hell out of her. She liked *that* feeling. But now she had to soothe Bella's hurt feelings. Was it wrong to send up the warning shot about Will? What did that kid have to offer Bella? It was too early to tell. She had a blinding flash of insight—or maybe that was the UV lamp the manicurist just switched on to dry her nails. Whatever. The point was . . . *Mmmm, the foot massage feels really good,* she thought. What was she thinking before? Something to do with Bella wanting to be treated like an equal.

In Gia's eyes, no man was Bella's equal. That's what Gia should've said, and would.

The facialist seemed to be reading her mind. "Your friend is very sensitive. Very tender. I could tell by her thin skin. Tan, but thin."

"I'm worried about her," said Gia. "I don't want her to get hurt. She's shaky right now. I had to say what I was thinking! It'd be wrong to keep it to myself. In some ways, having psychic power is a pain in the ass."

The manicurist said, "I'll tell you a joke, take your mind off your friend."

"I love jokes!"

"Okay. Did you hear about the gambler who came to Atlantic City in a fifty-thousand-dollar car and left in a three-hundred-thousand-dollar bus?"

All the women laughed, including Gia. "That's awesome! But why would he rather drive a bus than a slick car?"

The manicurist said, "Not driving the bus. A passenger on the bus."

"But why take the bus if he had his own wheels?"

"No, he lost the car."

"Like, in a parking lot?"

The manicurist and facialist lifted their pencil-thin, arched eyebrows at each other. The pedicurist said, "Yes. He lost the car in a parking lot."

Gia beamed. "That *is* funny."

Chapter Twenty-Four

Red Alert

Fredo's rickshaw was parked on the boardwalk outside Nero's Palace. He'd been taking an afternoon spin daily while the girls did . . . well, actually, he had no idea how Gia and Bella spent their afternoons. They slept all morning. God help the poor slob who interrupted Gia from her glitter dreamworld. Fredo once crept into their room and nudged her shoulder to see if she wanted to go with him to La Dolce Vito for an almond croissant. She nearly tore his hand off.

Lesson one of living with guidettes: Do not disturb their beauty sleep. You might lose a limb.

For the week they'd been at Nero's, Fredo, Gia, and Bella had fallen into the routine of doing their own things during the day, rendezvousing in the suite at nine to go out to dinner. Sometimes, their boys came along. Fredo had mixed feelings about Ponzi. On the upside, he often paid. On the downside, he acted like a prick whenever Gia wasn't there. Will was cool, though. After dinner, they'd play roulette until Gia's win percentage started to dip. Then they'd go to Providence or Midnight for dancing and drinks.

Meanwhile, the safe was filling up with stacks of cash. They put in more every night. They had to be closing in on Fredo's magic number, the amount he needed to return to Seaside Heights in triumph. If Gia's "gift" stuck around for another few days, he'd be golden.

His skin was golden, too, approaching bronzed. He spent part of every day on Gorilla Beach, soaking up sun and the vibes. Just being around the guido population was making him feel like a part of it. The gorillas had started to nod at him when they saw him. He nodded back with the same cool nonchalance. They accepted him, maybe even liked him. And not only the dudes. He'd caught girls looking at him, too. Erin, the cute pit boss, watched him at the table every night, closely. She was supercute, and her gaze made him nervous. A few times, he'd wondered what she'd look like out of that boxy, unflattering yellow jacket she wore.

"To the Taj, Juan," said Fredo, settling into the seat of the wicker rickshaw. His regular pilot, Juan, a three-hundred-pound, forty-year-old Puerto Rican in cargo shorts, a safari hat, a purple wifebeater, black socks, and Teva sandals, greeted him as usual with a growl and his hand out. Fredo forked over a twenty, and they were off.

Although he felt a bit anxious being pushed from behind, Fredo enjoyed his daily tour. He envisioned himself as a pasha in robes, carried by servants in a Roman litter.

They rolled passed Fralinger's candy store. Fredo asked, "You want taffy, Juan?"

Without speaking, Juan pulled to a stop at the door of the store. Fredo hopped out, ducked under the rickshaw canopy, and went inside. He selected a brick of peanut-butter fudge and a bag of assorted taffy for Juan. He returned to find his rickshaw occupied.

"Hello, Mr. Lupo," said a redhead in an orange halter dress.

Fredo glanced at Juan, who shrugged. "Erin!" said Fredo. "So that's what you look like out of your uniform!"

Juan coughed and shook his head every so slightly.

Then Fredo noticed the girl was blushing. "Oh! I didn't mean . . . you look pretty, that's all." She looked red-hot, to tell the truth. "Can I, er, give you a lift?"

"That's be great, thanks," she said, smiling.

Fredo slipped in next to her. Their rickshaw was designed to fit up to three people, or two fat tourists from Texas. There was plenty of room for a skinny guido and a slight ginger. But Erin sat close enough to Fredo to touch thighs.

"I hope you and your friends are having a pleasant stay at Nero's," she said.

"Were you following me?" he asked, suspicious. Growing up Lupo would do that to anyone.

Her cheeks had bright red splotches by now. "I wanted to talk to you, get to know you better. You kind of stand out."

Was Erin flirting with him or calling him a human ostrich? Not to say that she couldn't be doing both. "It's just that pretty girls don't usually jump into my rickshaw."

Erin smiled. "I can't imagine why." She put her freckled hand on his thigh.

He almost jumped through the canopy. "Now I *know* you're playing me. What's really going on here?"

Erin hesitated and removed her hand. He missed it terribly. They stared at each other. Fredo tried to concentrate on looking tough, and not crumbling in those green eyes—especially when they filled up and Erin started crying.

Instant flashback to the thousands of times his mom defeated him by crying. Donna Lupo would turn on the waterworks, and Fredo would give in to whatever she wanted. He felt his defenses start to crumble, but then he got a grip. *Not this time.*

"My boss accused me of helping you cheat. I have to prove I'm clean, or he'll . . . he'll . . . they have this room in the basement. The Boom Boom Room . . . I'm scared, Fredo." She cried louder.

Tourists on the boardwalk peeked under the rickshaw roof to see why a girl was crying. They glared at him, like he was some kind of monster.

Juan shook his head at Fredo. A warning?

"Who is this scumbag boss of yours?"

"Vito Violenti," she blubbered. "He said he wouldn't hurt me if I figured out how you and your friends were doing it."

He felt terrible for her. Almost on the verge of confessing to *something* just to help her. But they weren't cheating. "Gia thinks she's psychic. Maybe she does have powers, or she's just lucky. But she's square as a pizza box, and so am I. Your boss can make threats, but he can't bust us for gambling in a casino."

"This is humiliating," said Erin, wiping her tears. "I told him you're okay. But Mr. Violenti refuses to believe it. People have come up with some inventive ways to rig roulette. We caught one operator who planted a magnet under the table and switched a standard ball with one that had a ball bearing in the middle. He had a crew of three partners who placed bets.

"The casino lost a lot of money until we figured out what was going on. I don't know what happened to the operator and his partners. He was called away in the middle of a shift and disappeared."

Fredo swallowed hard. "What does your boyfriend think about all this?" *Whoa! Where did that come from?*

Juan made a strangled sound.

Erin did a double take at Fredo and smiled. It was like the first light of dawn after an endless night. "I don't have a boyfriend, or a husband. I haven't been on a date since I started working for Nero's. If you're hitting on me to distract me, it might work. But I'm not supposed to socialize with guests."

In the past, this would be when Fredo retreated or popped an Ativan or limped into the woods like a wounded animal. "Have dinner with me," he said, spitting a bit. "When's your shift over tonight? I can do early, late, whatever."

"I have the night off."

Not denied! Not rejected! Fredo's spirits soared like a seagull on crack. "Say yes. Just one syllable. You can do it."

The cutest nose in the world crinkled. After a few beats, Erin said, "Okay." She gave him her number. "Getting off."

Juan stopped the rickshaw. Erin stepped out, stumbling a bit as she exited, and headed back toward Nero's Palace. Fredo and Juan watched her for a while.

Fredo said, "I've got a friggin' date."

Juan said, "Nice work," and pushed on.

Chapter Twenty-Five

Batshit Being the Technical Term

"I'm having dinner with him tonight," said Erin.

"How'd you manage that?" asked Mr. Violenti.

"I cried," she said guiltily. Erin felt uncomfortable about this whole recon business. Using tears to manipulate the kid? It was like playing with loaded dice, or a stacked deck. She'd cheated to flush out an alleged cheater. Didn't seem right. "My gut tells me Fredo's a decent guy. Kind of shy and weird, but okay."

"He's a lying, cheating scumbag. Watch this. Look at 'em claw for scraps of meat."

Mr. Violenti, fifty-five years sleazy, spoke to her through the railing around the Jupiter statue. He was inside, feeding his pet gators. He flung a purple lobe of raw chicken liver into the moat. Writhing reptiles with yellow, snapping teeth broke the surface of the water. The pygmy alligators—only two feet long, but scary as hell—attacked the chunk. The water bubbled, then settled to eerie stillness. Erin had to keep herself from shuddering at the sight.

"Did you tell him we've got eyes on him?" asked her boss, hurling more chicken into the moat.

"Uh, I'm sure he knows the cameras are always on." A smoked-glass bubble hung overhead. Erin knew that one of the security slobs who lived, ate, breathed, and shat in front of the wall of monitors was ogling her right now. "Fredo's father is Luigi Lupo, by the way."

"I don't care who his father is. He's not in Seaside anymore. This is *my* town, and I call the shots. What do you know about the two skanks he's shacking up with?"

"They're just friends, actually. Nothing romantic."

"Do I look like I give a crap who's bangin' who?" he ranted. A pair of older women walked by at the moment. They gasped at his language. Mr. Violenti smiled and said, "Evening, ladies. Hope you're enjoying your stay. All-you-can-eat king-crab legs at the buffet tonight. Only twenty dollars per person!"

Erin noticed that Mr. Violenti's toupee was askew. It looked more than ever like a hit-and-run raccoon that dragged itself off the highway and crawled onto his head to die. Add to that the five o'clock shadow, loose jowls, and eyes filled with bloodlust, and the guy came off as batshit insane, *batshit* being the technical term.

"What're you looking at?"

"Nothing, sir."

He pulled a phone out of his pocket and found a photo of a man loitering in the lobby by the newsstand, reading a copy of the *New York Post*. "Who is he?"

Only the man's profile was visible, but Erin recognized him. "Goes by the name Arthur Ponzirelli, aka Ponzi or the Ponz. He's been staying in the hotel for two weeks now. Settles his bill in cash every day. A close friend of Giovanna Spumanti, Fredo's friend. Ponzirelli is most likely an alias. Our facial-recognition software program hasn't flagged him yet. He's good about keeping his face partially or completely away from cameras."

"I sent this photo to all the hotels in AC," said Mr. Violenti. "Got a hit from the head of security at the Borgata. This *fugazi* worked there last summer. His usual mark is a fat, middle-aged, lonely divorcée who's desperate for company. This concerns me. Take a look at camera fifty-four."

On his phone, he showed her the live feed of the roof pool camera (yup, there was an app for that). Gia Spumanti was just out of the water. She wore a zebra-print monokini that—oh, jeez—was completely sheer when wet. As Erin watched Gia walk to her orange lounge and bend over to arrange her towel, she thought, *That reminds me. Must make an appointment for my annual Pap smear.*

"Seen enough?" he asked.

"I'll say."

"Check out the other people."

Erin tore her eyes off Gia and looked at the other guests around the pool. They were *all* staring at Gia. Man, woman, child.

"Does she look fat, lonely, and desperate to you?"

"The very opposite, sir."

"You can understand why it concerns me that the *fugazi* is spending so much time with *her*."

"You think they're partners in crime."

Mr. Violenti raved, "They're all in on it! Every freakin' member of their crew. If you can't get anything out of Lupo tonight, I'm going to sweat the Spumanti broad tomorrow."

"Forgive me, sir, but that girl doesn't have a dishonest bone in her body. She might've hooked up with a con man, in which case she should be warned, not accused or threatened."

Mr. Violenti put his phone back in his pocket. He flung the remaining chicken meat out of the bucket and into the moat. The gators clawed and snapped until every morsel was consumed. "Go do something with your hair. Tie it back, or whatever. You're not gonna get any info out of Lupo if you look like Ronald McDonald's sister."

He should talk. "Yes, sir."

"And wear a decent dress, for Christ's sake. You can't afford something better on what I'm paying you?" He came through the moat's door panel.

"Actually, no, sir."

"Get the info out of Lupo, and we'll talk about a raise—and the manager job at Midnight."

He handed her the bucket and stalked off.

As she stared into the slimy remains, she wondered if she was working for the wrong man. Maybe, somewhere out there, she'd find a boss who treated her with respect and gave her a dream job to go with it. In the meantime, she'd do what Mr. Violenti wanted.

Chapter Twenty-Six

I See Tequila in Your Future

Bella took her afternoon run as always. Like every day, she finished her miles at Madame Olga's to cool down and hang out with Will for a while. But today he wasn't there.

Bella had some friends who freaked out if their boy went unaccounted for, for five minutes. Insecurity wasn't a good look on anyone. She didn't have a leash around Will's neck, and he didn't have to update her on his movements.

But he said he'd be around.

Maybe he was getting a burger. Or in the bathroom. Or he'd lied to her to get her off his freakin' back. Although Bella had yet to hook up with a boy who didn't become obsessed with her, she wasn't sure about Will's feelings. He liked her. But how much? He was a loner and might need space. He might be fed up with her for putting him off—damn Gia for planting that "you're vulnerable right now, don't rush" seed in her head.

One thing Bella did not tolerate, for any reason: the dip. The dip was when a kid avoided you in a sneaky, shady way, like if he pretended not to notice you when you were dancing near each other at a club. Or he said he lost your number when he had it programmed into his phone. Or he saw you coming and then slipped out the back door.

The dip was a pathetic, moby-dick move.

Bella was afraid Will was pulling it on her.

She jogged by Madame Olga's storefront three times. Will's celebrity portraits were lined up. His chair and stools were set up. His sketchpad was leaning against the chair, a cup of coffee on the floor next to it. In a mystery movie, it'd be like the detective rushing into the room and finding the killer's lit cigarette burning in the ashtray.

Bella slowed to stop. A year ago, she would have swallowed her hurt feelings and jogged away. She'd let the kid off the hook. Will didn't owe her anything. They'd spent some time together. They'd kissed. He'd bought her a Philly cheesesteak and taught her a few tricks with a Sharpie. Not like they'd smushed or declared undying love or made a commitment to go to Great Adventure together. But Bella believed that Will, unlike 99 percent of guys out there, saw past her boobs, straight into her soul.

"Screw it," she said, and marched into the store.

Madame Olga was in her curtained booth, finishing up with a client. "I see big change coming. In the next one or two years, you'll have great opportunities. You should stop worrying so much about money. It'll come."

The middle-aged man's voice said, "You think?"

"I'm sure of it."

Bella sat on the couch and waited for their session to end. After a minute, he came out, grinning ear to ear. Madame Olga emerged from behind the beads.

"Bella, I sense you've been exercising." Yeah, she needed powers to see Bella's sweat and workout clothes. Putting her hand to her temple, Olga added, "I also sense you're searching for something or someone."

"I'm looking for Will," said Bella, trying to keep the impatience out of her voice.

"Are you ready for your reading yet? I'll tell you everything you need to know. Free of charge."

"Maybe tomorrow. So, is Will around?"

"He's not here today. The muse takes him sometimes. He's probably at his apartment, not eating, drinking, sleeping, or bathing. It's like a demonic possession."

"His sketchpad, though," said Bella gesturing toward it, propped up against his chair. "And the coffee."

"You're very observant. You could be a psychic, too, if you weren't so cynical. Sometimes, I set up his chair and coffee. Many people wander in for a portrait and get a reading instead."

"He's at his apartment? Is it nearby?"

"Come in for a reading. I insist."

Bella groaned. Olga wasn't going to give her Will's address until she told Bella's future. Why bother? Olga would just serve up trite predictions that could apply to anyone off the boardwalk. Then again, Madame Olga might believe her own bullshit.

"Okay," said Bella, going into Olga's booth and handing over her . . . hands.

Madame Olga examined Bella's palms. "Yes, I can see you've had hard times. You've had love, and lost it. Someone hurt you badly, and you've got a lot of anger bottled up. You're in a limbo state. You used to have focus, but now you don't know what you really want. Uncertainty troubles you deeply."

"Isn't uncertainty and confusion why people come to psychics?"

"Your parents. They are sad for you."

"For me?" Bella was desperately unhappy *for them*.

"You have to forgive. Then the sickness will leave the house, and you'll all feel healthy again."

Bella pulled her hands out of Olga's grasp. "That's not friggin' funny," she said with acid. "Tell me you see tequila in my future, but don't talk about my family. You don't know anything about it."

"I know you're in pain, and you're worried about your loved

ones. I worry, too, Bella. William came to Atlantic City when he was just sixteen years old. Did you know that about him? He was a runaway. He's had more heartache in twenty-five years than most people see in a lifetime."

"What happened to him?"

"It's not for me to say. I only tell you because I'm worried you see Will as a stepping-stone. You're using him to get over a past love or to forget your problems. I don't like it."

This professional liar was going to judge her? "Will is a sensitive soul. I know. But all due respect, you should stay out of our relationship. If you can't tell how I feel about him, you're a bigger bullshitter than I thought. Will's a grown man. He doesn't need a gatekeeper."

Madame Olga whistled low. "Good answer. I sense genuine passion. Okay, I give you his address. But you must bring him food and make sure he eats it."

Bella felt both relieved and wary of what she'd find at Will's place. He'd been in the grip of a muse? What did that even mean? She had him by the shorties?

Olga scribbled an address on a piece of paper. She handed it to Bella. "I see travel, by land. Someone you know will impress you with their generosity. In the not too distant future, you'll have two children. A girl and a boy."

Bella was stunned, yet oddly pleased. "Anything else?"

"Something bad is brewing for those closest to you. If I were you, I'd watch my back."

Chapter Twenty-Seven

A Good Hard Whiff of Gorilla

"Where is everyone?" Gia asked herself out loud. She'd been waiting for Fredo and Bella, alone, in the suite since eight. The little hand was almost on the ten already! She was starving. They had reservations at a pier restaurant called Buddakan, a fancy Chinese place famous for boneless spareribs and lobster fried rice. She'd skipped lunch in anticipation of this meal. Her blood sugar was ant-belly low.

For the fifteenth time, Gia tried Bella's cell. It went to voice mail. She called Fredo.

"Speak," he said, finally picking up.

"*Wherethefuckareyou?*" she ranted. "I've been waiting for hours. My tan's faded three shades."

"Sorry, Gia. Something came up. You know that redhead pit boss?"

"I love Erin. What have you done to her?"

"Nothing! We're on a date. She just went to the bathroom. Tell me how to close."

"I don't believe it." Why would adorable Erin go on a date with Fredo? No offense to him. Gia loved the kid. But he'd been hit a few times with the grundle stick at birth, and Erin was supercute.

"I friggin' swear!" he hissed. "Now help me."

"Where are you?"

"Buddakan."

Gia nearly threw the phone across the room. "You used the reservation with *her*? I'm starving!"

"Don't hang up. Give me a closer. One line."

Sighing, Gia's love for Fredo trumped her hunger. "When she comes back from the bathroom, say, 'I was having so much fun talking, I forgot how nervous I am.'"

"Really?" he asked, doubtful. "That won't make me sound like a neurotic asshole?"

"You *are* a neurotic asshole. Trust me. If you pretend to be someone you're not, she'll switch off. Girls can sniff out a fake in two seconds flat."

"She's coming. Gotta go."

"Bring me spareribs!" Gia shouted at the phone, but he'd already hung up.

What now? Order room service? Go out by herself? She could call Ponzi and ask him to take her out, but he'd spent so much money on her, it was starting to feel awkward. He paid for everything, but asked for nothing in return. Any other boy who'd dropped thousands on her would demand at least a blow job. All Ponzi wanted to do was make out. When they were in the casino, he kept her mouth attached to his, as if she were his oxygen tank. But whenever they got serious on the couch in private, he made an excuse and left.

Could be, he had a contagious ESP.

He should trust her enough to tell her. For all she knew, he had a wife tucked away somewhere. How well did she really know him? A guy who dropped paper but didn't bend her over the bed? It didn't feel right. She'd just given Fredo a lecture about how girls could sniff out a fake in one inhale. It was entirely possible Gia hadn't taken a good hard whiff of her own gorilla.

Gia pictured Ponzi's shining smile, his pearly whites lined up in neat rows. Was that the mouth of a master manipulator? Did creeps have flawless teeth? In the movies, the telltale sign a character shouldn't be trusted was blackened stubs embedded in red, diseased gums. Maybe Ponzi's perfect smile was also the perfect disguise.

Like crabs at dawn, doubt crawled up Gia's spine. Who was Ponzi? What did he do when he wasn't with her or playing high-stakes poker? How did he really feel about her?

Only one way to find out. Gia called him.

"Great timing," he said. "I just stepped out of the poker game for a break. How was Buddakan?"

"I didn't make it over there. Meet me at Morton's Steakhouse in thirty minutes."

A ten-ounce porterhouse, *two-pound lobster, and bottle of Chianti later* . . .

"You like your meat," said Ponzi, licking the corner of Gia's mouth.

She burped lustily in agreement.

"What now? To the tables?" he asked.

"Fredo said we should take the night off. He doesn't want to 'tempt the gods,' he said. I had no idea Fredo was so religious."

"You've heard the saying 'no atheists in foxholes—or casinos.'"

What did foxes have to do with it? she wondered. Unless *foxhole* was his word for "kookah." Then the connection between foxholes and religion made sense. When a guy was in her foxhole, he always said, "Oh, God! Oh, God!"

"So, Ponzi, we've been hanging out for a week now."

"Best week of my life." He pulled her in for a pouf-quaking kiss. Then he smacked his lips. "I think I just sucked the last bite of lobster out of your teeth."

"Yummy."

"Maybe there's some steak in there, too," he said, coming in for another mackwich.

"Wait. I wanna talk."

He leaned back, his fingers making tiny circles on her shoulder. "You're gorgeous."

True. "Just shut up and listen. We never talk about your life away from AC. You let me ramble about Brooklyn and my family all night long. But I don't know a lot about you."

He looked panicked. "Not much to say. You're a psychic. You tell me."

Gia thought about it. "I can't guess specifics. But I think you try really hard to cut off your emotions. I think you're scared of getting with me. You're either afraid of having a relationship, or maybe you aren't sure about me because of my power. Like you think my power is emancipating."

"Emasculating?"

"Whichever one means you've got a mangina."

Ponzi paused. "A *what*?"

"Just saying." Gia peeked at him through the veil of her peacock lashes. "I appreciate your being romantical, and how much you love to make out. But if you really loved and respected me, you'd smush me raw tonight."

Ponzi raised his arm and yelled, "Check please!"

Chapter Twenty-Eight

Hell Isn't This Hot

The waitress brought the bill. Ponzi was afraid to look. He opened the leather envelope, scanned down to the bottom, and nearly swallowed his tongue. Three hundred and fifty bucks.

"Leave a big tip for Maggie," said Gia.

Who the heck was Maggie? Oh, yeah, the waitress. "Of course," he said, gritting his teeth. "I'm sensitive to that, as a former waiter."

"Where?"

"When I was in high school, I worked at the Clam Dungeon, a seafood restaurant in Hoboken. My dad was the maître d' there." *Whoa*, he was revealing biographical information that no one needed to know, especially not his next mark. He really had to be careful with this girl. And now she'd forced the issue about sex. He'd been avoiding it, afraid of what he'd say during the act, and after, when lulled by postorgasmic stupidity.

It was put-up time. Ponzi was not going to let this mark go, considering his huge investment in her. He took out his wallet—cash reserves were dangerously low—and took out four hundreds.

"Leave five," said Gia.

Before he even knew what he was doing, he slapped another benjamin on the stack. "Why do I get the feeling you're testing me?"

She shrugged and drained the last drop of wine from her glass. "Because I am."

"Making sure I meet your standards?" He liked a challenge. "Go ahead. Ask me anything."

"Carry me," she said, holding out her arms. He must have looked confused. "We all have our sexual quirks. I like to be carried. I knew a guy once who liked to watch a girl bounce on a balloon until it popped."

"That does sound hot," he said, swooping her into his arms. She weighed nothing. Carrying her like Tarzan, he walked out of the restaurant and onto the boardwalk. She squealed and giggled the whole way. People looked at them and smiled. Ponzi absorbed the positive vibes, their tacit approval of an affectionate, attractive couple having fun on a Saturday night. He hoisted her up, tossing her in the air.

She screamed and then dissolved into giggles. Ponzi heard genuine laughter come out of his own mouth, and almost dropped Gia in shock.

"To your room?" He was prepared to carry her to the end of the earth if she asked.

She thought for a second, then said, "That way."

He headed for the ramp between Nero's Palace and Bally's that connected the boardwalk to Gorilla Beach. With one smooth move, he spun her around so that she was riding piggyback, her smooth tan arms around his neck, and her legs wrapped around his waist.

"Why is it called piggyback?" she asked. "I feel like a monkey."

"And you look like one, too."

"Hey!" she said, laughing, swatting his cheek. "Go right."

He went right.

"I mean left."

"To the Gorilla Beach Bar, or the actual beach?"

"The bar," she said.

He delivered her to a chair at the bar, the ocean in front of them and the boardwalk behind them. The moonlight and ambient neon from the boardwalk gave her skin an angelic glow. Her eyes, dark as the sky, shimmered like the stars.

Lame poetic rhapsodizing? *Fuck me,* he thought. Ponzi was officially off the rails. A smitten jerkoff. Was there any hope for him? He wouldn't relax until he'd stolen her blind and was a thousand miles away from Jersey. In the meantime, he'd enjoy Gia, in every way a man can enjoy a woman. She'd demanded it!

She called the bartender. "Tanner!"

The guy leaned over the bar to kiss her cheek. "Welcome back, Gia." The kid was *way* too good-looking for Gia to kiss. Red-hot jealousy burned through Ponzi's gut.

To Gia, he said, "You make fast friends."

"Tanner, I have a special request from the kitchen." She motioned the kid in close and whispered in his ear.

When she finished, Tanner said, "I'll see what I can do."

"You rock."

"I'm curious," said Ponzi after the bartender left. "And jealous. Your lips were way too close to his ear. Should I be nervous?"

Gia played with her weave. "They must be cold."

"Who?"

"The waitresses." She pointed her square nail at the rear view of five girls in identical red bikini uniforms, clamoring around the bartender station for their orders.

"They should wear skirts or tops at night," said Gia.

"You're right," Ponzi said, distracted.

"What's wrong?"

How could he explain? "I didn't notice them." Usually, he made a point of ogling the Gorilla Beach Bar's waitresses. He planned it in his day. But he didn't notice them when he was with Gia. "I only have eyes for you." How many times had he used that cheeseball line on rich divorcées without ever understanding what it meant?

Oh, yeah. Ponzi was in *way* over his head.

The bartender returned with a plate covered by a napkin, and a glass of water. He winked at Gia, and she squirmed in her chair, excited.

"I'm gonna give you a trust test," she said to Ponzi. "I blindfold you and put something in your mouth. You have to eat it, or I won't believe you really love me."

"I'm kind of full from dinner." Blindfold? No way. Ponzi had a deep fear of being in the dark and out of control.

"You're no fun." Gia pouted, her bottom lip quivering. He'd love to put her lip in his mouth and suck on it. If he didn't do her trust test, he might blow the whole con.

"I don't see why you need to test me, but if it's that important to you . . ."

"Yay!" Gia tied a spare napkin over his eyes, tight. "Okay, open wide."

He did as she asked. A morsel hit his tongue. Salty, pliant. "An olive," he said, chewing. Okay, he could do this.

"Next!"

Another round object. Sweet, sticky. "Maraschino cherry."

"Okay," she said. "Open up."

A long, thin, crunchy thing. He bit down, and his tongue caught fire. He ripped off the blindfold. "What was that?"

"A serrano chili pepper," she said, laughing.

"You're crazy," he said, eyes bulging.

"Come on, it's not that hot."

"Hell isn't this hot!" he wheezed, breaking into a sweat.

"Here," she said, offering a glass. "Chase it with this."

Ponzi took a long draw on the glass. Ugh, not water. Something sour and salty. His scorching mouth puckered violently, and it felt as if his lips were sucked backward into his skull. He started coughing, in great heaves. "What. Was. *That*? Battery acid?"

"A pickle back. Pickle-juice shot."

"I'm dying," he gasped.

"You'll be fine in a minute."

He felt woozy. "I hate pickles!" Then he blacked out.

Chapter Twenty-Nine

Venus on the Oyster Shell

The taxi pulled to a stop outside Will's place. Bella had expected a condo building. But his apartment was inside a *Boardwalk Empire*-era brownstone. It reminded Bella of the town houses in her own neighborhood of Carroll Gardens, except for one major difference. Will's neighborhood was like a war zone. His old-fashioned house was covered in fresh graffiti. She cringed at the stench of overflowing trash cans on the street. Only a few blocks from the Taj Mahal Casino, it was as if she'd arrived at the slums of India. When Bella approached Will's door, a stray dog who'd been rooting in the garbage nearby tried to steal the bag of burgers she carried. She growled back, and the mutt ran away.

This was where Will lived?

He might be taking the starving-artist thing a bit too seriously.

Bella grew up solidly, proudly middle-class, a third-generation American and daughter of a small-business owner. She was the first of her family to go to college. She accepted that wealth probably wasn't her destiny. She'd never be rolling in dough—unless it was pizza dough. But she'd be okay.

Apparently, Will was not doing okay. The Brooklyn projects looked like the Ritz compared to this. Hoping that the shabby exterior was a front for a gleaming, luxurious interior, Bella found Will's buzzer on the rusted plate and pushed.

No response. She leaned hard on it. Nothing.

She might've hightailed it out of there, but a man exited the building. She caught the door before it locked closed and went in.

Only five units, one on each floor. Will lived on the first floor. She knocked on his door, pounding on it. No response, although she heard thrash punk coming from inside. She tried the knob. It opened.

Her heart beating to the manic music, she crept into the apartment. She knew she was in the right apartment because Will's old Ducati motorcycle was parked in the middle of the living room, a small puddle of engine fluid pooling under it. Otherwise, the room was sparsely furnished with junk that might've been pulled off the street. A lumpy couch, small TV, a scarred table. It reminded Bella of the Prison Condo.

One lamp with a soft bulb shone the way toward the rear of the apartment, where the music came from. Bella passed a kitchenette, clean with the lonely look of disuse. Will wasn't a cook. Too bad. Bella loved to cook. She and Tony had shopped for, prepared, and consumed many memorable meals together. After their first few nights together, Bella realized they cooked better in the kitchen than the bedroom.

"Hello?" Bella called.

No answer, but she could barely hear herself think with the music so loud. She walked by a bedroom alcove, a futon on the floor, tightly dressed with a clean white comforter. In the back of the apartment, she came to a closed door. Not knowing what to expect, she gathered her courage and pushed the door open.

The room contained several lamps with high-wattage bulbs, iPod speakers, cans of paint, and jars of brushes. And Will, shirtless, in jeans, bare feet, and a black, studded belt. He was on his knees, facing the rear wall, a brush in his right hand. In his left, a bottle of beer. He was bent close to the wall, doing detail work on a figure. An animal? She couldn't tell.

All four walls, and the ceiling, were covered, layered, with figure paintings. Bella drew her eyes away from the artist to take in the art. It seemed to be a complex mural that reminded Bella instantly of paintings she'd studied in art history class, specifically the work of Sandro Botticelli. One whole wall was devoted to Botticelli's most famous work, a fleshy Venus rising from the ocean on the half shell, escorted by angels, her golden hair streaming behind her like ribbons. But Will's Venus wasn't a blonde. She was a brunette, with perky boobs, a belly-button ring, and muscular legs. Will's angels weren't pink, chubby cherubs. They were winged dragons, the kind of images you'd find in tattoo parlors and comic books.

Studying the wall to her left, Bella took in the lush forest scene. He'd painted nudes. Male, female, she-males, writhing on top of each other in crazy positions. It was a Roman orgy to make Cupid blush. One wall was an ocean view, a beach with umbrellas, people, the glowing sun. It was so realistic, right down to the nipple piercings on a pair of iron-pumping gorillas, Bella could smell the sea. The ceiling was a sky at night, the moon, constellations, and the Milky Way.

Bella's eyes couldn't take it all in. Each mural was amazingly detailed. Every inch of space was covered, just covered, with figures and scenery. The woods scene had hundreds of animals and creatures in trees and on the forest floor. She simply didn't know how to appreciate the murals. From far away, or up close? Each face seemed so distinct.

Checking to see if Will was even aware of her presence yet—he wasn't—she moved closer to examine Will's brunette version of the goddess of love. He was working on her shell—not a clamshell, but an opalescent oyster. Bella studied Venus's face.

It was like looking in the friggin' mirror.

Will stopped painting suddenly and spun around. "Bella! What are you doing here?"

"I brought burgers," she said weakly, holding up the bag.

He stared at her, his mouth wide-open. "You're not supposed to see this."

He looked different without black eyeliner. His hair was washed and hung down like bangs. She'd never seen his bare chest and was pleasantly surprised by his muscle definition. He was slim, but buff. She could count his abs. He switched off the music so they could talk.

"These murals are . . . I'm blown away. Speechless. I can't believe what I'm seeing," she said. "How long have you being painting this room?"

"Three years. On and off. You're the first person to see it."

"In three years?"

"I'm kind of a loner."

"I see a familiar face here," she said, pointing to the goddess.

"Are you mad?"

"Are you freakin' kidding? I love it."

"You don't think it's creepy?" he asked carefully.

Bella took that into consideration. "No. I'm flattered. You made me look beautiful."

He smiled. "If you like that one, then you'll love the two dozen others I've done since I met you."

"Where?"

He showed her each figure. None of the others was as large as the Venus. But the mini-Bellas were just as amazing. He'd put her head on the body of a panther, an eagle, an exotic dancer with six gigantic boobs, and in a crest of sea foam.

Since she was thirteen, boys had been telling Bella she was beautiful. But Will made her believe it. Bella was his subject, and his muse. She'd inspired Will. And she felt inspired right back, by him. She felt as if she could do anything.

But there was only one thing she *wanted* to do.

"Any other girls make the wall?" she asked, scanning the other images.

He grinned. "A few. But they got painted over quickly enough."

"Who's this?" she asked of another female face that appeared often in the murals, usually as an insect or rodent. Will paused. A sensitive subject? "It's your mom, right?"

He nodded. "And this is my dad." He pointed to another figure, set apart, in the corner. "I'm covered in paint. Do you mind if I clean up?"

Following him into a small bathroom, she watched him scrub his hands and wash his face and neck. Beads of water trickled down his ripped back and chest. "You brought me dinner?" he asked.

She realized she was still holding the bag of burgers. "Are you hungry? Olga made me promise to feed you. She gave me your address."

"I owe her, again." After he dried off, they went into the living room. He found a bottle of Coke in the fridge. They sat on the lumpy couch and dug into the burgers. They ate in silence, but the air between them was warm and comfortable.

"Sorry about the bike. It dominates the room, but I can't leave it on the street."

"Tell me about your parents," she said. "Unless you don't want to."

"I've got nothing to be ashamed of. *They* do. Mom was a drunk when I was growing up. Dad was addicted to betting at Yonkers Raceway. Harness racing, guys on little carriages whipping horses. Five nights a week, year-round. If Dad got lucky, he drank his winnings. If he lost, there was a lot of screaming and fighting. Sometimes, it got physical. I spent a lot of time ducking for cover, or stealing food from my neighbors' kitchens. They kind of let me do it, out of pity. As soon as I could, I left home. I met Olga almost as soon as I got off the bus. She 'sensed' we had a future together and took me in. I lived in her house with her other kids and worked for her until she let me sell my drawings out of her store. I finished high school right here in AC. I wasn't a great student, though. The only thing I've ever been good at is drawing faces."

Bella's heart ached for him. Not having a loving, supportive family? It was inconceivable to her. She'd been raised in the same house with her parents, her grandparents, and, eventually, her aunt Alicia and Gia. They had dinner together every night and were in each other's business constantly. To be neglected and abused by your own flesh and blood? That was the ultimate nightmare. And Will had survived it.

"Please don't look at me like that," he said. "It's killing my appetite."

"How did you get by?"

"I got lucky. I met some people who helped, Olga and an art teacher. She encouraged me and paid for me to take some classes. Eventually, I saved enough money to buy the bike and rent this apartment. I've almost got enough to move to a better place."

"Do you talk to your parents at all?"

"Never again would be too soon," he said. "They have no idea where I am."

"Your mom is an alcoholic and your dad is a gambler. And you came to a casino party town. On some level, you want them to find you."

"I didn't plan on coming to AC, or anywhere. I hid on a departing bus, and it stopped here. Totally random. I have looked up my parents. They're on Facebook. She's sober and goes to AA. He's in Gamblers Anonymous. So, if you think about it, this is the one town they'll never visit."

"So even after they got sober, you still don't want to talk to them?"

"Too much under the bridge," he said.

"That's sad."

"It's ancient history. I'm numb to it. I don't really think it makes that much difference in my life now. I'm twenty-five years old. By being on my own for so long, I've got a jump start on other kids my age."

He had no friggin' idea what he'd missed by not having a close, loving family. Maybe that was a blessing. "I couldn't have survived," she said.

"You'd be surprised what you're capable of. I think you could handle any curveball life threw at you."

Bella put down her burger and cleared the wax paper off his lap. Then she threw a curve at him. Closing the distance between them, she kissed him. He returned it, wrapping his arms around her and holding her tight. *No more holding back,* she thought. The seed of doubt was gone.

Before they got too intense, he pulled away to ask, "Are you doing this because you feel sorry for me?"

"I do feel sorry for you. But that's not why I want you."

"Then why?"

"Your orgy scene really turned me on. That chick with six boobs . . . mad sexy."

Chapter Thirty

Wound Up Like Spaghetti
on a Friggin' Fork

"Stand back! Everyone, stand back," yelled the paramedic, a thirtyish black woman. The crowd gave Ponzi some air.

Her partner, a younger guy with dreads, put an oxygen mask over Ponzi's face. "Oh, damn!"

A dark circle appeared, and grew, around Ponzi's crotch.

"How much did he have to drink tonight?" the woman asked Gia.

"A bottle of wine."

"Medical history of high blood pressure, fainting, or panic attacks?"

"Not since I've know him."

"How long is that?"

"A week?"

"Vitals stable," said the paramedic. "He's slightly dehydrated. Probably just passed out. Is he allergic to anything?"

"He fainted after he did a pickle-juice shot," said Gia. If he was allergic to pickles, they were doomed. He might as well be allergic to bronzer or tequila. Or sex. Maybe he was allergic to sex! That would explain why he'd avoided it. "He might have a sensitivity to kookah."

"Kookah?" asked the female paramedic.

"You know, foxhole."

The woman gave Gia a suspicious look. "Are you on something?"

The guy said, "He's stable. Breathing steady. Let's load him up."

"Where are you taking him?" asked Gia.

"AtlantiCare Regional Medical Center. It's around the corner, behind the Nero's parking lot."

"Do I get to ride in it with you?"

"Unless you'd rather run alongside," said the woman.

"Yay! I've never been in an ambulance before!" Even though Gia was upset and scared about Ponzi, she felt excited about that.

Both paramedics stopped loading Ponzi on the stretcher to gape at her. "Patient's name?" asked the woman.

"Arthur Ponzirelli," said Gia, pleased to be useful and know the answer.

"Sounds fake."

They hoisted the stretcher into the ambulance. Gia had trouble climbing aboard. The first step was really high. She had heels on, and a supertight skirt. Plus, she was kind of height challenged.

"A little help?" she asked.

The guy yelled, "Get your ass in here, now!"

Jeez. No need to yell. She yanked up her skirt, climbed onto the step on her knees, then pulled herself in. The man was driving. The woman was in the back, checking Ponzi's heart rate and pulse. "Is he okay?" asked Gia.

"Stable."

"Good."

The siren went on, and the ambulance raced to the hospital. It was only a few blocks. They pulled up to the emergency room entrance. Gia climbed down the steps again and followed the stretcher as the paramedics crashed through a set of doors into the ER. It was kind of exciting, like being in a hospital TV show. "Male, midtwenties, possible anaphylactic shock, possible alcohol poisoning."

"Does he have ID?" asked the nurse, a fortyish white woman in green scrubs.

"His name is Arthur Ponzirelli," said Gia.

"Sounds fake," said the nurse.

"That's what I said," agreed the paramedic.

"It's real," said Gia. "I've been with the kid for a week."

The nurse found his wallet in his pants pocket. It was empty except for cash and an expired Florida driver's license. The nurse showed it to Gia. "This says his name is Boris Karloff."

Gia's brow crinkled. "Who the hell is Boris Karloff?"

"You don't have any clue who you've been hanging out with, do you?" asked the nurse, clucking.

"You're slut-shaming me? Seriously?"

"You can be a slut with a clue," said the male EMS. "Ponzirelli? As in Ponzi? Like the original pyramid schemer? Your boyfriend took the name of a con man, a grifter."

Pyramid scheme? Sounded like a bikini-line styling option. "It's not my fault he passed out," Gia whined.

"Can you describe what happened right before he passed out?"

"He ate a hot chili pepper, and his face turned bright red. He started panting like crazy. Then he drank pickle juice and said he hated it."

"Could explain dehydration and a panic attack," said the nurse. "Why'd he drink it if he hates it so much?"

"He didn't know what it was. I gave it to him as a joke. Ha."

"What *else* can you tell us about him?" said the nurse.

"He's a good kisser?"

The three hospital workers shook their heads at her. Talk about judgey! She hadn't done anything wrong. Except giving Ponzi the hot pepper, which was pretty funny, and then the pickle juice, which was also funny, *at first*. But it'd gone horribly wrong. Gia thought but didn't say, *Waaa!*

The nurse brought her to admitting. Gia spent the next hour filling out forms. She left most of the boxes blank or put question marks in them. Ponzi's date of birth? Insurance info? Home address? She knew *nothing* about the kid after being with him almost every night for a week.

An exhausting hour later, Gia returned to the emergency room with a throbbing headache. She looked around for Ponzi, until another nurse informed her that John Doe regained consciousness and insisted on leaving the hospital.

"Who the fuck is John Doe?" cried Gia, at wit's dead end.

At almost dawn, she clicked in heels the two blocks back to Nero's Palace. She tried Ponzi's cell phone. No answer. She was bone tired, but wired with worry. Where *was* he? Was he okay? When she found him, she'd apologize for almost killing him. And then, she'd kill him for . . . possibly lying about his name and everything else, too.

When Gia got to the suite at Nero's, she called out, "Bells? Fredo?"

No one home at six in the morning? Where *were* they? Gia called their numbers. No answer. She'd never felt so confused and alone. Her friends were who knew where, probably blowing through the cash that *she'd* won for them with *her* gift.

It wasn't right. They should be here to talk her down. On no sleep, having witnessed a near-death experience, Gia's emotions were as wound up as spaghetti on a friggin' fork. If Bella and Fredo cared at all about her, they'd have called or texted. It'd been, like, all freakin' night since she'd heard from either of them. Feeling bleak, Gia had a self-pitying thought.

"They'll turn up when they need money," she said to the empty room.

As if on cue, the door opened. Bella raced inside, amped up on adrenaline. She was still wearing her running clothes from yesterday afternoon—or a sunrise run on the beach? Masochistic, either way.

"Gia! You're up. *Cool.* Listen, I need money," said Bella.

Gia shook her head. "I'm like a human ATM to you. I open my mouth, and cash spits out"

"It's not for me. It's for Will. You should see the dump he lives in. But he can't leave. He's stuck there. His soul is on the walls. He's been painting them for three years and—"

"And he hit you up for a loan? Like Bobby used to all the time?" asked Gia in a rare mean mood. "Yeah, freeloading is *so* sexy."

Bella narrowed her eyes. "What's your problem?"

"Forget it."

"You've got a stink face, Gia."

"I'm just a little tired of your being . . . what's that thing that feeds off something else, sucking the life out of it one drop at a time?"

"Vampire?"

"I mean the thing that lives in your intestines from bad sushi."

"Parasite?"

"Right! You're the parasite," said Gia, "and I'm the host."

Bella's eyes blazed with anger. "How many times have I helped you when you were flat broke?"

"We're not talking about the past. The past is over. I mean right this freakin' minute. Now. The future. And, truth be told, you used to slip me twenties. I've been giving you hundreds."

"I gave you whatever I had. A lot of times, more than I could afford."

"You always put a price on it, though. A little jab about how I should learn to take care of myself. A comment about how I should get my shit together. Like I'm not *trying*? I think you *like* watching me struggle, so you can feel superior," said Gia, shocked by the harsh words and true emotions. She hadn't even realized she felt this way until she'd expressed it.

The rant kept flowing. "Your starving artist? Anyone can see this kid is in trouble. He's barely getting by. But it's so typical of you to need to be needed. Just like with Bobby, and just like with your mom when she was sick."

Bella's neck turned red under the bronze, and veins popped. Gia braced for an explosion. But it didn't come. Bella swallowed the bomb.

"You got nothing? Really?" asked Gia. "Do what you always do. After all we've been through together, you still don't trust me to say what you're really feeling."

"I'm not sure how I feel. I definitely don't like getting screamed at first thing in the morning."

"No one tells me anything! Not even you. Liars, fakes, and users. Everywhere I look."

"What are you talking about?" asked Bella. "Something happened."

Seeing the expression on Bella's face, the worry and love, even after she'd just ripped her a new foxhole, Gia's anger dried up. She wasn't mad at Bella anyway. She was upset about Ponzi. "I got played, Bells. Ponzi isn't who he said he was. So much for my excellent judge of character." Gia told Bella the story. The stress and exhaustion caught up with her. When Bella sat her down on the couch and gave her a guidette hug, Gia let a gusty sob escape.

"Waaa!" she cried. "For real!"

"At least he's gone. He knows he's busted. He must be in the wind by now."

"I don't have anyone to cuddle with."

"That does suck. But it's a temporary problem."

"How can I trust anyone ever again?"

"I bet you'll feel different after a couple drinks."

Gia nodded. "You spent the night with Will?"

"He's a good person. You're a hundred percent wrong about him. He hasn't asked me for a freakin' penny. But you might be right about me. I do feel the urge to care for him, although he doesn't need me to. He's the definition of self-reliant. I want you to hang out with him, get to know him."

"Maybe he has a gorilla juicehead friend?" sniffled Gia.

Bella laughed. "I doubt that."

"I'm sorry about what I said before. I know you didn't stay home with Aunt Marissa to feel better about yourself. You did it because you've got a giant heart."

Bella shrugged. "At college this year, I took Psych 101, and we studied 'caregiver syndrome.' It actually sounds a lot like the way you described me. I never thought of myself that way. But, now, I can see it."

"Is there a syndrome for being so desperate for love that you get suckered by every jerkoff on the Jersey Shore? Honestly? It's the story of my friggin' life. Frankie and I toasted the New Year together as a couple, but he was already seeing Cara—*for months*. And he's just one example. Every boyfriend I've had has lied, cheated, used me, or accused me of using him, or lying to him."

"So you've got some trust issues."

Gia groaned and held her stomach.

"It's not that bad," said Bella.

"No, it's my food baby," groaned Gia. "It's crowning. I had a huge dinner last night."

Bella laughed. "Bathroom's that way."

"Help me." Gia held out her arms.

"Never, ever, *ever,* say I don't do enough for you," said Bella, pulling Gia to her feet.

Chapter Thirty-One

How to Grow a Pair in One Fell Sploosh

Fredo and Erin walked down a fluorescent-lit hallway of the hotel, below street level. In a cruise ship, the area would be called steerage, where the poor people and staff lived, belowdecks.

"Here I am," said Erin, when they got to her door. "Compared to your suite, it'll look like a broom closet. But it's home."

Did he dare go inside? That would mean he was accepting the unspoken agreement to have sex. As Gia instructed, he asked himself, *What would a gorilla do?* He pictured those hulks on Gorilla Beach in this position. They wouldn't hesitate. They'd go for it. But those dudes probably had a lot of experience.

Fredo was dying to get naked with Erin—with any girl, really. By Jersey Shore standards, he was the worst kind of freak: a twenty-five-year-old virgin. He'd had opportunities with hookers and women who tried to get on his dad's good side. Right when he was about to get it in, Fredo's mind would start reeling questions. *Does this girl have kids? Do I know any of the other five thousand dudes she's been with? Is she counting the seconds until I stop? Would this woman even talk to me if my name wasn't Lupo?* Instant boner crushers. He'd watch his hard-on deflate like a punctured inner tube. And, damn if the women didn't look relieved at the sight.

But Erin wasn't a whore. She didn't even know who his father was. She had no reason on earth to get with him, except that she wanted to. Like that was remotely possible.

What the hell was really going on?

The ginger hottie stepped through the threshold into her room. She spun around, her hair floating around her shoulders in soft, red puffs. "Are you coming in?"

Fredo stood in the hallway, not quite ready to cross that Rubicon. "Why are you doing this?"

"Doing what?"

"Showing me your room."

She smiled, slow and sexy. "Why do you think?"

"I wonder about your motives."

That triggered something in her eyes. She glanced up and down the hallway. Her voice low, she said, "Just come in. People can hear."

"I'm finding it hard to believe a beautiful girl like you really craves a piece of this," he said, gesturing to his bod. "So you must have an ulterior reason."

"There is only one reason I'd ask a man into my bedroom," she whispered. "I'm not . . . whatever it is you think I am."

He'd insulted her. Great. Now she'd slam the door and tell him to go screw himself. Her offer would be off the table. He'd be full of regret and self-loathing. Or, in other words, back to the regular programming.

Except Erin didn't slam the door. She took his shirt by the fist and said, "*No one* tells me what to do." Then she kissed him. It was jarring at first, like jumping into an unheated pool. But then the kiss turned molten. Erin snaked her arms around his back and pulled him into a Full Frontal, boob-crushing, superpowered Guido Hug.

Like being tasered, a jolt shot through him.

"Are you okay?" asked Erin, stepping back.

"Ignore that."

"Are you having a seizure?"

Something strange *was* happening to Fredo. A totally new feeling. He'd heard others speak of it fondly. They called it confidence.

Going with it, Fredo placed his hands on Erin's hips and guided her body into his, pressing himself against her softness, and letting himself respond without embarrassment or fear.

"Oh!" she said, feeling him on her belly. Instead of shying away, though, Erin sighed and wriggled against him.

Fredo leaned down and kissed her, openmouthed, with tongue. Her lips parted for him, and—sploosh!—Fredo registered a sudden heaviness, a new gravity, in his soul and in his briefs.

His balls grew three sizes that day. Fredo crossed the threshold into Erin's room, knowing he'd broken important barriers tonight. The door closed. For once, Fredo was on the right side of it.

Chapter Thirty-Two

Lucky in Lurve

Erin had been beaming all day. The roulette operators and chip counters made comments like "Someone got lucky last night" and "I'll have what she's having." Erin laughed along. She'd laugh at anything today.

It was just so wrong. And yet, Erin hadn't felt this happy in years. After Fredo rocked her world, she felt a pang of guilt for deceiving him initially. Her seduction had begun with bad intentions. During their second course at Buddakan, though, Erin stopped pretending to have a good time and started having one. The realization was so unsettling, she had to excuse herself to the bathroom. When she returned to their table, he said, "I'm having so much fun, I forgot to be nervous." Exactly what she'd been thinking.

They had other things in common, too. They both loved lolcats vids of kittens in baskets with little bow ties. They shared a childhood terror of Barney the dinosaur. Each was an only child with a workaholic father and an overbearing mother. Erin was also the target of vicious adolescent teasing. Fredo had been taunted for his Ichabod Crane body and passive nature. The cause of Erin's hazing? One word: ginger. In the afterglow last night, Fredo told her freckles were kisses from the sun and likened himself to Apollo. It was corny, but when he kissed the speckled bridge of her nose, she was touched by the sentiment.

All day, she'd tried to clear her conscience about spying on Fredo and his friends because . . . well, maybe her conscience would never be 100 percent clear. She'd have to tell Fredo the truth about why she'd agreed to go out with him in the first place. Tonight. After her shift, when they were alone again. He'd be angry, but she hoped he'd understand.

When Fredo and Gia arrived at the roulette area at ten o'clock as he promised, Erin was overcome with joy to see him again. The two grinned moronically at each other.

"Hello, Erin," said Fredo.

"Ready for another big night?" she asked suggestively and, she hoped, subtly.

"Whoa, what's with the swampy looks? *Did you two hook up?*" asked Gia, instantly elated.

"No!" said Erin, glancing at the other players and at Steve, the roulette operator, now giving her the fish-eye.

"None of your freakin' business, Gia," said Fredo, but he looked proud of himself.

"I knew it!" screamed Gia. "We need champagne over here!"

"We'll start with five hundred dollars," said Fredo, laying cash on the table.

Steve changed the cash for their lucky magenta chips. Gia closed her eyes and announced, "Red." While the ball spun, she did her ritual of making the sign of the cross, kissing her fingers, then blowing a kiss. The regulars who'd flocked each night to bet along with her did the same thing. A dozen people blowing kisses in sync really was a happy sight. For the first time, Erin let herself enjoy it.

The ball bounced and then settled.

"Ten. Black."

"Signal jammed, Gia?" asked Fredo.

"Just a glitch. Let's go again." She meditated on the color for a second, then said, "Black. This time I'm sure."

"You sure you're sure?"

"I'm friggin' positive."

That drew a few more gamblers to the table, passersby who overheard the girl in head-to-toe black vinyl and fingerless, faux-leopard-fur gloves stamping six-inch heels on the floor, screaming, "Black, black, black!" Twenty gamers joined in, crossing themselves, blowing kisses, and chanting along.

The ball came to rest. Steve said, "Twenty-one. Red."

A collective groan rose up from the table like a toxic fart. Steve and the chip collector raked in the chips.

Erin felt a chill, the cold snap of a losing streak. She'd seen this happen too many times. It was a palpable sensation, registered by sensitive gamblers and hard realists. A handful of players felt it, too, cashing in their chips, and moving to another table or out of the casino for the night.

Gia had never been wrong twice in a row in over a week. Fredo was a wise gambler. He'd recognize the streak was over and quit while he was ahead. Or, Erin feared, he'd go temporarily insane and start doubling his bets. It was a ridiculously predictable phenomenon. Gamblers who won big at first felt entitled to keep winning forever. No matter how big the losses, they believed they were one spin or one hand away from winning again. In the end, they usually lost everything they'd won, and more.

With a sinking heart, Erin watched Fredo double his next bet to $1,000. Gia did her best, but she made the wrong call. Again.

Fredo got frustrated. "What the fuck, Gia?"

"I'm trying!" she pouted. "I don't know what's wrong. I'm seeing a color in my head, but it's not coming up."

It was agony to watch. The table was poison to other gamblers now. No one else would come near it. Erin glanced at the eye in the sky. Surely, Mr. Violenti was watching and rubbing his sausage fingers together with despicable glee.

Another loss. "Mother*focker*," screamed Fredo. "We're down

seven thousand dollars. If we bet another seven, and you hit, we'll be back to zero." He went into his pocket and pulled out a wad of cash.

When gamblers played to break even, it was a bad sign.

"Fredo, don't," Erin whispered. Steve's and the chip counter's heads turned toward her. It was against casino policy to advise a gambler in any direction, to keep playing or to stop. Erin didn't care.

"I can't leave seven G's on the table," Fredo said.

Gia said, "It's okay, Erin. I got it this time. I can feel it from my pouf down to my peeptoe. It's black. If it's not black, I'll eat this chip."

"All of it, on black," said Fredo. He was determined. His jaw set and gnashing, he moved the chip pile into the black bar. The ball was put in motion.

It went around the wheel. Fredo fidgeted.

At the very last second, before Steve called, "No more bets," Fredo moved the pile into the red bar.

"What're you doing?" asked Gia, frantic.

"I've got a feeling, too. A feeling like your wires are crossed, and betting the opposite is the way to go."

"No! Move them back!"

"Too late," said Fredo.

The ball settled into a slot. "Six," said Steve. "Black."

"I frickin' *told* you!" blasted Gia.

"I can't believe it," said Fredo, dumbfounded. Glancing at Erin, he said, "You did this. You broke our streak."

"Me?"

"You can't be lucky in love and gambling at the same time," he said. "Everyone knows that."

He's mad at me? "I tried to stop you."

"It's not her fault, Fredo," said Gia. "It's *your* fault! You should apologize to me and Erin."

But he was already gone, storming off like a six-foot toddler. A metallic taste of guilt and regret landed on Erin's tongue. In a way, their loss tonight *was* her fault. She was part of the casino culture that systematically separated hardworking people from their savings and paychecks. She'd overseen the losses of millions of dollars. It was her job to make nightmares happen.

Gia reached into her Hello Kitty, sequined tote and gave $100 bills to Erin, Steve, and the chip counter. It was awful to see Gia upset.

"Are you okay?" asked Erin.

"Meh. I was more bummed about losing my psychic gift than the money. But I got the last bet right. So I still have my power."

Oh, you poor deluded girl, thought Erin. "Just the same, I'd call it a night."

"For what it's worth," said Gia, "I'd rather be lucky in love than gambling."

Bzzzzzzzz. Erin's phone vibrated in her suit pocket. "Hello?"

"Lobby, now," said Mr. Violenti.

She found her boss by the statue of Jupiter, inside the security gate, holding a bucket. It was feeding time again. He threw a hunk of gristle into the moat. The gators snapped, the water roiled. "So Lupo dropped a bundle. Good. But he's still way up for the week."

"The streak is over," said Erin. "He'll steam through the rest in the next few days." Secretly she hoped Fredo would have the good sense not to.

"But his girlfriend told him to stop betting," said Mr. Violenti.

"Gia's not his girlfriend . . ."

He was smirking at her. So he knew about last night. Of course he did. "You told me to get close to him. And now you're angry about it?"

"I find it interesting that he lost a fraction of his winnings the day after you two spend the night together. That's convenient."

Mr. Violenti flung more fat into the moat, and his raccoon toupee tilted an inch to the left.

Erin's stomach tightened. "What are you getting at?"

"That little fight when he stormed off? I bet it was rehearsed. Now he's got an excuse to leave town with all my money, and you come off looking like a loyal employee for following my instructions."

"You're wrong," she said, panic rising.

"The capper was that the little brunette didn't seem to care about dropping twenty thousand dollars. Why wouldn't she cry or stamp her tiny feet or beat on her tan boobies? *Because it was part of the act.* You've been in on this scam from the beginning."

"Not true."

"I can't trust you anymore. You're done in the pit."

"What about the Midnight manager job?"

He doubled over laughing, the sick son of a bitch. "You don't really believe I'd ever give that job to *a woman*? Do I look retarded to you?"

"Now that you mention it . . ." The askew toupee wasn't helping his case.

Then he threw the rest of the beef gristle into the moat. "Just look at those suckers snap! God, I love them. You're freakin' fired. Clear out by noon tomorrow."

Chapter Thirty-Three

Scumbags Are My Weakness

Bella begged off betting tonight. She and Will were having dinner at Flagrante Delicto, a schmancy Italian restaurant in the hotel. She shimmered in a silver-lamé, strapless sheath dress and strappy stilettos, and fantasized about walking into the place and watching Will's expression change when he saw her. She laughed to herself, feeling that a *woww* was waiting for her.

A hand cupped her elbow from behind. "How's it going, hot wenis?" a deep voice growled in her ear.

In a flash, Bella grabbed the asshat's hand and bent his wrist forward in a karate move she called the Pussy.

The guy dropped to his knees. "Jesus, Bella! Let go!"

"Tony!" Her ex. She released him. "What are you doing here?"

Rubbing his wrist, he stood up. "Drove down from Seaside an hour ago, on an errand for my grandfather."

Was he stalking her? "In my hotel?"

"As a matter of fact, yeah. But I wanted to find you, too. We've got some unfinished business."

As far as she was concerned, they were done, done, done. Nothing left unsaid. "How did you know where to find me?"

"From Gia. She's my errand for Giuseppe."

They barely knew each other. "What's going on there?"

Tony shrugged. "No clue. He won't talk about it."

Bella made a mental note to ask Gia later. Her phone vibrated. A text from Will that said I'M HERE. WHERE U?

She texted ON THE WAY. To Tony, she said, "I'm late to meet someone."

"Just give me a few minutes, Bells. I've been thinking about you nonstop since you left town."

"Oh, for Christ's sake. Get over it."

They were standing within ten feet of the restaurant entrance. The last thing she needed was for Will to come looking for her and find her in an intense discussion with Tony. Will was well aware that he wasn't her usual type, and seeing her with Tony, a classic guido gorilla, might make him insecure and jealous.

"Come on," she said, grabbing Tony by his bruised wrist— "Ouch! Careful!" he whined—and leading him to her favorite statue of Venus, in the lobby. "Get back there." She directed him behind it, so they'd be hidden from view. "You've got two minutes."

He grinned. "You look good, Bella. Have you been working out? I mean, more than usual?"

Rolling her eyes under her glittered lashes, she said, "I'm outta here."

"No, wait. I don't mean anything. That's my fallback opener. You know that."

Tony was the manager of a gym. He pretty much started every conversation on the subject of abs, lats, and pecs. "Waiting," she said.

"Gia told me about Marissa, and how Charlie took off while she was sick. I had to tell you how sorry I am. If I knew what you were going through at the time, I wouldn't have been such a dick— not that it's ever okay to be a dick. Why didn't you tell me?"

A fair question. She'd thought about that, too. Instead of relying on Tony when she could have used the emotional backup, she'd frozen him out. He sensed her backing off, and like any guido would, he reacted with anger. When Gia accused her of feeling superior and needing to be needed, something clicked in Bella's head. For all her caretaking abilities, she was incapable of letting others take care of her. "I should have told you and let you help. I just couldn't talk about it. I didn't want to turn Mom's illness into my problem. And confiding to anyone outside the family felt like airing dirty laundry. I wanted to circle the wagons."

"I understand," he said softly. "When my parents died, I didn't talk about it to anyone, except my grandparents, for a year. I'm not blaming you for anything. I just hope you know you've got a friend in me. I'm here for you, no matter what. How is Marissa? Is she okay?"

Tony looked genuinely concerned. Seeing the sympathy on his face made the heavy armor Bella had worn for months suddenly fall off her shoulders. She felt lighter and freer and wanted to talk. "Mom's fine. She's still recovering from her treatment. But the doctors say she's in remission. She needs to be tested every six months, but things look good."

"And your dad?"

Bella shook her head, her chin buckling. "Can't go there."

"How about you?"

She smiled at Tony, the kid she'd loved hard for a while there, and felt only gratitude for their relationship. No more anger. No hurt feelings. He'd asked her for friendship, and now she was ready to have one.

"Better now," she said. "I was angry at the world and put a lot of it on you. It's not fair. I really am sorry about cutting you out."

"*I'm* sorry."

"We can both be sorry," she said.

"We have so much in common."

The last ripple of anxiety about their past smoothed over. "Do you wanna hang out later? Gia and Fredo are around here somewhere. I'm having dinner with my new friend, but we can meet up after."

"Friend? With benefits? Already?"

"I've been in AC for over a week! And I haven't been sitting around picking my nose."

Tony laughed and pulled her into a Guido Hug. He kissed her bare shoulder and said, "Thanks for asking, but I gotta get back to Seaside. I think the water's safe for you and Gia to come back, too."

"Why?"

"Donna Lupo has put out the word that you can come back, as long as you bring Fredo with you."

So Donna missed her boy. Well, he'd grown up *a lot* since she'd last seen him. "I don't control him. And I'm not sure we want to come back. Maybe," said Bella. Doubtful. Why leave AC when she had a boyfriend, her BFFs, and a great place to stay right here?

"If you do come back, you know where to find me," he said.

"Doing curls and making kissy faces to yourself in the mirror at the gym?"

"Exactly."

Bella rushed into Flagrante Delicto. Will wasn't there. But he'd texted not two minutes ago . . . another one came in. DINNER'S OFF he wrote.

The hell? Bella hadn't spent an hour flat-ironing her weave, shaving her limbs, and gluing on glittered lashes to get blown off at the last second.

She called him. "What's your problem?"

"I lost my appetite," he said gruffly.

She could tell he was walking through the casino from the bongs and pings of the slot machines. She turned her stilettos in that direction. "Talk to me, or else."

"Or else what?" he asked casually. "Or else you'll go behind the statue of Venus and make out with some juicehead? Too late. You already did that."

Just as Bella feared, he did come looking for her. "That was my ex. He's here on business and we ran into each other." Even as she defended herself, she knew it sounded lame. If he told her he'd gone behind the statue with an ex, Bella would've kicked him to the curb.

"That brainless side of beef used to be your boyfriend? If you're interested in a guy like that, I'm not interested in you."

"Nothing happened. We were just clearing the air."

From the background sound, Bella could tell Will had exited the casino and was on the boardwalk. She took a shortcut through the elevator bank and was outside in the neon glow soon after.

"I don't own you, Bella. You can do whatever—"

Cutting him off, she said, "Tony is a friend. He wanted to ask how my mom was feeling, since she's just out of the woods with cancer."

She spotted Will leaning on the railing nearby, overlooking sand dunes and the ocean. He was pressing the phone to his cheek, his mouth opened, surprised. "You never told me."

Walking toward him, she said, "I'm telling you now. And there's more. My father was so freaked out, he left home. I woke up one morning, and he was gone. Packed his bags and disappeared in the middle of the night. He was a coward, and I'll never forgive him for it." The last part, she was close enough to say to Will's face. She leaned on the railing next to him. "You're not the only person who's been disappointed by the people you love. I know what it feels like, too. But I'm not your mother or your father. I ran into Tony and made peace with him after months of bad blood. Settling up with him makes me feel even better about being *with you*. I got dressed up tonight for *you*."

Will shook his head. "Seeing you with that guy only made me realize just how different we are. You looked good with that kid. You fit. You talk the same language. I don't speak guido. Now that you set things right with Tony, you can get back together."

"Tony and I broke up because I couldn't open up to him. So now I open up to you, and you're dumping me anyway?"

"It's a preemptive strike."

Bella hauled back and jabbed him in the solar plexus. One of her signature moves in the sparring ring.

The air punched out of him, Will collapsed to his knees, gasping for breath. Bella squatted to get on eye level with him. "Just so you know, that's how guidettes say, '*Fuck you.*'"

Stomping back into Nero's, Bella collided with Fredo, who was also in a snit. "Where are *you* going?"

"Out of here," said Fredo.

"Wait for me!" Gia bounced up behind them. Seeing Bella's expression, Gia asked, "And?"

"Will is a scumbag."

"Told you he wasn't your type. Then again, Bobby and Tony were jerkoffs, too. So maybe that is your type."

"Yeah, scumbags are my weakness," said Bella.

"Can we *go*?" pleaded Fredo.

"To Gorilla Beach," said Gia. "Tanner will hook us up."

Bella did a double take. "Something's changed about you, Fredo."

"I just lost twenty thousand dollars!"

He looked taller, brighter, and studlier. Testing her theory, Bella gave him a Guido Hug—and he didn't squirm. "You lost something else, didn't you?" she asked, laughing.

Gia said, "Yeah, he did! *With Erin.*"

"The ginger? She's hawt."

"We want juicy details."

Fredo shook his head. "A guido never tells."

Gia and Bella stopped in their tracks.

"Wow," said Bella.

"I know," agreed Gia. "The transformation is complete."

They got to the Gorilla Beach Bar and grabbed seats. As they settled, Bella noticed that three or four of the juiceheads gave Fredo the nod. Two came over to him for fist bumps.

"Yo, bro. Washapnen?" asked one, a massive creature of six feet and 250 pounds.

Fredo said, "Rebate, my man! This is Gia and Bella. Girls, meet Rebate."

The cousins shook his hand, which was like trying to grab hold of a basketball. He said, "Fredo, man, I thought you were okay before. But now. Dude. Shock and Awe right there."

Gia said, "I'm Shock!"

Bella pointed at her chest. "Awe."

Rebate laughed. "We're hanging at the end of the bar. Check in later."

Gia asked, "We? You and your girlfriend?"

"Me and my boys. Six of us."

"Do they all look like you?"

"Nah," said Rebate. "They're much bigger."

Bella gasped. Couldn't help it. To be bigger than him, his boys would have to be monster-truck size. Fredo promised to say hey in a few. Once Rebate had lumbered away, Bella said, "Explain."

"I've been coming to the beach a lot. Got to talking to some of the guys. No biggie."

"Wrong," said Gia. "Hugie. You can introduce us to hotties! Get Rebate back here!"

"I feel something strange," said Bella. "It's like I had a dork brother who I loved but was kind of sad. And now I have a hot bro who puts the OG in AC."

Fredo—not blushing, meanwhile—shook his head. "Stop."

"Seriously, it's pride," said Gia. "We're proud of our bro. He's all guido'ed up. Right before our eyes."

Bella nodded. "It goes by so fast. It seems like only yesterday . . ."

"It was only a few weeks ago," he said, laughing. "Okay, girls. Enough. I get it. I owe you both a lot."

"You can start by apologizing for yelling at me," said Gia. "*Tanner!* You are awesome. I love you, kid."

The sexy bartender brought over three margaritas for them. He leaned in to accept an over-the-bar Guido Hug. Bella noticed that Tanner closed his eyes when Gia kissed him on the cheek. *Hmm, interesting.* Tanner gave Fredo the nod and a fist bump. Jeez, everyone loved Fredo! He'd become the mayor of Gorilla Beach while the girls were off hooking up with asshats.

"Thanks, man," said Fredo. "Okay, Gia. I'm sorry I was a complete douche bag before. You had an off night, and so did I. I should have rolled with it like you did, and next time, I promise I will."

"Apology friggin' accepted," said Gia.

"Let me just float this out there," said Bella. "How do you guys feel about going back to Seaside? Like, if people there missed us and wanted us to go back?"

"Like who?" asked Gia. "Maria? I'd go back to say huzzah."

"I'm not going back until I hit my magic number," said Fredo. "I know we might lose it all trying to reach my goal. But I can't go back yet. I'm not there. We're close, though."

"What's the magic number?" asked Bella.

Fredo shook his head. "If I tell you, I jinx it."

"Okay, then," said Bella. "We stay."

Chapter Thirty-Four

Snatch

From under a purple hoodie, goofy sunglasses, and a bushy fake 'stache, Ponzi watched Gia, Bella, and the Italian stork Fredo leave Nero's Palace together and hit the boardwalk. From a safe distance, he followed. The girls were wearing club outfits, footwear not fit for the slats of the boardwalk. Among the throngs of dumpy, bland tourists in cargo shorts and T-shirts, they were exotic creatures of the night. Gia's vinyl dress was tight enough to be her own skin.

His pulse, and penis, surged at the sight of her. A hater hard-on? He hated himself for having it. Despite that she'd nearly killed him with a pepper and pickle juice, he still lusted for her. The last thing he saw before he blacked out? Her face, laughing at him. Yes, his pain was hilarious. His agony was comedy of the highest order. Panic attacks were serious and not to be laughed at! If he could, Ponzi would bury that bartender Tanner in the sand up to his neck, then force peppers down his guido throat.

Ponzi had other plans for Gia. He'd thought about how to exact his revenge on her for an entire night and day. He sent his soiled trousers to the hotel laundry service. The laundress called and asked, "Were you aware there is a large stain in the front of your pants?"

He practically bit his lip off to keep from screaming at her. "That's why I sent them to be cleaned."

"It'd be helpful to know what caused the stain, sir."

Groan. "I don't see why that matters."

"Determines which stain remover we use. If it's blood, we'd do a peroxide rinse. If it's a margarita, we'd use Clorox and a cold wash. Can you tell us exactly what the substance is? Considering the size of the stain, it would really help to know what we're dealing with."

"Urine," he whispered into the phone.

"What was that, sir?"

"Urine," he said slightly louder.

"One more time?"

"It's piss! Human piss! Okay?"

"That's what we thought, sir. Thank you." He could have sworn he heard her, and a few other people in the background, giggling. In the end, though, she did a good job on the pants.

Ponzi trailed Gia and her crew back to the scene of the crime, to the Gorilla Beach Bar. From his spot on the boardwalk, he gnashed his teeth and watched the three guidos talk to some steroid-abusing freak. That cumsucker Tanner brought them drinks. Gia leaned across the bar to kiss him hello, then they sat down. Convinced they were parked at the bar for a while, Ponzi walked quickly back to Nero's Palace.

Ducking under security cameras, he sneaked up to Gia's suite. Using the key card he'd pinched a week before, Ponzi went inside and closed the door behind him. There were no cameras inside a hotel room, by law. He relaxed, but only for a moment. The adrenaline rush of his break-in kept the situation in his pants acute. The faster he got out of the room—the hotel, Atlantic City, the United States—the better.

He made a beeline for the closet safe. Ponzi took a few deep breaths and examined the unit. Same as in every other room. The safe required a four-digit combination. He'd had three tries to open it. Three wrong attempts and the mechanism would shut down for twenty-four hours or else the guest would have to call hotel security to gain access.

He tried the combination that would open half the boxes in the hotel. "One, two, three, four, open the friggin' door," he said.

The digital display on the safe read FAIL.

He'd remembered Gia's birth date from her driver's license. "Six, six, nine, zero," he said, punching the numbers.

Another FAIL message.

"Shit!" he exploded.

Now what? He thought back to the night Gia had opened the safe in his presence. What had she babbled about? She won so much money, she had to spread it around to the maids. *Won and done,* she'd said while punching the safe combo.

Won and done.

Or was it . . . ONE and done? Ponzi thought.

His fingers trembled at the keypad. This was his last chance. Exhaling deeply, his concentration laser sharp, he pressed and said, "One, one, one, one."

The safe door swung open.

Chapter Thirty-Five

No Crocadillies Were Harmed During the Writing of This Book

Gia woke up but couldn't open her eyes. At some point during the night, her upper and lower sets of peacock lashes, glue, and mascara fused together. She'd need a crowbar to open her eyelids.

Stumbling, she felt her way into the bathroom and splashed her face with warm water. Bits of sticky gunk came off in her hands (not that she could see it yet). Eventually, she was able to soften the glue, peel off the false lashes, scrub away the makeup, and see the morning.

Or was it afternoon?

The last thing Gia remembered, she, Bella, Fredo, and Tanner were toasting with mile-long frozen margarita glasses. Tanner poured a shot of mescal into the red straw so their first sip would be a brain freeze of straight alcohol.

"To good luck, bad luck, and all the luck in between," said Tanner. *"Alla salute!"*

Oh, Gawd. Just the memory of drinking made her stomach lurch. Gia held her fingers to her lips—noticing with relief that all of her nails were still intact—and went for the toilet. She opened the lid and bent over it.

A wet, green creature coiled in the bowl opened its calzone-size jaw and snapped at her, missing her nose by half an inch.

Gia closed the lid.

Clearly, she was hallucinating from the mescal. It was true, what they said about eating the worm. She might be asleep still. If she wasn't drugged or dreaming, how could she explain a . . . whatever that was . . . in the toilet?

Backing up, Gia's legs bumped into the bathtub. Glancing behind her, she saw her favorite lime-green bedmate in the tub. "Crocadilly!"

Why wasn't she in bed where she belonged? Gia grabbed the stuffed animal and held her protectively. In her peripheral vision, she noticed movement in the tub. Something had been hiding underneath Crocadilly. Ecch, it was another of those green, bumpy creatures. It turned its football head toward her and opened its jaw to show razor-sharp teeth. Then it dashed across the tub in her direction, scrambling to scale the slippery sides.

She screamed, tore out of the bathroom, and slammed the door behind her. Clinging to Crocadilly, she said, "Waaa! I really gotta pee."

She went to the minibar in the living room, climbed over the tiny sink, and relieved herself. *Ahhhh.* Feeling much better, she reasoned that her pee probably contained a lot of the tequila toxins. Her brain would stop hallucinating monsters in the bathroom. Gia inched back and slowly opened the door.

The creature in the toilet had flipped up the lid with its snout and was looking right at her with yellow eyes. The thing in the tub made horrible scratching noises, its nails clacking against the sides.

Gently she closed the door.

And screamed again.

From the couch, Bella moaned, "Shut up, Gia! Jesus, my head."

"Bella! The bathroom's been invaded by Smurf alligators!"

"What happened last night? I didn't sleep in bed?"

"Me neither," said Gia. "I woke up on the floor."

"I don't remember coming back last night."

"But we did. And we're intact. All ten nail tips, check it out." Gia fanned her hands for inspection.

"Nice."

"But we've also got a serious infestation in the bathroom."

Bella cupped her crotch. "I have to pee."

"Use the bar sink."

"Good idea." Bella took care of business. "Is Fredo here?"

"Ooops," said Gia. "Forgot about him."

They fumbled into his bedroom. Fredo wasn't on the bed. Or the floor. But the girls' underwear was strewn all over the room, hanging from the light fixtures, scattered across the dresser and the TV, littered on the floor. A mound of it was on the bed.

Bella picked up a pair of her black lace drawers. "I don't remember making a laundry pile in here."

Gia picked up her zebra-print push-up bra. "Was I wearing this last night? And it's in Fredo's bed this morning?"

"Don't freak out. You're still wearing your clothes from last night."

Gia checked. Her bra was still strapped on. "Whew. So Fredo's not here. Maybe he got lucky again last night."

"Yeah. Maybe he hooked up with one of those sexy waitresses from Gorilla Beach."

The cousins burst out laughing.

"Hey! I'm sleeping here" came a voice from the bed.

The mountain of panties and thongs moved. Both girls screamed. Fredo emerged from underneath with leopard-print panties over his face. "Where am I?" he asked, panicky. "Why am I seeing spots?"

"You're in your bed," said Gia, snatching the drawers off him.

"Oooh, my head."

Bella asked, "Any idea why you're sleeping with our underwear?"

Fredo seemed as baffled as they were. "What happened last night?"

"We got hammered at Gorilla Beach," said Gia. "After that, no clue. But we did get back to our room. Better than waking up in a Dumpster."

"True." Fredo flung his legs off the side of the bed and stood up.

The girls reared back in horror. "Fredo! Cover your braciola!" screamed Gia.

On reflex, he grabbed the nearest thing in reach and held it against his privates.

Bella said, "Not my baby doll!"

He dropped the black silk garment and picked up a pillow. "I'm hitting the can," he said. "Then we'll try to figure out what happened last night."

Fredo walked past the girls and into the bathroom. Two seconds later, he exited. "Funny thing. I thought I saw a pair of pygmy gators on the bathroom floor."

"Told ya," said Gia to Bella.

"Wait, they're *really* in there? I had a crazy dream that we brought them here last night on a room service cart. After we, er, rescued them from the lobby moat by that statue of Jupiter," said Fredo.

"Rescued? You mean, we stole them?" asked Bella. "I don't remember that at all."

"Oh, shit! We are *fucked*," said Fredo. "Erin told me the gators are her sadistic boss's pets. He'll kill us if he finds out we have them."

Bella took a peek. "They're actually kind of cute. Except for the teeth, and the eyes. And the smell."

Gia said, "I've got a genius idea!"

"I doubt that," muttered Fredo.

"Bells, remember last summer, when I rescued that sand shark? We talked, but only with our brains. I was, like, the shark whisperer. Maybe I can do it again. The gator whisperer."

"And tell them what? To crawl back to the swamp they came out of?" asked Bella.

"No swamp. Moat," said Fredo.

"So we take them back to the moat," said Bella.

"We can't just waltz down there with a pair of stolen reptiles. The lobby is full of people."

"I'd lead them back into the ocean anyway," said Gia. "So they can be free."

"Gators are freshwater animals," said Fredo. "They'll die in salt water."

"Oh, *now* you're the expert," said Gia. "I'm the one who can communicate with animals. I'll ask them what *they* want."

Bella shrugged. "Worth a try."

"Are you friggin' kidding me?" asked Fredo. "Okay, whatever. Go have your telepathic chat with the gators. I'm packing my stuff and getting the hell out of here. Vito Violenti does not have a sense of humor."

Gia said, "You can start by folding our drawers neatly and putting them back where you found them."

Fredo let out a low moan. "I'm sorry. Honestly, I don't know how that happened."

"I'm going in," said Gia. She took a deep breath, exhaled, and opened the bathroom door.

The gators were free from the toilet and the tub and on the floor. With her mind, she said, *Friends! Friends!*

The gators scrambled at her with alarming speed, their jaws snapping.

Gia slammed the door. They heard two thuds on the other side as the gators hurled themselves against it.

"Okay, not friends," she conceded.

"Noooo!!!!" Fredo's voice came from the living room.

Bella and Gia found him, frozen, staring into the closet.

He was as white as Twinkie filling. "The money," he gasped. "It's gone."

"It's in the safe," said Gia, but then she, too, saw the open door, and the stacks of cash gone.

Fredo reached inside. "Wait, there is something in the back." He removed the item. "A jar of pickles?"

"Oh, shit," said Gia.

Fredo shook the jar in Gia's face. "What does this mean?" he demanded.

"You see pickles and you automatically think I had something to do with it?"

Bella said, "Well, yeah."

"You blame me, too?" asked Gia. "It was Ponzi. I sort of played a trick on him with a serrano pepper and pickle juice. I guess this is his way of getting me back."

"Stealing sixty thousand dollars?" yelled Fredo.

"I'll find him," said Gia.

"First things first," said Bella. "We have to do something about our bathroom infestation. We can't take them back to the moat, and we can't leave them here."

"Why not?" asked Gia.

"Even you don't tip the housekeeper enough to clean up two alligators," said Bella.

"If Violenti finds out we gatornapped his pets, he'll feed us to them," said Fredo.

"We have to move them to a safe place where there are no cameras, and warm freshwater," said Bella.

"I've got an idea," said Gia.

"Not again," said Fredo.

"I know the perfect place."

"Bullshit."

"Trust me. All we have to do is catch them and dump them. Catch and dump. Sounds like my last five boyfriends."

Chapter Thirty-Six

The Atlantic City Dump

Bella called room service and ordered two raw steaks. While they waited, the girls got dressed in monokinis, bathrobes, and flip-flops.

Fredo threw on jeans and a polo and paced the suite muttering, "Sixty grand. Gone. Hopes, dreams, self-esteem. Stolen. I'd puke, but I'm afraid to go in the friggin' bathroom."

"Use the minibar sink," said Gia.

The three roomies rearranged the furniture into a makeshift gator chute leading from the bathroom door to Gia's open zebra-print hardshell suitcase. When room service arrived, they dropped the steaks inside as bait.

"I'm sad for zebes," said Gia in mourning for her suitcase.

Bella said, "Think of it this way: Zebes must die so the gators can live. We know they're hungry, so they'll go right for the meat. I'm going to open the bathroom door. They move fast, so get ready. If they try to climb the furniture, nudge them back toward the suitcase."

"Nudge them with what?" asked Fredo.

"Your foot," said Bella.

"They'll bite it off!"

"Here we go, on three. One, two, *three!*"

Bella opened the door, and the gators were out in a flash.

Those little lizards could run! They scrambled right into Gia's suitcase.

"Close it!" yelled Bella.

Gia kicked the top closed and fell on the suitcase, latching it, capturing the gators inside. She jumped back onto the couch. Bella and Fredo plopped down on either side. The three of them stared at the suitcase as it rocked and thudded on the floor.

"I'm in shock that worked," said Bella.

"Almost too easy," said Gia. "Maybe they understood me when I said 'friends.'"

"Onward to phase two, and hurry up," said Fredo. "We have to find that prick Ponzi."

Gia and Bella nodded at each other. Pulling out the handle of the suitcase, Bella turned it upright and tilted it onto its wheels. They went out the door of the suite and toward the elevator.

The girls stepped inside and pressed the button for the eleventh floor. A pair of blue-hairs with visors and ortho sneakers were already in the elevator.

"Pardon me, dear," said one of the old ladies. "Your suitcase is shaking."

Gia said, "My vibrator must have accidentally turned on."

That pretty much killed the conversation. The girls got off and made a right to enter the spa at Nero's Palace.

"Can I help you?" asked the receptionist. A new girl. They didn't recognize her.

"We'd like to visit the sauna," said Bella.

"Planning on moving in?" she asked, pointing at the suitcase.

Gia said, "I couldn't decide which outfit to put on after my shower, so I brought a few with me. I hope that's okay. I don't want to cause any trouble."

Bella almost laughed out loud at that. If anyone, anywhere on the planet, caused trouble, it was Gia, whether she wanted to or not.

"I'll need your room keys to verify access to the spa," said the receptionist.

They knew this was coming. They couldn't give their key, though. It'd leave an electronic record that they'd been there. Gia said, "Oh, shit! I forgot my card! I hate to go all the way back to my suite to get it. Tell you what. I'll just call my uncle Vito to vouch for me."

"Uncle Vito?" The woman's eyes widened. "Vito Violenti?"

"Yeah, do you know him?" asked Gia, all sugar and smiles.

"No need to call him. Just be sure to tell your uncle what a nice time you had here today. The sauna is straight through the green-glass door and down the hall."

"We know the way," said Gia.

Fortunately, the place wasn't crowded. The busy hours were early morning and early evening. In the middle of the day, people were having lunch or at the beach. They weren't taking a nooner sauna.

"First left after the locker rooms," said Gia.

Bella wheeled the case along behind her. It was hard to manage. The beasts inside were pretty heavy, plus they were doing somersaults in there. If not for her karate muscles, Bella might not be able to handle it.

"This is it," said Gia.

Nero's Roman Baths included a Jacuzzi, a cold bath, and a near-scalding bath. When Bella and Gia had come earlier in the week, they'd tried the recommended cycle of dips, going from cold to hot, which caused an all-over tingly sensation. Sort of like when you ate too many corn dogs and went on a roller coaster, but sexy. Between the two still-water baths bubbled the gigantic Jacuzzi. Its temperature was what Bella imagined a Florida swamp to be. Maybe a little hotter.

"Think they'll boil?" asked Gia. "I really don't want to hurt them. They look like alien babies. Or giant pickles."

"They're not babies," said Bella. "They're fully grown pygmies. And they're not going to boil. We sat in the hot tub for an hour."

"But we got pruney."

"Gators don't prune," said Bella.

"Says you." Gia frowned. "I'm gonna kill Ponzi when we find him."

"Same. Let's deliver this package first. Check the sauna."

"No one here." The baths were empty, as were the adjacent sauna and steam rooms.

Bella turned the suitcase on its side. "On three."

"Why is it always three? On four," said Gia. "Just to be different."

"Yeah, we really need to change our routine since we dump kidnapped alligators into hot tubs all the freakin' time."

"One, two, three, *four*!"

The cousins unlatched and opened the suitcase top and tilted it so the gators slid into the Jacuzzi. Gia checked inside the case. Critter scat was smeared all over the shredded lining.

The stench was suffocating. "Close it!" gasped Gia.

Bella kicked the lid closed and locked it. More evidence to destroy. Then they sat down on zebes, spent. The gators weren't immediately visible under all those bubbles. But every so often, eyes or nostrils rose to the surface.

"Should we wait, warn people?"

"Let's go. We'll report an anonymous gator sighting on the way out."

Wheeling the empty case back down the hallway, they walked by a group of robed women, moms-on-a-bender suburban types, chatting with each other, carrying bottles of Orangina.

Gia whispered, "You don't think they're going to the hot tub, do you?"

"Hope not," said Bella. "We can't risk it, though. Come on."

Gia followed Bella, who made a U-turn right into the spa room. They had only a few seconds before the group came in.

"On four."

Gia didn't think they had time to count that high. She gave her movie-quality bloodcurdling scream. Bella joined in as loud as she could, screeching as if she'd seen a werewolf, or a zombie. The crowd of ladies came running in. Gia and Bella frantically pointed at the bubbling tub, babbling about sea monsters and dragons. The ladies peered into the Jacuzzi, shouting and pushing to get a look.

The receptionist came running in. Just at that moment, one of the gators swam to the surface and snapped in the ladies' direction. They all started howling.

Bella said to Gia, "Now we leave."

They hustled the hell out of there, suitcase trailing behind them. "I hope none of those ladies get bit on the foot," said Bella.

"Just think about it," said Gia. "No big toe, no flip-flops."

"That would suck."

Chapter Thirty-Seven

Just Got Out of Open-Heart Surgery

Fredo didn't really care if the gators lived or died. He just wanted his money back. He'd counted and caressed the stacks just last night, before they went to the casino. And now, nothing. That cash was going to buy the respect of his father and jump-start his next venture, which was sure to be a huge hit. He hadn't a clue what that venture would be. But he was due—way past due—for success. But the grifter stole his chance out from under him.

Under him. The phrase made Fredo think of a particularly breathtaking moment with Erin.

"I'm the biggest asshole in the world," he cried to the empty room. Cringing, he remembered flashes from last night, but only the parts he wished he could forget. He'd yelled at Erin after he and Gia lost at roulette. No excuse for that. He'd let his frustration take over. It'd serve him right if she never spoke to him again.

He found his phone among the pieces of lingerie on his bed—he had a vague memory of measuring his chest against the girls' bra sizes—and called her number, intending to beg forgiveness.

"Hello?" asked an unfamiliar female voice.

"I'm looking for Erin Gobraugh."

"I'm sorry. She left Nero's and had to turn in her company phone. Her calls have been forwarded to my line."

"Left?"

"That's a euphemism."

Erin got fired? The day just got worse and worse. "And who are you?"

"Customer service," the woman said. "Is there anything I can help you with today?"

"Yeah, tell me where I can find Erin."

"Even if I knew, I wouldn't be able to tell you that, sir."

He hung up.

Did his rude behavior have anything to do with her getting fired? God, he hoped not. Fredo checked his phone again, to see if he had a message or another number for her. Nothing. She was the first woman he'd been able to relax with, get naked with, and he lost her after one day. *Pathetic.*

A knock on the door.

"Ginger Snap?" asked Fredo, picturing Erin on the other side. She'd come back to him!

He flung the door open. A mushy-faced dude with a barrel chest in a shark suit and a dead raccoon on his head asked, "Mr. Fredo Lupo?"

"I guess."

"I'm Vito Violenti, the hotel and casino capo. May I come in?"

So this was the gator banger, the guy who made crooked gamers and dealers disappear. "I'm kinda busy right now," Fredo said, knees knocking.

"Just a few minutes of your time," said Mr. Violenti, pushing his way into the suite. "These are my associates."

His associates—twin no-neck goons—had been lurking in the hallway. The room got a lot smaller when they came in. The overgrown juiceheads had massive upper bodies and (probably) shriveled raisins for balls. Fredo got a black eye just looking at them. They stood behind Mr. Violenti with their bulging arms dangling—too big to cross.

Mr. Violenti found and picked up the TV remote. "I'd like to show you something."

"You're not my type," said Fredo.

"Funny guy? Good. What I'm gonna show you is frickin' hysterical." The casino boss turned on the TV and used a security code to access a blank channel. A picture came on-screen, a view of the Roman Baths. A gaggle of dumpy women were clustered by the hot tub, staring at the Jacuzzi and weeping. While Fredo watched, something floated to the surface of the water, jaw snapping. The women screamed and drew back. Five heavily armed guards burst into the room and hustled the women out. A maintenance crew with a cart of cleaning equipment filed in. Then, two uniformed men with metal poles and cages.

"They'll have to close the spa for the day to drain and scrub the hot tub," said Mr. Violenti. "The hotel will have to compensate those poor women for the emotional trauma. Animal control needs to be paid off. I'll get fines from the city for reckless endangerment. Plus veterinary bills to examine and treat the gators. Also repairs to fix the damage to the railing around the moat."

"Why are you telling me?" asked Fredo. "I've got nothing to do with it."

Mr. Violenti cackled, as did the goons. "You watch TV makeover shows? They show secret footage of some ugly cow who gets a new dress and fresh coat of war paint?"

"Yeah," said Fredo.

"Then you're a freakin' faggot," said Mr. Violenti. The goons laughed on cue. "I've got some secret footage of you. Check this out." He switched to a different channel. "This is from early this morning, at four forty-eight a.m."

The scene was the hotel lobby, nearly deserted except for a few guests and some staff. The statue of Jupiter loomed over the space, the "sky" glittering with stars. Fredo noticed three people stumble into the frame.

"That's you, Lupo," said Mr. Violenti. "And you've got two hot chicks with you. Congratulations. Usually, there's a security guard over here. He went to take a piss, unfortunately. He no longer works for Nero's. Usually, there's a blubbery nerd watching the lobby-camera feed to sound the alarm in an emergency, but he fell asleep at the switch. He's been shit-canned. The late-shift concierge who is supposed to be at the check-in desk sneaked away from her post to play a quick game of craps. She's been fired, too."

On-screen, Gia and Bella were on either side of Fredo, essentially holding him upright. They all seemed pretty wasted, but Fredo could barely keep his feet under him. The girls propped him up on the fence surrounding the statue and the moat. Fredo watched himself, for no apparent reason, climb the ten-foot fence and threaten to throw himself in. Gia and Bella grabbed at his pants legs. He kicked them off, which unbalanced his perch and sent him toppling off the fence and into the moat. The gators woke up and advanced lazily toward him. Fredo fumbled for a weapon in his pockets, found his vial of Ativan, and threw a handful of pills at them. The reptiles snapped them up like candy. He climbed the statue of Jupiter and held on to his chiseled hips, Fredo's face right up against Jupiter's crotch. The gators tried to bite his ankles, but he was just out of reach. The girls on the other side of the fence were jumping up and down, yelling at him to be careful.

After a few minutes, the gators got sluggish, then stopped moving. On-screen, Fredo climbed down to check the animals. Their limbs were limp. Their mouths hung open. They looked dead.

"I love this part," said Mr. Violenti.

Holding the seemingly dead gators to his chest, Fredo keened and rocked. He wept and looked "sky"-ward, pleading with the gods to forgive him for the accidental murder. The girls convinced him to move. From the inside, he somehow unlatched the gate's maintenance door and exited the moat, carrying the apparently deceased gators with him. From there, Fredo sort of remembered what happened next. They brought the animals to the room on the room service cart by the elevators. They put one in the tub. Had Fredo tried to flush one down the toilet? There was the urban myth about a woman sitting down to pinch a cannoli and a tiny gator swam up the sewer pipes and took a bite out of her ass.

"One more video," said Mr. Violenti.

The image was of Erin, by an elevator bank, talking on her phone and looking at the ceiling. This video had sound.

Mr. Violenti's voice said, "Figure out how Lupo's doing it. You get answers, I'll give you the Midnight manager job. Do what you have to."

Erin smiled and said, "Yes, sir. Thank you!"

The screen turned to snow.

Fredo's eyes burned. He struggled to stay in control. "Well, that was a lot to take in all at once."

"The betrayal of your girlfriend at the end," said Mr. Violenti, tsking. "She screwed you for a job. That's got to hurt. What exactly did you drug my pets with, by the way? The vet needs to know."

"Ativan."

"That's like Valium? You kids with your pills. You're all popping some shit. Friggin' addicted generation."

"I happened to have a medical condition that—"

Mr. Violenti interrupted Fredo by slapping him across the cheek. "Time to settle up, Lupo. You're running a big tab. The hotel charges, the incidentals related to the drugging, kidnapping, and recovery of my pets, destruction of property, comps and payoffs to injured parties. You owe me thirty thousand dollars. Payable"—he checked his watch—"now."

Fredo held his stinging cheek. "I'd like to report a robbery. A con man broke into the suite and stole sixty thousand dollars from our safe last night."

"You mean the known grifter your roommate invited into this suite numerous times? For all I know, she paid him for his services. Or she gave him the combination of your safe when she was drunk. Either way, it's not my problem."

"Mr. Violenti, sir, you might not be aware that my father, Luigi Lupo, is an important businessman in Seaside Heights."

"I had a nice conversation with Luigi twenty minutes ago. Your father is a great man. The tops. I got a lot of respect. He sends his regards."

Fredo blinked. "Did he send anything else?"

"Unfortunately, no. He said, and I quote, 'Fredo's a grown man. He's responsible for his own debts. Makes a father proud when his son is no longer a burden.' End quote."

If what Mr. Violenti said was true, Luigi had effectively pried Fredo's lips from the family teat. Dad was not going to help him, now or again. It'd been one thing to *want* to prove himself, to dream of returning home as a conquering hero, like Caesar or Augustus. Even if he'd feared the possibility of defeat, he'd never expected his family to abandon him if it actually happened. That wasn't the Lupo way. They stuck together. But, from what he'd just heard, Fredo had been cast out.

His money gone. Spurned by his family. His girlfriend turned out to be a *due facce,* aka a two-faced bitch. He could try calling his mom, but that would be the ultimate humiliation. Gia and Bella, his summer sisters, would try to help him. But he'd die if they got hurt. No, he made a silent prayer that they didn't march in here until Violenti left.

"I don't have the money," said Fredo. "I *did,* but that *brutto figlio di puttana bastardo* stole it."

"I appreciate the Italian," said Mr. Violenti. "Kids these days have no respect for the mother tongue. Even 'ugly bastard son of a whore' sounds like poetry in Italian. Makes me hungry for fettuccine puttanesca, actually."

"We can continue this conversation after lunch, if you'd prefer," said Fredo, trying to get rid of him before the girls got back. Turned out, he got his wish.

"We're done talking. Boys." Mr. Violenti signaled the goons, and they grabbed Fredo under the armpits. "Take him to the garage."

They dragged him into a private elevator to the casino's parking lot. He assumed they had a secret corner or private space where they did the wet work. Or maybe they planned to put him in the trunk of their car and drive him to the Pine Barrens to thrash him and leave his body for the turkey vultures. Best-case scenario? They'd pound him in the parking lot and leave him a splotch on the pavement.

I don't wanna be a splotch, he thought. *I don't wanna be pulverized and washed away with a hose.* Fredo asked himself, *What would a gorilla do?* He'd beat his pecs or growl. He wouldn't feel terrified, like Fredo. This might be . . . the end. In his head, Fredo said his good-byes. *Good-bye, Ma! You hovered like a UFO and taught me to be afraid of everything, but I love you. Good-bye, Pa! You tried to show me how to be a man, but I failed you. Good-bye, Gia and Bella, my only true friends. We should have had more time to party together.*

"This is it," said Goon One.

Fredo was confused. They stopped at Area 3, a well-populated parking level. Dozens of people were milling around. Not a beat-down? For some reason, that made Fredo even more nervous.

Then he noticed the vintage, white Caddie convertible with the red leather interior. His pride and joy. The one thing he valued most in the world.

Mr. Violenti stroked the tail fin of the car in a disgustingly pervy way. "She's sexy, right? Sweet stuff. Whack material. I've always wanted a vintage Caddie like this. I have a fantasy about me and this car, a broad in the front seat, her head in my lap, driving on Route 66 all the way to Vegas."

"Please," begged Fredo. "Anything but the car."

"The second I saw this baby, I fell in love. I had to have her. And I will have her."

"It's like you're asking me to give up my heart," said Fredo, his voice quaking. "The Caddie is a part of me. Whenever I get behind the wheel, my troubles dissolve. This car isn't just four wheels and an engine to me. It's my saving grace. My dignity. It's the one thing I've got that no one else does. I won't just hand it over. You want this car, you're gonna have to fight to the death for it." Fredo put up his dukes.

The twin goons and their boss snickered at him. "Can you believe this little fart is Luigi Lupo's son?" Mr. Violenti recovered and wiped a tear from his eyes. "Hey, kid, have you heard the one about the guy who came to Atlantic City in a fifty-thousand-dollar car and left in a three-hundred-thousand-dollar bus? That guy, Lupo, is you. We'll give you a minute to say good-bye."

"I'll never give you the keys and you'll never find them. I've got them hidden in a safe—"

"You mean these?" Fredo's rabbit-foot key chain dangled from Mr. Violenti's fingers. "In a sock in the dresser drawer? You call that *safe*?"

Fredo felt tears forming, but he would not cry. That'd be a degree of embarrassment he'd never recover from. He tried to grab the keys. Goon Two pushed him back and Fredo landed on his ass on the pavement.

"Consider us even," said Mr. Violenti, opening the Caddie door and slipping into the driver's seat. "Ahhh, like nailing a virgin. I wonder if Erin Gobraugh would agree."

"I hate you," said Fredo.

"In that case, you'll want to leave my hotel immediately. Boys, escort Lupo back to his suite and help him pack."

"What about that other matter, Mr. V?" asked Goon One.

"I'll be right there. Just a quick spin around the block first." Mr. Violenti put the key in the ignition. The Caddie purred to life. Fredo felt an irrational resentment that the car started for another man.

Fredo could hear the Caddie's motor roaring all the way back to the hotel, but maybe that was just his mind playing a cruel trick on him. He walked ahead of the muscle so they wouldn't see the anguish on his face.

His phone rang.

"Hello?" he asked, numb.

"It's Erin."

"Oh."

"You sound strange."

"Just got out of open-heart surgery," said Fredo. "Your boss took my car. Gia's boyfriend stole our money. And you screwed me for a job. I thought you really liked . . . whatever. I should have known you were faking. I *did* know, but I let myself believe."

"I do like you. I defended you! I told Mr. Violenti you were innocent, and he fired me."

"I guess you whored yourself for nothing."

She paused. Her voice catching, she said, "That's not fair."

"Do you always do what your boss tells you? Were you sleeping with him, too?"

Long pause. Then Erin hung up.

I guess it's true what they say, thought Fredo, utterly defeated. *Gingers have no souls.*

Chapter Thirty-Eight

America's Most Wanted Dickhead

"Fredo's not here," said Gia. "He has no money, and no other friends. Where did he go?"

"I'm sure he'll walk in the door any minute," said Bella. She found a few sheets of hotel stationery and a ballpoint pen. It wasn't a sketchpad and a Sharpie, but she would make do. "I'm going to draw a portrait of Ponzi and we'll ask around if anyone has seen him."

"Like a wanted poster. America's most wanted dickhead."

"Describe him."

"You know what he looks like."

"Not really. Whenever we were all together, you and Ponzi were making out. I never got a good look at his face, just the back of his head."

"All right. His shoulders were about this high." Gia held her wrists in the air, like she was tree-branchin' the Invisible Man. Then she made a circle with her arms. "His waist was this far around." She patted her tummy. "His braciola hit me here when I wore four-inch wedges. Okay! Let's see what you got."

"I got nothing! I need a description of his *face*. You must have a picture on your phone."

Gia checked, scrolling through her photo album. "Here's one. Meh, he turned his head at the last minute. Same thing with this one. The next is just a blur. He ducked out of the shot here. It's like he purposefully bombed each photo."

"He did, Gia. It doesn't matter. Just try to picture his face in your mind. Start with his hair."

"He had dark hair, slicked-back gorilla style. He was tan. I think he had brown eyes, but maybe dark hazel. He had a nose, a mouth, cheeks, and chin. Definitely a neck. Okay! Whaddaya got?"

Bella groaned. "I need details. You've got to give me something specific to work with. Use your gift."

Gia nodded and closed her eyes. "Calling my gift. Hello, gift! Come in, gift. Yeah! I'm seeing something. A fuzzy image, focusing . . . okay, I got it. Every inch is as clear as if it's right in front of me."

"Locked in?"

"Yeah. It's about seven inches long, tilting to the left. A big vein running along the right side, red and shiny on the tip . . ."

"You're joking, right?"

Gia pouted. "I can't to do it, Bells. I'm stuck. My gift is gone."

"How can you not remember the kid's *face*? You were with him every night for over a week."

"I don't know!" said Gia guiltily. "We were always making out—or drinking. Or on the couch with the lights out, or walking side by side. He wore aviators. Honestly? I can see a face, but it's fuzzy, like the camera in my head moved, too. His only really memorable feature was big white teeth."

"Handsome enough to suck you in, but bland and forgettable. The perfect face for a con man." Bella worked with the little information she had. She drew a basic oval-shaped face and put some aviators on top of a classic male nose. She used Will's technique of exaggerating the one distinctive feature—his wide, toothy smile. "How's this?"

"Wow! That's friggin' incredible. It really looks like him. Can you make the nose a little longer? And the cheeks a little sharper? . . . Yeah, that's perfect! You're amazing, Bella! You should get a job working for the cops as a sketch artist like on *Law & Order*."

Looking at the drawing brought back images in Bella's mind of Ponzi. She tweaked it further. The final version was as close to his face as she was going to get without him standing in front of her.

"I feel like an idiot for trusting him," said Gia, glaring at his likeness. "I'm a good judge of character. How did he fool me? Don't give me that look. I *am* a good judge of character. It's just that the range of what I consider 'good' is pretty wide."

"Ponzi is a professional. It's his job to fool people, and he's obviously talented at it. Don't beat yourself up."

"Do you hate me? About Ponzi and the money?"

"I never thought of it as mine. I feel bad for you and Fredo."

Gia shrugged. "A week and a half ago, we had nothing at all. Since we got here, we had a great time. We got rockin' nail tips and hair extensions, ate some incredible food. I had five men massaging my body at the same time. It was fun while it lasted."

"I don't think Fredo sees it that way, though. It's fucked up, but his pride is wrapped up with the money. We can't let him lose it."

"That makes me feel sick with guilt," said Gia. "We have to track down Ponzi and then murder him."

"I'll trace a copy of the portrait so we can split up and cover more ground. You work the casino and hotel lobby. I'll hit the boardwalk and beach. We'll meet back here in an hour."

Chapter Thirty-Nine

Going Down

Gia tore through the hotel and casino, showing the portrait to bellboys and concierges, security guards and blackjack dealers. No one had seen the handsome-yet-anonymous man with the shades and teeth.

A pair of gorilla juiceheads approached her. "Twins!" she squealed. They'd walked out of one of her favorite wonderland fantasies, and into her real life. "It's Guido D and Guido DM."

"Giovanna Spumanti?" asked one.

"Holla!"

"Please come with us."

Before she could say, "Lead the way, hotties," the twins encircled her upper arms with their hands, pulled her out of the lobby and into a private elevator, going down.

"What's going on?" she asked.

"Hotel security," said Guido D.

"You found Ponzi?"

But the twins didn't speak. Gia felt a pang of fear, but that was squashed when she looked in the mirrored doors of the elevator car. Despite the stress of the last twenty-four hours, Gia was pleased to see that she looked superfine, especially with a gorilla on each arm. Gorillas were the most flattering accessories a guidette could have. If she'd put on lashes and a pair of hoop earrings, she'd be savage.

The elevator doors opened into a dank basement, which was cool. Not *cool* as in "sick." But *cool* as in "cold." Gia didn't need a thermometer. She could tell the temperature by nipple. They registered a shivery fifty degrees.

"The basement? What's going on? Just tell me. I'm great at keeping secrets," she said. "Except if the secret violates the girl code. Then I'd be honor-bound to spill it."

Even in full flirt mode, Gia couldn't get the gorilla twins to break their silence. It was creepy—but exciting.

"This is like a gangsta movie. And I'm the sexy girlfriend, you know, the mole."

Guido D said, "The moll."

"We're going shopping?"

They came to a metal-plated door and pushed it open. Inside the room, she saw a chair, a naked lightbulb hanging from the ceiling by an electrical cord, and some mechanical equipment.

A man stood against the cold, black cement wall. He was fat and old, with pockmarked skin and a bizarre hat. "Welcome, Ms. Spumanti. Have a seat."

The gorillas escorted her to the metal folding chair. "Do I know you?" she asked, getting comfortable. "You look familiar. If we met last night, sorry, I don't remember much."

"We haven't met. My name is Vito Violenti. I'm the casino manager and president of the hotel. The capo."

"What? The crappo?"

The old dude smiled, and Gia leaned away in the chair. His teeth reminded her of the gators'. He smelled like a hot dog left on a picnic table after a summer rain. Maybe it was the roadkill wig.

"We call this the Boom Boom Room," he said. "Do you have any idea why?"

"You're a Black Eyed Peas fan?"

"This is where we take people we think might be stealing from

Nero's Palace. Sometimes, we have to use enhanced interrogation techniques to get them to confess. Do you understand? Have you ever heard of pouring liquid into someone's mouth while they're lying flat on a board?"

"You mean like upside-down margaritas? I'm kind of hung-over, but I'm down for it. Hair of the dog. Or whatever you're wearing." Gia tapped the top of her head.

The Guido Twins laughed, then quickly shut up when Mr. Violenti snarled at them. "I'd like to discuss your uncanny ability at the roulette table," he said.

"You mean my gift. I'm psychic."

"Really. Would you mind proving it?"

"Sure!" said Gia, sitting forward. "This'll be fun."

"I'm thinking of a number between one and ten . . ."

"That's too hard. Make it one and five."

Mr. Violenti paused. "Fine. I'm thinking of a number between one and . . ."

"Five."

"Right. So what is it?"

"I just said."

"Between one and five."

"*Duh*. Am I right?"

Mr. Violenti glared at her. "But what's the number?"

"Are you, like, hearing challenged? Maybe your wig is clogging your ears."

His lip twitched. "Let's try this again. I'm thinking of a number. A new number. What is it?"

"Between one and what?"

"Five."

"Don't tell me the number! I'm supposed to guess."

"Young lady," he asked, "are you fucking with me?"

"Ewww, gross. No offense, but I don't do chodes."

Mr. Violenti turned toward the twins. "Is this girl speaking English?"

"I speak guidette," said Gia. "I'm still waiting for you to think of a number."

"Okay."

"You're doing it?"

"Yes," he said.

"It's three. Am I right? Look at his face! He's in shock. I hit it, bitches," said Gia. "I got the sight."

"Actually, I was thinking the number four. You were wrong. You're not psychic. You're not gifted. And I want to know *now* how you won at roulette." Mr. Violenti nodded at the twins. Guido D stepped forward and picked up her hand. "Start talking, or we'll have to use some advanced interrogation techniques. The Japanese invented one I particularly like," Mr. Violenti said, eyes glowing dementedly.

"But I've got nothing to confess. I just used the power of my brain. It's a natural talent. I was born this way. Like Lady Gaga."

"Go ahead," he said, nodding at Guido D. "Pull off her fingernail."

The gorilla took Gia's index finger and started twisting her nail, which quickly snapped off.

"Hey!" she said. "That cost thirty bucks!"

"What the hell?" Guido D's jaw dropped, and he stared at the nail in his hand. He went to her middle finger and twisted that tip, which broke off easily. The gorilla seemed completely stunned. It was almost as if he expected her to be writhing in pain, as if he'd ripped off a real nail or something.

"Give those back," she said, angry now, swiping the tips out of his palm. "Look at this," she said, fanning her hand. "Now I have to go back to the salon. I hope you're gonna pay for this."

Mr. Violenti shook his head. "I've got to give it to you, Ms. Spumanti. You've got balls."

"You bet your old-man ass I do. Ziiing."

His mouth twitched again. He might want to see a doctor about that. "It's time for you to take your balls and go home," he said. "Boys. Get this garbage out of my hotel."

The twins lifted her by the upper arms again and dragged her out of the Boom Boom Room, up the elevator, into the lobby, and toward the nearest exit. Then they threw her out on the street. She landed on top of a pile of luggage. When Gia got back on her feet, she recognized the metallic-pink suitcase. It was Bella's. Gia's smaller zebes suitcase was there, too, along with a few full garbage bags and Fredo's black leather duffel.

Lucy the housekeeper came through the exit doors and carefully placed Gia's makeup case on top of the pile. "I'm so sorry, Gia. I was told by hotel security to pack up all your things and have them brought out here."

"You put my clothes *in trash bags*?" Gia asked, horrified.

"They took your big zebra suitcase. 'Evidence,' they said." Lucy looked as if she was about to cry. "I feel terrible, Gia. You've been so nice to me."

"It's not your fault." Gia, hated to see anyone upset. Searching her pockets, Gia came up with her last bill, a hundred. "Here, take this."

"No."

"It's okay. I want you to have it."

Lucy took the bill, hugged Gia quickly, apologized one more time, then ran back into the hotel.

That was it. Her last dollar. Gia sat down on Bella's suitcase. She'd been evicted for the second time in three weeks. No money, no place to stay. Her clothes in trash bags like she was a homeless person—which she kind of was.

"Lemme go!" came a hysterical voice behind her. She turned around to see four security guards carrying some poor kid by his limbs through the hotel doors.

"Oh my freakin' Gawd," said Gia. "Fredo?"

Struggling and flopping, Fredo yelled, "Put me down, you ass-holes!"

So they did. Dropped him like a moldy fish on the sidewalk. Gia rushed over and helped him to his feet. Fredo's face was red and wet, as if he were sweating or . . .

"Are you crying?" she asked.

"No!" he said.

"What do you call those drops of water shooting out of your eyes?"

Covering his face with his hands, he said, "Erin lied to me. And I lost my car! The one possession I truly loved. I lost it. It's gone, forever."

"Oh, no," said Gia, rubbing his back. "Did you check the parking lot?"

He pulled away from her. "It's not *missing*, Gia. That fat bastard Violenti took it to pay off our debt. Now I've got *nothing*. Absolutely nothing. And it's. All. Your. Fault!" He grabbed his duffel and stormed off.

"Where are you going?" she called after him.

"None of your freakin' business."

Gia was crushed. As dorky as Fredo was, she'd grown to care about the kid. She felt protective of him. She knew she wasn't responsible for their getting thrown out of hotel, losing all their money, and his car . . . okay, maybe she was a little bit to blame. Maybe a lot to blame. Sadness and desperation settled into her small bones, and she could only think of one thing to say:

"Waaa!"

Chapter Forty

The Ballad of Pretzel and Kookah

"Fredo just left?" asked Bella twenty minutes later when she found Gia by the hotel exit. "Did he say where he was going?"

"He wouldn't even look at me," said Gia.

"Maybe he took a bus back to Seaside."

"Holy shit. I just got the manicurist's joke about a guy coming to Atlantic City in a fifty-thousand-dollar car and leaving in a three-hundred-thousand-dollar bus. It's not funny because it's true."

Although they were cousins the same age, Bella thought of herself as Gia's big(ger) sister. She was knee-jerking into caregiver syndrome. But what else could she do in the situation? Someone had to figure out their next move. Should she call Will? If she apologized for the body blow, maybe he'd let them crash at his place for a day or two, or store their stuff.

Gia blinked up at her. Without two sets of lashes and makeup, her face was as smooth and innocent as a baby's. It reminded Bella of when they were kids. Gia and her parents would come to Brooklyn to visit, or Bella's family went down to Toms River where the Spumantis lived until their divorce. Bella used to get so excited about seeing her cousin Gia. She'd burst out of the car and sprint up the walk to Gia's house. They'd run at each other and collide on the front lawn, rolling around like puppies. Their parents—two happy couples back then—would watch their daughters, then go inside to catch up and cook a huge meal they'd eat all day with digestive rest periods between courses. Now both their parents' marriages had ended. The cousins were grown. Like it or not, prepared for it or not, they had to rely on themselves.

Reading her mind, Gia said, "Should we call Uncle Charlie?"

Bella's dad. "I haven't spoken to him since he left." He'd called her a million times. But Bella wasn't ready to forgive, if she ever would be. So what if he'd been a rock her whole life? When Bella and her mom needed him the most, he turned to dirt.

"Grab your bags. When I took a cab to Will's place, I remember passing a cheap hotel with a vacancy sign. We can park there until we come up with a plan."

"The plan before the plan?" said Gia. "Fine. Whatever. Is it far? These bags are heavy."

"Fifteen minutes, tops."

Two hours later . . .

"Where is this place?" whined Gia. "My feet are gonna fall off."

Bella was hopelessly lost. She'd think they were going in the right direction, then she'd lose her bearings. Every wrong turn had them circling deeper into the heart of the grime district.

Gia said, "Wasn't there an Atlantic City serial killer a few years ago? He attacked tourists who'd wandered off the main strip? Or am I just making that up?"

The slums of Atlantic City weren't as bad as, say, parts of Harlem or Bed-Stuy. But, *damn*, these mean streets gave Newark a run for its money (meaning, you'd best run, son, before someone took your money). They hoofed past a bombed-out building with shattered windows and heard something crash inside. A pack of wild dogs stormed out of the building, barking and snarling. Gia stepped over broken bottles in her platform heels, while Bella side-stepped gutter puke.

A garbage can fell over behind them, the clatter echoing in the alley they'd mistakenly walked down. Bella felt a presence behind her. Spinning around, she saw a moving pile of rags. A homeless man. He was crawling out of a makeshift cardboard-box shelter. He wore filthy pajamas, as if he'd rolled out of bed and kept rolling through a mile of filth. His face was so dirty, Bella couldn't guess his ethnicity. The matted black hair hadn't been washed since the Bush administration. Bush the elder.

"Stop right there," he said, his voice hoarse from disuse.

"Is he tan or gross?" whispered Gia.

Bella wasn't looking at his face. She had eyes only for the rusty kitchen knife in his right hand.

"Money, phones, cards, Pods. Throw 'em on the ground."

"We don't have money," said Gia. "*Duh!* That's why we're in funky town."

"Drop the bags," he growled. "Now!"

Bella did as she was told. Her parents had lectured her many times on how to handle a mugging. Just throw your stuff and run like hell. Only problem: Their backs were to an alley wall. The only way out was around or through the mugger, who, by the look and smell of him, was a drunk or an addict. No one could stand the stench if he weren't massively wasted. His habit made him unpredictable.

"Karate-chop him," whispered Gia.

If he weren't holding a knife, Bella would have already wheelhoused him to the ground. She'd sparred with and crushed dudes twice his size at the gym. But they weren't loco junkies with sharp weapons.

"Just do what he says," whispered Bella.

"But my clothes. What's he gonna do with a Lycra halter dress?" To the mugger, she said, "Honestly? You don't want my stuff. It won't fit you. It's tight on me, and I'm a Smurf."

He took another step toward them, his odor strong. "Just do it!" he yelled.

"Fine," said Gia, dropping her bag on the ground. "Jerkoff."

Bella's reflexes were primed to react. Instinctively she assumed a ready-position fighting stance. The mugger noticed and seemed to hesitate. But then he took another step toward them.

"It that your real hair or extensions?" he asked, waving the knife at their heads. "I can tell it's a weave. Human hair, or synthetic?"

"Were you a stylist in a former life?" asked Gia.

"Human hair or synthetic!"

Gia said, "It's human hair. Who do you think we are? A pair of cheap bitches? Hooker, please."

"I want it."

"Tough," said Gia. "You can have my clothes, but you're not taking my hair. You know what I paid for these extensions?"

"Yeah, I do," he said, grinning a rotten smile. "I can sell the hair for more than your trashy dresses."

In a flash, the mugger rushed toward them, knife out. It was the single most terrifying moment of Bella's life. She'd stared down raging bullheads in bars and fought off a date rapist in a hot tub. But this guy was desperate, fearless, with nothing to lose. The crazy look in his eye distracted Bella and she waited two seconds too long to react. Gia heaved a trash bag at the guy and ducked. Bella unfroze in time to crouch protectively over Gia.

The sound of barking echoed in the alleyway. "Get away!" shouted the mugger.

Bella peeked over Gia's head. Two stray dogs were attacking him. They tore at his pajama legs, ripping the already frayed fabric to ribbons. The mugger's scream meant the white blur of a dog had bit into flesh. He tried to kick away the small dogs, but they kept coming at him. One had springs for legs and jumped up, snout open, to bite the guy on his wrist. The knife clattered on the ground.

Seizing the moment, Bella squared off to do a classic spinning high kick, landing it on his jaw. The mugger collapsed in a heap, out cold.

As soon as the enemy was down, the dogs stopped barking and biting. They sniffed the mugger's motionless body, then turned their attention toward Gia and Bella.

Gia was jumping up and down, clapping. "That was incredible, Bella! You nailed him!" Gia knelt down, her arms open, and made kissy sounds to the dogs. "Our little heroes! Come 'ere." The dogs pranced over to her and accepted vigorous rubdowns.

Now that the fur had stopped flying and Bella's pulse was returning to normal, she could see how tiny the dogs were. If she had to guess their breeds, she'd say one was a Pomeranian, and the other a dachshund. Bella had heard tragic stories about people adopting purebred dogs, and then, when they couldn't handle the responsibility or training, they drove to parks or faraway neighborhoods and dumped their pets on the street. She wondered if that could have happened to these two.

"Are you sure you want to touch them?" asked Bella. "They're probably covered in bugs."

"These dogs just saved our lives. After a bath, they'll be little princesses. Er, let me double-check that . . . yes, two princesses. Look at this little wiener dog! And this fur ball! Adorable. They're ours now. We owe them, big-time."

"Are you sure?"

"I'm sure," said Gia. "Come on, danger babies. Get us out of here."

Just like that, the dogs showed them the way out of slime city. The cousins followed the dogs for a few blocks and came to a main road. A block farther along, they could see the ocean, which meant the boardwalk was nearby.

"You see?" said Gia. "The puppies know what's up."

"But we're right back where we started."

"Wrong. We went out sad and alone. And now we're mommies to Pretzel and Kookah."

"Only you could sugarcoat a mugging," said Bella.

"My shot glass is always half-full."

"We're still broke with nowhere to go."

"Meh. I say we're the two luckiest bitches in AC. The *four* luckiest bitches."

The dogs barked affirmatively.

Bella laughed. "Pretzel and Kookah?"

"The wiener is Pretzel. And the fluff ball is Kookah."

"Makes sense."

Music. Gia's cell was playing Kaskade. "Phone! Maybe it's Ponzi, calling to give our money back."

Bella snorted. "You're delusional."

Gia checked caller ID. "Maria?" she answered.

"I need you," cried the newlywed. She could barely speak. "You have to come back to Seaside, immediately."

"What's wrong?"

"Stanley moved out," sobbed Maria. "We're getting a divorce."

Chapter Forty-One

Up Shit Creek Without a Plunger

"It all went to hell, that's what happened!" ranted Maria, a soggy tissue in her shaking hands. The wedding portrait of her and Stanley hung on the wall behind her. It looked awesome. Gia felt kind of bad things didn't work out with Will, the artist, and Bella. But Gia put that out of her mind for now. Also, the travesty of Ponzi. And that she and Bella nearly got mugged a short while ago.

Gia had never seen Maria look this bad, not even blind drunk, sprayed with whipped cream, and falling down the stairs at Karma. Maria was so upset, she didn't complain about paying the cousins' $100 cab fare from AC. Her blond hair hadn't been flat-ironed in days, her permanent French manicure was cracking, and—the sign something was seriously wrong—Maria was pale. Well, her version of pale, which was like a normal person after a week in Bermuda. But if Maria was a shade lighter than latte, she might as well be naked.

"How long has Stanley been gone?" asked Bella.

"Since I called you."

"Two hours ago? Does he even know he's been kicked out?"

Maria said, "When the door crushed his nose, he got the friggin' message."

"Did he cheat?" asked Gia. Impossible. He had a face and body only Maria could love.

The five of them—Maria, Gia, Bella, Pretzel, and Kookah (the dogs had already had kitchen-sink baths)—sat on the couch in the living room. The bungalow had changed so much since Gia and Bella had lived there last summer. Maria and Stanley had renovated the original house from floor joists to roof, as well as annexed the house next door, doubling the number of bedrooms, bathrooms, and living space.

Maria said, "No other woman. It's even worse. He tried to turn *me* into another woman. He doesn't really want me. He wants a wifey to sit around the house, rolling fresh pasta, looking classy. Someone like Donna Lupo."

Bella said, "I thought you wanted to be a wifey."

"I did, at first. I looked at those women and thought they lived the good life. No jobs. No responsibilities. Spending all their time buffing and polishing themselves, wearing the right clothes, the right shoes, drinking the right wine. But that's not me. I've been wrong my whole life! Three times divorced. A high school dropout. Not saying I'm proud of those things, but that's who I am. The only thing I ever did right was run Tantastic. I was good at that. I was happy having my own business. Don't look at me like that, Gia. I know I was lonely. But you can't expect every part of your life to be perfect at the same time. You'll always have troubles. Before I got back together with Stanley, I had one major problem—no man. Now I've got no job, no true friends—present company excluded—and I'm bored out of my freakin' mind talking about clothes, recipes, and plastic surgery. Stanley expects me to cook dinner for him—every friggin' night! And if we eat out, forget pizza at Three Brothers or nachos grandes at Spicy. We have to go to the right restaurants with the entire Lupo crew. I'm sick of being right! I wanna be wrong again! If I have to wear fur in this heat again, I'm going to kill myself."

Gia stroked Pretzel's back, making her purr. "This hot dog

thinks she's a cat. Honestly, Maria? When I saw you at the Cowboy Club at your bachelorette party, I didn't recognize you. I was like, 'Who's that bimbo talking with Maria's voice?'"

"I thought, if a little change was good, then a lot of change was even better," said Maria, pressing her face into Kookah's soft fur. "But now I regret it all. The face, the hair, selling Tantastic, marrying Stanley. I'm not me anymore. I'll take the loneliness if I can just be myself again."

"You can go back," said Gia.

"How?" sobbed Maria. "I sold the salon and gave up my apartment. Stanley owns this house. I threw him out, but, legally, he can evict me anytime."

"You're married," said Bella. "Doesn't that make half the house yours?"

"He owned the buildings before we got married."

Maria really was up shit creek without a plunger. Gia's parents split of five years ago was still fresh in her mind. She remembered the war waged over candlesticks that no one really wanted. They had seventeen years' worth of possessions and life to divide and dismantle. Maria and Stanley had been married only three weeks.

"I've got the wedding money, but that's it," said Maria. "It's in a joint savings account."

"It's something," said Gia. "First thing we need to do is dye your hair back to lethal brunette. And your skin is scaring me. Second stop at Soleil for a myst. Then we shop for new clothes at the Toms River Mall."

"I might need a bigger size," Maria said. "I've gained ten pounds in the last month."

"I hate to have to give the reality check," started Bella.

"Then shut up," said Gia.

"New hair and clothes are superficial changes," said Bella. "Maria's real problem won't be fixed that easily."

"She can't function with flat blond hair! She needs her pouf to think. It'll double her brain capacity."

"Makes sense," said Bella. "Let's go."

For dinner later, the five bitches celebrated their successful shopping day at Spicy, a Mexican restaurant on the boardwalk in Seaside. Pretzel and Kookah had new outfits, too, matching silver jumpers and rhinestone-studded collars.

"When I grow up, I wanna be a cougar like you," said Gia to the restored Maria. "God *damn*, woman. You look as hawt as last summer, minus ten years. You've got a glow tonight, and I don't mean bronzer."

Maria stroked her freshly dyed hair, radiating joy. "I feel like myself again. Thank you both, so much. You're my real friends. Those plastic bitches don't care about me. Only you two really understand." So much for joy. She started blubbering, mascara running.

"Jeez, Maria, get a grip," said Bella.

"Are you hormonal?" asked Gia. "You haven't had a cocktail yet or I'd say you were in weepy-drunk mode."

"I need a shot," said Maria, rallying. "Waitress! Tequila emergency!"

The waitress came over to their table. "Round of margaritas. Rocks. Salt," said Maria. "A nachos grandes con carne with a side of beans and rice. A couple chicken tacos, hard tortilla, and some chimichangas, too." Turning to the girls, Maria said, "What are you guys having?"

"Hungry?" asked Bella, smiling.

Gia turned toward the waitress and said, "We need a bowl of water for the dogs. A chicken burrito and . . . Whoa. Erin!"

Hearing her name, the waitress looked up from her order pad for the first time. "Gia?" asked the former pit boss. "Bella?"

"Whatthefuckareyoudoinghere?"

"I got fired," said Erin, apparently surprised to see them, too. "This was the only job I could find for sixty miles."

"All roads lead to Seaside," said Maria.

"At least the Parkway and the Turnpike," agreed Bella.

"You got fired?" asked Gia.

"Didn't Fredo tell you?"

"He's not talking to us since we got thrown out of Nero's, too. That place isn't good enough for the likes of us," Gia said, and burped defiantly. She introduced Erin and Maria. "Where are you staying?"

"In this boxy condo on Hancock Ave. It's all cinder block and depressing as hell. I feel like I'm in prison."

Gia and Bella groaned. "We know the place," said Bella. "Frickin' Stanley."

"You know Stanley Crumbi? He's my landlord. Nice guy, although, he seems kind of manic."

Maria let out a sob.

Erin said, "Um, I'll put in your order."

After their feast, Erin gave them the check and said, "My shift is over. It's great seeing you guys again. Pleasure to meet you, Maria."

"Sit down with us," said Gia. Reluctantly, Erin pulled up a chair. "Maria is going to start looking for work soon, too."

"I was just telling Gia and Bella about my fantasy job," said Maria. "I'd love to be the hostess at a nightclub like Karma. Just circulating and talking to people, dancing and drinking all night."

Erin nodded. "My fantasy job is at a club, too, but more behind the scenes, managing the business, booking DJs and bands. I worked three different jobs at Nero's and learned a lot on every level. I was actually up for the job of managing the on-site club, but I got canned instead. The final stab in the back was when my boss said he'd never trust a woman to manage Midnight. He dangled the carrot, but hit me with the stick."

"Bastardo!" spit Maria.

"Yeah, major disappointment. But that's how the tortilla chip crumbles."

Gia said, "I hate men who think they're better than us just because they grow hair on their asses. It's not fair. I bet if you and Maria teamed up, your club would kill Midnight, or Karma."

The six bitches left Spicy together, bemoaning their bad situations, and moaning from refried-bean gas.

Bella said, "If only we had start-up capital and a location."

Maria said, "I do have that wedding money."

"How much?"

"Gia! That's rude."

"Twelve grand," said Maria. "Not enough to build a club from the ground up."

"We don't have to. Come on." Gia tugged the rhinestone leashes. The dogs heeled and kept apace while Gia clacked down the boardwalk.

"The bungalow's the other way. Where are you going?" asked Bella.

"I've got an idea."

Chapter Forty-Two

Hindsight's a Bitch, Bitch

"'Here lies Fredo Lupo, a bitter disappointment to his long-suffering parents.'

"'Here lies Fredo Lupo, nonvirgin. He got it in once in his whole freakin' life, and then he threw it away.'

"'Here lies Fredo Lupo, skinny mama's boy who died alone. No girl. No friends. No car. No respect. No purpose in life.'

"'Here lies Fredo . . . ' Eh, that's enough," said the man to himself, sitting up from his prostrate position on the rubber floor mat behind the bar at the shuttered Cowboy Club in Seaside Heights. It was ten o'clock on a Thursday night. He could hear the pounding house music and the sound of partying from Bamboo next door. Every beat and peal of laughter reminded him sadly of his own failure.

Fredo had been hiding out in his empty, dark club since he arrived back in Seaside. The bus ride was an agonizing journey into humiliation, regret, heartbreak, and nausea. If he could have vomited his soul into a plastic bag, he would have been grateful for the relief. How could he have yelled at Gia and Bella like that? He didn't deserve them. They were better off without him.

Self-pity had no friends. It had no family. Fredo had never felt less connected to himself or his roots. Mostly, he was ashamed of the way he'd behaved. What he'd said to Erin was unforgivable. He'd hit her with unfair low blows. Regardless of what that bastard Violenti said, Fredo believed Erin let him into her bedroom with honest intentions. Maybe she was spying, at first. But, at some point, she switched allegiances. Otherwise, why would Violenti fire her? No way could Erin fake what happened in bed between them, and afterward, when they cuddled for hours. In the parking lot, he'd been bullied and manipulated. In the grip of terror and self-doubt, he'd believed Violenti's lies.

Like Karma, hindsight was a bitch. The three emotions he hated most—regret, shame, and guilt—raged in his heart. He was sick to death of feeling powerless and afraid.

Something had to change. "*I* have to change," he said out loud. "I'm not who I want to be."

He got off the floor and poured himself a stiff shot of amaretto. He'd been through half a bottle of it. He'd gone to AC to get cash to reinvest in the club. When it'd opened on Memorial Day a few months ago, his dad gave him until August 1 to make it work. It was now the third week in July. He had one week left to create a miracle. Too ashamed to go to his parents' house, Fredo would hide here. Come August, he'd have to face reality. For now, he'd drain the bar inventory by himself.

"Carpe diem," he said, and shot the amaretto. "Or should I say, *crappy diem?*"

Putting the empty glass on the bar, he though he heard rhythmic knocking, as if the pounding beat from Bamboo were beating down the door of the Cowboy Club.

It persisted. To ease his mind, he went to the front door and opened it.

"There you are," said Gia. "Way to ditch us at Nero's, you douche bag. Bella and I almost got mugged and raped and killed. Step out of the way. We're here to look the place over."

The petite guidette bulldozed by him with two tiny dogs on rhinestone leashes. "Kookah and Pretzel, don't mess on the floor."

To Fredo, she explained, "When they get excited, they pee and poo."

"Who doesn't?" he muttered.

Bella came in behind Gia. "'Sup, Fredo? I'm not mad at you, even though you left us to rot in AC. But, *damn*, bro, you might want to look in a mirror. And brush your teeth."

Following Bella, in walked . . . Maria Crumbi? As a brunette in slutwear with five-inch bondage heels? She looked like she'd been hit by Hurricane Gia.

"I'm back, Fredo," she said. "Didn't think I'd set a stiletto in here again after my bachelorette party train wreck. But just goes to show: you never freakin' know."

"True," he said, amazed to see the three women—and two dogs? Where the hell did they come from?—in his club. Then he felt a chill, as if he'd been poked on the taint with a Popsicle.

Spinning around, Fredo couldn't believe his eyes. He rubbed them with his fists and made a *wiki-wiki* sound. In the club doorway stood Erin Gobraugh, a soft halo of pink around her red head from the neon lights next door.

"This is business, not personal," she said, frosting him with her glare. "If you lay a pinkie on me, I'll rip your nads off."

"Fair enough," he said, and stepped back so she could come inside. His heart overflowed with amaretto sweetness at the sight of her. "How is this happening? How did you find me? Not that you were looking. What's going on?"

Gia said, "Don't think, Fredo. Life is better when you don't think."

"I'm sorry for everything," Fredo said to Erin. "I was a huge dick."

She ignored his apology, but he felt a subtle change in the air temperature around her. She'd warmed two or three degrees. If he kept it up, maybe she'd let him pinkie her after all.

Gia said, "So, bitches, whaddaya think?"

"It's small," said Erin. "Half the size of the clubs next door."

Bella said, "No matter what we do to the place, we can't compete with Karma and Bamboo. They own the weekends, Thursday to Sunday. And the Inca owns Monday nights."

Gia said, "So we open on Tuesdays and Wednesdays. The hump days. We can call it the Hump Club."

Erin crinkled her adorable Irish nose. "Sounds like a stripper bar."

Fredo had to interrupt. "You want to relaunch my club?"

"Shhh. The women are talking," said Gia. "Go make yourself useful and mix drinks. Do you know how to make a Scooby Snack, like at Beachcomber?"

"Malibu rum, Midori, and milk, right?"

"Less talk, more pouring," said Bella.

Fredo got to work and listened.

Maria twirled on the empty dance floor. "We can do a lot with a little. Remember the great lighting at my wedding?" She stopped spinning. "The wedding. It seemed like yesterday. We were happy then. . . ."

"As a couple, maybe. But you weren't happy with yourself," said Bella. "You were faking."

"That's right," said Maria. "Keep reminding me."

"Drinks ready. Even if you give the place a makeover," said Fredo, "my lease ends on August first. My father wants to turn it over to a warehousing company for twice the price. And there's no staff. To reopen, we need bartenders, waitresses, custodians, security."

They considered his points while shooting Scooby Snacks. The situation was dismal, but Fredo felt nothing but joy. It was a tremendous lift to be surrounded by hotties (and doggies). *Women are a miracle,* he thought. Just being near them was like flipping the hope switch.

"I know some people," said Gia.

Bella nodded. "Me, too."

Fredo said, "You can't pay them with kisses. We need seed money."

Maria said, "I've got it. And we'll have more after we sell the mechanical bull."

"No way! We're keeping it. We'll hire a go-go dancer to grind it all night long," said Gia.

"Who's going to be in charge?" asked Fredo.

Bella said, "Equal partners. Just like in AC."

"Because that worked out so well."

Gia said, "Just go with it, Fredo. We were a winning team for a while there. We can do it again."

Erin piped in, "We need a name. And not the Hump Club."

"The Horny?" suggested Bella.

"Rudey Tuesdays?" said Maria.

"Smush." That was Gia. "Shoregasm!"

"Clever, but too sexy? We don't want the obscenity police breathing down our necks," said Bella.

"It's true," agreed Fredo. "You can be sexy, but not that sexy. Wait! I've got it. We'll name it after all of you."

"The Squirrel Monkeys?" asked Gia.

Fredo said, "Venus."

Maria said, "What? Penis?"

"Venus! Sexy and classy. I love it. Yay!" said Gia, jumping, clapping.

The dogs sensed her excitement and started running around in circles and barking so hard their front legs lifted off the ground. The fluffy one seemed to have a little seizure. And then . . .

"Oops," said Gia. "I'll clean that up."

Maria said, "That settles it. We hereby christen the club—with dog urine—*Venus*."

Chapter Forty-Three

Depunk'd

Bella watched from the open door of Venus as Will Lugano parked his Ducati on the curb outside. He double-checked the address and seemed confused. He would be. The sign outside still read COWBOY CLUB. Will got off his bike and came forward. Bella shuffled back into the dark doorway. She wasn't ready to talk to him yet.

She was happy to see him, though. Will looked okay. The cloud over his head was a little darker than usual. Hugging the wall, Bella stayed hidden. Will entered the club and walked right by her. She followed him as he made his way inside.

Earlier that day, Bella had Erin call Will, and even wrote her a speech to say. Erin delivered it perfectly while Bella listened in. "Hello, Will Lugano? My name is Erin Gobraugh. My partners and I are renovating a club in Seaside Heights, and we'd like to hire you to paint murals on the walls. It's a rush job. You'll have to come to Seaside immediately, and you'll have only three days to do the work. We open on Tuesday, four days away. The theme is Venus. Sex, love, life, beauty. We're thinking lots of nudes, maybe some tasteful orgy scenes. But nothing too graphic. No actual smushing. And friendly animals, too."

Will asked, "Are the animals participating in the orgy?"

Bella had to hold her lips not to laugh.

Erin mouthed, "Is he serious?"

Will's deadpan tone didn't always signal a joke. Bella shook her head.

Erin said, "No animals in the orgy scenes. Just scattered around looking cute. Maybe watching?"

Bella nearly laughed out loud again at the idea of peeping cats and horses. Will asked, "How did you get my name and number?"

Erin said, "Google. I found your website. You are cheapest portraitartistinatlanticandoceancounties.com, right? And you did a wedding portrait of Maria and Stanley Crumbi."

"Ah, the Seaside connection." Then Will wavered. Bella suspected he was connecting the dots and didn't want to risk returning to Seaside in case he'd find her there. Bella gave Erin the signal to mention money.

"Let me tell you the fee." Erin quoted a number. A life-changing number. Bella knew he had his principles. But he couldn't turn this down.

"I'll see you in an hour," he said, and hung up.

Bella had been waiting for him to pull up since then. She'd been thinking nonstop about what had happened between them. A lot had been said. But a lot hadn't been said. He'd cut off their relationship out of fear of being hurt. Considering his family history, Bella understood that, for Will, being in love and being hurt were the same thing. She'd reacted the only way she knew how—lashing out in anger. But with a few days between Will's preemptive strike and now, Bella could see the underlying reasons for his actions. If he didn't love her, he wouldn't have dumped her. It sounded crazy, but it made sense. In the last few days, Bella couldn't deny her longing to see him, to touch him, to help him break out of his fears and create a new life for himself with her in it. His face wouldn't get out of her head. Simply, she missed him. She wasn't done with him. Besides that, Will really was the best man for the job.

She kept ten paces behind him as he walked deeper into the club, his motorcyle helmet under his arm. He slowed, reacting to the burst of light in the main room and taking in the buzzing hive of activity.

"Tanner?" asked Will. He'd spotted the familiar face behind the bar.

"Bro," said Tanner, busy stocking and cleaning up the space. "Welcome to Venus. You know Jim, right?"

Will nodded at Jim, also behind the bar at Venus. Bella hadn't realized they all knew each other, but it made sense. AC, for locals, was probably just as small as Seaside. Tanner caught Bella's eye and glanced at her funny. She waved him off, letting him know she didn't want Tanner to acknowledge her or call attention to her. She wanted to watch Will take it all in, without his seeing her yet. He might leave if he knew she'd hired him. Maybe if he saw all the familiar faces first, he'd be more likely to stay.

Bella watched as Will noticed the DJ on the stage platform, setting up her gear. "Koko?"

She waved at him. "Hey, Will! Haven't seen you since my last reading at Madame Olga's."

"I thought you were at Providence."

That was where Gia and Bella had met DJ Koko, that amazing night when Bella and Will kissed for the first time. Gia and Koko had bonded, doing shots during her break. She was one of Gia's first calls. Another was to their Nero's housekeeper Lucy Garcia, who was, at the moment, polishing the dance floor.

Of freakin' course, Will knew her, too. Bella watched them hug. Lucy later told Bella that Will had done a portrait of her three daughters last year and refused to let her pay for it. In exchange, she cleaned Madame Olga's booth once a week.

Apparently, Will also knew Maggie, a former waitress at Morton's. Bella had seen her jogging on the boardwalk every day, and they had, a few times, run together. Maggie confided to Bella that she was bored at work and wanted to try something different. Maggie agreed to come to Venus, at least temporarily. She waved at Will from where she was cleaning the back booths.

Bella watched Will come to a complete stop in the middle of the room when a big man, built like a manatee, in a black T-shirt with the words VENUS SECURITY printed on it, came toward him. But then Will said, "Juan!" They fist-bumped a greeting. "So weird to see you without a rickshaw on the boardwalk, man. What's the deal here? It's like AC tipped over and spilled into this club."

A great visual. Of course, Will saw things that way.

Juan, who hardly ever talked, said, "It's not Seaside. It's the twilight zone."

"I'm looking for Erin Gobraugh," said Will.

Juan caught Bella's eye, too, but she shook her head and mouthed, *No*. He shrugged and pointed Will toward the offices in back.

"Thanks," said Will.

But Erin was already walking toward him. Bella could see from his body language that he recognized her, too. He had to be putting the pieces together by now. If he was, though, he didn't say anything to Erin.

Barely glancing at Bella behind him, Erin said to Will, "Mr. Lugano?" He nodded. "Thanks for coming on such short notice. Come this way to the office to meet the other partners."

He followed her, and Bella followed them. Erin installed Will in the office, alone. The redhead closed the door and came over to Bella.

"He's all yours," said Erin.

"Not necessarily."

Bella's moment of truth was upon her; she felt the nerves kick in. What would she say to him? Would he feel cornered? Taking a deep breath, Bella turned the office doorknob and went in.

He was leaning against the wall. When she came in, he dropped the bike helmet. She walked behind the desk.

"Have a seat," she said.

He sank into the chair opposite. "Bella," he said the name like a prayer. "You're a partner in a club? How'd that happen?"

"One of life's curveballs."

"Are all these people out there from AC?"

"Gia makes fast friends. It's either her personality or her big tips."

He nodded. "Are they getting big bucks, too? They must be, or why leave regular gigs in AC on such short notice otherwise. Good for them. Good on you and your partners for paying people what they deserve."

Bella smiled, but her heart was pounding. Just being near him made her pulse race. Was he reacting the same way? She couldn't tell. "Let's talk about supplies," she said. "There's a hardware store on Route 37. You can take Erin's car to get paint, canvases, whatever you need. Fredo can help carry stuff, but if you need—"

"I don't deserve this."

"You're a great artist. You should have jobs like this every week."

"I don't mean the job. I mean, your letting me back into your life. That night, I saw you in another man's arms, and my heart exploded like a hand grenade. I overreacted and then I acted like a punk."

"You think Picasso ever overreacted?"

"He was a jealous maniac," said Will.

"Artists are passionate."

"You can't let me off for shitty behavior that easy."

"Who said I was letting you off?"

He bit his lip. "I'd never presume . . ."

"What's with the hair?" she asked, daring to make direct eye contact and to see up close how he'd changed. "No spikes? No eyeliner?" His naked face was sweet, vulnerable—but strong, too. It was a sign of strength, Bella realized, for him to show himself to the world. Will was done hiding behind the punk mask.

He paused. "I'm trying something new."

"I like it. It's you. The real you."

"Of course you understand. I knew you would. I wanted to show you the real me from the beginning, but I was afraid. I've been running scared for a long time, Bella. And then I met you. Right from that first moment at the wedding, I've felt an intense desire to live another way, to think another way. I want to be more trusting and optimistic like you. Our breakup pushed me over to the other side. The world isn't shutting me out. I've been keeping myself out. Breaking up with you was the last act of self-sabotage I will ever commit."

His words quieted her nerves. She believed him completely and was humbled by his revelation. Bella felt her heart expand. This was more than physical attraction. Her influence had changed him for the better. She'd inspired his life, not only his art. And he'd inspired her right back to look deeper at the reasons people in love pushed others away. Bella found it in her heart to forgive.

"It's awful I had to lose you to gain insight into myself," said Will. "Glad as I am to have it, I am so freakin' sorry about what happened, Bella. I haven't stopped thinking about you for a minute. I hope we can be friends."

"Friends? Fuck that."

She came around the desk. He met her halfway, and they fell into a hot kiss. Breaking apart, she said, "Just so you know, this is how guidettes say, 'You're forgiven.'"

Chapter Forty-Four

Hands Full of Sudsy Wiener

Gia stepped out of the shower in the bungalow, dripping wet. She was supposed to be at the club with everyone else, but the dogs needed to be walked. After their beach tour, Gia got sweaty and decided to rinse off.

She padded back to her bedroom—the same room she'd lived in last summer with the porthole, round window, and ocean view—to get dressed. But she stopped short (no pun intended) when she saw a man in her room, pawing through the dresser.

"Stanley! Get away from there! What is it with guidos and panty drawers?"

"Gia?" He turned around and instantly lowered his eyes. "Damn, woman! Put on some clothes."

She was wearing a hand towel. She slipped on her leopard-print robe. "What're you doing here?"

"It's my friggin' house! I don't need a reason to be in my own place. But if you have to know, I came for socks. Maria kicked me out without letting me pack a bag." Softer, he asked, "Have you seen her? Is she still pissed off?"

"Do you even know why she's upset?"

"She's crazy! How am I supposed to know what goes on in her head?"

"You think you're upset now. Have you checked your joint savings account today?"

Stanley turned white. "What?"

"Maria's opening a new business. I can't tell you what it is yet. Calm down, Stanley. I know the idea of spending one penny makes you hyperventilate. But she needs to work, and it's a good investment."

Stanley's face turned strawberry-daiquiri red. "I feel dizzy. I need to sit." Falling on Gia's bed, he moaned, "How can Maria *do* this to me? She treats me like garbage. She spends all my money. I'm dying, here. I'm losing my hair."

"Since you only had one hair to begin with, it's not such a loss. I need a favor. If you help me, I can help you with Maria. She still loves you. But she doesn't think you love the real her."

"Who kicked me out? The real Maria or the *fugazi*? 'Cause one of them almost broke my nose."

"It's not like it was so great to begin with. Now, *as I was saying* . . . you have friends all over Jersey, right? I need you to locate a kid. I met him in Atlantic City. He's holding some money for me."

That got Stanley's attention. "What's the story?"

Gia filled him in about Arthur Ponzirelli.

"Man, you got played," he said, shaking his head. "Suckered by a pretty face. Why am I not surprised?"

"Are you gonna help me or make me feel worse?"

Stanley considered her proposition. "Okay, Gia. I'll take fifty percent of whatever you get back, after I find him."

"Make it thirty percent and we have a deal." Fredo wouldn't be happy about that. But third of whatever was more than a third of nothing. The new math?

"Give me the details again," Stanley said. "Tell me everything about this douche bag you know is true."

"He's twenty-seven and grew up in Hoboken. He hates pickles

and might have a medical history of panic attacks and hot-pepper-related fainting. My gut tells me his first name really is Arthur. His father was the maître d' at the Clam Dungeon in Hoboken. He might have a good friend or ex who's an orthodontist."

Stanley nodded. "Give me a few days."

Twelve hours later . . .

Gia gave Pretzel a bath in the club's bar sink. The puppy had had a little accident, then slipped on her tiny legs and landed in the poopie. Poor baby. Gia was using the sink's spray nozzle when she heard her Kaskade ringtone. Hands full of sudsy wiener dog, she fumbled to answer the phone, holding it against her ear with her shoulder.

"Found him," said Stanley.

"You rock."

"I called a business associate in North Jersey. This kid—Arthur Sanders—is semifamous in certain circles. He's also wanted by Hoboken PD, so if you do find him, you got leverage."

"Sanders? That does *not* end in a vowel. Unless *s* is a vowel?"

"It's not. It *is* the symbol for cash, though. There's a reward out for his arrest. Two grand."

"That prick," whined Gia. He was wanted by the cops? On top of lying about being a guido, he'd done crimes? She felt a rush of dread. Had she almost smushed with a . . . "What'd he do?"

"Nonviolent cons. He scammed an old lady out of her life savings. My friend pointed me toward Arthur's mother, who moved from Hoboken to Belmar when her husband, the restaurateur, died ten years ago. Very nice lady. Kind of batty, and nearly deaf. I called her and said I was an old friend of Artie's from Hoboken High. Asked if she'd seen him recently. Turned out, he'd been by her place the day before. Bought her a new chair and a TV."

"He's in Belmar?" asked Gia. "That's, like, twenty minutes away."

"Mom said he's planning on taking a trip, a long one, out of the country. He's leaving in a few days."

"No shit!" Pretzel looked sad. "Not you, baby."

"Sanders hangs out in Belmar at a bar called the Four Leaf Clover. Want me to pick him up?"

Gia's skin buzzed with anticipation. She'd *love* to have Stanley send in the goon squad. "I've got a better idea. Thanks, Stanley. Truly, you're a rock star. A porn star!"

"I take cash or personal check. And tell Maria I'm moving back in, whether she likes it or not. I need access to clean socks. My feet stink."

"So buy some at Rite Aid."

"I'm not buying new socks when I have drawer full of them at home! You know how much socks cost?"

"Like five bucks for a dozen?"

"Exactly," he said. "I'm not made of money, you know."

She hung up, then dialed a number she hadn't called in months.

"Frank Rossi," he said, answering with his first and last name like he worked in a freakin' insurance company and not the firehouse.

"It's Gia. You still babysitting Cara?"

He paused. "We broke up."

"What happened? Got sick of sleeping with Huggies pull ups and a night-light?"

"She was pissed I didn't put a dollar under her pillow when her baby tooth fell out."

Gia gagged. "Seriously?"

"No, but she did order off the children's menu at Luna Rosa. Embarrassing."

Pause. "Yeah, well, the reason I'm calling is that I need a favor. You cheated on me with Cara, and you lied to my face about it. I'll be mad at you for the rest of your life, or we can neutral it right now."

"Okay. What do you want me to do?"

Chapter Forty-Five

Venus Gets Whacked

"Another employee quit?" Mr. Violenti roared to his underling. "That's four people in the last three days!" He'd been enjoying a peaceful moment, feeding his gators a whole roaster chicken and watching them tear it apart.

The hotel concierge—what was this idiot's name again?—cowered in his presence. It took everything the kid had to say, "Yes, sir. The last to go was the receptionist at the spa. She got an offer at triple her current salary to work at a new nightclub in Seaside Heights."

"The same freakin' club? Frickin' poachers," screamed Mr. Violenti. "I pay to train these people, and then a shithole in Trash Town steals them out from under me? What is this club? Who runs it? I want information."

The idiot looked at his notes. "It used to be called the Cowboy Club, but they changed the name to Venus. The space was rented by Fongul Industries, but I can't get any further details. It's a shadow organization, almost like it doesn't really exist."

"That's all you got?" asked Mr. Violenti, trying to rein in his impatience. When will his people *get it*? He doesn't want to know what they don't freakin' know! He might as well fire every one of these useless fucktards! If he could clone himself and work every job in the casino and hotel, he would. He *will*. Until technology catches up to his fervent wishes, he'd suffer through the incompetent idiots he was forced to surround himself with.

The idiot added, "Venus opens on Tuesday night."

"Venus is gonna get whacked," Mr. Violenti said, hurling two more whole chickens by their plucked drumsticks into the moat. "Now get out of my sight."

The cringing idiot scurried away. Mr. Violenti wiped off a fleck of chicken skin on his slacks. He had a bad feeling about all these ex-employees working at the same place. As he built his empire, he'd cut some corners, violated some codes, and broken a few of what the New Jersey gaming commission called "laws." When he had the staff under his thumb, he didn't worry about being ratted out.

But now they'd wriggled free of his grasp and were together, comparing notes.

"Fuck!" he shouted in the direction of the gators.

"That won't work," said a passing tourist.

"Huh?" he asked the broad in the floppy hat.

She pointed at the moat. "Gators don't breed in captivity. Yelling the F-word won't help."

Repressing his rage, he said, "Thank you, madam, for sharing. Now if you'll excuse me, I've got a baby club to kill."

Chapter Forty-Six

Doing It with the Lights On

Since the miracle of her son's birth, Donna Lupo hadn't spent more than three hours out of touch with Fredo. The last three weeks had been like sawing through an umbilical cord made of oak.

The first week? Donna was frantic with worry. Fredo left a note saying he was going out of town, not to worry, and that he'd be in touch. She had no idea where he'd gone. Whenever she called his cell phone, it went to voice mail. She begged her husband to call the service provider and track Fredo down via GPS. But Luigi refused.

"I know where he is," said her husband. "I've got eyes on him. He's safe. Leave him alone."

Despite the reassurance that her baby was alive and protected, Donna cried every day. As fast as she could stroke on mascara, her tears washed it off. Despite having had two eye lifts in the last five years, Donna's lids puffed like thick-crust pizza dough.

"I'm a mother!" she pleaded to her husband. "A mother worries!"

"Get over it," said Luigi.

The second week without Fredo, Donna fell into a depression. She attempted to ease her mind by pouring herself into her new friendship with Maria Crumbi. They had seven-course dinners and went to the mall nearly every day. Donna fretted away the extra calories, but Maria got fat. Before long, Donna's strategy failed. She never thought it possible: eating and shopping didn't fill the empty shell that was her heart.

She was lonely. She missed her son.

Until he'd run off, Donna hadn't realized how much she relied on Fredo for companionship. Sure, she had a posse of cronies to fill the hours. But they weren't blood. They didn't satisfy the deep craving for the love and connection she felt only in the company of her baby boy.

By the third week of Fredo's disappearance, Donna got angry. How dare her son abandon her like this? After all she'd done for him? If it weren't for her, he wouldn't even be alive! She'd devoted her life to Fredo, and he repaid her by leaving her in a rambling mansion with a husband who barely grunted at her over the dinner table?

If she ever saw Fredo again, she'd kill him.

Donna was having such murderous thoughts while driving home from her plastic surgeon's office after a Botox touch-up. She steered her car down Boulevard and came to a stop at a red light by the Cowboy Club. Fredo's latest fiasco. The place had been empty for the last few weeks, and Donna knew her husband wanted to unload it in August.

Then she saw the club door swing open, and out came a woman who looked exactly like Maria Crumbi, circa a year ago, only fatter. A closer look, and Donna's lipo'ed chin dropped. It *was* Maria Crumbi! She wore a black pouf and a ridiculous leather minidress with cage platform heels.

As Donna watched with horror and fascination, Maria carried a bag of garbage behind the building and heaved it into a Dumpster. Then she teetered back to the front entrance and disappeared inside.

"What the hell does she think she's doing in Fredo's club?" Donna asked herself out loud.

A disgusting thought popped into her head. Were Fredo and Maria Crumbi holed up together in there, like a secret lovers' hideaway? Donna had heard a rumor that Stanley Crumbi was living in one of his other properties for the last few days.

The thought was sickening on so many levels. As soon as the light changed, Donna hit the gas and left a burned-rubber mark to pull into a parking spot. She tore out of the car and into the club.

Expecting the place to be dark and empty, she was blinded by the bright lights inside. Fresh-paint fumes hit her hard. Everywhere she looked, people were doing things. A kid in jeans and a splattered T-shirt was rolling up drop cloths on the floor in front of a freshly painted wall. She glanced around and noticed that every wall had been painted with Roman-style nudes, a hundred of them, some wearing sunglasses, with poufs, dripping with bling. Some wore fuzzy fur boots or leopard-print panty/bra ensembles. A blurring of old world and new that, if she weren't seething with confusion and anger, would have blown her away. The style reminded her of that painting she'd hired some cheap hack to do of Fredo years ago, and of the Crumbi wedding portrait.

"Can I help you?" A guido behind the bar was talking to her.

"Where's the fuck is Fredo?" she demanded.

"He's in his office."

So he *was* here. With Maria? Who were all these people? Donna clomped toward the back of the club. She flung the office door open.

On the desk, which she'd picked out for Fredo herself, lay a woman on her back. Donna's only son, her baby boy, was on top of the girl, his pants down around his ankles.

"Argghh!" Donna's French-manicured hands slapped over her eyes.

"Ma?" choked Fredo.

Donna heard movement and dared to peek again. Her son, her

only love, was now upright, his pants buttoned. The girl on the desk (not Maria Crumbi, thank freakin' Gawd) was standing next to Fredo, holding his hand.

"Although this isn't how I hoped you two would meet, Ma, I'd like you to meet my fiancée, Erin. Erin, this is Ma."

Donna said, "Your . . . *what*?"

"I know it's sudden. But I love her. She loves me."

Shocked, Donna couldn't speak for a minute. Then she took a step toward her boy, put her hands on his cheeks, gave him a kiss on the lips, pulled back, and said, "Fredo, you break my heart!"

Then she turned her back on the couple and ran out of there.

"Ma, wait!" he called.

Her only son, engaged! Three weeks away from her, and this happened? The nightmare of nightmares. A redheaded gold digger got her hooks in Donna's pure, innocent son! The worst part: she was definitely *not* Italian. This Erin might as well have the map of Ireland tattooed on her face. Tears, mascara, and fumes temporarily blinding her, Donna didn't see where she was going and collided with someone in the hallway.

"Get out of my way!" she yelled.

"Donna! What're you doing here?" asked her former friend, now enemy, Maria Crumbi. "You remember my bitches of honor, Gia and Bella?"

The two girls who'd humiliated her son and then had stolen the money from Mama Lupo's bingo game at Our Lady of the Perpetual Sorrow were back to cause more trouble. The short one waved and said, "How's it hanging?" The tall one had the good sense to keep her trap shut. The three of them clustered together looked like a magazine ad for tackiness.

Donna said, "You, Maria Crumbi, are dead to me. You are no longer my friend. Your husband can consider his business with Luigi over. I hold you two girls personally responsible for corrupting my son. Enjoy your last minutes in Seaside Heights. I'm gonna have you ridden out of town on a stretcher. You'll have tire tracks on your asses. I'm gonna slap you so hard, I'll bruise your whole family. I'm gonna—"

"Ma! Shut up," said a loud voice from behind her.

Donna didn't at first know who spoke. The deep growl that had apparently come out of Fredo's body was unrecognizable to her. She'd never heard him raise his voice before. "Do not talk to me that way! I'm your mother!" said Donna, having to look up at his face. Fredo seemed taller than she remembered. It was as if he'd grown half a foot in the last three weeks. Or maybe he was standing upright. Had he been bent in a crouch for the first twenty-five years?

"You have no right to threaten my friends or insult my fiancée," he said, pulling the redheaded harlot into a Safety Sidehug, just as Donna had trained him to do.

Donna smiled at the sight. Even though he'd been on top of the girl a few minutes before, when in public he was a good boy. A polite, neutered, sexless boy.

"This is gonna hurt, Ma. But you need to see this." As if he'd read her mind, Fredo pulled the girl into a full-frontal hug, putting his hand on her rear end, squeezing her against him so hard she might as well have been behind him. "I'm Guido Hugging, Ma. I'm not afraid of anything anymore. I haven't popped an Ativan in days. I even took a dump with the lights on this morning!"

Erin nodded. "He looked at it, too. We both did."

Gia, the tarty brunette with the doll face, said, "Group Hump!" She attached herself to Fredo from behind, pressing her chest into his back. Maria and Bella, too, clamped their bodies onto Erin and Fredo, making a five-person assault on Donna's propriety.

"Hey, Mrs. Lupo. Get in here," said Gia. "Once you Guido Hug, you never go back."

"I can't," she protested, although, to be honest, she was tempted. She'd been so lonely. Her husband wasn't the most affectionate of men. But how could she participate in the degradation of her pure baby boy? No, she would not.

"Ma, it's okay," said Fredo, waving her in. "You can do it."

"Fredo, I'm afraid," she said, sensing a momentous shift in the nature of their relationship and in the character of her son. In the press of female flesh, Fredo ceased to be her baby boy. She'd lost him. But Donna had a strange feeling that she'd gained something even more valuable in its place. A grown man to talk to. A daughter-in-law to spend Sundays cooking with.

"Is this really what you want?" Donna asked. "You choose these floozies over me?"

"You're my ma, Ma. That'll never change. But I need other women in my life."

Fredo's arm, longer than Donna remembered, reached for her and pulled her in. She struggled at first, but then she let herself be enveloped by the warm, open arms of her son, and the women who were physically, emotionally, and professionally attached to him.

It wasn't that bad, actually. Three weeks of loneliness and anxiety sloughed off Donna's skin as if she'd had a full-body microdermabrasion. She felt something she'd never before felt about Fredo: pride. Maybe it wasn't a curse on her house that Fredo got engaged. They could have children soon. Perhaps a baby boy who needed a strong, protective *nonna* to care for him.

After a few moments, the arms loosened, and the group broke apart. Donna stepped back, wiped a tear from her eye before anyone noticed. "I won't run you all out of town after all."

Gia said, "Yay! No tire tracks!"

Donna squinted at her. This girl really was a dim bulb.

"I'm glad you're here," Gia continued. "You can see what a balls-to-the-wall hottie your son has turned into. But I've also got a job for you, if you want it."

"Oh?" asked Donna, wondering what kind of "job" this girl expected a woman of her maturity to perform.

"You enjoy getting revenge on your enemies, am I right?"

"Yeah?"

"Your son has an enemy. A dirtbag who ripped us off in Atlantic City. Wanna help us get revenge on him?"

"I'd really appreciate it, Ma," said Fredo.

Donna looked at each of them, including Bella and Maria (whose style crisis made her wince), and saw the genuine respect and desire for her to join their crew.

What could a mother do? "I'm in."

Chapter Forty-Seven

The Setup

Arthur Sanders sat at the bar at the Four Leaf Clover, nursing a beer and watching the Mets on the TV. They were losing by a landslide. He was glad he hadn't placed a bet to beat the spread. He needed to conserve cash. He'd already blown through the money he'd stolen in Atlantic City. He'd bought his mom some new stuff. Not that she appreciated it. Arthur opened the box of a brand-new HDTV and his mom said, "Your sister, Angie, comes for dinner every Sunday night with the kids. She's a good girl." A brand-new couch from Pottery Barn arrived and she said, "Your brother, Chester, visits every Wednesday to watch *Top Chef.* He's a good boy."

Everything he did, she came back at him with the guilt. That was why he hardly visited. She pecked at him, peck, peck, peck, until he had to get away or let her tear him to pieces. He had to get out of town soon anyway. An old friend told him some goombah was asking around about him in Hoboken—a bad sign. He should be on a plane to the Bahamas already.

In his career as a gigolo grifter, Arthur had ripped off retired grandmas, lonely divorcées, merry widows. Sometimes he had regrets about his work. Even though he saw it as a free-market exchange, on some level he knew it wasn't right to trade sex for gifts. If he'd been successful at any other profession, he wouldn't be in the oldest one. Charming women was the only area where Arthur truly shone.

His latest con, however, went beyond minor regret. It'd left a bad taste of pickle, cotton candy, and shame in his mouth. Gia wasn't his usual mark. And she hadn't treated him like a beefcake-flavored chew toy, either. She'd treated him as an equal. She was so generous with her money. If he'd asked for the safe's contents, she would probably have given it to him. She'd been good to him all around, including riding with him in the ambulance and going to the hospital. Then again, she was the one who put him there. Regardless, he was a little bit in love with her. Maybe a lot in love.

Whatever. His feelings didn't matter. He couldn't undo what he'd done. It would have been the perfect crime except for the nagging tug of doubt. Could he and Gia have had a real relationship? Lived a straight life? If he put his mind to it, Arthur could get a real job, work as an actor, or a model. Then again, if he put his face out there, every woman he'd swindled would come out of the woodwork. No, the smart move was to get out of the country and try his luck on vacationing desperadoes in the Caribbean.

Jingle. The door of the bar opened.

A woman draped in a lynx coat with diamond jewelry on her neck, wrists, and ears came in followed by a huge dude in a black tank top, black jeans, and deep tan. A gorilla juicehead, as Gia would say. The woman was older, around fifty, but she was slick and put together, with straight black hair and bangs, face and neck skin tight (probably from face-lifts), and intense blue eyes.

"Forget it, Frankie," said the woman to her much younger boyfriend. "I'm done with you."

"Please, Donna. I'll do anything. Just one more chance." He was begging, but he seemed stiff, embarrassed. Fake? Or just awkward about being dumped in a public place?

The woman, Donna, didn't seem embarrassed. She was enjoying making a scene. "I told you, Frankie, that if you weren't willing to do . . . what I needed you to do, there was no point in our being friends. Just leave me alone, wouldya?"

"But I care about you."

Ha! Arthur didn't believe that for a second.

Donna said, "I'm not interested in your feelings. Now leave me alone, before I get mad."

Head hanging on massive muscled shoulders, the kid shuffled out of the Four Leaf Clover. Donna yelled, "Bartender! Prosecco, please."

"On me," said Arthur. "If that's all right with you."

She turned toward him, and he could see the doorknob-size diamond pendant around her neck. This woman stank of green. And, apparently, she liked her men young.

Arthur said, "If you don't mind my saying, you are an extraordinarily beautiful woman."

"Slow down, Romeo." Her voice was throaty, sexy. "Don't worry. I'm flattered. A young man like you, noticing me?"

"Well, you did make a dramatic entrance. If you don't mind my saying, that kid isn't good enough for you." Holding out his hand, he added, "I'm Ponzi."

"Donna," she said, shaking his hand. He didn't let her go for three seconds too long. He was frozen, like a deer in headlights, by the size of her ring. He could retire with that beauty.

The bartender brought her wine. Arthur put a twenty on the bar. "Keep the change." If he weren't softening the mark, he wouldn't leave a penny behind on the bar.

He raised his beer bottle. They toasted and drank. Before he could continue his usual patter of polite flattery, the mark's expression changed.

"I'm so embarrassed," she confided. "I should have ended it with Frankie in private, but he kept following me around. Ever since my fantastically rich husband died and left me all of his money, young men like Frankie are suddenly attracted to me."

"You are a gorgeous, sexy woman."

"That's what Frankie said, too." She laughed, throaty and deep. "Look, I know what's what. I'm down with . . . whatever a young man like you would find appealing about me. It's just that I like variety, okay? I won't have anyone falling in love with me and making emotional demands."

Arthur blinked in shock. He'd never before met a woman who was so direct. Ordinarily he'd be suspicious. But, given his urgent need to round up quick cash and get out of the country, he'd go with it. Donna liked variety? Fine. He'd milk the MILF until she got bored of him. One week with her might be enough to get him in the air.

Donna finished her wine and checked her diamond-studded gold watch. "I've got to go. It's been nice meeting you, Ponzi."

She was leaving? So soon? "We're just getting to know each other," he said, a little panicked.

She looked him over slowly. "I'm having a little party with a bunch of my girlfriends. It's informal. Just come as you are. My friends and I, we enjoy . . . games. Do you like to play *games*?" she asked, puckering her lips suggestively.

"I love games."

"This game, it's sort of kinky. Sort of goth. It's an exclusive gathering in a secret room in the basement of a church."

"What, like a cult thing?"

"You could say that."

"Human sacrifices at the altar?" he asked, a little nervous.

"Nothing violent. Just some harmless . . . *games*." She winked sexily.

Ponzi considered it. What the hell? It was one night. If he got creeped out, he'd leave. "I'd be honored to come, Donna."

"Great." She wrote down the time and place on a napkin— Thursday night in Seaside—and left. He could see her black Mercedes pulling out of the parking lot.

Chapter Forty-Eight

Sex on the Beach

New Club Grand Opening!!!
Have a Shoregasm at VENUS!!!
DJ Koko Spins 9:00 PM to 3:00 AM!!!
Grand Mixer Tanner's Signature Cocktail, the Black Out, Only $6!!!
TUESDAY NIGHT! BRING THIS FLYER FOR ONE
FREE TEQUILA SHOT!!!

• • •

"Who wants to pass out flyers?" asked Bella over breakfast.

"Me!" Gia was glad to do it. The frantic work inside the club and the overcrowding at Maria's bungalow was making her "claustropubic," she said.

"Claustro*phobic*," said Bella.

They were living together in the porthole-window bedroom at the bungalow. Tanner and Jim, Will, Erin, Fredo, and DJ Koko occupied the other bedrooms. The place also served as the off-site break house for Venus's AC commuters Lucy, Maggie, and Juan.

"It's like a college dorm," said Bella. "Fighting for the bathroom. People eating each other's food. No privacy. No downtime. I can't believe I was resentful I didn't get to live like this at NYU!"

"And Maria is the twisted dorm mother," said Gia. Sharing a

bedroom with Bella took Gia back to their family reunions when they were kids. They'd stay up all night with a flashlight, telling each other stories about the hottie husbands they'd have one day.

"You sure you don't mind passing out flyers?" asked Bella. "I'm helping Will with the finishing touches on the murals or I'd do it myself."

The murals were spectacular. Gia especially loved the Venus with Gia's head, the sun god Apollo with Fredo's, Diana, moon goddess, with Erin's. Will had painted Jupiter and Juno, the king and queen of the gods, with his and Bella's heads. Maria's head appeared on the body of a creepy Cupid, flying all over the murals, arrows and bow in a quiver.

Tanner walked into the bungalow's kitchen, bare-chested in nylon shorts, and said, "Can I help, Gia? I'd love to hit the beach."

Gia did a double take. He'd been yummy all along, but now Gia was seeing him with his shirt off for the first time. Holy cannoli, the kid was freakin' hot. He'd been loading and organizing the bar. A week's worth of hauling and lifting cases of booze had pumped his body to prime gorilla. She'd be thrilled to have him at her side today.

"Ready when you are," said Gia. They sorted out puppy care. Bella would take Pretzel. Gia and Tanner had Kookah. They weren't two blocks along the boardwalk when Kookah slipped her rhinestone collar and took off like a shot after a seagull.

Gia screamed, "Come back!" She chased after the fluffy puppy, but lost sight of her almost immediately. "Help! I've lost my Kookah! Has anyone seen my Kookah? I need a bone for my Kookah!"

A pack of gorillas on the beach thought her cries were freakin' hilarious. In a different context, Gia would have laughed, too. But this was serious. The dog that saved her life was missing. Calling her name, running along the beach, Gia stopped to catch her breath under the pier, among the forest of wood pillars supporting it.

She looked up and saw a figure jogging toward her on the horizon. It was Tanner, who'd sprinted after Kookah the second she broke free and gotten ahead of Gia in a flash.

"Got her." Tanner held the naughty fur ball in his arms. "For such tiny legs, she's friggin' fast!"

"Thank you, thank you, thank you!" Gia sang, cuddling the puppy and putting the collar back on, a notch tighter. Then Gia launched herself at Tanner and showered him with grateful kisses and a Guido Hug. One of her kisses landed on his lips.

"Finally!" he said. "All summer you've been giving me those frustrating cheek kisses. I'll rescue your dog again for another one."

"What's your last name?"

"Aeillou."

"Ends with a *u*? That's definitely a vowel."

"My name has all *five* vowels, in alphabetical order."

Gia's kookah, the one she carried with her wherever she went, felt suddenly unleashed. She fastened the dog's tether around one of the pier pilings and said, "Wanna cuddle?"

"What about the flyers?" Then, reconsidering, he said, "Fuck the flyers."

Anyway, Gia had thrown her stack in the air when the dog took off. The wind would scatter them, doing their work for them.

While Gia and Tanner rolled around under the pier for a few hours, Kookah watching and digging in the sand happily, Gia realized that the guido she'd been looking for at Gorilla Beach had been right in front of her the whole time.

Opening night! So far, everyone Gia had called or texted had shown up. Tony was here, fist-pumping with all his gym-rat friends. Giuseppe and Tina Troublino, Tony's grandparents, also showed up to wish Gia and Bella good luck. Frankie arrived with his brother and sister-in-law and a bunch of off-duty firefighters. Donna Lupo came, along with ten of her closest bitches. Luigi Lupo was there, too, along with a dozen henchguidos straight out of central casting's open call for goombahs. DJ Koko cranked. Tanner mixed Black Outs (Kahlúa, vodka, and Red Bull) for a thirsty crowd. The partners had taken a vote and decided against VIP table service at Venus. Their club would be democratic, for the people. Everyone was equal upon stepping through the door. Just like their equal partnership.

Gia danced over to Maria's perch on a stool at the entrance to the club, checking IDs. "How many so far?"

The cougar checked her clicker. They had to keep track of how many people were inside. If they reached the maximum capacity of four hundred (it was a small club), they'd have to set up a waiting area on the street, which they hadn't yet gotten a permit for. Erin thought to apply for one. She knew all the ropes, the hoops, and how to jump through them. Fredo was right alongside her, greasing the right wheels in Seaside to make things happen.

Maria said, "We're up to two hundred already." It was only 10:00 p.m.

"Why aren't you happy? You're back in biz, and it's a huge success!"

"I am happy. I'd be friggin' ecstatic if I didn't feel sick to my stomach. I must've had a bad oyster at lunch."

"You've been feeling sick for days," said Gia, concerned.

Maria waved it off. "I need a drink. Can you bring me a glass of milk?"

Gia blinked. "Did you say *milk?*"

"Make it a dirty milk with a shot of olive juice."

"This is your cure for the pukes?"

"It sounds gross, I know," said Maria. "I've been obsessed with it lately, though. Also ice cream and pickles."

"Chocolate or vanilla?"

"Strawberry."

"Whoa, that is weird."

Another wave of people came into the club. Maria dutifully clicked them off on her counter. Gia asked, "Is Stanley here?"

"He refused to come. He's sulking in the Prison Condo."

The groom had no choice but to move into the room Erin had vacated. Maria wouldn't have him back, not that there was any room for him at the bungalow now anyway. Although Gia loved the beach house, it was her third residence in as many weeks. She longed for the feeling of home. But what home? The Toms River house she grew up in, pre-divorce-bomb, when her parents were still together? Or the Brooklyn brownstone with Mom, Bella, and Aunt Marissa? Although she and her mom had been welcomed there when they moved in, Gia couldn't shake feeling like a permanent guest.

Gia felt rudderless. She wasn't sure where she belonged. Despite the packed club and thundering house music, the flowing drinks and smiling faces, opening night was bittersweet for Gia. Despite having great friends, new pets, and a new boyfriend, she felt a bit lost.

"Check out the geezers," said Maria out of the side of her mouth.

Gia looked up. Two middle-aged men were walking toward the entrance. "They're not geezers. They're my family! Daddy!" Running toward the two men, Gia jumped into the shorter one's arms. "What are you doing here?"

"Ooof," said Joe Spumanti, catching her on the fly. He gave his daughter a brief squeeze, then let her down to her heels.

She turned to give her uncle Charlie, Bella's dad, a hug, too—an ambivalent Safety Sidehug. He was her uncle, but he'd been a terrible husband and father this year. He said tersely, "Hello, Gia. Is Bella here?"

"She's behind the bar." Gia wasn't sure how Bella would feel about seeing her dad. They hadn't spoken since he left Brooklyn. Uncle Charlie excused himself and went to find his daughter.

Gia introduced Joe to Maria. She burped, then cupped her hand over her mouth. "Oh, crap. I'm gonna hurl." She ran around the side of the building toward the Dumpster in the alley.

Joe said, "Friend of yours?"

"She's my cougar role model," said Gia. "I can't believe you're here!"

Joe picked up the clicker that Maria had dropped. He handed it to Gia, who took over Maria's perch. "Is she okay?" he asked.

"Too much ice cream and pickles."

"She's kind of old to be pregnant."

Gia's brown eyes snapped open. "What did you say?"

"Nauseous, food cravings. Thick around the middle. Is she crying a lot, too? Rhonda went through all that when she was pregnant last year. And your mother, too, from what I remember."

Gia reeled from the revelation. Maria, preggers? Did Maria even know? Even more mind-blowing, Joe Spumanti, Gia's estranged dad, had been the one to figure it out. Surreal.

"What are you doing in Seaside?" asked Gia. "How did you know where to find me?"

"Charlie got a text to come for the opening night of your club. So, this is it?"

"You like?" Bella sent her dad a text? She never said anything about that.

"It's cool."

"Yeah."

The awkwardness and tension from Christmas hadn't gone away. Predivorce, Gia had been a total daddy's girl. But since then, they had nothing to say to each other. Joe was a man of few words. After the split, from Gia's perspective, it was as if he didn't speak at all. His silence was contagious. Joe was probably the only person in the world Gia hesitated to speak her mind to.

She could sit there, feeling angry, hurt, and disappointed, or she could tell him how she really felt. Fredo was downright inspiring when he stood up to his mom. That Bella had reached out to Charlie gave Gia courage, too.

"Dad, I'm glad you're here." She clicked as a few newcomers went into the club. "Remember when I came to see you and Rhonda and the baby at Christmas?"

"Of course," he said, arms crossed over his chest like a bouncer. He was still handsome, for an old guy.

"Are you sure? 'Cause I felt kind of invisible the whole time. You totally ignored me. I tried to talk to you, and you'd just walk away."

"The baby cried," he said, obviously uncomfortable. He shifted on his feet as if he were about to escape.

"I got the feeling just being in the same room with me made you nervous. You used the baby as an excuse to get away from me. Before the divorce, we were inseparable. You took me with you everywhere. Now you can't wait to get away from me."

"Gia, please."

"It's my club! I'll bitch if I want to!"

"I guess I deserve to get yelled at," said Joe.

"I don't want to yell. I just want you to love me again."

He frowned, and Gia flashed back to the night her parents told her they were splitting up. Mom cried and begged Gia to understand. Dad sat on the couch, arms crossed like now, sulking in angry silence.

"Fine, ignore me again," she said. "As friggin' usual."

"You know I love you. You're sizing this up wrong."

"I'm telling you how I feel, and you say I'm wrong. Just forget it. Thanks for coming to Venus. Have a great time."

It was his cue to leave, but he didn't. "Gia, I know I've let you down. I never meant to, I swear. This is hard for me to explain. You just . . . you look so much like your mother. Right after the split, it was painful to be around you. I kept thinking about how we used to be as a family. I turned to stone inside. Then you and your mom moved, and I met Rhonda. I let my new life take over. But I felt lousy about us, Gia. The guilt was always there. And that only made it harder to fix things. I just didn't know where to start."

It was the most words in a row he'd spoken to her in five years. Although it pissed her off to hear how unfairly he'd treated her, Gia understood the impulse to ignore a problem, hoping it'd go away. How many times had she done the same thing? She could see how he'd dug the hole deeper with each passing year, until it started to cave in around them.

"I'm not Mom," she said. "She wanted the divorce. Not me."

"I know that. I'm not saying I reacted rationally. Being an idiot has nothing to do with logic. I really wanted to explain myself to you at Christmas, but the baby kept . . . okay, the baby was an excuse. It's easier to change a diaper than open a vein."

"So what now?" asked Gia, feeling the tension fade.

He shrugged. "We could dance. Like we used to."

When Gia was a little girl, Joe would put on his Springsteen records and they'd dance for hours in the living room. She'd take flying leaps off the couch into his arms, and he'd spin her around until they fell on the floor dizzy and snort-laughing.

At that moment, Maria reappeared, wiping her mouth with the back of her hand. "Better now. Sort of."

"Here's the clicker. I'll be inside dancing," said Gia, taking Joe's hand. "About twenty people came in while you were puking. Oh, yeah. You've got a garlic knot in the brick oven."

"Huh?"

"You've got a mini-Stanley growing in your uterus."

Maria's expression was priceless. Her hand went to her Lycra-encased belly. "I think I'm gonna throw up again."

Gia and Joe didn't wait to watch that Technicolor event. They went inside, hand in hand, and hit the dance floor. As soon as they started moving, Gia was transported back in time to when she was her dad's everything. They were the only two people on the crowded dance floor, just like they'd been in the living room.

Chapter Forty-Nine

Fuggedaboutit

Bella pinch-bartended. There were just so many people! Tanner and Jim couldn't handle the action, so she and Will helped pour. She made countless vodka tonics, seven and sevens, Bacardi and Diet Cokes. Tanner had premixed a vat of triple sec and lime juice for margaritas. All she had to do was add tequila and ice. You'd think bartending would be easy. Pour booze into a plastic cup. But when five people came at her at once, screaming their orders and pushing $10 bills at her, it was hard! When a prissy guidette screamed, "I said *gin*, sweetie," after Bella had poured vodka, she felt totally flustered.

Clearly, she had no future in bartending.

At her side, Will was a controlled explosion of energy, mixing, making change. With his hands busy, he was downright chatty. Same thing with a Sharpie in his hand. If there were a way to draw portraits and bartend at the same time, Will would be in heaven.

It was a huge turn-on for Bella to watch him in action. He'd changed his look to fit in, too, with a new fade haircut to Bella's specs. Reluctantly Will submitted to a light Mystic tan. With darker skin, his blue eyes were mesmerizing. She'd gaze into his eyes and could almost see her future. Tonight, he wore jeans, a spiked leather belt, and a wifebeater with a button-down, black, short-sleeved shirt on top. When Bella suggested he buy a pair of Pumas, he drew the line.

"I am not wearing white sneakers. Absolutely no way."

"But motorcycle boots?" she asked. "Really? They're so butch."

"Since I actually ride a bike, I need them. You are not taking my boots. You can have my hair, my skin, my clothes, my art, my life. You already have my heart. You can have every part of me, but you are not taking my boots."

"Hello? Are you listening to me?" A guido snapped his fingers in front of Bella's face, bringing her back to present.

"Don't be an asshole or I'll spit in your drink," she said. "What'll you have?"

She poured and mixed until her fingers pruned. Will suggested she take a break. But Bella was not leaving his side, not with all these girls clamoring for his attention. Word got out that he was also the mural artist, and every girl here wanted him to do her portrait.

In the fresh press for drinks, Bella barely looked at the customers' faces. Someone tried to grab her hand when she passed him a drink. She looked up, ready to tear the guy's face off.

"Daddy?" It was Charlie. He looked awful, as if he'd aged twenty years since she'd seen him last.

"Bella," he said, and—shockingly—started crying.

"Dad, stop. There's no crying in Venus."

Will came over to her. "Problem?"

"It's my father." To Charlie, she said, "How did you find me? I told Mom not to let you know where I was."

Will put his hand out. "Hello, Mr. Rizzoli. I'm Will Lugano. Bella's boyfriend."

Charlie pulled himself together to shake Will's hand. "You're the kid who sent me the text to come here tonight?"

"Yes, sir."

"Um, *what?*" asked Bella.

"Can you give us a second?" Will said to Charlie. He pulled her back. "I found his number on your cell phone."

"Where do you get off interfering in my personal business? You know what he did to my mom. To me."

"He was an idiot. And you need to forgive him anyway. He must have sent you a hundred texts. I knew you'd never back down, so I sent him the message about the club opening."

"You have no right." The crowd was building up at the bar. Dozens of people waved money in their direction. "Wait a friggin' minute," she yelled at them.

Will put his hands on her shoulders and squeezed. "You need your family, Bella. Cutting off your dad is like cutting off your legs. Yeah, he did a despicable thing. You don't think he knows that? Jesus, look at him! He's miserable."

"He deserves to be," she said, daring to take a peek at Charlie. He really did look awful, haggard and defeated. So freakin' sad. Bella's heart tightened at the sight. Her caretaker instinct kicked in. She wanted to help him. "No! I'm not knee-jerking into taking care of everyone else."

Will smiled sweetly at her. He really was gorgeous, especially with a tan. "What's wrong with taking care of the people you love?"

"I lose myself."

"But caring for the people you love is *who you are*. Okay, you might veer toward the extreme. But things come full circle. You help someone else, like you turned my life around. And now, I'm doing it for you. Find a way to forgive, or you'll suffer more than Charlie in the long run."

"Practice what you preach. You're not about to forgive your parents."

Will shook his head. "My parents are addicts. They should never have had a child. There are things they did that simply can't be forgotten. Because of you, though, I'm trying to forgive my parents in my way. I can't have a relationship with them. But I'm not hiding anymore. That's a major step."

He can forgive, but not forget. Will was asking Bella to do both. "I can't," she said.

"You can do anything. Go. I'll be fine back here."

Bella nodded and stepped under the trapdoor of the bar. Charlie was waiting. He immediately wrapped her in his arms. He'd lost so much weight. Her pudgy papa had turned into a lean cuisine.

"I'm so sorry," he repeated until Bella's defenses shattered, and she found herself hugging him back. "I was so terrified she was going to die, I couldn't stand to be around and watch it happen."

"I'm not sure I can stand to be around you."

"I'm dedicating the rest of my life to making it up to you both. I've been talking to your mom. She's letting me move back home, by the graciousness of her heart. I told her I won't come back unless you okay it."

"Mom's taking you back?"

"She's generously allowing me to sleep in the basement."

Bella laughed. "On that disgusting old futon down there?"

"I'll sleep on a dirt floor if I have to. With the rats. And the mold. And the oil burner that leaks. She can throw a rind of cheese and a crust of bread down the stairs once a day, and I'll thank God for the blessing."

"You deserve to suffer."

"I agree! I want to suffer for what I've done."

"Where have you been all this time?" Bella asked.

"I traveled around for a while, stayed with cousins in Naples."

"Italy?"

"Florida. The last two months, I was in Philly with Joe and his family. He's here, too." Charlie pointed out Uncle Joe and Gia on the dance floor, going crazy, as if they were the only two people out there. Seeing the two of them having fun together undid the knots in Bella's heart. If Gia and Joe could bridge their divide, then Bella would forgive Charlie, too.

"If Mom says you can come home, I'm okay with it. But I'm serious about making you suffer. For a long, long time."

"Thank you, Bella," Charlie said, awash with relief. "I don't deserve you. But I'm the luckiest man on earth to have you for a daughter."

They joined Gia and Joe on the dance floor. DJ Koko started spinning deadmau5, Gia's favorite. The four of them made a square and she felt connected, grounded, back in the safe place, where nothing could hurt her, called home.

Chapter Fifty

When Anchovies Attack

"What a dump," groaned Mr. Violenti as he pulled up to the club in what had, until recently, been Fredo Lupo's white Caddie convertible with the red leather interior. He loved his new acquisition. He parked carefully and killed the engine. A cluster of Shore kids hung around outside, smoking. No neon signage or velvet rope? You call this a nightclub? Looked more like a neighborhood social club that catered to grumpy men with cigars and stories about the old days.

His enforcers, the Costello twins, Lou and Elvis, were in the backseat. Not moving. Just sitting on their fat asses like they had all night.

"Open the friggin' door, you mooks," instructed Mr. Violenti.

Lou sprang into action, opening the driver's-side door. The boss man stepped out, righted his jacket lapels, and strode in his Italian leather shoes to the entrance.

A fetching brunette with a curvy body sat on a stool outside, playing hostess. A barrel-chested Mexican with a VENUS SECURITY T-shirt loomed next to her.

"Good evening," said Mr. Violenti. "Is this Venus?"

"Yup," she said. "We don't have a sign yet, but this is the place."

"May I introduce myself?" he asked, taking her hand. What

glorious hands! Dark and cracked as alligator hide. And her lips. Frosted as a pink doughnut. Her hair was captivatingly black, with a striking platinum streak. "My name is Vito Violenti, businessman and bachelor."

"I'm married. And probably knocked up. I don't know for sure yet. I'm gonna pee on a stick later. But right now, I could vomit a river."

Charming! What refreshing candor! To the security guard, Mr. Violenti said, "All of the good ones are taken."

The man didn't speak. He didn't nod. He stared, though, as if he could see through Mr. Violenti's skull and directly into his brain.

"Ahem," said the boss man. "We're going in."

The giant Mexican didn't object, so he nodded to his twins, and the three of them walked into the club. Once inside, Mr. Violenti assessed the scene. Crowded bar, with people waving twenties at three different bartenders. A packed dance floor. The thud of monotonous house music the kids loved for some inexplicable reason. He inhaled and picked up the scents of drying paint, spilled beer, Axe body spray, Aqua Net, sweat—and money. The place reeked of money.

This was his special gift. His version of ESP. Mr. Violenti could tell, in one deep whiff, if any venture would be a success. This rinky-dink watering hole with the amateur murals and plastic cups and bad lighting? It was worth a friggin' fortune. Soon to be *his* fortune. Whoever ran the place just got himself a brand-new, controlling partner, whether he wanted one or not.

To the twins, he said, "Follow me."

Picking his way toward the back of the club, Mr. Violenti bumped into a familiar freckled face on the edge of the dance floor. "I should've known it was you poaching my staff," he said to Erin Gobraugh. "So you landed on your feet. Or your back."

"Who let this reptile in here?" asked Fredo Lupo, appearing at Erin's side.

"Fredo, *paesano*! We meet again."

Fredo put his hand on Erin's shoulder. She put her hand over his. It was almost touching to see them like this. Despite Mr. Violenti's best efforts to poison their relationship, they were still together.

"I'll ask you to leave our club," said Fredo.

"Not so fast, Fredo. I'm generously offering myself to be your majority partner in this entertainment venture. You still owe me, remember."

"You called us even right before you stole my car," said Fredo.

"Since you poached half a dozen people from my hotel staff, I deserve a finder's fee."

Erin's face turned another shade of red. "You mean the staff you underpaid, threatened, manipulated, and lied to?"

"I always knew you could manage a club, Erin. I was only teasing you when I fired you. You can come back to Nero's and manage Midnight. Now go powder your face or whatever you do in the bathroom. Let the men talk business."

Fredo whispered something in Erin's ear. She said, "I'm not leaving you." The couple smiled supportively at each other.

"Ahem. You need a protection policy," Mr. Violenti said.

"I have insurance."

"Not the kind I'm talking about." The twins laughed menacingly on cue. "You never know when a fire might start, or kids might break in and smash up the bar, or the entrance is hit by a truck. Also, you need someone to handle waste management."

Fredo shook his head. "This isn't Atlantic City. Things are different in Seaside Heights."

"People bleed here," said Mr. Violenti. "Their bones break."

The twins pounded their fists into their open palms. The gesture was old-school. Kind of stupid. No wonder Fredo and Erin laughed when they saw it.

Fredo said, "In Seaside, a man stands with his whole family. I've got the Lupos at my back. We handle our own protection and waste management."

"You mean your father, Luigi, who told me to put you on the Atlantic City bus? That guy?"

"Uh, boss?" said Elvis. "Look around."

Mr. Violenti tore his eyes off Fredo and saw that a circle had formed around them—a circle of big, hairy guidos and guidettes, closing in. And all of them were mimicking the twins, hammering their fists into their palms.

"Meet my cousins, aunts, uncles, nieces, nephews, and friends."

Luigi Lupo, built as solid as a submarine, stepped forward and clasped Mr. Violenti's shoulder. "I'm Fredo's father. We finally meet. Now tell my son the truth. We never spoke on the phone. I would never okay you stealing my son's car or threatening him. Not on your life, which is getting shorter by the second."

The hand on Mr. Violenti's shoulder tightened like a steel vise. "So I exaggerated to make my point."

Erin said, "Now tell Fredo the truth about me."

Luigi squeezed harder, and Mr. Violenti's knees shook. "I lied, okay? I lied to my advantage. That's what businessmen do. You understand that, don't you, Luigi?" The circle of Lupos tightened. The twins huddled close at Mr. Violenti's sides.

Luigi said, "In Seaside, we might cheat, steal, and bend the truth. But we know where to draw the line. We've got honor."

Mr. Violenti scoffed, "You're a small fish in a small pond. A puddle! You're nothing, Lupo. You're a friggin' anchovy. You're all anchovies!"

"That may be true," said Fredo, "but we've got strength in numbers."

In a flash, the cousins, uncles, aunts, nieces, and nephews sur-rounded them. They grabbed Mr. Violenti and the twins by their respective limbs. Then the AC sharks were carried through the club and out the door on a wave of anchovies. They were uncer-emoniously hurled into the gutter. Mr. Violenti could appreciate the irony. This was how he'd had Fredo ejected from Nero's.

"The Lupos manage the waste at Venus. We'll start by flushing the three of you," said Fredo, wiping his hands of the AC rot. He held up Mr. Violenti's toupee. "I'm nailing this to my wall. Now get out of here."

The brunette cougar watched the ousting from her perch on the stool, the Mexican next to her silent as the moon.

Mr. Violenti struggled to his feet. He rubbed his aching behind. He'd be black-and-blue tomorrow. "Come on, fucktards," he said to the twins. "We'll never speak of this again. Now let's get out of here."

"Boss," said Lou. "Where's the car?"

Mr. Violenti spun around. Their parking spot was empty. "Did you see anyone take my Caddie?" he asked the brunette.

"What Caddie? Juan, did you see a Caddie parked here?"

The giant Mexican shook his head and grinned malevolently.

"Boss, look," said Elvis.

On the ground in the empty parking spot, next to an oil stain, lay a piece of paper. "What's it say?" Mr. Violenti asked.

"It's a map," said Elvis. "It says, 'U R here,' with a little drawing of a building with musical notes around it. A club! Venus!" The goon had peanut butter and bananas for brains. Following with his finger, Elvis continued, "From 'here,' there's an arrow pointing a few blocks to the right, then a few to the left, to a building. It's got a picture, and a sign."

"What's the sign say?" asked Mr. Violenti.

"'Seaside Heights Bus Station.'"

Flipping the piece of paper over, Elvis saw another drawing. A hand with the middle finger extended. On the finger? A long, squared fingernail with a whiskered leopard face on it.

"What now, boss?" asked Lou.

What else could they do? Mr. Violenti consulted the map.

With his own middle finger, he pointed. "This way."

Chapter Fifty-One

Daddy Knows Best

Gia, Bella, and their dads had decided to get some air. They'd been dancing for a while, and the old dudes needed a break. Hanging outside the club, the girls listened to Charlie tell a story about taking care of Joe's baby the other night. Part of his agreement with Joe and Rhonda was that, if he was going to mooch their spare bedroom, he had to help around the house, and with the baby. So when Georgina cried at three in the morning, Charlie got up, fed her, and changed her. Proud of his work, he held the baby, who smiled, then unloaded a Fralinger's store's worth of fudge into her diaper.

"She can crap twice her size," said Charlie, laughing. "She's a miracle baby!"

Joe was laughing, too. "Just like Gia."

"Me?"

Joe nodded. "Tiny baby, sweetest face, could melt a stone. And a devil diaper bomber."

"I still do some tremendous work in the bathroom," said Gia.

Bella held up her hand. "I can testify to that!"

The four of them cracked up and it felt like good old times. Gia didn't want it to end. She flashed back to those family reunions, grilling burgers and hot dogs at her old house. Joe and Charlie rocked mullets back in the nineties and wore jean jackets with the sleeves cut off with high-belted jeans and tucked-in T-shirts from Bruce Springsteen concerts. Denim suits and mullets! They thought they were so gangsta! Gawd, Gia just had a brilliant idea. She'd find one of those photos of the two brothers-in-law circa the "Hungry Heart" era and have Will reproduce it in a painting! They could hang it at Joe's house, and every time he looked at it, her dad would crack up and think about how thoughtful his (first) daughter was, and how much he friggin' loved the hell out of her.

Squee!

Bella squinted at Gia. "What're you so excited about?"

"I'm happy we're all together and having a blast, duh." Gia would tell Bella about the Mullet Twosome idea when she could get her alone later. She'd love it.

"You guys about ready for another round?" asked Gia. To Joe, she added, "Dad, I want to introduce you to the genius behind our club's drink, the Black Out. His name is Tanner and he's a really awesome bartender."

"Is he your boyfriend?" asked Joe.

If it was possible to smile and frown at the same time, Joe was doing it right now. Any conversation about boys always made him queasy, going back to first grade when Gia kissed her first guido.

Uncle Charlie said, "If he's anything like Bella's new friend Will, then Tanner has to be a decent guy. Relax, Joe. The girls are grown women. They should have boyfriends."

"I know that. But no sex until you're married!" Joe laughed.

"Okay, Dad," said Gia, rolling her eyes, smiling. The guy was tragically not funny. But his lame attempts cracked her up anyway.

Bella laughed along. "I'm glad you like Will," she said to Charlie. "I think he's a keeper."

They were about to go inside and get another round of drinks when a white Caddie convertible pulled up to the curb.

"Block me!" said Gia, moving Joe to stand between her and the street. Bella, too, moved so that she was obscured.

Charlie asked, "Who is that?"

"The guy who broke my nail," said Gia. "He stole Fredo's car, too."

After a minute, Vito Violenti and the Twins disappeared into the club.

"That guy stole this car from your friend?" Joe asked. "We should steal it right back."

Bella said, "Yes!"

"How?" asked Gia, following Bella and Charlie as they jumped into the backseat. Joe took the driver's side and Gia the passenger seat.

"Whaddaya mean *how*? We hot-wire it," said Joe, who reached under the steering-wheel panel and pulled out some wires.

Gia was, like, *pause*. "Daddy? You know how to hot-wire a car?"

He grinned at her as the engine turned over and purred. "Ahhhh. Just like old times. I was young once, too, Gia."

At that moment, Gia had never loved her father more. He was a true American guido.

Charlie said, "Just like old times."

"What does that mean?" asked Bella.

Charlie and Joe just laughed. "Ready to roll?" asked Joe.

"Wait!" yelled Gia. "I have to leave a note." She found a piece of paper on the floor and scribbled directions to the bus station, and a simple hand drawing that was her personal message for Violenti. "Done."

Joe steered the car out of the spot. Gia threw the note in the vacated space. They he slammed the gas and they roared down the street, hooting and tearing up the Seaside night.

Chapter Fifty-Two

The Smackdown

Arthur Sanders, aka Arthur Ponzirelli, aka Arthur Buongiorno, took a taxi from Belmar to Seaside Heights for this kinky, goth church human-sacrifice party with the horny MILFs. He wore a vintage Giorgio Armani suit that had actually belonged to his father, a legendary swordsman/douche bag. Arthur had learned the tricks of the trade from his father. While Arthur's mom stayed home, cooking and cleaning, her husband racked up the gumars. Revoltingly, around the time Arthur turned sixteen, his father's girlfriends started hitting on him.

He'd been cursed with a pathologically unfaithful father and a long-suffering martyr for a mother. But he'd been blessed with a face and body that women could not resist—especially older women. Just as his dad attracted North Jersey floozies, Arthur was catnip to Shore cougars.

"Forty bucks," said the cabdriver, pulling to a stop outside Our Lady of the Perpetual Sorrow, a church on Grant Avenue in Seaside. Arthur paid the fare.

"No tip?"

"Always floss before bed."

"Asswipe!" screamed the driver before speeding away.

Arthur looked up at the classic brick church with the double arched doors and the cross on top. This was the right place. In his head, though, he hadn't pictured a building quite so holy. He'd imagined a club that was a converted church, or a modern building. Having sex in a real, classic church rubbed hard against his Catholic upbringing. Arthur started to walk away.

His cell rang. "Hello?"

"Where are you? We're all waiting," said Donna.

"I'm outside."

"Come in, walk down the stairs to the left, to the basement. It'll be worth your while." Then she hung up.

Arthur exhaled. Oh, why *not*? Truth be told, he'd only been to church a few times as a kid. His dad parked him in the pew and then sneaked into the rectory to bang the church secretary. If Donna Lupo and her friends got off on nun play, who was he to judge?

He followed her directions and found the basement. He walked deeper into the dark space, toward the sound of voices. A light shone from under a partially closed door. Slowly, he crept toward it, then pushed it open.

"There you are!" said Donna. "Come in, Arthur. I saved you a seat."

Something was wrong. The other women weren't hyperstyled rich-housewife types like Donna. Some appeared to be homeless women. Others looked like working-wage slaves, or blue-collar wives. Still others were lace-and-silk-shrouded silver-haired grannies. And the room didn't have a satin-sheeted altar at the center of a circle. It had long rows of tables and plastic chairs and, at the front, a dais and a card table with a round cage full of Ping-Pong balls.

"I'm not . . . I thought . . ."

"Right there, sweetbuns," said Donna, leading him to a chair at one of the long tables. "Here's your card and a pile of chips. Good luck! Oh, before I forget, you have to put twenty dollars in the basket. That's right. Take out your wallet and drop some cash right in here. That's a smart boy!"

Dazed, Arthur took out his wallet and put a bill in the basket. He noticed that it was stuffed with cash. That perked him up. Whatever was really going on here, Arthur planned to leave with the contents of that basket.

A priest swept into the room, his black cape and purple scarf fluttering behind him. He had a thick mustache, sideburns, and wore a black fedora. A heavy gold cross hung from his clerical collar. "Hallo, a-friends. I a-see some a-new faces tonight. *Bene!*"

The priest bowed to a withered fossil in the front row, with a black doily pinned in her hair. "*Buona sera,* Mama."

"*Buona sera,* Padre Guido," said the ancient crone.

Arthur looked around, still totally confused. The priest started blabbing about an upcoming church potluck and a gently-used-clothing drive for the homeless shelter. His voice whistled between Arthur's ears. Did this mean no fucking? He looked at the card Donna had given him.

A bingo ballot?

"They say *bingo,* but I say *bimbo,*" whispered a girl who slipped into the empty seat to his left.

Gia!

"She says *bimbo,* I say, 'I'm gonna beat your ass until you don't have one.'" Bella, the amazon with the boobies, took the chair to his right.

Gia whispered, "Relax, *Arthur.* We're not gonna kill you."

"Yet," said Bella.

"We just want our money back."

"*Attenzione!*" called Father Guido. "I'm a-gonna call-a the first a-number. Make a-bingo, and you win the basket. Oh-keh? Here-a we go."

The priest cranked the cage handle and called a number. Incredibly, Arthur hit it. Despite the surrealism of the situation, he had a shot at winning the prize basket.

"You were conning me from day one," whispered Gia in his

ear. "For the record, my feelings for you were real. I thought I got lucky the day I met you."

Her hot breath so near to the sensitive skin of his ear . . . well, he hoped he wouldn't have to stand up anytime soon. "It was business, Gia. Not personal."

"Making out in the moonlight, saying you had eyes only for me, was business?"

"Yup." It was half-true. He was always planning on cleaning her out, but he cared for her, too.

Donna, who sat in front of him, turned around. "Shhhh," she hissed, then winked at Gia and Bella.

Obviously, he'd been set up. Donna got him here so Gia and Bella could get their revenge. But it wouldn't be sweet. He said, "The way I see it, I broke even with you."

Father Guido called out more numbers. Incredibly, Arthur's card was on fire. He had *B, G,* and *O* covered. Only two more lucky calls and he'd win the basket and get the hell out of there.

"You stole sixty thousand dollars from our safe!" said Bella. "You'd have to give us your kidney to call it even."

"Sixty grand? Try three. Barely." To Gia, he added, "I spent more than that on dinners and drinks for you and your friends. I had to soften you to the consistency of pulp."

"Soften? Are you saying I'm fat?"

"It's a grifter term. Doesn't matter. I could've spent twice as much, and you still wouldn't trust me."

Gia shook her head. "I did trust you."

"Is that why you tested me with that pepper?'

"It was just for fun. I never got to apologize about that. I am sorry I made you wet yourself."

Bella said, "Fredo counted the money the morning of the robbery. He swears it was sixty thousand dollars."

"And I swear there wasn't more than three."

Bella said, "Gia? Whaddaya think?"

"You know I'm bad at math." Gia frowned.

A few more bingo numbers were called out.

"The gap between three and sixty thousand is wide enough to drive a truck through," said Bella.

"That's between you two and Fredo," said Arthur. "I'm done with all of you." Standing, he shouted, "Bimbo! I mean, *bingo!*"

Father Guido slapped his hand on his cheek. *"Mamma mia."*

Arthur brought his card to the front of the room. Father Guido confirmed Arthur's winning numbers. Arthur grabbed the cash.

"Oh-a no! Not again!" said the priest, who grabbed Arthur by his lapels. "You're not-a stealing this-a money!"

What? No! He *won* the cash, fair and square.

"Stop him!" yelled a few grannies, who got out of their seats and rushed toward the front of the room.

"Get offa me!" Arthur shrugged off his jacket to get free of the priest. But then a horde of bingo grannies, bag ladies, and house-wives surrounded him, and they looked mad. They grabbed at his clothes. He struggled, but there were too many of them. Before long, they'd torn off his suit and were going for his boxers.

If he were watching this scene from above, he'd think, *Man, this is kinky.*

In all the commotion, he heard an old lady yelling, "Captain Morgan? This is Mama Lupo. I'm at Our Lady. A young man is trying to rob the church!"

The cops were coming? Now Arthur had to get serious. He el-bowed a few old ladies out of the way and knocked the priest off his feet (now he was going to hell for sure). He made a rush for the door, only to be clotheslined by Donna, the woman who'd lured him here. His head hit the floor when he fell. His vision was cloudy. Donna's face appeared above him, shimmering around the edges.

"That's for Fredo," she said.

Gia's face appeared. She said to Donna, "You never told me how Frankie was as an actor."

Donna said, "He was horrible! Only a moron would have believed him for a second! Frankie should stick to putting out fires."

Arthur's head started to clear. He thought he understood what was going on here, but he was still a bit fuzzy.

A cop with a mustache burst into the room, almost as if he'd been waiting just outside the door. He dragged Arthur to his feet. "Fair warning: I hurt my shoulder playing skeeball with my kids at the arcade, so I'm using my gun tonight instead of the nightstick."

Arthur Sanders, aka Ponzirelli, aka Buongiorno, whimpered, "This can't be happening."

"Whatever you say, chief," said the cop. "Can I get the man's clothes?"

Four dozen bingo players ignored the question.

"Fine, I'll book him and fingerprint him at the station in his boxers. It won't be the first time."

Gia stopped the cop at the door. "One second," she said, then gave Arthur a sloppy, saucy kiss. "Good-bye, Ponzi. That's the last kiss you're gonna get for a while. From a girl."

Chapter Fifty-Three

Heard the One About the Girl
Who Came to Seaside in a Honda?

"To the mother of my child!" said Stanley, holding up his beer.

"To Maria!" toasted Gia, Tanner, Bella, Will, Fredo, and Erin.

Kookah and Pretzel yipped.

The eight of them (not counting dogs) were having dinner and drinks at EJ's on the boardwalk to celebrate the triumphant opening week at Venus and Maria's pregnancy. The dinner was also a farewell. Bella and Gia were heading back to Brooklyn in the morning.

"Please stay," said Erin. "The club is rocking. You'll have money, an apartment, and a job. You've got friends." The red-head's freckled brow crinkled with sincerity. She really didn't want them to go. Gia leaned across the table to give her a kiss on the cheek. Mmm, tasted like gingersnap.

"What apartment? Not the bungalow. You're all evicted," said Stanley. "We're expecting a baby! We need room."

"Just how fat do you think Maria's gonna get?" asked Bella.

He was right, though. The Crumbis needed space. Maria's pregnancy hormones were overflowing like beer from a broken tap. When she wasn't vomiting or quaffing pickle-and-strawberry smoothies, she and Stanley were smushing. Loud, and hawd, from what Gia could hear, even with two pillows pressed to her ears.

Bella said, "We'd love to stay, but we have to be back home. I've got to see my mom and hear from her own lips that she's taken my dad back. And then I'm starting my sophomore year at NYU."

Fredo asked, "What's your excuse, Gia?"

"I go where Bella goes. We're a twofer."

Tanner understood. At least, he said he did. They'd had a fun few days, but their connection was just too young to change her life for. Then again, sometimes a casual fling turned into a major relationship. Stranger things have happened. Gia would keep an open mind about Tanner. For now, she was glad she had a boy to bring to their quadruple date.

"You'll come back, though, right?" asked Maria. "You can't make me go through this pregnancy alone."

"Whaddaya mean 'alone'? I'm sitting right here," said Stanley.

Maria said, "You're useless! Where's the corn dog with sauerkraut I asked for last night?"

"It was four in the freakin' morning!"

While Maria and Stanley argued, Gia smiled to herself, thinking about her good-bye with Joe after the club opening. They made a plan to talk every Sunday at noon and that she'd go to Philly the last weekend of every month. Gia was determined to hold up her end of the bargain.

"What about you guys?" asked Fredo, gesturing between Gia and Tanner.

Tanner said, "We're playing it by ear."

"And you two?" Fredo asked Bella and Will.

Will said, "The plan is to make some money—"

"That's always the plan," said Stanley.

"—and enroll at Parsons art school in Manhattan for the winter term. Bella invited me to live at her house in Brooklyn, so that'll save me a bundle."

"Not a freebie, though. We're putting him to work," said Bella.

"They haven't painted the interior in twenty years," said Will. "So I'm going to give it the royal treatment."

Gia said, "You do realize the brownstone has five stories."

Will gulped his beer and nearly choked on it. *"Five?"*

"Didn't I mention that?" asked Bella, grinning. "You'll be stuck there for at least a year with me and my whole family. We're always in each other's business, yelling, screaming."

Will cringed. "You make it sound so peaceful and relaxing."

"You'll love it." Gia raised her vodka cranberry. "To our Seaside family!"

They all clinked glasses and drank.

"One thing still bugs me," said Fredo. "Arthur Ponzirelli still got away with all that money."

Gia rolled her eyes. "You got your Caddie back, *and* a hot new club, *and* a hot new fiancée. You're still bitching about money?"

Stanley said, "I'd be bitching, too, Fredo."

Draining her glass, Gia said, "I have an announcement to make."

"This should be good," said Maria.

"Okay, remember how we divided our AC winnings equally? Well, I sort of took out an advance. Before Ponzi stole it."

"How much?" asked Fredo.

Gia counted on her fingers. "All of it? Minus three grand."

"So Ponzi told the truth," said Bella.

"So did you," said Gia.

"Me? What're you talking about?"

"Come outside, and I'll show you."

Gia pushed back her chair, told the waiter they'd all be right back, and led the group out the street-side exit of the restaurant.

Giuseppe Troublino was sitting on a bench outside. When he saw Gia, he said, "You're ten minutes late. It's not nice to keep an old man waiting. Here." He handed her an envelope. "I got you a deal, so you've got some walkaway cash."

"How much?"

"Fifteen grand."

Gia handed the envelope to Fredo. "This belongs to you."

Bella said, "Can someone tell me what's happening?"

Giuseppe smiled and handed Bella a set of car keys. "These are for you."

Gia Guido-Hugged the old man. "You rock, Giuseppe."

Bella said, "I still don't get it."

"Remember how you said the gap between three and sixty grand was wide enough to drive a truck through? Well, here it is." She walked over to the shiny black Cadillac Escalade, brand-new, parked at the curb. "It's for you, Bella, to make up for my trashing the Honda."

"How . . . what . . . I'm in shock," said Bella, her eyes big as man-hole covers.

"As soon as we started winning," said Gia, "I called Tony's grandpa and asked him to scout around for a good deal. When we'd saved up enough, Tony drove down to AC and picked up the cash. Giuseppe and Tony installed the zebra-print leather seats themselves. So? You like?"

Bella sputtered. "But this is a brand-new Cadillac! The Honda was a piece of shit!"

"*And????*"

"You could have bought yourself something," said Bella, jumping inside the Escalade, running her hands all over the leather seats. "I'm mean, I'm *loving* this truck. Don't get me wrong. My panties are soaked! But Jesus frickin' Christ, Gia. This is huge. It's too much."

"First of all, too much? Huh? Does not compute," said Gia, excited by Bella's intense reaction. "Second, a gift is only worth having if you can give it away. Fourth, you've been slipping me loans and helping me out for years—and you never once asked me to pay you back. This is my payback. I still don't think it's enough."

"You skipped the third reason for buying it," said Will. He'd opened the back door of the truck, lifted the dogs inside, and climbed in.

"Third? Yeah, third, I need a ride back to Brooklyn, and I want to do it in style."

Chapter Fifty-Four

Run 'Til We Drop

The cousins waded into the Atlantic Ocean all the way up to their thongs. On the beach, the puppies, in their leopard-print vests, dug up buried cigarette butts and bottle caps in the sand.

"Do we have to do this? I don't want to get the leather seats wet," said Bella.

"We have to," insisted Gia. "It's tradition."

Last summer, right before they left Seaside Heights on July 31, they ran into the waves and got soaked pedicure to pouf. Gia conceded it wasn't the brightest idea to get salty water on the Escalade's new leather seats.

"Whale sperm," said Gia.

"Why the ocean's salty?" asked Bella.

"Yeah."

"I've heard that."

"If I had one complaint about this summer," said Gia, "it's that I didn't fall madly in love with a hot guido. But I feel falafel about it."

"Philosophical?"

"Whatever. I'm only twenty-two. I need to have experiences, not commitments. So I haven't met the father of my four or five tan babies yet. I can wait. The point is, I came to the beach to find a gorilla juicehead, and I wound up finding myself."

"Where were you?" asked Bella.

"At the bar, *duh*."

After a few more minutes, they had enough of tradition and falafelizing. The cousins tipped their trucker hats to the horizon, scooped up the dogs, and returned to the Escalade. Bella loved her new ride, as deeply as she had ever loved anything in her life. "Have I thanked you enough for sneaking around behind my back, lying, and stealing to get me this truck?"

"Anytime."

They didn't get four blocks before a SHPD cruiser pulled up behind them, lights flashing.

"Not again," said Bella.

Captain Morgan appeared at the driver's-side window and leaned down. "Ladies, I heard you were heading back to the city today."

"So you had to pull us over?" asked Gia.

"The man I arrested at church the other night, one Arthur Sanders? Turns out he's swindled women from Fort Lee to Cape May. You girls wouldn't know anything about that, would you?"

"Nope," they said in unison.

"The Hoboken police are offering a two-thousand-dollar reward for Sanders's apprehension."

"Wow! Are you getting it?" asked Gia.

Captain Morgan's mustache curved slightly. "I'm not refusing to take it. I wonder if I deserve it, though. I got an anonymous phone tip about an hour before Mrs. Lupo reported the church robbery."

"Really," said Gia.

"The caller said it'd be worth my while to park the cruiser outside Our Lady of the Perpetual Sorrow that night."

"Maybe the caller owed you a hundred bucks from a loan you made earlier this summer," said Gia.

"Then she should pay me back a hundred and take the two thousand for herself."

"She wants you to have it. Her way of saying, 'Thanks.'"

"Then I will keep it. My way of saying, 'You're welcome.'" Captain Morgan thudded the roof of the Escalade. "Have a safe trip back to Brooklyn. Keep those dogs on their leashes. I'd hate to scrape them off the highway."

"Got it," said Gia.

He climbed back into his cruiser, gave them one siren blast, and drove away.

Bella put the car in motion and quickly reached the HURRY BACK! sign that marked the town border. "So long, Seaside! See ya next year!" they yelled. Kookah and Pretzel yapped. Minutes later, they were on thunder road.

"Floor it, bitch," said Gia.